# CONTEMPORARY BRITISH WOMEN WRITERS

# CONTEMPORARY BRITISH WOMEN WRITERS

## Texts and Strategies

Edited by

### Robert E. Hosmer Jr.
*Lecturer in English, Smith College*
*Northampton, Massachusetts*

MACMILLAN

First published 1993 by
THE MACMILLAN PRESS LTD
Houndmills, Basingstoke, Hampshire RG21 2XS
and London
Companies and representatives
throughout the world

ISBN 0–333–56532–0

A catalogue record for this book is available
from the British Library.

Printed in Hong Kong

# Contents

# Notes on the Contributors

**Brett T. Averitt** is Associate Professor of English at Westfield (MA) State College, where she teaches courses in British and American literature, the structure of the novel and linguistics. She has written and published essays on several women writers, including Muriel Spark, Penelope Mortimer and Cynthia Seton. She is also a poet and has written a volume of poetry on friendship and other topics. She is co-founder of the Northampton (MA) Women's Center, an organization devoted to the study of women's past and current lives.

**Clare Boylan**, born and educated in Dublin, began her writing career as a journalist, working as a reporter, feature writer, and editor. In addition, she has reviewed books for Eireann radio and television and contributed to several magazines. In 1983 she published her first novel, *Holy Pictures*, described by William Trevor as 'sharp as a serpent's tooth'. That was followed by a collection of fifteen stories, *A Nail on the Head* (1983) and another novel, *Last Resorts* (1984). Most recently, a third novel, *Black Baby* (1988) and another collection of short stories, *Concerning Virgins* (1989) have appeared; critical response to those volumes has confirmed the promise discerned in her earlier work. In addition, she has written the introduction to the Virago and Penguin reprints of Molly Keane's *Taking Chances*.

**Robert Owen Evans** was educated at the University of Chicago and the University of Florida. He pursued additional graduate work at Harvard University. In the course of a long and distinguished career as teacher and scholar, Professor Evans served as Professor and Director of the University Honors Program at the University of Kentucky, and as Professor and Director of the General Honors Program at the University of New Mexico. In addition, he served in 1977 as President of the National Collegiate Honors Council. He is the author/editor of eleven volumes and the author of more than fifty scholarly articles, and a novel.

**Ernest H. Hofer** was educated at Brown, Oxford and Cornell. His academic career has veered toward the administrative; he spent six years in Heidelberg, Germany as Associate Director and Acting

Director, University of Maryland European Division; eight years as Associate and Acting Head of the English Department at the University of Massachusetts; eight years as Faculty Dean at the University of Massachusetts. He founded and was Director from 1966 to 1988 of the Oxford Summer Seminar, Trinity College, Oxford. Meanwhile as Professor of English, he taught during the entire tenure of his administrative period, especially in the areas of his special research: Henry James, Hawthorne, the contemporary British novel and the Bloomsbury Group. He has published in *The New Yorker*, in England on the British novel, and lectured on Henry James, Hawthorne and Oxford on both sides of Atlantic.

**Robert E. Hosmer Jr.** was educated at Holy Cross College, Smith College, the University of Massachusetts/Amherst and Trinity College, Oxford. He is currently a Lecturer in the Department of English Language and Literature at Smith College. He formerly taught at the University of Massachusetts, where he received the University's Distinguished Teaching Award, and at Mount Holyoke College. He has published widely on contemporary British and Irish writers, particularly Anita Brookner, Edna O'Brien and Muriel Spark. He also regularly reviews for *Commonweal*, the *Boston Globe* and the *New York Times*. A specialist in Anglo–Saxon poetry and the teaching of writing, he is the author of the *Guide* to the seventh edition of *The Norton Reader*.

**Ann Hulbert**, a Senior Editor of *The New Republic*, works on the literary section of the magazine. She has written for *The New Republic*, *The New York Review of Books*, *The Times Literary Supplement*, *The New York Times* and other publications. Her biography of Jean Stafford was published in the spring of 1992.

**Joseph Hynes** is Professor of English at the University of Oregon, where he has been a member of the Faculty since 1957. He has been a Visiting Professor of English at the Daido Institute of Technology in Nagoya, and an Exchange Professor at the University of Tubingen. His special interests include modern literature, Henry James, contemporary British fiction, and experimental fiction. His publications on James, Dickens, Graham Greene, Evelyn Waugh, Henry Green, J. F. Powers and Doris Lessing have appeared in such journals as *American Literature, ELH, Texas Studies in Literature and Language,*

*Criticism, Twentieth Century Literature, Modern Language Quarterly,* and the *Iowa Review.* His critical study, *The Art of the Real: Muriel Spark's Novels* appeared in 1988.

**Walter Kendrick** is Professor of English at Fordham University, New York City. From 1986 to 1988 he was Senior Editor of the *Village Voice* and the *Voice Literary Supplement.* He is co-editor, with Perry Meisel, of *Bloomsbury/Freud: The Letters of James and Alix Strachey 1924–1925* (1985), and the author of *The Novel Machine: The Theory and Fiction of Anthony Trollope* (1987), *The Secret Museum: Pornography in Modern Culture* (1987), *The Thrill of Fear* (1991) and numerous articles and reviews in academic and popular journals.

**Jenny Newman** has a particular interest in contemporary British women's fiction, which she teaches for the Department of Continuing Education at Liverpool University, Chester College and the University of Massachusetts Summer Seminar at Trinity College, Oxford. Her recent editing of *The Faber Book of Seductions* (1988) brought her considerable praise as well as a highly popular round of television and radio appearances. Her co-written novel, *Connections,* was shortlisted for the 1989 Constable Trophy.

**Jean Sudrann** is Mary E. Woolley Professor of English Emeritus of Mount Holyoke College (South Hadley, MA) She received her BA degree from Mount Holyoke, her MA and PhD from Columbia University. She holds the honorary degree of Doctor of Humane Letters from Mount Holyoke. Her publications include essays on both Victorian and modern novelists in *Victorian Studies, ELH, Antioch Review, Studies in the Novel* and *The Dickens Quarterly.*

# Introduction

From Jane Austen to Virginia Woolf the literature of England has been graced with first-rate fiction written by women. Nevertheless, no English generation has contained as many talented women novelists as contemporary England now enjoys. *Contemporary British Women Novelists: Texts and Strategies* brings to the attention of readers and teachers of literature a selection of writers – all of them women, all of them English (with the exception of the Anglo–Irish novelist Molly Keane and the Scots writer Muriel Spark) – demonstrating a renaissance in English literature. It can be argued that the most exciting contemporary writing is being done by women; several of England's rich collection of talent have earned international critical and popular acclaim. The work of Muriel Spark, for example, is known and appreciated throughout the English-speaking world and beyond, as a substantial number of her novels have been translated into other languages. Yet other women writers included here merit greater attention than they have heretofore received. It is our hope that this volume will bring these exciting and talented women writers to an even larger audience of new readers.

The chapter on each writer consists of four parts: a substantial critical essay written in clear, jargon-free, accessible prose with parenthetic documentation and minimal notes; a primary bibliography ('Writings by X') that is as exhaustive and up-to-date as possible; a secondary bibliography ('Writings About X') that is selective rather than exhaustive; and a brief biographical sketch.

Subsequent volumes will deal with other contemporary women writers not included here. Two additional volumes are planned: one, to cover a number of modern/contemporary women writers like Murdoch, Lessing, Drabble, Figes, Gilliat, Lehmann, O'Brien, and Bainbridge; the other, to present some of the dissident voices in contemporary fiction like Winterson, Desai, Gordimer, and Jhabvala.

Robert O. Evans's 'Sybille Bedford: A Paradise of Dainty Devices' examines Bedford's major fiction from *A Legacy* (1956) to *Jigsaw* (1989) and illuminates the extraordinary craft of this neglected writer by minute attention to technical elements and rhetorical strategies. Evans probes well beneath the prose surface, uncovering structures of enduring strength, intricately and paradoxically constructed from

those 'dainty devices'. His essay derives added strength and dimensions through references to Bedford's non-fiction, to the work of
writers in the great tradition of European letters (Tolstoi and Stendhal)
and English literature (Milton, James), to modern European history
and through a judicious use of biographical detail.

My own essay, 'Paradigm and Passage: the Fiction of Anita
Brookner', focuses on three of the ten novels of this art historian
turned novelist who, in the course of only ten years as a fiction
writer, has achieved not only a McConnell Booker Prize (1984) but
extraordinarily apt comparison to writers like James, Woolf, and
Proust. Taking exile to be the central concern of Brookner's fiction, I
have attempted to combine the Biblical paradigm of that experience
and what Stanley B. Greenfield took to be the formulaic expression
of that theme in Anglo–Saxon poetry, then apply it to *Providence*
(1982), *Hotel Du Lac* (1984), and *Latecomers* (1989). That process reveals some of the ways in which Brookner foregrounds exile as what
Joseph Brodsky has called both 'a linguistic event' and 'a metaphysical condition'.

Ann Hulbert's essay, 'The Great Ventriloquist: A. S. Byatt's *Possession: A Romance'*, focuses attention on this writer's latest and clearly
most important novel. Deeming the novel a 'tour-de-force of university fiction', Hulbert illuminates the strategies by which Byatt
foregrounds linguistic and critical matters while juxtaposing the
narrative of two contemporary literary scholars with the tale of two
nineteenth-century artists. The result, in Hulbert's estimate, is a
twice-told tale post-structuralist critics would be wise to heed.

In 'The Real Magic of Angela Carter', Walter Kendrick cross-
sections the fictions of Carter, perhaps the most daring and experimental writer included here, and describes them mostly aptly as
'bizarre amalgams of tale and essay, delicacy and grossness, studded
with literary allusion and jewelled here and there with poetry'.
Kendrick's richly synthetic critical approach, drawing upon the
insights and strategies of recent theory, enables him to reveal the
dynamics of the fiction of this feisty, sometimes irreverent, always
provocative contemporary writer.

The fictions of Isabel Colegate chosen by Brett Averitt for her
essay, 'The Strange Clarity of Distance: History, Myth, and Imagination in the Novels of Isabel Colegate', lend themselves to a particularly rewarding analysis when Averitt uses a device she calls 'the
Keats code' to show the interplay of history and individual creativ-

ity. From the discussion, Colegate emerges as a mythmaker who maps out her own reading of history, subverting commonplace causal connexions while calling into question received understandings of major historical events and notions of human behaviour.

When Jean Sudrann examines the novels of Penelope Fitzgerald, she foregrounds matters metaphysical and epistemological to show just how Fitzgerald understands the dynamics of human personality within a larger scheme of things. Sudrann's discussion derives its resonance and persuasive power from her ability to combine the insights of narrative theory with Scriptural and cultural insight.

Ernest Hofer's essay, 'Enclosed Structures, Disclosed Lives: the Fictions of Susan Hill', offers a poetics of space as a reading guide to the work of this contemporary novelist. Hofer demonstrates not only how physical and fictive structures intersect in Hill's fiction, but how, by manipulating the relationship between physical space and character development through a dynamics of shifting distances, Hill has crafted fictions of keen psychological insight and Gothic pleasure.

Clare Boylan ('Sex, Snobbery and the Strategies of Molly Keane') describes Keane as a writer who renders 'an energetic dissection of human nature'. Boylan locates sexual politics at the center of Keane's fiction, and demonstrates how, from her early novel, *Taking Chances* (1929) to her latest, *Queen Lear* (1989), Keane has revealed a vanished era in all its insufferable, class-based claustrophobia.

Reviewing Muriel Spark's extraordinary literary achievements, Joseph Hynes isolates a number of techniques and choices that characterize her craft in 'Muriel Spark and the Oxymoronic Vision'. These recur with such consistency that Hynes is led to speak of 'the persistence of some definite Sparkian preoccupations'. His essay makes generous and judicious use of insights drawn from psychology and theology as well as literary theory and history in qualifying the unique excellences of this prolific writer.

Jenny Newman's 'See Me as Sisyphus, But Having a Good Time: The Fiction of Fay Weldon' devotes attention to specific textual strategies while illuminating the evolution of Weldon's feminism. Newman puts what she learns at the service of a larger endeavour. What emerges is a fascinating exercise in cultural decomposition and literary composition.

Like all books, *Contemporary British Women Writers* has been a long-term project and over two years have elapsed between my idea and the creation of the volume you now hold. During that time I received assistance, support, and encouragement from a number of sources. Scholarly research assistance was so generously given by the staff of the Williston Memorial Library, Mount Holyoke College, South Hadley, Massachusetts, that words are inadequate; I must, however, single out Kuang-Tien Yao, Interlibrary Loan Librarian, and Kathleen Egan Norton, Reference Librarian: it is no vacant cliche to say that this book would not have come to be without their patient, cheerful, and thoroughly professional guidance.

To Barbara Kozash, Office Manager – Humanities Cluster, Smith College, I owe thanks for so many tasks performed so efficiently and for such good cheer, day in, day out.

To Margaret Cannon, Editor at Macmillan, I extend genuine gratitude for the kind of belief and support found with decreasing frequency in the world of publishing today, and for extraordinary patience and skill devoted to this transatlantic project.

My greatest debt remains to the nine scholars who have contributed to this volume; from the extraordinary range of their knowledge and the generosity of their hearts they have given so much, and just for the cause. Thank you. While I am indeed in their debt, so too are all those who now love this literature as well as those who will come to love it through our book. The words of William Wordsworth, at the end of *The Prelude*, aptly express what each of us had in mind from the very beginning:

> What we have loved,
> Others will love, and we will teach them how.

Northampton, Massachusetts

# 1

# Sybille Bedford: A Paradise of Dainty Devices

ROBERT OWEN EVANS

When last I wrote about Sybille Bedford, for Jack I. Biles' *British Novelists Since 1900* (New York, AMS Press, 1987), I began with a quotation from a strange prayer by Aldous Huxley: 'Faith is not believing in something which our intelligence denies. It is the choice of the nobler hypothesis. Faith is the resolve to place the highest meaning on the facts which we observe.'[1] It still seems to me a sure stepping-stone, for while the writing of the two novelists – close friends for many years – is immeasurably different, both are dedicated to exalted themes, to that higher purpose Huxley called 'the nobler hypothesis'.

Sybille Bedford's higher purpose is, I think, particularly clear in her first and most important novel, *A Legacy*, though it is also discernible in her last and most recent book, *Jigsaw* (New York, 1989). When Weidenfeld and Nicholson published *A Legacy*, in 1956, the reviews were generally laudatory and enthusiastic, but most of them seem to have missed the point. Typical perhaps was the judgment of Evelyn Waugh, who wrote that *A Legacy* is a book 'of entirely delicious quality, witty, elegant, and uproariously funny' in his notice in the *Spectator*. It is all of these things, but it is also much more, a book with serious and important themes, as I shall try to illustrate, and also one which is technically very complex, laden with sophisticated, rhetorical devices aimed at drawing the reader into her scheme, far beyond the scope of most first novels. But while *A Legacy* was Sybille Bedford's first *published* novel, it was by no means an initial effort. Twenty years earlier (1936) in Sanary, that unfashionable part of southern France where the Huxleys also had a house, she tells us Maria Huxley found time from her busy schedule to type parts of a novel for her. That juvenalia, we now learn from *Jigsaw*, was refused by all the publishers to whom it was submitted, and the author now seems to agree with their judgment. When *A Legacy* finally did appear, it came after twenty years of training and education. The reviewer for the *Daily Express* who thought 'it reads like Nancy Mitford at her most brilliant' failed to discern the forest for the trees.

*A Legacy* begins, as Shakespeare often began his plays, with the dashing display of wit that blinded some of the reviewers but contributed to a verbal economy we have not seen the like of since, perhaps, *Pride and Prejudice*, with some new twists to tried and true devices, and high comic intensity.

The story, told by a narrator, Francesca, begins with the first nine years of her life, which she spent 'bundled to and fro between two houses', a town house on Voss Strasse in what is now West Berlin, the family home of the Merz family, the parents of her father's first, deceased wife, and a chateau in southern Bavaria, in the Vosges, purchased by her father for her mother. The chateau was as beautiful as Voss Strasse was ugly. But it is Voss Strasse that sets the immediate tone, Francesca's House of Seven Gables. She was not, however, born there. That would have been unthinkable. *Cela ne se fait pas parmi les gens de cet milieu.* Instead a flat was rented in Charlottenburg for the birthing, chosen because it had street access for the horses. The Von Feldens, her father's family, liked their animals to live at home, not in livery stables. In Charlottenburg only a thin wall separated Francesca's mother's bedroom from the sound of horses chomping at night, which Caroline found 'consoling'. Bedford says it was the beginning of the century, but we may assume, since there is a heavy autobiographical dimension to the novel, the year was 1911, the year Sybille Bedford was born.

The house she was not born in but moved to after three weeks backed on the Imperial Chancellery and belonged to Arthur and Henrietta Merz, upper Jewish bourgeoisie, descendants of the former Henrietta Merz, who rose from the ghetto to keep a fashionable salon frequented by such notables as Goethe, Mirabeau, Schleiermacher, and the Humboldts, in the glorious days of *Sturm und Drang* and the glittering intellectual accomplishments of eighteenth-century Germany. The Merzes, however, had not lived up to the excitements of their ancestor, nor even to the remarkable financial accomplishments of the generation that followed, the fortune-founding and scientific discoveries of the Oppenheim(er)s, Mendelsohns, and Simons. By 1911 they lived in absolute isolation.

## A ROSE BY ANY OTHER NAME

What else might we expect from a family called Merz? In German the word means *cull* or *reject* (related to *ausmerzen*, to *sort out* or *take away*), and they are certainly rejects, even from the lively threads of German Jewish society of the era. (A portent perhaps of what was to become of that whole milieu after 1933.) The other names Bedford calls up – she too can call spirits – make it all too clear. The Mendelsohns are, no doubt, the bankers, Joseph and Abraham, founders of the great fortune, or perhaps their descendant Franz, born in 1865, who lived until 1935, former President of the German Chamber of Commerce who became in 1931 President of the International Chamber of Commerce. Nor should we forget that the family descended from Moses Mendelsohn, the Jewish philosopher known as the 'German Socrates'.

I am not so sure about the Oppenheims (or Oppenheimers), though there was a Franz in the nineteenth-century who became a noted economist. His brother Carl was also well known, as a physiologist and chemist. And there were of course Simons everywhere – a very different circle from that of the first Henrietta Merz, less brilliant but in its own way no less distinguished. In any case we would not expect the second generation to be the equals of Goethe and Mirabeau. Schleiermacher must surely have been Fredrick Ernest Daniel, noted theologian and philosopher. The Humboldts were either Baron Alexander von Humboldt, scientist and diplomat, or his brother Wilhelm, the linguist, or both. (Had I to choose I think I might favour Wilhelm, for Henrietta Merz herself was no mean linguist and 'like George Eliot . . . spoke English, German, French, Italian, Spanish, Latin, Greek and Hebrew, and unlike George Eliot she could also read in Swedish'.) No traces survived at Voss Strasse.

No music was heard there. Schubert and Haydn were aliens. No Corot landscapes were added to the Delacroix. The Merzes were too busy 'adding bell-pulls and thickening the upholstery'. No animal's foot sullied the carpeting. The newspaper the family read – rather, had read to them by the butler Gottlieb – was the *Kreuz Zeitung*, already much out of date and devoted mainly to recording births, deaths, and marriages. Money was handled (literally) by the butler and always in crisp new bills. Banknotes were considered unsanitary; 'the problem of change was not envisaged' (*A Legacy*, 17).

High drawing-room comedy laced with sparkling wit – little wonder the reviewers responded with enthusiasm. And it gets better, Grandpapa Merz, turning ninety, still took carriage exercise in the afternoons, accompanied by a 'shapely leg'. But there were no shapely legs to amuse him in the Merz circle where even the younger relatives had already done their seventh season at Marienbad. To this dilemma Gottlieb found a solution in the Prussian aristocracy where 'long, well turned legs' were natural to the caste. This point, five pages into the novel, marks Bedford's introduction to the Prussians and the point at which one of her major themes begins; that is, Prussianism (or the Prussian Problem), one of the ingredients which, mixed into German history, brought about three disastrous wars within a century.

Look more closely at those Prussian ladies who pass as shadows in Arthur Merz's carriage, sisters and widows of line officers – none of them well-off. Gottlieb paid them for their innocent services – or were they really quite so innocent? Bedford supplies a nice list of their names (her list of ships that pass in the afternoon – her version of a descent from the sublime to the ridiculous?). Fraulein von Bluchtenau (from German *blicken*: I might translate as 'one of a shining appearance' or, figuratively, 'Miss Well Scrubbed'); Fraulein von der Wahenwitz ('Miss Senseless'); Frau von Stein (German *stone* or *rock*, 'Mme. Hard Face or Hard Nose', though *Stein* can sometimes mean a piece at the game of draughts – but surely that would be too far-fetched); Frau von Demuth ('Mme. Humble'); Fraulein zu der Hardeneck ('Miss Hard Neck' or 'Stiff Nose' – she was mortally offended when Grandpapa tried to slip a banknote under her garter); Frau von Kummer ('Mme. Trouble'); and finally Fraulein von Kalkenrath ('Miss Quick Lime' – who left in a huff and had to be hastily replaced).

A single example of the traditional, ancient art of casting character by the name given might suffice, but I list all the shapely legs to show there is nothing accidental here. The author is playing a complicated cross-language word game, perhaps at such length in hopes the reader cannot miss her point. No other English novelist I know is as clever at cross-language word games as Bedford, save perhaps Anthony Burgess. His invention of the argot 'Nadsat' in *A Clockwork Orange* is as brilliant and more pervasive, though it is based on a kind of clipped Russian instead of familiar German. Often, of course, such word games are monolingual, played in the language of the text, but even so they can become very complicated, as for instance in Shakespeare's wondrous passages of oxymora in the speeches of both Romeo and Juliet. After such verbal fireworks Bedford pulls in on the reins to introduce a new question – money. Money, after all, lies close to the heart of the realistic novel, and who could deny that *A Legacy* is really aimed at the realistic portrayal of unvarnished truth? 'Young Russleben owes everywhere', Gottlieb announces during luncheon. Then a rather crude below stairs joke: 'He is being pressed by his tailor.' Suitable for a butler, though not germane to the novel, but the real purpose lies deeper – to permit the introduction of Francesca's father Julius. Bedford rarely resists an opportunity for verbal play. Here she names the tailors Fasskessel and Muntmann, but the slightly obtuse Julius automatically ignores those names. He simply cannot understand why anyone would go to a German tailor. From this delicate and comic beginning Bedford is able to push her readers into acquaintance with the rest of the family, the sisters Flora and Melanie (who was Julius's first wife) – both died young of consumption. Then the second son, Fredrick Merz, a man of mediocre intellect but at times stout instincts, university-trained, well placed by the family in a government career but doomed never to rise because he has brought his French mistress Jeanne with him to Berlin. (Jeanne, however, grows into a stronger character later in the novel.) From the first she is unacceptable at Voss Strasse. In that age of rubber tubs she brought with her from Paris a silver bidet. Fredrick has set her up in a hat shop – realistic enough, though why mistresses were thought to have a talent for selling hats (or gloves) is one of those mysteries of civilized Europe that remains to this day unsolved. The day after Henrietta Merz died, Fredrick married her.

Introductions to other important characters follow. Eduard Merz, the elder son, and his wife Sarah Genz-Kastell, the Frankfort aniline heiress, a rich, 'clear-brained woman, elegant rather than beautiful' (17). And Eduard (Edu) himself, a rake and a gambler, now a bankrupt bailed out eleven times by the family or by Sarah. Finally she had enough, sued for a financial separation, offering Edu either a generous allowance or divorce. In twentieth-century Germany women of the upper classes were not, as some people believe, mere chattels of their husbands. Still an action like Sarah's, accompanied by a newspaper announcement stating that she would no longer be responsible for his debts, caused a storm of scandal. It also drove Edu to the money lenders, an act that drove his father Arthur Merz into a fury: 'Who does the fool think he is, a Goy?'

No doubt Eduard did think of himself as a Goy or at least the social equal of the class with which he associated. That was a time when the sons of Jewish magnates were accepted in Germany with no sign of prejudice. Money and lifestyle were what mattered. The changes that occurred twenty years later, when Hitler and his Nazi gang came to power, could not have been dreamed of in 1911. The Kaiser would have turned in his grave had he known that a German government would come to consider its greatest task a final, permanent solution to what they called 'The Jewish Problem'. By filling in the backgrounds as she does, with the wit and insight of a very skilful novelist, Bedford, like Joseph Conrad, enables us to *see* how it took place. This is heady stuff and subtle, too. Through such portraits we come to understand better what the holocaust was all about without her ever directly mentioning it.

Sarah's shocking reaction to her husband's gambling debts is a small mechanism for suggesting the larger question, which 'goes without saying'. The closest she comes is in a short passage describing the Kaiser when he learned what Sarah had done. He 'was furious. He made a scene at Eulenberg . . . for fifteen years he had tried to get rid of anti-semitism . . . those Kastells thought they owned the world . . . those debts would have to be paid' (27). His Majesty considered sending a letter of sympathy to Grandpapa Merz, a tremendous indiscretion, until 'Bulow persuaded him to keep his oar out'. And that of course is what a large number of the German nobility did, *kept their oars out*, turned their attention to Prussian military schemes, leading twice to world war – until, it appears, fairly late in the Second World War, they had finally had enough. They plotted to destroy the tyrant in his bunker in East Prussia.

This is indeed very serious business, though we come to it through delicious comedy. That tone continues, somewhat mitigated, when Bedford next describes the von Feldens, the other side of Francesca's family, her father's people. Julius rose from a line of Bavarian country gentlemen of cultured if not intellectual interests, bored by the abstract and by letters, more French than German: 'The French Revolution was still alive with them as a calamity, and of the Industrial they were not aware' (32). No Felden had borne arms since the Reformation, 'their home was Catholic Western Continental Europe, and the centre of their world was France. They ignored, despised, and later dreaded Prussia; and they were strangers to the sea'. (32)

## MISTRESS OF A DRIFTING PREDICATE

How Bedford brings the two milieus together in service of her themes is perhaps the major accomplishment of this remarkable novel. Far too complex for a mere essay; hence I concentrate now on one linguistic aspect of her technique. After all, language is what novels are made of, but it is really languages, English, German, and French, that are the tools Sybille Bedford uses with such mastery. (She is also fluent in Italian, though she does not need it until *Jigsaw*.) Most of her quotations that are not in English are left for the reader to translate himself. Often it is not necessary to know German or French to arrive at the meaning of a passage, though doubtless it helps. Like many other writers Bedford does not place too great a burden on her readers.[2]

Even a long dissertation might not suffice to describe all of the devices Bedford seems to have at her fingertips, but one – because of the brilliant way she handles it and because of its relative rarity in English – is worth some attention. The Greek name for this figure of speech is *anacoluthon* (that is, *wanting sequence*). The Greeks considered the declarative period (sentence), much as we do, as comprised of two distinct parts. The first is the *protasis* and the second the *apodosis*. (Schoolmarms translate loosely with *subject* and *predicate*.) *Anacoluthon* occurs when the second part does not follow logically from the first, or when the predicate is omitted altogether. The commonest form of this is what Henrich Lausberg calls the 'absolute nominative'; that is, constructions which have to do with correlative particles (as *either . . . or; both . . . and*).[3] Handbook writers sometimes cite as a good example a passage from Thucydides, where he writes, 'If the attempt succeeds . . .', leaving the *apodosis* for the reader to fill in from his own mind. For instance, 'It will be a good thing', or something along those lines. Bedford uses this device often and to a very good ends. (Perhaps she has been influenced by her training as a journalist.)

For example, at one place in *A Legacy* there is a conversation between Count Bernin and Father Hauser, a Jesuit who has arrived in an attempt to help solve the dilemma caused by Johannes (Julius's younger brother) after he escaped from the Prussian military school at Benzheim. For two pages we read what almost seem like headlines:

Presently Count Bernin said, 'There is too much involved.'
And presently, 'I can't help it that old Felden hasn't got his wits
about him.'
'Besides it's too late.'
'You are not my spiritual adviser, you know.'
'I did not start it. I never liked it.'
'*You* know, if anybody does. I am not building for myself. Nor for
my time . . .'
'Oh those men. They're still in the house. They are nothing.
Automata. Cut off. With their Nation and their duty to State.
They are blind men who must be led.'
'Yes, if you like, used. On occasion *used*.'
'Pride? *My* pride?' (92–3)

One full page of the novel. Out of context, to someone who has
not been reading the book, it seems meaningless. But for the atten-
tive reader the predicates, or lapses in the conversation, come magically to mind. That is of course the way effective rhetorical figures are
supposed to work. Moreover, with Bedford such conversations draw
us towards the theme she is presently examining, for this passage
has to do with the Prussian militarists at Benzheim (and in Berlin),
and with a Prussian attitude towards life in general as well as the
natural family desire to shield Johannes. Given his character and
upbringing, the whole idea of a military school is revolting, and as a
matter of fact the Benzheim method of education should disgust any
right-thinking person. Shall the family then force Johannes to return? Or not? If not, what will the political implications be? If so, the
moral implications? (One of the appeals of Bedford's writing is that
the author, through the persona of her narrator, seems invariably to
be on the side of right – ethical – thinking.)

Also this passage cuts a bit deeper than ethical considerations –
into modern German history. It focuses our attention on a dream
that failed (and receives little attention these days), the dream of
Catholic empire, a dream broken under the yoke of Prussianism that
paved the road to the wars that followed and eventually to the
horror of Nazi control. What Bedford is doing – how consciously I
cannot say – is reminding us of some important threads in German
history, which, had they been pulled differently by the gods, might
have forestalled the terrors of world war and of holocaust.

The novelist has selected a large and very important subject, and
that is one reason *A Legacy* should be seen as a major accomplish-

ment. I am not suggesting we rank it with Tolstoi's *War and Peace* or Stendhal's *Rouge et Noir*, but it takes on tasks of similar magnitude. It deals with noteworthy subject matter. It is not of course the only contemporary novel to face such a challenge. There exists, for instance, a striking parallel in a novel by Anthony Burgess, the *Napoleon Symphony* – so striking one is almost tempted to believe Burgess had been reading Bedford. In one passage Napoleon is conversing with a young German named Stapps who has tried to assassinate him. But Napoleon was no Hitler, who hanged his would-be assassins to the wall of Plotzensee prison with strands of barbed wire and came to rejoice in their death throes.[4] Burgess writes:

> N came round to Stapps' front . . . 'The what? What was that word?'
> 'The *Volk*. Untranslatable. The German people becoming aware of their destiny.'
> 'Oh, my God.'
> 'You don't understand. You're not a German. You don't know our language and literature and folklore. You don't weep with joy at the smell of the German forest or the German sunrise over the German mountains.'
> [Stapps then breaks into poetic ecstasy.] '*Habt Acht. Uns drauen üble Streich . . .*'
> 'Oh, for Christ's sake . . . shut up . . . that fucking gibberish, do you hear?'
> '*Baragouin?*' [French for gibberish]
> [Now Burgess] The boy knew the word or guessed at its meaning. Very coldly he said: 'You see what I am trying to say when I say you do not understand the *Volk*. We are the only pure race in Europe and must remain so. Our tongue is the old pure Aryan. France is a mongrel country full of Jews. We must keep ourselves clean. Once our blood is mixed with the lower races we become cursed of God. Jesus Christ turns his back on us.'
> 'He was a Jew, man, what the hell do you think you're saying?'
> 'In him was the *echt* [German, *pure*] blood of the Aryans.' (136)

Burgess is quite capable of horrifying civilized readers and does so in this dreadful passage where he reminds us that as far back as Napoleon's time the worst ingredients were already present in Germany: the seeds of anti-semitism; the blood myth of the *Volk*; *lebensraum*; racism – and that mixed together in the German melting pot, in proper proportion, with a dash of German romanticism, they spelled *Hitler, Nazi, Madness.*

That, too, is one of Bedford's themes, presented more delicately, with a lighter touch, but with much the same technique – by reported conversation wherein much of the predication is omitted or drifting. The reader fills in the missing sequence and thereby automatically allies himself with a certain point of view, the one the writer intended. The author persuades him to force upon himself, through the words that arise in his own mind, the correct reaction.

Perhaps this rhetorical trick will seem a little clearer if we look at another, shorter passage from Burgess, a dinner conversation with Napoleon and Josephine, when the subject of divorce is first broached:

Napoleon: 'The national interest alliance attempt on my life at Schönbrunn a male heir you understand must under.'

The reader completes the protasis. 'You must under' becomes 'You must understand,' but Burgess really says a good deal more than that. Not only is Josephine obligated to understand she is being replaced, but she must also go under; that is, accept the divorce, accept the need for a male heir. Later the passage continues in the author's words, 'So she undered, eyes closed, hearing everything, hearing the whole of the Tuileries startled to movement like a flurry of bats in a cave if one screams by her scream'. As with Bedford in the passage previously quoted, this is very economical writing, leading the reader miles from the literal statement, and thereby much enhancing the depth of the novel by the use of rhetorical devices. Also the passages are parallel in subject matter as well as technique (coincidence?), but I am not suggesting Burgess borrowed anything from Bedford or even that he has read *A Legacy.* Parallel passages do not prove much anyhow, except that in this case two expert linguists happen to deal with much the same topic and use similar devices to put across their points.

The tragedy of rising anti-semitism in Germany, which Bedford documents in her portraits of the Merzes (and elsewhere), will be instantly understood by most readers (at least those who were alive during World War Two), but some readers may perhaps conclude – I think erroneously – that the Merzes themselves share some responsibility for their fate. She is not of course saying that they brought racism down upon their own heads, but rather that with their narrow vision they were unable to adapt to the kind of prejudice-free society the Kaiser sought. They became stunted and uncreative and hence easy prey for stronger forces. I do not believe that Bedford means to say so much, and certainly it would be a very unpopular view to espouse these days, but if I am mistaken and that is, by implication, what she is saying, then we should applaud her honesty for recording social history as she sees it. Right-thinking writers tell the truth even when it is not very pleasant. That is not to say Bedford is revisionist in her declaration. On the contrary, *A Legacy* is written with great sympathy for the fate of German Jews, and later (in *Jigsaw*) Bedford even suggests she herself shares a Jewish ancestor somewhere in her background. I think she would like it to have been the first Henrietta Merz.

It is more difficult for Americans, or the insular English, to understand the dream of Catholic empire that flourished for a short time and then failed – which she presents largely through the character of Count Bernin. She views it as another thread in the German matrix, which, forced out of proper proportion, contributed to the Germany that fell hostage to the Nazis. Notice her use of a conversation between Caroline Trafford, the narrator's mother, and Count Bernin to enforce this suggestion:

> Bernin: 'I began by representing the corner of the earth I was born in, Baden; later it was Germany. But whether Germany or France or Montenegro, the true statesman is a Steward entrusted with the welfare of the larger whole.'
> Caroline: 'Has this ever been a working concept in international politics?'
> B. 'There's a leaven. In many quarters. Among men in all kinds of positions. We are all placed to serve the greater end.'
> C. 'Abolition of armies and navies?'
> B. 'That may well be one of the aspects.'
> C. 'Social justice?'
> B. 'Helping the poor is always a rich man's duty.'
> C. 'When there are no more poor?'
> B. 'Are you not putting the cart before the horse?'
> C. 'You have not told me: What is your horse?'
> B. 'Spiritual unity, without which there can exist no other. Reestablishment of our Faith. The old Faith, to which you have just returned. I regard it as a happy omen.'
> C. 'Count Bernin, are you quite mad?' (251–2)

The reader can of course answer from the safe harbour of history that indeed he was quite mad. Not so vicious as the Prussian imperialist bent on conquest, nor so morally bereft as the anti-semitists, nor so dangerous as the racial purists like Stapps in Burgess's *Napoleon Symphony* with their insane romanticism about the *Volk* and the pure Aryan blood. But nevertheless mad!

Such rhetorical devices (and others) emphasize major themes in *A Legacy*, but they accomplish more.they help drive the reader inexorably to the points of view the author espouses and wishes them to share. Sometimes Bedford is a bit of a nihilist about it all (as if the decline of German civilization were inevitable?); other times she can be more explicit even providing gnomic directions for the reader, as when she writes, 'The moves that shape the future seldom shape their intended ends; the course of self interest is seen as a beeline only at the moment, and this history of individuals, groups, and countries is the sum of these'. If anyone still doubts what the novel is really about, consider the following passage, which occurs after Count Bernin (a good man at heart even if quite mad) undertakes to support Johannes after his escape from Benzheim. The militarists want the boy returned, and the case has become (or almost become) a *cause célèbre* which may even threaten Bismarck's coalition government. Bernin has written to Lieutenant-General von Schimmelpfennig (another name game; Lieutenant-General Bad Penny) that the whole business of Johannes's escape has become a farce; it would be wiser/saner for the people at Benzheim to say the boy is ill, or been shipped somewhere else, and to play down the whole stupidity. For response the general's ADC, an undersecretary from Bismarck's Chancellery, and Captain Montclair (from the military school) present themselves at Bernin's gates. They want the affair kept out of the papers and believe that the way to do this is to send him back. It is at this point we receive some instruction from the author herself:

[Eighty years ago] nearly everybody believed in the intrinsic desirability of a United Germany. The Empire . . . was a Historical Necessity. Yet everybody up to Bismarck was dissatisfied with the form of Empire itself. Liberals had worked for Union in the hope of cutting down the power of Princes; Prussian nationalists with the intention of establishing hegemony over Austria; Free traders to get rid of archaic monetary conditions, Democrats to extend the franchise, Labour leaders to unite the working class,

Socialists to expand trade unionism and the Army to expand the
Army. The first fruits were the Imperial Constitution of Versailles,
new tariffs, anti-socialist legislation, Alsace-Lorraine, Bismarck
and the lasting enmity of France. Bismarck had to take a coalition
government.

I rest the case – that *A Legacy* is a realistic, ethical novel concerned primarily with the great tragic events that swept across
Europe in the late nineteenth- and early twentieth-centuries. Since
many of these events are still too close for us to understand them
thoroughly, the novelist can, and does, provide something the social
historian cannot. More, I believe, than just an intimate view by a near
participant. That is why *A Legacy* is so much more than remarkably
witty, drawing-room comedy, the mode Bedford chooses to promote
her themes. It is an explanation of an extremely important segment
of recent history, important if indeed it is possible to learn anything
from past events. It is also, admittedly, a comedy in another sense,
Balzac's in *La comédie humaine*, where the intention of the writer is
beneath it all the improvement of human conduct that the future
may become better than the past.

## THE REST OF THE FICTION

It seems convenient to divide Bedford's other fiction into two
periods, the novels *A Favourite of the Gods* (1963) and *A Compass
Error* (1968), which follow fairly soon upon the heels of *A Legacy*, and
then two very recent pieces, 'Une Vie de Chateau' (*New Yorker*,
February 20, 1989, pp. 38–48) and *Jigsaw: An Unsentimental Education:
A Biographical Novel* (1989).

The two earlier works, novel and sequel, really constitute a single
story covering two generations. Both deal with human conduct
without the historical skeleton or the large themes of *A Legacy*,
without most of the pyrotechnical devices that are such an important
part of *A Legacy*, works painted on much smaller canvas.

*A Favourite of the Gods* is the story of Constanza, once again told in
the first person through the voice of a young girl, her daughter
Flavia. The novel begins with mother and daughter on a train from
Italy bound for Nice, where Constanza plans to catch the Calais
express. She is travelling north to be married for the second time.

Suddenly she discovers that her ruby ring, her only memento from her Italian father, is missing. A jewel of slight monetary worth but, she claims, great *valeur sentimentale*. Because of this mishap the Calais connection is missed. The two travel on towards Toulon, eventually disembarking at an unfashionable seaside town at an unfashionable season. (No doubt much of the portraiture here is of Sanary.) They take rooms in a hotel (later rent a villa), and send telegrams of explanation to the abandoned fiance, Lewis, who never does appear in the novel. 'It doesn't look,' says Constanza, 'does it, as if we were getting off tomorrow or the next day?' (20).[5] They stay there eleven years.

This is Constanza's book, though Bedford turns back to tell the story of her American mother who married an Italian nobleman and eventually left him because (to his utter astonishment) of his infidelities. Like her daughter she took herself off – to London, to Brown's Hotel – and in time arranged a marriage for her daughter to a young ambitious man. Indeed Simon was so ambitious that he divorced Constanza to marry a woman better equipped to serve his goals. Then years later Constanza makes another marriage contract which she will not honour, perhaps, Flavia suggests, because she was considering alliance with Lewis primarily for Flavia's sake. After eleven years Constanza finally meets a Frenchman, separated from his wife, with whom she believes she can find happiness. And she is right, for Constanza is, after all, a favourite of the Gods.

Bedford sketches her characters surely with more than a touch of humor, from the inviolable principessa to the young Constanza experiencing her first sexual awakening. Social comedy with hints of serious themes here and there, perhaps shaded a bit by Henry James's *Portrait of a Lady* or even *Daisy Miller*. At one point Flavia asks, 'Mr James, what is wrong with human affairs?' And her kindly old mentor can only answer, 'Wait for Evolution' (136).

Sometimes, as in *A Legacy*, there is a gnomic quality to the conversations, as Constanza to Flavia on marriage for love: 'One doesn't marry like that, just like that. For a bit of love' (154). Or the trusted maid, Mena, on the relation women sometimes have with their husbands: 'Some women get to hate their men' (165). It seems clear Sybille Bedford is no romantic. One wonders what she would have to say about the Sanseverina in Stendhal's *La Chartreuse de Parme* or, perhaps, Elvira Madigan. And her feelings on the insanity of war as a political solution are hardly disguised: Simon to Constanza, 'May

I only remember it in my nightmares. People going through it is the final proof that we are all insane' (177). There is a good deal about war in this book, especially World War One. Most of the time it reflects the horror of writers to the dreadful slaughter, though their memories may rely heavily on the anti-war novelists, like Remarque (*All Quiet on the Western Front*) or Hemingway (*Farewell to Arms*). War of course changed between 1914 and 1939, and some writers, like Hemingway, revised their views (*For Whom the Bell Tolls*), but Bedford remains remarkably constant. In this book we hear Anna, the old principessa, upon being told World War One brought on revolution in Germany: 'Whatever that means, they won't stand for another war'. And Constanza responds, 'Nobody will that' (202). Bedford reflects the feelings of that time, the period between wars, with great accuracy, though she of course knows better, having lived through the terrors of World War Two. But she does not change her position. Constanza says it very well, speaking of Michel Devaux, the man she finally picks. 'Now he's alone and writes books . . . He tells us that the first step towards sane government is the renunciation of war as an instrument of policy . . . *Que voulez-vous, mesdames, c'est un homme a principes*' (267).

These are samples of two of her grand themes, marriage and war. Earlier, through Constanza she has had her say about religion (or at least about the church), a subject that appeared more prominently in *A Legacy*. Here a young Anglo–Catholic has come on a visit to Rome. 'How do you feel about Infallibility?' Constanza asks him. 'That's easy, like the Immaculate Conception and all that. God is omnipotent, isn't he?' 'But why should God want to make the Pope infallible?' 'Because we are the One True Church'. [Shades of Count Bernin in the former novel.] 'Do you really believe that?' And Constanza a moment later, 'I'm not at all certain . . . It does seem odd that everybody else should be wrong, the Protestants and the Greeks and the people who think there isn't any God at all; the Buddhists, too' (47–8).

But Bedford does not spend much time on religion in this novel (and indeed the time she spent on it in *A Legacy* was more concerned with politics than theology). She lacks the theological interest of a Graham Greene or an Evelyn Waugh. Though she does not ignore the subject, her women tend to approach it with a certain flippancy. Religion is not a major theme like marriage or war, but it is not quite ignored. More proof that *A Favourite of the Gods* is not just social comedy. If we need more evidence, consider Constanza's death, in a ditch in France during World War Two, 'riddled by German machine gun bullets'.

It would be even harder to dismiss *A Compass Error* on grounds of levity. Flavia's story is far less light-hearted than Constanza's, and she does not share her mother's luck. The story begins with Flavia alone in the villa on the French seacoast. Anna is dead, and Constanza has fled with her lover, keeping her whereabouts secret from everyone save Flavia because discovery could ruin Michel's divorce case. Flavia then has her first introduction to sex, like Constanza at the same age only, in Flavia's case the affair is Lesbian with an older woman.

Flavia is supposed to spend the summer cramming for her university entrance exams. She is a rather intellectual, lonely girl, and picks up with an artist's family and goes to bed with the wife. One wonders how much the portraits drawn here may owe to that summer of 1936 when Sybille Bedford and the Huxleys were at Sanary? In *Jigsaw* the author tells of such a summer when she was supposedly cramming for a translator's exam (which I believe she never passed despite her complete fluency in French). Her relations with Maria Huxley were, in the later book, mainly economic; she could usually count on Maria for a loan in times of dire necessity. In *A Compass Error* (most appropriate title) Flavia is not so fortunate as her mother. She forms another relationship with a woman, Andree, and against her better judgment reveals Constanza's and Michel's retreat. Their escape is spoiled leaving Flavia with a burden of guilt. What Flavia suffers from is a compass error rather than a deliberate betrayal, a breach of judgment and conduct with her seductress. So Constanza and Michel are never married. Flavia never goes to university. The end results (from the epilogue) are domestic tragedy, though in time Flavia is able to 'come near to absolving herself' (270). The war begins. Michel spends it in a corner of Occupied France as a conscientious objector (not a very salutary part to play), Andree, the *femme de monde* who seduced Flavia, is decorated by both the British and the French, Constanza dies in the evacuation, and Flavia simply continues to exist. The ending is filled with irony, and the Flavia we find at the last bears only a diminished resemblance to her creator.

The books should of course be read together as one long work dealing with many vital issues of those times. One at least is quite new; that is, how one should behave in the face of totalitarian menace. Nothing like the Nazis had happened in the living memory of any civilized European (or for that matter American). They provide a sort of scheme upon which to test one's own ethical values, but they do not attempt to reveal the causes of contemporary history in the way *A Legacy* does. Put together they seem important; *A Legacy* is a giant.

Some of the techniques developed in the first published novel reappear in the two later books, but largely without the fireworks. Like Milton's *Paradise Lost*, having done it once, who could ever do it again? There are of course a few new devices, and some of the old ones get refurbished. For example, the catalogue of Henrietta Merz's followers reappears in *A Favourite of the Gods* in near contemporary terms. We meet Asquith, Keir Hardie, Winston Churchill, and Lloyd George only a few lines apart from Cezanne and Picasso, Stravinsky and Debussy. And on almost the same page G. B. S., H. G. Wells, D. H. Lawrence, E. M. Forster, Marcel Proust, T. S. Eliot, the Sitwells, Exra Pound, Gerard Manley Hopkins, and even D'Annunzio. The texture, laden as it is with much contemporary reference, provides a plus value for the reader.

## ENCORE ROMAN – UN RETOUR

The works of fiction heretofore discussed all appeared within the period of a dozen years. There followed some two decades in which Sybille Bedford published little (or no) fiction. Then in 1989 two major pieces appeared, one, 'Une Vie de Chateau', a fairly long piece in the *New Yorker* (20 February 1989), and shortly thereafter *Jigsaw: A Biographical Novel* (New York, Alfred, A. Knopf, 1989). As a matter of fact both works are highly biographical and deal directly with materials and events already familiar to readers of *A Legacy*. The short piece in the *New Yorker* tells us more about her relationship with the Merz family in Berlin and continues with a fairly extensive view of life at Feldkirch, in Bavaria. The events, however, are not exactly the same as those we met in the earlier novel. Some new factual material appears, and it is possible to ascertain points at which *A Legacy* is indeed very much fiction and where it is not. The *New Yorker* story is told in what is very much *New Yorker* style – the editors seems to like nothing better than vignettes from the life of Europeans (should I add preferably intellectual Europeans – at least those who write well?). However, the stylistic fireworks, the paradise of dainty devices, that make *A Legacy* so extremely interesting are largely omitted. The scenes add to our knowledge of Sybille Bedford's unusual childhood. They are well written. But the story reminds one of the early chapters of *A Legacy* with the lights turned down – way down.

*Jigsaw* proceeds in much the same manner, though it is only fair to Sybille Bedford to add that she did not simply excise bits and pieces from this work for the *New Yorker* piece. Though they deal with similar subject matter, the author's early life, they have separate identities. *Jigsaw* digs much deeper of course, beginning with life in Germany at Feldkirch. She starts with a passage delineating her father's impatience waiting for her mother to join him in a carriage for a visit, perhaps a shopping trip to Karlsruhe. One presumes the incident is reasonably factual, as a child might recall it. Before we have gone a dozen pages, we are brought face to face again with the complicated affair of Julius's younger brother, Johannes, which occupied such a paramount position in *A Legacy*. We discover that the fictional incident (or more accurately incidents) in *A Legacy* was actually based on a real scandal, the Allenstein affair, to which Sybille Bedford says, 'I owe my existence'.

Thence from these 'Antecedents' (her title for the first chapter) to 'Fugitives' (early life with her mother in Italy), to 'In Transit' (England, Italy), 'Anchorage' (some stability in France, fairly reminiscent of *A Favourite of the Gods*) to 'Landslides' (Sanary, London, Sanary). This brings us to the verge of World War Two. *Jigsaw* is no doubt heavily biographical and explains much about the author that we did not previously know or could even guess. For instance, she was largely self-educated, did not attend university, always planned to become a writer, etc. Where fact stops and fiction begins is not really discernible, and perhaps not very important. Does not every good writer draw heavily on his own experience, molding it into the stuff of fiction? Some of the personages are real and appear under their own names, the Kislings and the Huxleys. Some are disguised, the Falkenheims, the Nairns, the Desmirails, though they, too, were real people and some of them still live and keep in contact with the author. Her mother and Sybille are 'a percentage of ourselves . . .' (author's note) One wonders what percentage? For instance is here sexual awakening – anything but exciting – real or fictional? It probably does not matter, and Sybille Bedford does not play to the prurient in her readers.

There is a good deal of discussion of anti-Semitism in the book, all of it from what right thinking people would have to consider the proper viewpoint. For instance, the Nairns are Jews. The sister Toni explains to Sybille about Rosie's lover, who is a prominent English judge. And Sybille, 'He can't be against Jews if he – well if he loves one'. And then Toni, 'You know nothing about the social anti-semitism of the English . . . in Germany it's the plebs (she used a horrid sounding German word, *der Pöbel*) who are the anti-semites, here it's the nobs. It's their natural order of things' (128). Anti-semitism is of course one of her favourite – and most important – themes, but considering what she has to say on the subject we should keep in mind that she is writing now out of the 1930s, not the present. This passage rises from Hitler's Germany, before the war began. The writer is so disgusted with anti-semitism that she seems almost to have invented (?) for herself a Jewish ancestor, her own Henrietta Merz. I have no idea whether this is factual or not. In any case it is hardly important; she would have held the same views, I am sure, had she been a blond, blue-eyed Aryan. (We tend to forget that, in the Nazi scheme of things, one who had no Jewish ancestors before the middle of the nineteenth-century was Aryan.)

*Jigsaw* provides some other interesting tidbits, such as that the early novel Maria Huxley helped type (about which I once puzzled) was actually called *An Expense of Spirit*. But two things it does not do. It does not show the remarkable stylist with her rhetorical devices that wrote *A Legacy*. As in the *New Yorker* piece the fireworks are toned down or never appear at all. This I think is disheartening, but perhaps we should be thankful for what we do get. Second, *Jigsaw* ends rather abruptly just before the war began, encouraging one reviewer to ask when we can expect a sequel bringing us up to date. Did Sybille Bedford's mother actually suffer the fate of Constanza in *A Favourite of the Gods* and *A Compass Error*, to be gunned down in the evacuation by German machine-gun bullets – it hardly seems likely from what we find in *Jigsaw*.

## NON FICTION

I certainly do not intend to suggest that Sybille Bedford spent nearly two decades between the two periods of fiction doing nothing. She continued working as a journalist, flying to Dallas to cover the Kennedy assassination, for example, and also produced four sub-stantial, remarkable pieces of non fiction. These are in short:

*The Trial of Dr Adams* – an account of a famous murder trial. As it happened Dr Adams was acquitted and, I used to believe, rearrested as he left the courtroom, but Sybille Bedford has corrected me. He lived on a free man and perhaps still lives.

*The Sudden View* – (in the American edition called *A Visit to Don Otavio*). This is to my mind the best travel book about Mexico since Graham Greene's *Another Mexico*. It appeared in 1960 and is an account of a trip Bedford made with another woman identified only by an initial. It turns out she was Esther Murphy Arthur, wife of the grandson of the former President of the United States, Chester A. Arthur. (A letter from Mrs Bedford suggests there may be some fictional elements here, too.)

*The Faces of Justice* – a very accurate account of the workings of justice in the courts in England, Germany, Austria, Switzerland, and France, first appearing in 1961, so stimulating it has been used as a textbook in classes on comparative law both in Germany and the United States.

*Aldous Huxley: A Biography* – first printed in 1973, a mixture of literary criticism and personal reminiscence of Huxley, and the family, by a close friend and admirer. We learn in *Jigsaw* that she has been a lifelong fan of Huxley's works. When the Huxleys finally left for the United States, Sybille Bedford inherited their London flat. For all I know it may be the one she still occupies. Unfortunately the book did not fare as well with some American academic reviewers as it deserved. Bedford's favourites among Huxley's novels were perhaps not theirs.

### Notes

1.  Aldous Huxley in Gerald Heard (ed.), *Prayers and Meditations: A Monthly Cycle Arranged for Daily Use* (New York, Harper, 1949).
2.  Writers in the English Renaissance, Ben Jonson for instance, loved to lard their works with erudite Latin quotations, to add stature and authority to their words, most of which were translated in the following sentence (often rather badly, too). Some modern novelists have adopted their practice, for example, Umberto Eco in the Italian (and American) bestseller *Il Nome della Rosa*. There, however, the Latin passages seem to me to be quite extraneous to the meaning, being developed in the vulgar tongue. But other rhetorical devices often lend even the contemporary writer a hand, particularly the tropes and figures of speech. For instance Robert Graves, who was classically educated, makes great use of these, usually adapting them to English.

American writers on the whole seem a little less conscious of the nuances of style represented by the figures. Ernest Hemingway is perhaps an exception. Note, for instance, his repetition of the Spanish word *nada* in his short story 'A Clean Well Lighted Place', where the refrain underscores the existential theme of the tale.

3.   Henrich Lausberg, *Handbuch der Literischen Rhetorik* (Munich. 1960, #924).

4.   One cannot help thinking of such *good* Germans as Dr Adam von Trott zu Solz, an architect of the East Prussian plot, where Colonel Schenck von Stauffenberg placed a bomb at Hitler's feet during a conference in the bunker at Rastenburg. Hitler's life was saved by sheer accident when another officer pushed the attache case containing the bomb away, perhaps to make room for his feet. Hitler was so incensed he arrested all known relatives of the plotters, including their children; however, only two Stauffenbergs eventually paid the supreme penalty. But several thousand others, many of them no doubt quite innocent, lost their lives. There has been much controversy about how many. Nazi sources claim 5,764 persons were executed in 1944 and another 5,684 the following year, but these figures may be excessive. Adam von Trott, with many others, died in the manner described.

5.   For all their charm Bedford's women have a tendency to be a bit zany. The only comparable, outrageous incident I recall from contemporary British fiction occurs in Nancy Mitford's *The Blessing*, where the heroine, stranded in a Paris railway station, without money, sitting on her suitcase and in tears, is picked up by a gallant Frenchman, who, on the way to a taxi, drops her mink coat in a trash receptacle, promising to buy her a sable.

## A BIBLIOGRAPHY OF WRITINGS BY SYBILLE BEDFORD

*Robert O. Evans and Robert E. Hosmer Jr.*

## Novels

*A Legacy* (London: Weidenfeld and Nicholson, 1956. New York: Simon and Schuster, 1957; Penguin, 1964; Ecco Press, 1976).
*A Favourite of the Gods* (London: Collins, 1963. New York: E. P. Dutton, 1984).
*A Compass Error* (London: Collins, 1968. New York: E. P. Dutton, 1985).
*Jigsaw: An Unsentimental Education: A Biographical Novel* (London: Hamish Hamilton, 1989. New York: Knopf, 1989).

## Stories

'Une Vie De Chateau', *The New Yorker* (20 February 1989): 38–48.

**Books**

*The Sudden View: A Mexican Journey* (London: Gollancz, 1953. Later published as *A Visit to Don Otavio: A Traveller's Tale from Mexico*. London: Collins, 1960. New York: Atheneum, 1963).

*The Best We Can Do: An Account of the Trial of John Bodkin Adams* (London: Collins, 1958. American edition: *The Trial of Dr Adams*. New York: Simon and Schuster, 1959).

*The Faces of Justice: A Traveller's Report* (New York: Simon and Schuster, 1959. London: Collins, 1961).

*Aldous Huxley: A Biography. Volume I: 1894–1939* (London: Chatto and Windus, 1973).

*Aldous Huxley: A Biography. Volume II: 1939–1963* (London: Chatto and Windus, 1974).

*Aldous Huxley: A Biography* [Volumes I and II] (New York: Harper and Row, 1974).

**Articles**

'Lake Constance', *Holiday* (January 1960): 74–7.

'Black Forest', *Mademoiselle* (March 1961): 131+.

'Last Trial of Lady Chatterley', *Esquire* (April 1961): 132–6+.

'Truth and Consequences of French Justice', *Esquire* (June 1961): 73–4+.

'Way Home', *Reporter* (14 September 1961): 50+.

'Generations on the Gallows', *The Nation* (7 December 1963): 394–5.

'Ruby Trial: A Chance to Redeem a Tragedy', *Life* (28 February 1964): 36–6B.

'Violence, Froth, Sob Stuff: Was Justice Done?' *Life* (27 March 1964): 32–4B+.

'Lost Art of Civilized Touring', *Esquire* (November 1964): 126–31+.

'House of Lords', *Horizon* (Autumn 1965): 4–13+.

'This Blessed Plot, This Earth, This Realm, This Denmark', *Esquire* (December 1965): 212+.

'Her Majesty's Incorruptible, Imperturbable, Incomparable Judges', *Esquire* (October 1965): 78–82+.

'Worst That Ever Happened', *Saturday Evening Post* (22 October 1966): 29–33+.

'Authors and Editors', *Publishers Weekly* (7 April 1969): 18.


## A BIBLIOGRAPHY OF WRITINGS ABOUT SYBILLE BEDFORD

*Robert O. Evans and Robert E. Hosmer Jr.*

**Articles and Reviews**

Annan, Gabriele, 'High Romance' [*Jigsaw*], *The New York Review of Books* (27 April 1989): 22–3.

Bailey, Paul, 'A Legacy of Summer Nights' [*Jigsaw*], *Sunday Times* (7 May 1989): G14.

Benenson, Peter, 'Seen To Be Done' [*The Faces of Justice*], *The Spectator* (26 May 1961): 769.

Bicker, Alexander, 'A Cook's Tour of the Law Courts' [*The Faces of Justice*], *The New Republic* (26 June 1961): 26–7.

Colvin, Clare, 'Journeys in a Vanished World' [*A Favourite of the Gods* and *A Compass Error*], *The Times* (17 February 1984): 11.

Craft, Robert, 'Huxley at Home' [*Aldous Huxley: A Biography*], *The New York Reviewer of Books* (23 January 1975): 9–12.

Dinnage, Rosemary, 'Between Two Worlds' [*Aldous Huxley: A Biography: Volume II*], *Times Literary Supplement* (*TLS*) (20 September 1974): 1017.

Duguid, Lindsay, 'Outlandish Legacies' [*Jigsaw*], *TLS* (12–18 May 1989): 519.

Dyer, Richard, 'Bedford Puzzles Out a Vivid Life' [*Jigsaw*], *The Boston Globe* (10 May 1989): 52.

Evans, Robert O., 'Sybille Bedford: Most Reticent, Most Modest, Best', *Studies in the Literary Imagination* 11, ii (1978): 67–78. Reprinted in *British Novelists Since 1900*, ed. Jack I. Biles (New York: AMS Press, 1987): 207–20.

Jones, Richard, 'Kensington Ghosts' [*A Compass Error*]. *The Listener* (7 November 1968): 618.

King, Francis, 'Women, War and Crime' [*A Favourite of the Gods* and *A Compass Error*], *The Spectator* (18 February 1984): 21.

Leavitt, David, 'Living Large: Sybille Bedford at Home and Abroad', *The Village Voice Literary Supplement* (June 1990): 9–10.

Lindley, Robert, 'Best Way To Do It' [*The Best We Can Do*], *The Spectator* (14 November 1958): 655.

Murphy, Dervla, 'Global Warning' [*As It Was: Pleasures, Landscapes and Justice*], *TLS* (26 October–1 November 1990): 1144.

Nott, Kathleen, 'Novels' [*A Favourite of the Gods*]. *Encounter* (March 1963): 88–91.

Olney, James, 'Most Extraordinary: Sybille Bedford and Aldous Huxley', *South Atlantic Quarterly* 74 (1975): 376–86.

Partridge, Frances, 'Loving Mother and Mother's Lover' [*Jigsaw: An Unsentimental Education: A Biographical Novel*], *The Spectator* (20 May 1989): 36.

Plante, David, 'Once and Future Addictions' [*Jigsaw*], *The New York Times Book Review* (28 May 1989): 13.

Pritchett, V. S., 'The Vision From Limbo' [*Aldous Huxley: A Biography: Volume I*], *New Statesman* (20 September 1974): 384–6.

Raven, Simon, 'A Summer's Tale' [*A Compass Error*], *The Spectator* (25 October 1968): 593–4.

Sale, Roger, 'Huxley and Bennett, Bedford and Drabble' [*Aldous Huxley*], *Hudson Review* 28, 2 (Summer, 1975): 285–93.

Schott, Webster, 'Flirting With History' [*A Favourite of the Gods*], *The Nation* (4 May 1963): 377–8.

Steiner, George, 'The Last Victorian' [*Aldous Huxley*], *The New Yorker* (17 February 1975): 103–6.

Wain, John, 'Women's Work' [*A Compass Error*], *The New York Review of Books* (26 April 1969): 38–40.

Waugh, Evelyn, 'A Remarkable Historical Novel' [*A Legacy*], *The Spectator* (13 April 1956): 498.

Wilmers, Mary-Kay, 'Nonchalance' [*Jigsaw*], *London Review of Books* (27 July 1989): 12–13.

**Interviews**

Baker, J. F., '*PW* Interviews Sybille Bedford', *Publishers Weekly* (16 December 1974): 6–7.

## SYBILLE BEDFORD

Sybille Bedford was born 16 March 1911, daughter of Maximillian von Schoenbeck and Elizabeth Bernard. She married Walter Bedford in 1935. A reticent and private person, she has supplied no additional information to biographical sources. However, something more can be assumed from her literary work. The dust jacket to her latest book, *Jigsaw*, states she was born in Germany, and if we can believe the opening statements in *A Legacy*, in a rented flat in Charlottenberg in West Berlin. After her father and mother separated, she lived the early years of her life with her father in a chateau in southern Germany in much impoverished circumstances brought about by the ravages of World War One. This portion of her childhood is documented, probably with considerable accuracy, in her recent *New Yorker* short story, 'Une Vie de Chateau' (20 February 1989). There she attended school briefly and made her First Communion (also documented in the biographical novel, *Jigsaw*).

She left Germany to join her mother in Italy, at the resort Cortina d'Ampezzo. The stay in Italy proved rather short. Thereafter her youth was divided between residence in the south of France at Sanary, a village not far from Toulon, and London, where she was sent at first to friends of her mother's and later lived on her own in a bedsitter. She prides herself on being bilingual, English and French – which indeed she is – but she also has a fine command of German and Italian. The early times at Sanary are also documented, probably with some accuracy again, in her novels, *A Favourite of the Gods* and *A Compass Error*.

She was largely self-educated; like Virginia Woolf she attended no university but must have been a serious and voracious reader. Much can be interpolated from *Jigsaw*, but just how much is fact and how much fiction is difficult to tell. In her 'Author's Note' to the book she says: '. . . the Aldous Huxleys [are] themselves . . . My mother and I are a percentage of ourselves . . . These, and everyone and everything else, are what they seemed – at various times – to me.'

For details of her life following World War Two we shall have to wait for the sequel to *Jigsaw*. Throughout her early years it was her ambition to become a writer, and she has surely been that, a novelist of the first rank, a writer of non-fiction including a travel book, *The Sudden View* (later published in both England and the United States under the title *A Visit to Don Otavio*), and the monumental biography *Aldous Huxley*. She has also done her service as a journalist, writing articles and reviews, particularly about legal systems and issues; at the time of the assassination of President Kennedy, she was sent to Dallas to report firsthand for the English press. From the mid-1970s until the appearance of *Jigsaw* in 1989, Bedford largely ceased publication. However, that year marked the publication of not only that biographical novel but a short story in *The New Yorker*. There is reason to believe Sybille Bedford is presently engaged in writing a continuation of *Jigsaw*.

# 2

# Paradigm and Passage: The Fiction of Anita Brookner

ROBERT E. HOSMER JR.

It is a narrative as old as those told about Odysseus, Aeneas, Adam and Eve, Joseph, Moses, the Viking warriors, and countless other uprooted souls set adrift into uncharted waters or expelled into barren deserts. Exile, that harsh, often brutal, state of perpetual and self-renewing loss, that ur-experience of most peoples, and of most individuals, sweeps through the drama of human experience, changing forever its contours and signs. No wonder that it constitutes a resonant, heart-rending theme articulated in so many of the traditions, both oral and written, that we call 'literature'. When we think about exile within our own Western, Judaeo-Christian tradition, classic expressions of the theme spring readily to mind and loom large there: the Hebrew Scriptures, with particular emphasis on Genesis, Exodus, the Writings, the Prophets; the *Odyssey*; the *Aeneid*.

Certainly, the exile, under one guise or another, whether political, social, or religious we've always had with us, or so it seems. The familiar twentieth-century figure of the exile can boast an impressive spiritual pedigree, from Anaxagoras, Empedocles, and Ovid, through Dante, and on to Chopin, Hugo, Mann, Einstein, Chagall, Kundera, Milosz, and Brodsky. Some exiles have made of their experiences major works of art, while others have left lasting contributions in political and intellectual spheres: so many seem to have harnessed tremendous creative energies.

It is among the company of artists such as these that Anita Brookner finds herself, both personally and artistically. Born in London to a Jewish immigrant father from Poland and a mother whose parents had immigrated to England, Brookner, for all her British schooling and experience, to this day considers herself an exile living among a people essentially foreign to her; and her departure from the religious sphere of her family's Jewish heritage has only exacerbated her sense of dislocation.

In 1980 Brookner, then at the height of her career as an art historian of international reputation, turned her hand to writing fiction, an occupation that now engages her fully since her retirement from the Courtauld faculty (1988). In a *Publishers Weekly* interview Brookner explained her motivation for becoming a novelist, noting, 'It was most undramatic . . . I had a long summer vacation in which nothing seemed to be happening, and I could have got very sorry for myself and miserable, but it appeared to be such a waste of time to do that, and I'd always got a lot of nourishment from fiction. I wondered – it just occurred to me to see whether I could do it. I didn't think I could. I just wrote a page, the first page, and nobody seemed to think it was wrong. An angel with a flaming sword didn't appear and say, 'You shouldn't be doing this'. So I wrote another page, and another, and at the end of the summer, I had a story.' The result was a novel titled *A Start in Life* (1981), published in the United States as *The Debut*. Each succeeding summer Brookner followed the same schedule, working in her office, producing a first draft that would be the final draft (a distinction she shares with Muriel Spark); eleven novels have appeared thus far, earning her high marks in this second career.

Despite an astonishingly rapid rise in the world of letters, Brookner continues to feel an exilic grief and isolation. In a 1985 interview with John Haffenden, shortly after her fourth novel, *Hotel du Lac*, won England's most prestigious literary prize, she described herself as 'this grown up orphan with what you call success' (63), before announcing, 'I feel I'm walking about with the mark of Cain on my forehead. I feel I could go into the Guinness Book of Records as the world's loneliest, most miserable woman' (75). This is a woman for whom exile is not just the very marrow of existence: it is also the stuff of art.

In *The Poetics of Prose*, Tzvetan Todorov has noted that, 'No narrative is natural; a choice and construction will always preside over its appearance; narrative is a discourse, not a series of events . . .' (45). It will be my contention that a paradigm of exile, with elements rather clearly derived from the dominant Scriptural model, is the 'choice and construction' which presides over the narrative of Brookner's fiction, and that *nostos*, understood not only as 'the drive to return home' (Peter Brooks, *Reading for the Plot*, 38), but as the desire to create a home never before realized, empowers the narrative dynamics of her fiction. The paradigm acquires additional resonance when viewed within an evolving literary tradition and when valued not only as an integral component in the deep structure of each novel but also as a constituent element within that discourse we call narrative. That discourse foregrounds the concerns of exile, both within and without the novel, and privileges the experience of this writer to an extraordinary degree.

## EXILE: A BIBLICAL PARADIGM/AN ANGLO–SAXON FORMULA

The Jews are perhaps the most experienced exiles, indeed exiles *par excellence*, if you will, and their story begins with the patriarch Abraham. The call of Abraham and his subsequent journey as a voluntary exile toward the Promised Land is but one of two proto-types in Hebrew history, however. The other is expulsion or invol-untary exile, the sentence of endless wandering with Cain as the marked, archetypal outcast, stranded in a perpetual exile, alien to all, even himself, restless, rootless, without a home. Looming large on the horizon of Hebrew history as well is Moses' leading the people from Egypt which combines both prototypes in a sojourn of forty years' wandering. Yet that episode is dwarfed by an event so cata-strophic to the Jewish community that it is known simply as 'the Exile'.

Between 598 and 586 B. C. E. most of the inhabitants of Judah and Jerusalem were deported to Babylon; the city was sacked and looted and, most cruelly, the Temple was levelled. In Babylon a Hebrew community was reconstituted and remained there, substantially, until the edict of Cyrus in 538 B. C. E., an official release allowing the Jews to return home and rebuild the Temple (515 B. C. E.). Perhaps only the Psalmist's eloquent lament of Psalm 137 can recapture the existential anguish of the Exile. Wretched isolation. Alienation. Trauma. Deprivation. A seeking after identity. A longing for 'home'.

Life in exile 'with the memory of their spiritual or ethnic, divine or geographical, real or imaginary homes' (Leszek Kolakowski, 'In Praise of Exile', *Times Literary Supplement*, 11 October 1985: 1133) kept alive with them, caused the Hebrews to re-examine their lives, re-evaluate their conduct, and re-constitute their religious and cultural heritage. These people came to understand that their journey from Jerusalem to Babylon somehow replicated the journeys of their forebears; this homelessness, with its corollary loneliness, fostered a renewed sense of *nostos*. Within such a context, they understood that the journey would continue, that there would be a return to the Land of Promise; the quest for home was parallelled by a search for identity. Self-examination produced intense self-awareness and the need, nearly obsessive, to create order from the chaos of deportation and exile. Yet the importance of Exile lay not just in its existential and spiritual dimensions: this traumatic time, marked not only by separation from the Promised Land and its Temple, but also by spiritual and emotional suffering for those Jews who clung to their beliefs and rituals, was a period of remarkable literary activity. The impulse to create order extended from the personal and existential to the spiritual and literary; indeed none of these dimensions of the Hebrew experience can be separated from the others. Both Ezekiel and Second Isaiah, resident in Babylon, prepared the biblical materials that bear their names. So, too, Jeremiah, exiled to Egypt, collated texts, culled materials from them, infused them with his spirit and style, and bequeathed a document distinguished for the force and insight of its teaching as well as the literary excellences of its crafting. And this was the time when that school of men, known collectively now as the 'Priestly Writer', collated and codified so many Hebrew traditions into some of the most beautiful, spiritually-resonant material in the Pentateuch.

Efforts to clarify the literary dimensions of the Exile for textual purposes, and to discern inner resonances among 'literary expressions' of the theme can be enhanced by uncovering a paradigm in texts. One distinguished scholar of medieval literature articulated a paradigm for Anglo–Saxon poetry; that paradigm can be applied not only to Scriptural texts (such is not my purpose here, though) but also to the fiction of Anita Brookner.

In 'The Formulaic Expression of the Theme of "Exile" in Anglo–Saxon Poetry' (*Speculum* XXX, No. 2, April 1955), Stanley B. Greenfield traced patterns of 'words and phrases which, by virtue of their repetition in the same grammatical-metrical patterns in the same or other poems, may be termed formulas' (200). That investigation led him to posit what he called 'four aspects or concomitants of the exile state: 1. status; 2. deprivation; 3. state of mind; 4. movement' (201). These 'aspects' function as elements establishing a paradigm (i.e., 'a model of reality . . . constructed to explain significant phenomena').

Key phrases uncovered in the Anglo–Saxon poems he scrutinized caused Greenfield to characterize the first aspect, 'status' as 'joyless' or 'wretched'; the second aspect, 'deprivation' to apply to joys and comforts, but particularly to loss of 'home'; the third aspect, 'state of mind', as 'humbled' or 'troubled'; and the fourth, 'movement in or into exile', not only as a turning away from home and endurance of hardships, but as a seeking. Greenfield's paradigm provides a short-hand grammar of exile simultaneously emphasizing the existential dimension of the experience and tracing the literary construction of those texts which present the narrative to us.

In 'The Condition We Call Exile', (*New York Review of Books*, 21 January 1988: 16–20), Joseph Brodsky has said that exile is both 'a linguistic event' and 'a metaphysical condition', an opportunity to ponder 'the meaning of what has happened to you'. Though he does not mention the Biblical experience or Anglo–Saxon poetry (or the fiction of Anita Brookner, for that matter) Brodsky has un-wittingly illuminated aspects of all three for readers.

And it is against this backdrop that I would like to consider three of the novels of Anita Brookner, this self-described 'sort of Jewish exile' who feels that she 'walk[s] about with the mark of Cain on my forehead'. I mean to suggest nothing as neatly paradigmatic, nothing so precisely supported at the linguistic level as Greenfield's analysis, only what I discern as a consistent, perhaps loosely paradigmatic concern with this major theme in Anita Brookner's fiction, a concern expressed with such evolved precision and enhanced resonance that it might well be considered the dominant expressive interest of her fiction.

## PROVIDENCE

Brookner's first three novels bear such striking resemblances to one another that they can be considered together as delicate variations on a single theme: the plight of a painfully sensitive, lonely woman on the cusp of middle age, who, despite keen intelligence and con-siderable learning never does quite 'get things right'; critical, intro-spective and disciplined, this woman is victimized not so much by her romantic idealism, which causes her to wait for a Prince Charm-ing whose loving presence will fill her absence, completing her identity and granting her perpetual happiness, as by her own inabil-ity to assert herself aggressively enough to attract (and retain) his attentions. In each novel, literature – both the reading and writing of it – is a self-consuming activity which substitutes for 'real life' and displaces those energies that ought be directed elsewhere if that love 'without [which] there can be no reason to hope' (*The Debut*, 83) is to be a functional reality. Of the three novels, the second, *Providence*, combines excellences of style with thematic integrity to such an extent that it can be considered not only the best of the lot but a model of typicality.

'Kitty Maule was difficult to place.' With the emblematic resonance that only a thoroughly-accomplished stylist can achieve in a novel's very first line, we are introduced to Brookner's protagonist in *Providence*: a young woman of impeccable manners, precise speech, and fashionable, if slightly outmoded, style, Kitty is an academic, a specialist in the Romantic tradition who holds an appointment at a small British college; during the summer term that constitutes the bulk of the narrative present, she gives a seminar on Benjamin Constant's novel, *Adolphe*, a stunning study of failure which she describes for her students as 'an essay on alienation', (131), an ironically apt way to characterize her own life and this novel as well.

Born to a French mother and an English father who died before her birth, the child is caught between two cultures; her mother, a languid and melancholic figure given to reading romances, largely abdicated the child's upbringing to her own father, Vadim, a Russian acrobat who had met and married Louise, a young seamstress, and emigrated from Paris to London after World War One to establish a successful couturier house on Grosvenor Street. Known as 'Therese' at home, but as 'Kitty' to the outside world, she is a divided soul, caught between the suffocating, Continental house of her grandparents in Dulwich where she was reared and still spends weekends, and her own 'rational little flat in Chelsea' (6). Kitty is constantly moving back and forth between these worlds, between her French and English selves, considering herself, even in her late twenties, an 'orphan', and admitting, 'I am not anywhere at home. I believe in nothing. I am truly in an existentialist world' (88). That sense of cultural estrangement is intensified by acquaintances like the mother of a colleague who considers Kitty's 'very precise English' an indication of 'her being a foreigner'. And she is further divided by her participation in two distinctly different spheres of activity: the realm of literature which has given her expectations, both about what abstract values ought obtain in the world at large and about standards of human behaviour in particular, and the real world in which she lives.

Kitty Maule feels deprived of a distinct identity, of a reliable, articulated code of behaviour, and most importantly, of romantic love. As a result, she spends a good deal of time on the move, whether shuttling back and forth between Chelsea and Dulwich, travelling to France, or walking about the streets of London or Paris. In a grimly deterministic pattern, she travels, 'but she disliked travelling, which always seemed to increase her feelings of isolation, her sense of not belonging in any one clearly defined context . . . she was losing her identity', (102). Kitty knows that in order to create a satisfactory, functional identity, she must reconcile the disparate elements of herself and her experience; with penetrating self-analysis, she declares, 'I function well in one sphere only, but all the others must be thought through, every day. Perhaps I will graft myself onto something native here, make a unity somehow. I can learn. I can understand. I can even criticize. What I cannot do is reconcile. I must work on that' (51–2).

Kitty's manifest inability to make herself at home anywhere leaves her conflicted and terribly uncertain about how to behave: 'she was eternally uncertain about standards of behaviour and worried in case she formed or indeed gave a false impression' (103). Conflict and uncertainty manifest themselves in undue concern for appearance, an excess abetted by the smothering attentions of her grandparents who design and execute custom clothes for all important events in the life of their darling.

While certainly loved by her grandparents and loving them in return, Kitty finds that inadequate, given the expectations that literature has given her. She longs for her Prince Charming, that man whose presence will fill her empty soul and become everything to her; indeed, upon Maurice Bishop, a colleague described as 'a romantic and devout Christian', she has placed all these expectations in rather pitiful fashion. Though by the novel's end she has lost him for good, still, in the narrative present of the novel, she regards that day when she first saw him in the Senior Common Room as 'the best moment of her life' (25). For him, she becomes servile, typing his notes and feeding him, knowing that she is 'useful' though not 'indispensable' to him, yet relishing opportunities to create a home for him, for them both, in her flat while settling for little more in return than a smile, a wink, an occasional evening, or a little time together in Paris. Her fondest (and unrealized) desire is 'to be at one with him' (35); but what she takes as the promise of his presence is never fulfilled.

Kitty and Maurice Bishop are hopelessly mismatched, however: he believes in Providence, while she is utterly without faith; his identity is rooted in his faith, which allows him 'to make a unity somehow' of his own life. At one point, he declares to her: 'I can't tell you how simple life is when you know that you are being looked after' (55). His sense of being 'looked after' allows him to decode the signs of experience and extract messages and meanings; her utter lack of faith catapults her from brief flirtations with the God of her Roman Catholic mother, to various superstitions, to a clairvoyant to Nature, 'the great female corollary to God' (78).

If Brookner's great narrative strategy depends, literally and figuratively, on the paradigm of exile, then corollary to that strategy is what Michiko Kakutani, in a review of Brookner's most recent novel, *Latecomers* (*The New York Times*, 24 February 1989: C31) has called the 'schematic juxtaposition of opposites'. This may be a bit over-simplified, for the development of the schema always has an aesthetic fullness to it, but it is accurate and perhaps nowhere better illustrated than in one particular scene in *Providence*. Kitty and Maurice walk toward the basilica of Saint-Denis, 'which she perceived as a dungeon surrounded by abattoirs' (117).

> She was very disappointed with what she saw. The rose window was mean . . . She craved something elegant and rational, something that would allow her to keep her balance, for Saint-Denis, she felt, contained the unreason of God, and the Christ figure seemed to bar the door to her unworthiness (118).

For Maurice, however, the experience is a fundamentally different text, radically Other and not radically Self: 'Maurice, his eyes uplifted to the Christ, ignored her question; he stood transfixed, in the rain, his hair darkened by the damp drizzle, while she darted in the side door for shelter' (118).

Inside, 'she was in a vast necropolis, an indoor cemetery reserved for the rich, the famous, and the very dead . . . an inexplicable feeling of dread made her linger near the door' while 'he was quite oblivious to her presence, or had forgotten it, and she was too uncertain of herself to inflict it on him' (118). A typically Brooknerian strategy, this showing rather than telling that takes account of the reader as an active presence within the textual dynamic, inviting her/him to participation rather than mere acceptance. It is a strategy used repeatedly in *Providence*, particularly in these moments of what used to be called deeply-felt experience; Kitty, a word child herself, recognizes how Constant uses juxtaposition in *Adolphe* when she tells her seminar, 'the potency of this particular story comes from the juxtaposition of extremely dry language and extremely heated, almost uncontrollable sentiments . . . even if the despair is total, the control remains. This is very elegant, very important' (131). Anita Brookner has applied this principle of juxtaposition not only in individual scenes but also as a kind of metaphor for the whole experience related in her own novel and the results are indisputably 'very elegant'.

Kitty spends so much of her time seeking meaning, trying to reconcile opposites, attempting to develop her own identity through Maurice; in Paris, before Maurice has arrived, she acknowledges what we already know: after dinner in a bistro, she contemplates the return to her room: 'a sadness which she did not fully comprehend, set in, and the thought of sitting at a small table under a weak light in a bedroom furnished in shades of tired crimson, while she grappled with the task of writing her lecture . . . came to be associated in her mind with the thought of solitude, of exile. Exile, she thought. I have felt this before. But she could not remember in what context' (112).

Yet it is all futile: Kitty learns nothing from her exilic condition. Brodsky's declaration about the metaphysical dimension of exile obtains: 'to ignore or to dodge it is to cheat yourself out of the meaning of what has happened to you, to doom yourself to remaining forever at the receiving end of things, to ossify into an uncomprehending victim' (16). At the end of the novel she is back where she started, really no wiser, but certainly the worse for the wear. Like Ellenore in *Adolphe*, Kitty is a victim of disasters because she misjudges her man. She rationalizes her failure thus: 'I lacked the information . . . Quite simply, I lacked the information. She had the impression of having been sent right back to the beginning of a game she thought she had been playing according to the rules' (182). Just as she has failed to realize that in teaching *Adolphe* she was the text as surely as that novel, so she cannot appreciate what a reader of *Providence* can: both novels inscribe 'the painful astonishment of a deceived soul' (46).

## HOTEL DU LAC

Brookner's fourth novel, *Hotel du Lac* (1984), displays marked similarities to its three predecessors yet is distinct from them in its resolution, however tentative and fragile that might be. This, too, is a novel about a somewhat prim woman hovering about middle age, a disciplined, articulate romantic with longings for hero, home, and hearth. Edith Hope, a thirty-nine-year old novelist, endures a month-long exile at this venerable Swiss hotel and emerges with her own sense of self rather more sharply focused; though she may not appreciate the fullness of that 'very clear metaphysical dimension' Brodsky discerns as one of the truths of exile, she comprehends to a degree sufficient to avoid 'ossify[ing] into an uncomprehending victim'.

*Hotel du Lac* is not simply a character study nor is it merely an illumination of the harrowing existential state of loneliness endured by a contemporary woman; nor is it, as Brookner herself would have us believe, 'a love story pure and simple' (Haffenden, 73). Rather, it is an intensely metaphysical exploration of exile as both external and internal; it is very nearly a meditation on dislocation and displacement, while certainly a study of another woman 'difficult to place'. Brookner's novel sketches this portrait of a woman in whose experience we can discern all four elements of our paradigm, including that movement which takes *nostos* as its dynamic force, and the establishment of an integrated self with an articulated, if temporary, identity as its goal. In the process Brookner employs her customary schematic juxtaposition of opposites, yet here an enhanced literary self-consciousness whose style, allusion, and insight rescue the text from the genre of 'romance novel', enables Brookner to create a fiction which, while it renders vivid and precise an examination of the notion of romantic love and the position of women in contemporary English society, also offers incisive commentary on the dynamics of fiction-making.

The child of an Austrian mother and an English father, Edith Hope is another divided soul; the premature death of a father whom she loved, left her at the mercy of a mother foreign to others and particularly to her daughter. Edith has never felt at home among the English; she retains a sense of being a foreigner amongst these people whom she regards as 'flippant, never serious', a cultural estrangement made more striking by Edith's double life, for under a 'more thrusting name', ('Vanessa Wilde'), she is the author of bestselling romances.

At the age of thirty-nine, Edith has been sent by friends to a resort hotel in Switzerland 'to forget the unfortunate lapse which had led to this brief exile' (8): she had left her husband-to-be, a man of 'mouse-like seemliness', standing on the steps of the Registry Office, unable to go through with a 'safe', albeit loveless, marriage. From the second page of the text on, references and allusions to exile proliferate. Edith feels 'doomed for a certain time to walk the earth', while feeling very much like a prisoner working out her time. Before her departure from Heathrow, she had caught sight herself in a mirror, and murmured, 'I am out of place' (10). Staying at the hotel out of season, in the grey time between the end of summer and the onset of winter, Edith's sense of alienation is exacerbated, her sense of dislocation intensified by both geographical and psychological factors, as she contemplates 'the melancholy of exile', (52), the pain of 'this tiny exile' (117). What she recognizes about her own condition is likewise apparent to others at the Hotel, for most of the guests seem to dwell in the same kingdom.

Like Kitty, Edith feels deprived of home and love; like Kitty, she mourns for an absent father, to be replaced by a Prince Charming who will bring her both home and love. And like Kitty, Edith feels the absence of a mother who should have taught her the rules of the game, for she too quite simply lacks the information, at least until a certain point in the novel. The image of her Viennese mother, an aging coquette given to violent outbursts and babbles of German conversation with her sisters, haunts Edith's dreams and waking hours as well. Like Bronte's Jane Eyre, this motherless child embarks on a quest for fulfillment by substitution, seeking a mother in her man. Like Jane, Edith is left at sea, without instructions for navigating in a world of different women, and men. Like Jane, she seeks desperately to make a home for herself, and that home cannot be without a man; when told that she is a 'romantic', Edith responds by saying, 'No, I am a domestic animal' (98), and indeed she is both. Driven by a self-acknowledged 'unhoused' condition, Edith nearly sacrifices her ideals for the compromise of a loveless marriage, not once, but twice, so powerful is the appeal of this romantic myth.

Edith's state of mind can be described in several quick phrases: underlying unease; uncertainty; deeply introspective; and guilt-ridden. Comfortable neither with herself nor others, Edith engages in rather superficial sociability with others only because they feel sorry for her, or because they can use her as audience or foil. She establishes no meaningful, satisfactory relationships, either in England or Switzerland. For most of the novel, uncertainty characterizes her thoughts and actions, and how could they not, given her sense of deprivation and alienation: sitting in a cafe, alone, she wonders aloud, 'And what am I doing here, myself?' (45). Early on her mental state is clearly revealed when she whispers, 'I think I am rather unhappy' (94). While her deep introspection ('most of my life seems to go on at a subterranean level' (92)) may serve her craft well, it does avail much for life in the real world, since she lacks the 'maxims' a mother ought to hand on to her daughter. Unease, uncertainty, and introspection combine to make Edith Hope one of the most guilt-ridden figures in contemporary literature; this woman blames herself for the rudeness of others and assumes responsibility for the offensive behaviour of others. What movement there will be, is instigated when she recognizes her condition with particular poignancy:

> And now, paradoxically, in the blessed silence and dimness of her room, Edith felt her own fatigue dissolve, and the underlying unease, of which she had been intermittently aware during the writing of her letter, began to stir, to increase, to take over. And at this very late hour, she felt her heart beat, and her reason, that controlling element, to fragment, as hidden areas, dangerous shoals, erupted into her consciousness. (116)

Edith Hope teeters dangerously on the precipice of a complete nervous breakdown: status, deprivation, and state of mind do not cause her to stop dead, however. Her thought processes continue; though 'beneath the sorrow' that succeeds the scene above she feels 'vividly unsafe', she converts the energy of introspection to a review of 'the events that had brought her, out of season, to the Hotel du Lac' (117) and eventually emerges knowing and confident, if not triumphant.

Edith's characteristic physical movement in exile takes the form of well-nigh ceaseless walking while waiting for her time to be up. Her walking is sometimes aimless, sometimes directed, but always restless and uncomfortable, without progress or substantial accomplishment. All that passes is time. Indeed, this walking is emblematic of her own soul searching: this woman who feels 'unhoused' seeks a home for herself, but knows not where it could be. Admittedly 'homesick', she feels she 'must go home', but to what? Edith Hope is an existential wanderer, rootless and ruminative, without direction, without role model.

For both Kitty and Edith, literature with its encoded romantic messages compounds the problem, for the fiction which has fed them offers no exempla of practical value in the world. And certainly the other female guests at the Hotel du Lac present no models for Edith either.

Four other women are guests at this 'place guaranteed to provide a restorative sojourn for those whom life had mistreated or merely fatigued' (9): Iris Pusey, a wealthy widow; her daughter, Jennifer; Mme de Bonneuil, an aged widow discarded by her son; and Monica, anorexic wife of a Belgian nobleman sent to the Hotel for a cure. The Puseys are voluntary exiles; Mme de Bonneuil and Monica, involuntary. These last two, one a pathetic study in painful neglect, the other a vicious near-parody of vengeful condescension, pale in comparison with the first two.

The first appearance of Iris and Jennifer arrests Edith's attention:

> . . . an unexpected note of glamour in the person of a lady of indeterminate age, her hair radiantly ash blonde, her nails scarlet, her dress a charming (and expensive) printed silk . . . rings sparkled on the hand that brought a delicate lace handkerchief to her lips. . . . and into the salon came a girl wearing rather tight trousers (rather too tight, thought Edith) which outlined a bottom shaped like a large Victoria plum, 'There you are, darling,' cried the lady . . . (18)

Indeed, Iris Pusey indulges in a life of pampered excess and material comforts; left a substantial fortune by her late husband who always gave her 'a blank cheque' for spending sprees of madcap frequency, Iris lives without unease, uncertainty, deprivation, or introspection: as Edith herself notes, 'She knew from the outset what some unfortunates never learn; she knew that the best is there to be taken, although there may not be enough to go around' (111). Iris Pusey is a model of that mother who has passed along practical maxims ('A woman owes it to herself to have pretty things' (43); 'Romance and courtship go together. A woman should be able to make a man worship her' (73–4)). And she does her best, even at the age of 79, making a dazzling entrance for her birthday dinner:

> Her midnight blue lace was surmounted by a sort of spangled jacket, obviously extremely expensive; this in its turn was enlivened by several strings of beads, pearls, gold chains, and even a rather beautiful lapis lazuli pendant. Her hair had been regilded, and her nails were flawlessly pink . . . she looked quite splendid, in a baroque sort of fashion (105).

Brookner's juxtaposition of Edith against these ultra-feminine creatures needs no commentary, except perhaps to say that Brookner is
no feminist: 'You'd have to be crouching in your burrow to see my
novels in a feminist way. I do not believe in the all men are swine
programme', she told John Haffenden (70). Nor is Edith 'who was
drawn to Mrs Pusey's table from her own as if by some magnetic
force' (53). While the Pusey programme is not endorsed by the
novel, neither is it censured: it simply is. It is nonetheless true that
Edith's behaviour achieves more careful relief when set against this
backdrop.

When Brookner sets Edith next to the one significant male in the
novel, she employs that 'schematic juxtaposition of opposites' we
expect of her. Philip Neville is a wealthy, divorced businessman
staying at the Hotel du Lac; Neville fits Oscar Wilde's definition of a
cynic. Crisply pragmatic, he provides the maxims her mother never
offered: 'It is a great mistake to confuse happiness with one particular situation, one particular person' (94); 'Without a huge emotional
investment, one can do whatever one pleases' (94); 'You have no
idea how promising the world begins to look once you have decided
to have it all for yourself' (95). Echoes of Iris Pusey reverberate in the
dicta of this man who lives by the motto, 'assume your own central-
ity'. A shrewd, if amoral, judge of character, Neville knows Edith
('Edith, you are a romantic . . . you are misled by what you would
like to believe', 95); when he proposes a Jamesian marriage, urging
her to recognize her own self interest and pressing his case by
declaring, 'You face a life of exile of one sort or another' (165), she
consents, only to decline later after seeing him leave Jennifer's room
before dawn. At novel's end, Edith sends a terse telegram to her
lover David; she writes: 'Coming home'. But, after a moment, she
thinks that this is not entirely accurate and, crossing out the words
'Coming home', writes simply, 'Returning' (184).

Edith's exile is not over; Neville was correct, she will 'face a life of
exile of one sort or another', but it will be by choice, the result of her
having recognizing that the force of *nostos* will not accomplish its
goal. While she still professes the tenents of the romantic creed, she
refuses to accept marriage with Neville because it will be sexless: 'I
believed every word I wrote. And I still do, even though I now
realize that none of it can ever come true for me', she writes to David
(181). Edith remains a romantic, but a romantic who has achieved
some clarity of vision about herself, her world, and her future.

To judge from her literary activity during exile, Edith Hope has found it conducive to creativity, writing frequent, though unsent, letters to David and working on a new novel, *Beneath the Visiting Moon*. In both cases, writing is a nostrum for depression and a means of emotional control, not just what Edith calls 'her daily task of fantasy and obfuscation' (50), and 'the time-honoured resource of the ill-at-ease' (66). In the case of the novel, writing is something more, a self-acknowledged form of conversion therapy: 'To contain her anger . . . she tried various distancing procedures, familiar to her from long use. The most productive was to convert the incident into a scene in one of her novels' (102).

*Hotel du Lac* ends not only with a significant degree of acceptance and some optimism, but with what Barbara Hardy has deemed 'Edith's final affirmation of integrity', which shows that the metaphysical dimensions of exile have not been lost upon her; she will not be an 'uncomprehending victim', a victim, perhaps, but not an uncomprehending one. This fiction of one woman's random passage, written with elegance, cool formality, and wit, is the most satisfying of Brookner's first four novels not only in terms of narrative but also in terms of style.

## LATECOMERS

*Latecomers*, Brookner's eighth novel, is both like and unlike its predecessors. Like each previous novel, this one is essentially concerned with the experience of exile, only here perhaps in the most explicit detail yet; like Brookner's fifth novel, *Family and Friends*, which it most clearly resembles, this is a family saga of Jews displaced by the horrors of Hitler's Germany and translated to England. Here, as in the former and unlike in *The Debut, Providence, Look at Me, Hotel du Lac, The Misalliance*, and *A Friend from England*, Brookner occupies herself with more than one life: in *Family and Friends* it was Sofka Dorn and her four children; here it is Thomas Hartmann and Thomas Fibich and, to some extent, their wives and children, though Fibich dominates the narrative.

Yet the novel's most striking departure from her previous work does not consist, as a number of critics have suggested, in Brookner's concentration on male rather than female characters: she had in fact already done this with Frederick and Alfred Dorn in *Family and Friends*. Rather, the singular and distinguishing achievement of *Latecomers* can be located precisely in the way in which Brookner has dealt with exile here: this is the first novel in which the protagonist has come to terms with the experience by moving through deprivation and inner turmoil, through stoic endurance to heightened and grateful awareness of the richness of human life; in the process, by means of a kind of secularized conversion experience, Thomas Fibich's status has been transformed. Moreover, this is the first of Brookner's novels to impart a sense of optimism, buoyancy, and life-affirming aesthetic integrity to its narrative, making *Latecomers* the most satisfying fiction Brookner has created to date.

Thomas Fibich, the alienated, driven protagonist tormented by the railway station scene of his mother fainting on the platform as he escapes to England, deprived of a past he struggles to uncover, and unable to achieve even transient contentment, returns to his childhood home, Berlin, experiences a revelation, and finally emerges with the confident sense of himself he has so long sought. That state of exile which continued without end in both *Providence* and *Hotel du Lac* comes to satisfying and poignant closure for both protagonist and reader in *Latecomers*. What first Hartmann, then Fibich, is able to say can also be said of Brookner's achievement here: 'Look! We have come through!'

Half-way through *Latecomers* Thomas Fibich listens as his wife Christine recounts an afternoon's shopping with Hartmann's wife, Yvette, at Harrods. His mind wanders and that nearly continuous introspection to which he is given overlays his wife's narrative:

> He knew that he loved her. Yet he also knew, in an unrealized way, that his true life lay elsewhere, that it remained undiscovered, that his task was to reclaim it, to repossess it, and that for as long as it remained hidden from him he would be a sleepwalker, doomed to pass through a life designed for him by others, with no place he recognized as home. Increasingly, what he felt was a kind of homesickness, although he could not have explained this . . . And, to be honest, he felt in such need of a compass himself, so ardently desirous of an explanation, that practical suggestions died on his lips (128).

Initially it seems that Fibich and his life-long friend Hartmann will receive equal attention in *Latecomers*; within the first several pages of Chapter One they are described as 'metaphorically and almost physically twin souls' (8–9). Indeed, to avoid the confusion generated by their common given name, 'Thomas' (which derives from the Aramaic *t'ōma* meaning 'twin') nearly everyone refers to them by surname.

This common forename seems to imply a sort of spiritual twinning, and in fact they share much more than their name. Yet, these two men are strikingly different characters and Brookner uses schematic juxtapositioning to highlight how each negotiates that treacherous, random passage to 'the end'.

Five years older than Fibich, Hartmann's early years were spent in Munich; escaping to England and the nominal care of an aunt, he was sent to public school. A foreigner among natives, he felt himself an alien: 'doubly, even trebly an outsider' (6), Hartmann emerged from school not only with coping strategies, the most effective of which consisted of tactical manoeuvres for 'damage limitation', but with a consciously-chosen, functional amnesia (his motto about the past: an emphatic 'it is over'), an ability to create order ('he was exceptionally good at ordering subversive thoughts out of his mind' (105), and a carefully-developed and maintained good humour. For Hartmann, the experience of exile provided the opportunity to create order from the chaos of displacement and forge an identity achieved by force of a will that ignores the pain of a distant past while directing him to savour the pleasures of a comfortable, sensually-replete present; he has established a home for himself, a place within the world of business and family which accords him status, security, and joys both personal and domestic.

Fibich, on the other hand, is a different case study altogether: the experience of exile has proved to be something other for him. As the novel opens, he is a middle-aged man, still 'strikingly handsome' and unaware of it; an 'abstracted and uncommunicative' soul troubled by the past, serious, trustworthy, and honourable, but horribly burdened, for he carries with him a 'weight of existential anxiety' (54). Self-absorbed and distant, deprived of a past he cannot recover, this is a deeply introspective man: he 'needed all his spare time to himself, as if the task of discovering himself required all his best energies' (44). And indeed it does. Though he and Hartmann have worked industriously, first starting a greeting card company, then a photocopying operation, making 'a small fortune built on flair' (220), he has never enjoyed the rewards; though he has a home complete with devoted wife and handsome son, Toto, Fibich feels alienated, incomplete, and adrift. Unlike Hartmann, he is unable to say of the past, 'it is over', and get on with life; without an identity, he struggles to make that unity Kitty Maule also sought. In his quest 'to reach

enlightenment' (144) he has sought professional help, regularly con-
sulting an analyst, Mrs Gebhardt; nowhere in this novel does Brookner
use juxtaposition so skilfully as in this exchange between the two
men on this subject:

> Hartmann looked disappointed. 'And what does this woman
> for you?'
> 'She listens,' said Fibich, feeling faint at the prospect of describ-
> ing to Hartmann those wordless afternoons when he failed to find
> anything for her to listen to. 'She wants me to tell her about my
> childhood.'
> 'Tell her to mind her own business,' said Hartmann. 'You went
> through it once, why go through it again?' (145)

Hartmann's declaration. 'The present is my secret. Living in the
present' (145), prompts even greater introspection for Fibich. He
discerns something that Hartmann does not recognize about himself: '. . . he saw that Hartmann did in fact retain something of the
past, his past. Somewhere in Hartmann's past had been the unthink-
ing confidence of the loved child . . .' (146). Fibich apprehends a
distinct opportunity: 'he told himself that the testing time had
come, and that if he took no action at all he would perish' (147–8).
Act he does, returning to Berlin with that 'hunger for absent knowledge, a longing, a yearning, not for those losses to be made good
. . . but to be assuaged by fact, by circumstantial detail, by a history,
a geography' (147).

With the compass he formerly lacked Fibich returns to Berlin and
searches the landscape of memory for that absent knowledge:

> Restless and homesick, he entered upon an altered state . . .
> homesickness . . . restlessness . . . That was what his life amounted
> to, he could see it now; he was doomed from the start to have his
> condition unchanged. And perhaps death was the only resolution
> he would ever be permitted for his insoluble lifelong problems
> . . . This pilgrimage, undertaken for Toto, to answer Toto's ques-
> tions, to furnish Toto with a lineage that would survive the death
> of his parents, was, he thought, a rehearsal for the real thing, the
> true homecoming (198–9).

In Berlin, Fibich feels 'at home, and not at home' (205), traveling
to Dahlem, 'a suburb of silent villas painted yellow' (203), touring a

museum where he views 'the vast stone heads of a brutal ancient culture' (204), and finally resolving 'to go to the East, to try, once more, to find that illumination, that shock of recognition that would tell him that he had come home' (206). 'Face to face with the terror and the alienation and the longing' (207), he crosses to East Berlin. Once there, Fibich experiences that 'shock of recognition' for which he has so longed; freed of obligation, even fear and guilt for having 'abandoned' his parents, and graced by reflection from a distance, he comes to see his own life as 'precious' and 'blessed' through an epiphany of sorts:

> Everyone carries around all the selves that they have ever been, intact, waiting to be reactivated in moments of pain, of fear, of danger. Everything is retrievable, every shock, every hurt. But perhaps it becomes a duty to abandon the stock of time that one carries within oneself, to discard it in favour of the present, so that one's embrace may be turned outwards to the world in which one has made one's home. (210)

And the moment culminates in revelation:

> Fibich, sitting in the sun outside the Kranzler, watching the crowd, felt a great peace come upon him, recognizing at last that his purpose in life had been not to find his own father but to be a father himself. (210)

Fibich seizes the day ('Nothing to wait for now, he thought'), returns home, ending an exile both literal and metaphorical, having come to terms with experience and himself. No longer does he ignore the 'very strong, very clear metaphysical dimension' of exile; rather he has chosen to apprehend the meaning of the experience, converting his status from that of uncomprehending victim to that of comprehending participant. In sum, Fibich has 'come through', acknowledging that 'Life brings revelations' (234), which, not coincidentally, he sets forth in a touching memoir written for his son. Out of the experience has come not only personal renewal but literary creativity as well.

*Latecomers* is thus Anita Brookner's most developed treatment of the theme of exile, a novel in which the paradigm discerned in the very first of her fictions functions not only to delineate the narrative pattern with deft, draughtman-like precision but to impart a resonance that echoes throughout her fictional *oeuvre*, from *Providence*, through *Hotel du Lac* and on to this eighth novel.

## CONCLUSION

In *Providence* and *Hotel du Lac* Anita Brookner has imaged late twentieth-century women who are, in effect, exiles: solitary women overwhelmed when experience in the real world turns out to be not at all like the lives fed to them in literature. Deceived, disappointed, deeply introspective, and deprived, they wander through the maze of contemporary experience, shouldering the burdens of being stranded in a hostile, often meaningless world. Restless seeking after the 'information' that will enable them 'to make a unity somehow' characterizes their existence; they embark on an endless and cyclical journey, impelled by a *nostos* without realized destination: for them, there is no promised land, no 'home'.

Yet *Providence* and *Hotel du Lac* are not the same fiction writ twice and it is precisely the foregoing discussion of exile that provides not only one way of reading these fictions (and it is but one way), but also one way of distinguishing the works: whereas Kitty Maule's status remains that of uncomprehending victim, Edith Hope's shifts in the direction of comprehending victim. Kitty will never be more or less than she was (is); indeed, verb tenses are irrelevant here, for she dwells in a static and eternal present; she remains a divided soul, 'difficult to place', to the end; for her, exile will be a lasting and debilitating psychological reality – the metaphor is the reality. Edith, on the other hand, has made a unity of sorts, somehow; still believing in the truths of the romantic myth, she acknowledges that they do not obtain, at least for her, in the real world; her 'exile' to Switzerland has imparted some of the meaning of what has happened to her, enabling her to return, if not to the home she craves, at least to the place she knows.

In *Latecomers* the paradigm of exile informs a novel of fulfilment, for Thomas Fibich's lifelong exile, recapitulated in his return to Berlin years after his escape, ends with a home and identity full realized at last: status radically altered, deprivation removed, state of mind transformed, objectives achieved by painful movement of both body and soul, Thomas Fibich is no longer difficult to place, no longer an alien to himself and others, no longer in exile. His journey back to London from Berlin is indeed a homecoming, but one of decidedly transcendent, if not cosmic dimensions, for this Jewish exile has finally found his place within the great scheme of things. The revelation granted him 'sitting in the sun outside the Kranzler' has lifted that enveloping sense of doom and replaced it with an abiding, life-enhancing optimism.

At one point in *Providence* Kitty Maule cautions the students in her seminar on *Adolphe*, asserting, 'I simply want to make the point that in this period fiction, indeed all creative endeavour, becomes permeated with the author's own autobiography' (130). This principle applies, despite the risk involved in its application, to Anita Brookner's fiction.

Biographical criticism, lately very much out of fashion, can be fraught with errors of overreading and sometimes becomes a means of achieving willfully reductive ends, particularly in connexion with fiction by women. Numbers of male critics have dismissed Brookner's novels as mere transcriptions of her own life experience, and as such not entitled to consideration as real art, whatever that may be. Yet when they suggest that the fiction of many nineteenth-century female authors somehow mirrors their lives, Elaine Showalter and other feminist critics point the way toward an illuminating 'biographical' reading of Brookner's novels. Nonetheless, the enterprise of investigating whether or not the paradigm of exile has anything to do with Brookner's own life might seem a dubious endeavour at best, a wrong-headed and self-defeating exercise at worst, were it not for Brookner's own remarks on the subject.

Interrogated about the relationship between her life and work in nearly every interview she has granted, Brookner has responded candidly, admitting, for example, that *The Debut* is autobiographical (*Paris Review*, 150). But the barrage of complaints alleging that her first four novels are essentially and transparently autobiographcial transcripts, that these genteel, repressed heroines with their romantic longings are only figures in a four-part *roman a clef* elicited the response that such comparisons were 'inevitable' and 'a great bore' as well as this frank admission from the author: 'I have *been* that woman at times' (Kolson, 4-D). Certainly Brookner acknowledged the inevitable when she told John Haffenden that, 'One has to use one's own life; one has no other material. These novels [her first four] are a transcript from a random, rather unsuccessful passage through life' (70).

Integral to Anita Brookner's sense of self is her understanding of herself as an exile. Only child of Polish Jews (her father was born in

Poland, her mother in England). Brookner has described her parents as 'Exiles. Jews. Complicated people', amplifying that description with a remark that evidently includes herself ('That sense of exile is ineradicable' – Moorehead, 13), to judge from what she told Amanda Smith: 'I'm a sort of Jewish exile' (67).

My purpose here is not to initiate a discussion of how closely Greenfield's four-part paradigm applies or does not apply to Anita Brookner's life (such an endeavour would be futile and pointless), nor to explore whether or not she has escaped the fate of 'uncomprehending victim' ascribed to those who ignore or cheat themselves of the metaphysical dimension of exile discerned by Brodsky. Rather, it is to suggest some relationship between Anita Brookner's sense of herself and what many critics take to be the creation of a first-rate fictional *oeuvre*.

Her own 'explanation' of how she became a novelist is interesting, though certainly disingenuous and incomplete. At different times she has offered different explanations. In 1985 she told Amanda Smith that the boredom of a summer vacation (1980) when she could have been miserable prompted her to try her hand at fiction; by vacation's end she had finished the manuscript of *The Debut*. She offered John Haffenden another explanation which adds something to that: 'when deception is practised on you . . . you write novels out of that sense of injustice . . . or you go under' (60). And most succinctly she has suggested a theory of compensation, telling Shusha Guppy, 'My own life was disappointing . . . so I am trying to edit the whole thing' (152), by writing novels since the novel's imposition of structure on experience gives a sense of control.

Without denying the validity of any of these 'explanations', we might also turn to another, one which takes its source in the experience of exile. In response to an interviewer's query, Brookner declared, 'Silence, exile, and cunning, as Joyce said, those are the conditions for writing' (Kolson, 4-D). In writing about the 'intellectual in exile', Leszek Kolakowski has speculated about the relationship between creativity and exile:

> Creativity arose from insecurity, from an exile of a sort, from the experience of homelessness . . . any exile can be seen either as a misfortune or as a challenge; it can become no more than a reason for despondency and sorrow or a source of painful encouragement. (1133)

In his understanding of the metaphysical dimension of exile and its imposition of a radical, either-or-imperative, Kolakowski echoes Brodsky. Brookner has understood exile as an impetus to and opportunity for creativity; further, she has apprehended the metaphysical dimensions of the experience, and here an important distinction between the writer herself and some of her protagonists (Kitty Maule, even Edith Hope, and others) needs to be made: while a number of them have ignored the metaphysical dimensions of exile, thereby cheating themselves out of the meaning of what has happened to them and remaining uncomprehending victims, she has – if the progression I discern in the three novels discussed here has any validity – grasped the meaning of what has happened to her, neutralized the experience, and converted it to literary art of the highest quality. Exile has become an extended period of intense literary creativity for Anita Brookner. Might not Hartmann's motto, 'Look! We have come through!' be hers as well as Fibich's? *Latecomers* is Brookner's finest novel to date, not just for its excellences of thought and expression but for its satisfying sense of closure. Interviewed before she had finished the manuscript of that novel, she spoke in a most revealing way about Romanticism:

> For the first time Europeans felt that God was dead . . . The Romantics tried to compensate for the absence of God with furious creative activity. If you do not have the gift of faith . . . You have to live with absence. Nowadays I wonder if it is really possible to live without God, maybe we should dare to hope . . . I don't know. I'm not there yet. (*Paris Review*, 154)

This enigmatic remark, resonant with ambiguity, admits the possibility that Brookner's exile is also over, that the journey has ended in an unexpected presence.

### Notes

1. I am indeed grateful to Pascal Carys and Jonathan Cape Ltd. for permission to quote as extensively as I have from the works of Anita Brookner; I acknowledge their very considerable generosity.
2. This essay represents a substantial revision of '"By the Waters of Babylon": Exile and Anita Brookner's Novels', delivered on 5 April 1986, at a meeting of the Northeast Modern Language Association, Rutgers University, New Brunswick, New Jersey.

3.  I am grateful to the following people for their insight and contributions during my work on this essay: Anita Brookner, who has always been most patient and helpful in answering my questions – may this essay meet with her approval and repay some of the pleasure her work has given me; and Brett Averitt, whose conversations about the art of fiction and unqualified support have taught me so much. To both of you, my inadequate words of appreciation.

## A BIBLIOGRAPHY OF WRITINGS BY ANITA BROOKNER

### Novels

*A Start in Life* (London: Jonathan Cape, 1981. American edition: *The Debut*, New York: Linden, 1981; Vintage, 1985).
*Providence* (London: Jonathan Cape, 1982. New York: Pantheon, 1984).
*Look At Me* (London: Jonathan Cape, 1983. New York: Pantheon, 1983).
*Hotel Du Lac* (London: Jonathan Cape, 1984. New York: Pantheon, 1984).
*Family and Friends* (London: Jonathan Cape, 1985. New York: Pantheon, 1985).
*A Misalliance* (London: Jonathan Cape, 1986. American edition: *The Misalliance*, New York: Pantheon, 1986).
*A Friend From England* (London: Jonathan Cape, 1987. New York: Pantheon, 1988).
*Latecomers* (London: Jonathan Cape, 1988. New York: Pantheon, 1989).
*Lewis Percy* (London: Jonathan Cape, 1989. New York: Pantheon, 1990).
*Brief Lives* (London: Jonathan Cape, 1990. New York: Random House, 1991).
*A Closed Eye* (London: Jonathan Cape, 1991. New York: Random House, 1992).

### Books

*An Iconography of Cecil Rhodes* (Oxford: The Trustees of Cecil Rhodes, 1956).
Waldemar George: *Utrillo*. Trans. by Brookner (London: Oldbourne Press, 1960).
Jean-Paul Crespelle: *The Fauves*. Trans. by Brookner (London: Oldbourne Press, 1962).
Maximilien Gauthier: *Gauguin*. Trans. by Brookner (London: Oldbourne Press, 1962).
*Watteau* (London: Hamlyn, 1968).
*The Genius of the Future: Studies in French Art Criticism* (London: Phaidon, 1971. New York: Phaidon, 1971; Ithaca: Cornell University Press, 1988).
*Greuze: The Rise and Fall of an Eighteenth-Century Phenomenon* (London: Elek, 1972. Greenwich, CT and New York: Graphic Society, 1974).
*Jacques-Louis David: A Personal Interpretation* (London: Oxford University Press for the British Academy, 1974).

*Jacques-Louis David* (London: Chatto and Windus, 1980; London: Thames and Hudson, 1987. New York: Harper and Row, 1980).

'Rigaud: *Portrait of Louis XIV*, 1681', 'Delacroix: Scenes from the *Massacres at Chios*, 1824', 'Ingres: *The Turkish Bath*, 1862', 'Cezanne: *The Bathers*, ca. 1900', in *Great Paintings*, edited by Edwin Mullins (London: British Broadcasting Corporation, 1981; New York: St. Martin's, 1981.)

Margaret Kennedy, *Troy Chimneys*, introduction by Brookner (London: Virago, 1985; New York: Penguin, 1985.)

Edith Templeton, *The Island of Desire*, introduction by Brookner (London: Hogarth, 1985.)

Edith Templeton, *Summer in the Country*, introduction by Brookner (London: Hogarth, 1985.)

Edith Templeton, *Living on Yesterday*, introduction by Brookner (London: Hogarth, 1986.)

*The Stories of Edith Wharton: Selected and Introduced by Anita Brookner* (Volume I. London and New York: Simon and Schuster, 1988).

*The Stories of Edith Wharton: Selected and Introduced by Anita Brookner* (Volume II. London and New York: Simon and Schuster, 1989. New York: Carroll and Graf, 1990).

Wharton, Edith. *The Custom of the Country*, introduction by Brookner (New York: Penguin, 1990).

## Articles and Reviews

'Rousseau and the Social Contract', *Times Literary Supplement* (*TLS*) (8 February 1980): 149.

'Corinne and Her *Coups de Foudre*', *TLS* (14 March 1980): 287.

'The Bibliotheque Nationale', *TLS* (5 October 1984): 26.

'A Fortune and a Name' [*Marthe, a Woman and Her Family: A Fin-de-Siecle Correspondence*, edited by Frederick Brown], *TLS* (28 June 1985): 718–19.

'The State-of-the-Art Crowd' [*Painters and Public Life in Eighteenth-Century Paris* by Thomas E. Crow] *TLS* (29 November 1985): 1348.

'At the Height of Her Powers' [*The Mother's Recompense* and *Hudson River Bracketed*, both by Edith Wharton], *The Spectator* (28 June 1986): 29–30.

'The Bitter Fruits of Rejection' [*Barbara Pym* by Robert Emmet Long], *The Spectator* (19 July 1986): 30–1.

'In the Incomparable Spaces' [Francois Boucher 1703–1770: Galeries Nationales du Grand Palais, Paris], *TLS* (10 October 1986): 1137.

'Comedies of Good Manners' [*The Blush and Other Stories* by Elizabeth Taylor], *The Spectator* (29 November 1986): 32–3.

'Black Melancholy Mischief' [*The Stories of Muriel Spark*], *The Spectator* (18 April 1987): 29–30.

'A Stooge of the Spycatcher', *The Spectator* (25 July 1987): 13–4.

'The Madness of Art' [*Henry James: A Life* by Leon Edel], *The Spectator* (1 August 1987): 28–9.

'Quietly Excellent and Very English' [*The Gooseboy* by A. L. Barker], *The Spectator* (3 October 1987): 34.

'Stupidity Is In the Head of the Beholder' [*Three Continents* by Ruth Prawer Jhabvala], *The Spectator* (24 October 1987): 27–8.

'Beneath the Surface' [*The Bonfire of the Vanities* by Tom Wolfe], *The Spectator* (13 February 1988): 37–8.

'Memory, Speak but Do Not Condemn' [*A Far Cry from Kensington* by Muriel Spark], *The Spectator* (26 March 1988): 31–2.

'The Importance of Being Alone' [*The School of Genius* by Anthony Storr], *The Spectator* (25 June 1988): 39.

'The Perils of Biography' [*Deceits of Time* by Isabel Colegate], *The Spectator* (10 September 1988): 34–5.

'New Interests in an Old Setting' [*Loving and Giving* by Molly Keane], *The Spectator* (24 September 1988): 37.

'Moscow Before the Revolution' [*The Beginning of Spring* by Penelope Fitzgerald], *The Spectator* (1 October 1988): 29–30.

'Prize-winning Novels from France', *The Spectator* (10 December 1988): 39–40.

'Not Decadent Enough' [*The Road from Decadence: From Brothel to Cloister: Selected Letters of J. K. Huysmans*, edited and translated by Barbara Beaumont], *The Spectator* (18 February 1989): 29–30.

'Men, Women and the Whole Damn Thing' [*The Grown-Ups* by Victoria Glendinning], *The Spectator* (29 March 1989): 29–30.

'As Natural as Breathing or Going for a Walk' [*Passing On* by Penelope Lively], *The Spectator* (8 April 1989): 33.

'Decline and Fall of a Dandy' [*Baudelaire* by Claude Pichois], *The Spectator* (1 July 1989): 23–4.

'Of Love and Death' [*Falling* by Colin Thubron], *The Spectator* (16 September 1989): 43.

'The Girls of Slender Connections' [*A Natural Curiosity* by Margaret Drabble], *The Spectator* (30 September 1989): 35.

'Without a Hint of Melancholy' [*Other People's Trades* by Primo Levi], The Spectator (7 October 1989): 34.

'In Need of Considerable Gilding' [*The Fly in the Ointment* by Alice Thomas Ellis], *The Spectator* (4 November 1989): 31.

'Nostalgia for Something Awful' [*An Awfully Big Adventure* by Beryl Bainbridge], *The Spectator* (9 December 1989): 37.

'A Writer in Search of a Subject' [*The People and Uncollected Stories* by Bernard Malamud], *The Spectator* (20 January 1990): 31–2.

'The Appeal of Other People's Awful Families' [*The Other Side* by Mary Gordon], *The Spectator* (27 January 1990): 37.

'Eminent Victorians and Others' [*Possession: A Romance* by A. S. Byatt], *The Spectator* (3 March 1990): 3.

'Rosamond Lehmann', *The Spectator* (17 March 1990): 20–1.

' . . . and Dangerous to Know' [*Chicago Loop* by Paul Theroux], *The Spectator* (7 April 1990): 39.

'Three Women and a Dragon' [*Three Times Table* by Sara Maitland], *The Spectator* (14 April 1990): 33–4.

'Straying into the Path of Real Danger' [*Lies of Silence* by Brian Moore], *The Spectator* (21 April 1990): 31.

'A Master Unraveller of Balls of String' [*Those in Peril* by Nicolas Freeling], *The Spectator* (14 August 1990): 23.

'Daisy Pulls It Off' [*The Gate of Angels* by Penelope Fitzgerald], *The Spectator* (1 September 1990): 31–2.

'Catastrophe But Not the Death of Hope' [*Brazzaville Beach* by William Boyd], *The Spectator* (15 September 1990): 38.

'The Different Ages of Women' [*Friend of My Youth* by Alice Munro], *The Spectator* (20 October 1990): 37–8.

'Ending the Heartache' [*Rabbit at Rest* by John Updike], *The Spectator* (27 October 1990): 28–9.

'Living in the Mirror City' [*Janet Frame: An Autobiography*], *The Spectator* (24 November 1990): 39–40.

'Prize-Winning French Novels', *The Spectator* (5 January 1991): 27–8.

'Portrait of the Hero as a Fallible Man' [*The Noble Savage: Jean-Jacques Rousseau: 1754–1762* by Maurice Cranston], *Observer* (24 February 1991): 63.

'Sloughing Off Despair' [*Darkness Visible: A Memoir of Madness* by William Styron], *Observer (Sunday Section)* (3 March 1991): 59.

'Adventures of a Virile Woman' [*Colette: A Life* by Herbert Lottman], *Observer (Sunday Section)* (10 March 1991): 60.

'Unfortunate Women of Cambridge' [*Air and Angels* by Susan Hill], *The Spectator* (30 March 1991): 28.

'Alone in a Valuable House' [*Family Money*], *The Spectator* (4 May 1991): 30.

The Battle of All Mothers' [*The Battle for Christabel* by Margaret Forster], *The Spectator* (11 May 1991): 38.

'More than Sugar and Spice' [*Wilderness Tips* by Margaret Atwood], *The Spectator* (12 October 1991): 36–7.


# A BIBLIOGRAPHY OF WRITINGS ABOUT ANITA BROOKNER


## Books

Sadler, Lynn Veach, *Anita Brookner: Twayne's English Authors Series* (Boston: Twayne Publishers, 1990).

## Articles and Reviews

Alexander, Fiona, 'Anita Brookner: *Providence* and *Hotel du Lac*', *Contemporary Women Novelists* (London: Edward Arnold, 1990) 30–4.

Banner, Simon, 'Too Good to be True', *Guardian* (4 September 1985): 22.

Bayles, Martha. 'Romance a la Mode' [*Hotel du Lac*], *New Republic* (25 March 1985): 37–8.

Dinnage, Rosemary, 'Exiles' [review of *Latecomers* by Anita Brookner and *Baumgartner's Bombay* by Anita Desai], *The New York Review of Books* (1 June 1989): 34–6.

Epstein, Julia, 'Images of Melancholy', *Washington Post Book World* (24 July 1983): 6.

Gies, Judith, 'An Anachronism in Love' [*Providence*], *The New York Times Book Review* (18 March 1984): 17.

Glastonbury, Marion, 'Sentimental Education' [*Providence*], *New Statesman* (14 May 1982): 25.

Gross, John, 'Hotel du Lac', *The New York Times* (22 January 1985): C17.

Hale, Sheila, 'Self Reflecting', *Saturday Review* (May/June 1985): 35–8.

Hamilton, Alex, 'Finding the Art of Fiction', *Guardian* (27 May 1981): 12.

Hardy, Barbara, 'A Cinderella's Loneliness', *Times Literary Supplement* (14 September 1984): 1019.

Hosmer, Robert E., Jr., 'Anita Brookner', *The Dictionary of Literary Biography Yearbook '87*, 293–308.

Hosmer, Robert E., Jr., 'A Virtuous Woman, Who Can Find?' [*Family and Friends*] *America* (15 April 1986): 215–16.

Jebb, Julian, 'Unblinking' [*Hotel du Lac*], *The Spectator* (22 September 1984): 26–7.

Kenyon, Olga, 'Anita Brookner', in *Women Novelists Today: A Survey of English Writing in the Seventies and Eighties* (London and New York: St. Martin's, 1988): 144–65.

Lasdun, James, 'Pre-Modern, Post Modernist: Recent Fiction' [*Hotel du Lac*]. *Encounter* (February 1985): 42; 44–7.

Lee, Hermione, 'Cleopatra's Way', *Observer* (9 September 1984): 22.

Lee, Hermione, 'Drowning Tastefully in the Dark' [*Hotel du Lac*], *Los Angeles Times* (20 March 1988): 2; 12.

Lee, Hermione, 'A New Start in Life for Miss Brookner', *Observer* (21 October 1984): 10.

Lopate, Phillip, 'Can Innocence Go Unpunished?' [*Lewis Percy*], *The New York Times Book Review* (11 March 1990): 10.

Moorehead, Caroline, 'The Poet of Loneliness', *The Times* (21 March 1983): 13.

Parrinder, Patrick, 'Dreams of Avarice' [*A Closed Eye*], *London Review of Books* (29 August 1991): 18.

Rubin, Merle, 'Anita Brookner's Novels: Old Moral Choices without the Old Rhetoric', *The Christian Science Monitor* (1 March 1985): B3.

Rubin, Merle, 'Casting Moral Puzzles: A Novelist on Her Craft', *The Christian Science Monitor* (1 March 1985): B3.

Sudrann, Jean, 'Goings and Comings' [*Latecomers*], *The Yale Review* 79, 3 (Spring 1990): 414–38.

Taubman, Robert, 'Submission' [*Providence*], *London Review of Books* (20 May– 2 June 1982): 18–19.

Tyler, Anne, 'A Solitary Life Is Still Worth Living', *New York Times Book Review* (3 February 1985): 1, 31.

Wyatt-Brown, Anne M., 'Creativity in Midlife: The Novels of Anita Brookner', *Journal of Aging Studies* 3, 2 (1989): 175–81.

## Interviews

Caldwell, Gail, 'Anita Brookner's Shy, Discerning Eye', *The Boston Globe* (5 June 1989): 32–4.

Guppy, Shusha, 'Interview: The Art of Fiction XCVII: Anita Brookner', *Paris Review*, no. 109 (1987): 146–69.

Haffenden, John, 'Anita Brookner', *Novelists In Interview* (ed. John Haffenden) (London and New York: Methuen, 1985): 57–85.

Hughes-Hallett, Lucy, 'Great Expectations', *The Observer* (27 March 1983): 29.

Kenyon, Olga, 'Anita Brookner', *Women Writers Talk* (ed. Olga Kenyon) (New York: Carroll and Graf, 1990) 7–24.

Kolson, Ann, 'Exploring the Hearts of Hopeful Romantics', *Philadelphia Inquirer*, 4 March 1985, D1, D4.

'Novelist With A Double Life', unsigned interview, *Observer (Sunday Section)*, 7 August 1988, 13.

Smith, Amanda, 'Anita Brookner', *Publishers Weekly*, 6 September 1985, 67–8.

## Miscellaneous

*Contemporary Authors*, Volume 120, 57–62.

*Contemporary Literary Criticism*, Volume 32, 59–61.

*Contemporary Literary Criticism*, Volume 51, 58–66.

*Contemporary Novelists*, 142–3.

*Dictionary of Literary Biography Yearbook 1984*, 136–43.

## ANITA BROOKNER

Born 16 July 1928, the only child of Newson and Maude Brookner, Anita Brookner was educated at James Allen's Girl's School. After taking an undergraduate degree in history at King's College, University of London, she began her graduate study in art history at the Courtauld Institute; work there and three years' research in Paris earned her a PhD. A distinguished career marked by Brookner's being honoured as the first woman appointed Slade Professor of Art at Cambridge (1967–8) and her eminence first as Lecturer, then as Reader, at the Courtauld (1964–88), was further enhanced by four substantial, critically–acclaimed works in her field: *Watteau* (1968); *The Genius of the Future: Studies in French Art Criticism* (1971); *Greuze* (1972); and *Jacques-Louis David* (1980). Brookner's precise and meticulous scholarship, set forth in prose of unusual fluency and narrative power, particularly in the last study, established her as an internationally-recognized authority on seventeenth- and eighteenth-century French art, a scholar whose teaching abilities earned her a place as one of the Courtauld's most respected and popular lecturers.

In 1980 Brookner began to write fiction: her first novel *A Start in Life* (1981), published in the United States as *The Debut*, was an immediate bestseller. Since then she has published ten more novels, including *Hotel du Lac*, winner of England's most prestigious literary award, the Booker McConnell Prize, and, most recently, *A Closed Eye* (1991). Following her retirement from the Courtauld, Anita Brookner has devoted her energies to writing fiction while serving as a frequent book reviewer for *The Spectator*.

# 3

# The Great Ventriloquist: A. S. Byatt's *Possession: A Romance*

## ANN HULBERT

In our era of theory-saturated literary studies, it takes a tenured professor to set a clever novel in the groves of academe. Who else knows the orthodoxies cold, and has the liberty and leisure to have readable fun with them? The key is to be suitably self-conscious about anything so simple as a 'story' or a 'character', and then proceed to create just that. Handle it right, and you can offer old-fashioned mystery, comedy, and romance tricked out in new-fangled, self-reflexive style. You can, as A. S. Byatt does in her tour-de-force of university fiction, write a book that is packaged like a fat, glossy romance – and win the Booker Prize, too.

The escape from criticism into creative writing, as Byatt tells it, occasions a kind of conversion in one's attitude toward the word. One of her protagonists, Roland Mitchell, a dogged postdoctoral researcher at Prince Albert College, London, describes his heady sense of enlightenment when, toward the end of *Possession*, he suddenly thinks he might be a poet:

> He had been taught that language was essentially inadequate, that it could never speak what was there, that it only spoke itself. ... What had happened to him was that the way in which it *could* be said had become more interesting than the idea that it could not. (513)

Just how subversive a revelation that can be, challenging the reigning theories of linguistic indeterminacy, Byatt only slowly reveals. Her immediate aim is to make the most of multiple meanings and voices; her novel is the occasion for an exhilarating, virtuosic, and at times exhausting exploration of the many ways language has

55

of speaking. A scholarly authority on George Eliot, the Romantics, and Iris Murdoch, Byatt puts her expertise to energetic use. In *Possession* she becomes a nineteenth-century ventriloquist, and she ingeniously juxtaposes the previous century with the hothouse world of the contemporary academy. The donnish novels of Murdoch (to say nothing of David Lodge, John Fowles, Umberto Eco, and others) have clearly inspired her.

True to the requirements of up-to-date university fiction, *Possession*, is full of the fashionable rhetoric of literary theory. Byatt proves herself, as she says of Roland, 'trained in the post-structuralist deconstruction of the subject'. But it soon becomes clear that her facility with the professional jargon is accompanied by a mounting frustration with it. The two characters in the historical foreground of the novel, Roland and his equally sober literary companion, Maud Bailey of Lincoln University, 'know all . . . about how there isn't a unitary ego – how we're made up of conflicting, interacting systems of things. . . . We know we are driven by desire . . . ' (290). They often lapse into semiotic chatter, and the talk about textuality and sexuality is almost always an occasion for a satiric dig, not least at their emotionally straitened lives. It is also a prelude to serious doubt for Roland and Maud about the literary orthodoxy they officially endorse.

For as Byatt sends them off on one extraordinary quest – to uncover the secret romance between the famous (married) Victorian poet Randolph Henry Ash and the lesser known (and until now purportedly lesbian, or asexual) poet Christabel LaMotte – she also burdens them with another mission: to confront the glacial anti-romanticism at the heart of their studies and their lives so far. What better way to scrutinize the postmodern, post-Freudian, 'knowing' attitude than to compare it with the doubting, inhibited Victorian spirit? Especially since the juxtaposition offers an unexpected twist: lives in the age of sexual ultrasophistication turn out to be frigid, and passion thrives in the age of repression.

In playing out this contrast, Byatt takes a conventional novelistic approach; she interweaves the paths and preoccupations of her two couples. But within that old-fashioned structure, she mixes up styles, genres, voices in good postmodern manner. The tale of her contemporary pair is a detective story, and the mystery at its heart is the tale of her Victorian pair, which is a romance. The thriller is launched when Roland, browsing among his hero Ash's papers in the library, discovers drafts of an urgent personal letter to an unidentified woman.

Roland immediately recognizes the note as a possible clue to an unknown side of the fiercely intellectual poet renowned for his calm, exemplary life. In a moment of uncharacteristic impulsiveness, Roland slips the letters into his own Oxford *Selected Ash* and leaves the library, and the sleuthing begins.

In pursuit of Ash's mysterious correspondent, whom he quickly identifies as Christabel LaMotte, Roland is led to Maud Bailey, who is a distant relative of the poetess, an expert on her, and the guardian of some of her unpublished papers. They turn out to have more than a professional subject in common: they are both full of diffidence about personal entanglements. From here on, Roland and Maud's story, as they pursue the Victorian secret, traces the erosion (slowly) of their literary certainties and (even more slowly) of their emotional uncertainties.

The quest for the poets' hidden passion is a formal challenge to the scholars' habits. Roland, a dedicated textual editor of Ash, and Maud, a psychoanalytic critic of LaMotte, are at once queasy and excited about the personal probing they are suddenly drawn into. Byatt captures their ambivalence, and their initially combative relation, in a characteristic bit of well-tuned dialogue, initiated by Roland:

'I've never been much interested in places – or things – with associations – '
'Nor I, I'm a textual scholar. I rather deplore the modern feminist attitude toward private lives.'
'If you're going to be stringently analytical,' Roland said, 'don't you have to?'
'You can be psychoanalytical without being *personal*' Maud said. Roland did not challenge her. (230)

Inevitably, their pursuit becomes very personal, as they unearth letters that chart the at first hesitant, then increasingly intense conversation between Ash and LaMotte – and that break off at precisely the moment when the young scholars (in spite of their purist approach) are dying to know what happened next. Was the relationship ever consummated, or did Christabel in the end retreat into the quiet house she shared with her spinsterish companion? Roland and Maud set out to trace Randolph Ash's natural history expedition to North Yorkshire in June 1859, hoping to discover, by reading various clues in a new light, whether Christabel accompanied him.

Just because Roland and Maud depart from their strictly textual methods doesn't mean that Byatt endorses old-fashioned biographical hounding, or the newer feminist variation on it. She may be sceptical of high-flown theory, but she's also dubious about more reductive approaches. As she follows Roland and Maud in their tramp through Yorkshire on the trail of the poets, she interweaves her most merciless satire of two of the cruder varieties of literary analysis. Her targets are Americans, Professor Mortimer Cropper, keeper of the most complete collection of Ash relics at Robert Dale Owen University in New Mexico, editor of Ash's correspondence, and author of *The Great Ventriloquist*, a pompous biography of Ash; and Professor Leonora Stern, from Tallahassee, author of *Motif and Matrix in the Poems of LaMotte*, a study in which discussions of creativity inevitably return to discussions of female sexuality.

Roland and Maud dip into those tones on their trip, and so do we, thanks to Byatt's skillful parody of several pages of each. Writing of LaMotte's long poem *The Fairy Melusine*, for example, Leonora Stern discourses on feminine landscapes as erotic terrain and emphasizes the relation between watery scenes and orgasmic pleasures:

> The male fountain spurts and springs, Mélusine's fountain has a *female* wetness, trickling out from its pool rather than rising confidently, thus mirroring those female secretions which are not inscribed in our daily use of language (*langue*, tongue) – the sputum, mucus, milk, and bodily fluids of women who are silent for dryness. (267)

By now prepared to be impatient with their colleagues, Roland and Maud see that they completely miss the point. Stern digresses about LaMotte and autoeroticism, and Cropper speculates about the fear of sterility and decline lurking behind Ash's new interest in nature's procreative powers, but the younger scholars are onto the truth, which is precisely the opposite: the Yorkshire journey was the occasion of an all-consuming affair between Ash and LaMotte, and their poems can't look the same once that secret has been glimpsed.

Byatt's aim is to show that Maud and Roland are guided to their discovery by a much more imaginative sense of what words can mean than either of the Americans begins to grasp. The key to the young scholars' sympathetic comprehension of the poets is the opposite of sophistication. 'Something primitive,' they acknowledge, seizes them in their reading, 'narrative curiosity' (259). And something else, equally primitive, overtakes them at the same time: stirrings of their own desire – this from a pair who agree that their ideal is 'a clean empty bed in a clean empty room, where nothing is asked or to be asked. . . . Maybe we're symptomatic of whole flocks of exhausted scholars and theorists' (290–1). Though still studiously avoiding any admission of their growing interest in each other, they pore over the works of their heroes with new energy and vision.

Here Byatt agilely plays off the divergences and convergencies between the circumstances of her two couples. Roland and Maud are inspired by the act of sympathy required to bridge what they see as a huge gap separating them from Ash and LaMotte. 'It makes an interesting effort of imagination,' Roland puts it in his understated way, 'to think how they saw the world' (276) – and saw each other. Byatt invites her readers to join in that effort, plunging us into the same freighted material the professors peruse. She puts all her linguistic, parodic skills on display, almost as if she had set herself the challenge of imitating and interweaving as many Victorian genres as possible; short poems, long poems, personal letters, public letters, stories, journal entries (Ash's and his wife's, as well as those of LaMotte's companion and her niece), and more.

The effect of the sometimes dizzying collage is at first just as Roland says: there's a sense of real distance separating us from them. But before long that comfortably detached vantage is unsettled. Juxtaposing her contemporary style – abrupt swerves between documents and time frames – and the poets' old-fashioned style, Byatt unfolds a curiously anachronistic story. The great drama of their lives, as Christabel steps forth from her well-guarded seclusion and Randolph ventures onto uncharted emotional terrain, begins as a Victorian tale told in musty letters but becomes a surprising modern story of liberation followed by abandonment. In the chapter that culminates the poets' affair, Byatt springs free of her documentation and claims imaginative license to follow them on their fateful Yorkshire trip. As she begins, using only 'the man' and 'the woman' (297), it's momentarily unclear whether the excitedly apprehensive couple on the train are Randolph and Christabel or Maud and Roland.

Several further, suspenseful turns in the detective story reveal that the poets' lives have a ragged modern ending, their paths leading off in different directions and their messages to each other lost in transmission. The young professors, meanwhile, are on their way to an old-fashioned happy ending, two chilly souls warming each other at last. Having quoted Hawthorne in her epigraph ('When a writer calls his work a Romance . . . he wishes to claim a certain latitude, both as to its fashion and material . . .'), Byatt calls on the conventions of Romance to wind up the many threads of her mystery in a pleasantly implausible way.

But Byatt the literature professor can't resist a last word. Though the lives she has spun out have been fascinating, it's the books that finally count, she instructs near the end: language and imaginative reading shouldn't be eclipsed by biographical sleuthing. As she explains in a Victorian authorial intrusion, it's not easy to prevent words from fading into the background amid the drama of tumultuous lives: 'It is possible for a writer to make, or remake at least, for a reader, the primary pleasures of eating, or drinking, or looking on, or sex. . . . [Novels] do not habitually elaborate on the equally intense pleasure of reading' (510). That's because it's a tricky, self-reflexive matter, calling attention to the experience of reading in the course of that experience; it requires rousing 'the brain' and 'the viscera' so that the pleasure of encountering words on a page isn't merely 'papery and dry'.

That is the challenge Byatt has immodestly set for herself in her elaborate patchwork of 'original' texts. There's a triumphant, sometimes slightly irritating, exhibitionism at the core of that aim, for the many words we're meant to thrill to are, of course, all finally Byatt's own. At the close of the novel, just in case her readers haven't already fully enjoyed such pleasure and watched her characters enjoy it, she gives Roland a classic moment of readerly ecstasy. He goes back to a poem of Ash's with his new knowledge of the poet's passionate life:

> Roland read, or reread, *The Golden Apples*, as though the words were living creatures or stones of fire . . . He heard Ash's voice, certainly his voice, his own unmistakable voice, and he heard the language moving around, weaving its own patterns, beyond the reach of any single human, writer or reader . . . He saw too that Christabel was the Muse and Proserpine and that she was not, and this seemed to be so interesting and apt, once he had understood, that he laughed aloud. (512)

Byatt assiduously tends to all the 'primary pleasures' of description in her novel, entering into her characters' lives and above all their loves. She sees to it that Roland gets his girl in the end, though as he's said earlier, that's 'vulgar romance', certainly compared with the Victorians' high passion. But the real feat of her novel is in making it plausible – and important – that those poets wrote poems from their heads and hearts, and that Roland and Maud can now read them more fully than they ever have before. It's the kind of lesson more literature professors could stand to teach.

## Note

1. Reprinted by permission of The New Republic, (c) 1991, The New Republic, Inc.

## A BIBLIOGRAPHY OF WRITINGS BY A. S. BYATT

*Robert E. Hosmer Jr.*

### Novels

*The Shadow of a Sun* (London: Chatto and Windus, 1964. New York: Harcourt, Brace and World, 1964).
*The Game* (London: Chatto and Windus, 1967. New York: Scribner's, 1968).
*The Virgin in the Garden* (London: Chatto and Windus, 1978. New York: Knopf, 1979).
*Still Life* (London: Chatto and Windus, 1985. New York: Scribner's, 1985.
*Possession: A Romance* (London: Chatto and Windus, 1990. New York: Random House, 1990).

### Stories

*Sugar and Other Stories* (London: Chatto and Windus, 1987. New York: Scribner's, 1987).

### Books

*Degrees of Freedom: The Novels of Iris Murdoch* (London: Chatto and Windus, 1965. New York: Barnes and Noble, 1965).
*Unruly Times: Wordsworth and Coleridge in Their Time* (London: Nelson, 1970. New York: Crane Russak, 1973).
*Elizabeth Bowen: The House in Paris*, introduction by Byatt (London: Penguin, 1976).
*Iris Murdoch* (London: Longman, 1976).
*George Eliot: The Mill on the Floss*, introduction by Byatt (London and New York: Penguin Books, 1979).
*Grace Paley: Enormous Changes at the Last Minute*, introduction by Byatt (London: Virago, 1979).

*Willa Cather: A Lost Lady*, introduction by Byatt (London: Virago, 1980).
*Willa Cather: My Antonia*, introduction by Byatt (London: Virago, 1980).
*Grace Paley: The Little Disturbances of Man*, introduction by Byatt (London: Virago, 1980).
*Willa Cather: The Song of the Lark*, introduction by Byatt (London: Virago, 1989).
*Willa Cather: Death Comes for the Archbishop*, introduction by Byatt (London: Virago, 1989).
*Passions of the Mind: Selected Writings* (London: Chatto and Windus, 1991).

## Articles and Reviews

'The Obsession With Amorphous Mankind', *Encounter* (September 1966): 63–9.
'Wallace Stevens: Criticism, Repetition and Creativity', *Journal of American Studies*, 12 (1978): 369–75.
'Worldly Wise' [*The Realists* by C. P. Snow], *New Statesman* (3 November 1978): 586–7.
'People in Paper Houses: Attitudes to "Realism" and "Experiment" in English Postwar Fiction', in *The Contemporary English Novel* (ed. Malcolm Bradbury) (London: Edward Arnold, 1979).
'Marginal Lives' [*An Academic Question* by Barbara Pym], *Times Literary Supplement* (8 August 1986): 862.
'Obscenity and the Arts', *Times Literary Supplement* (12–18 February 1988): 159.
'Beginning in Craft and Ending in Mystery' [*The Penguin Book of Short Stories* ed. by Malcolm Bradbury; *The Oxford Book of Short Stories*, ed. by V. S. Pritchett; *The Dragon's Head* by W. Somerset Maugham, Saki and others; *The Green Man Revisited* by Roger Sharrock; *The Killing Bottle* ed. by Dan Davin; and *Charmed Lives*, ed. by T. S. Dorsch], *Times Literary Supplement* (13 May 1988): 527.
'Writing and Feeling',*Times Literary Supplement* (18–24 November 1988): 1278.
'The Trouble with the Interesting Reader' [*Romanticism, Writing and Sexual Difference: Essays on 'The Prelude'* by Mary Jacobus], *Times Literary Supplement* (23–9 March 1990): 310.
'After the Myth, the Real' [*The Van Gogh File: A Journey of Discovery* by Ken Wilkie; *Young Vincent: The Story of Van Gogh's Years in England* by Martin Bailey; *The Love of Many Things: A Life of Vincent Van Gogh* by David Sweetman; *Vincent Van Gogh: Christianity Versus Nature* by Tsukasa Kodera], *Times Literary Supplement* (29 June–5 July 1990): 683–4.
'Amatory Acts' [*The Chatto Book of Love Poetry*, edited by John Fuller, and *The Collins Book of Love Poetry*, edited by Amanda McCardie], *Times Literary Supplement* (31 August–6 September 1990): 913.
'Dickens and His Demons' [*Dickens* by Peter Ackroyd]. *The Washington Post Book World* (10 February 1991): 1–2.
'The Hue and Cry of Love', *The New York Times* (11 February 1991): A19.

# A BIBLIOGRAPHY OF WRITINGS ABOUT A. S. BYATT

*Robert E. Hosmer Jr.*

## Articles and Reviews

Bernikow, Louise, 'The Illusion of Allusions' [*The Virgin in the Garden*], *Ms.* (June 1979): 36–8.

Bradbury, Malcolm, 'On from Murdoch' [*The Game*], *Encounter* (July 1968): 72–4.

Brookner, Anita, 'Eminent Victorians and Others' [*Possession: A Romance*], *The Spectator* (3 March 1990): 35.

Campbell, Jane, 'The Hunger of the Imagination in A. S. Byatt's *The Game*', *Critique: Studies in Modern Fiction 29*, 3 (Spring, 1988): 147–62.

Creighton, Joanne V., 'Sisterly Symbiosis: Margaret Drabble's *The Waterfall* and A. S. Byatt's *The Game*', *Mosaic 20*, 1 (Winter, 1987): 15–29.

Cosslett, Tess, 'Childbirth from the Woman's Point of View in British Women's Fiction: Enid Bagnold's *The Squire* and A. S. Byatt's *Still Life*', *Tulsa Studies in Women's Literature 8*, 2 (Fall, 1989): 263–86.

Cunningham, Valentine, 'The Greedy Reader' [*Passions of the Mind: Selected Writings*], *Times Literary Supplement* (16 August 1991): 6.

Cushman, Keith, '*Sugar and Other Stories*', *Studies in Short Fiction 25*, 1 (Winter, 1988): 80–1.

Dinnage, Rosemary, 'England in the 50's' [*The Virgin in the Garden*], *The New York Times Book Review* (1 April 1979): 20.

Duchene, Anne, 'Ravening Time' [*Sugar and Other Stories*], *Times Literary Supplement* (10 April 1987): 395.

Durant, Sabine, 'Shavings and Splinters' [*Sugar and Other Stories*], *New Statesman* (15 May 1987): 30.

Dusinberre, Juliet, 'Forms of Reality in A. S. Byatt's *The Virgin in the Garden*,' *Critique: Studies in Modern Fiction* (Fall, 1982): 55–62.

Feinstein, Elaine, 'Eloquent Victorians' [*Possession: A Romance*], *New Statesman and Society* (16 March 1990): 38.

Hargreaves, T. 'Review: *Sugar and Other Stories* by A. S. Byatt', *Hermanthena* 142 (1987): 77–8.

Irwin, Michael, 'Growing Up in 1953' [*The Virgin in the Garden*], *Times Literary Supplement* (3 November 1978): 1277.

Jenkyns, Richard, 'Disinterring Buried Lives' [*Possession: A Romance*], *Times Literary Supplement* (2 March 1990): 213.

Karlin, Danny, 'Prolonging Her Absence' [*Possession: A Romance*], *London Review of Books* (8 March 1990): 17–18.

Kenyon, Olga, 'A. S. Byatt', in *Women Novelists Today: A Survey of English Writing in the Seventies and Eighties* (New York: St. Martin's Press, 1988: 51–84).

King, Francis, 'Grand Scale' [*The Virgin in the Garden*], *The Spectator* (2 December 1978): 26–7.

Lewis, Peter, 'The Truth and Nothing Like the Truth: History and Fiction', *Strand Magazine 27*, 2 (Spring, 1986): 38–44.

Lewis, Roger, 'Larger than Life' [*Still Life*], *New Statesman* (28 June 1985): 29.

Mars-Jones, Adam, 'Doubts about the Monument' [*Still Life*], *Times Literary Supplement* (28 June 1985): 720.

Merkin, Daphne, 'Writers and Writing: The Art of Living' [*The Virgin in the Garden*], *The New Leader* (23 April 1979): 16.

Murdoch, Iris, 'Force Fields' [*The Virgin in the Garden*], *New Statesman* (3 November 1978): 586.

Musil, Caryn McTighe, 'A. S. Byatt', *Dictionary of Literary Biography* 14 (1983): 194–205.

Paulin, Tom, 'When the Ghost Begins to Quicken' [*The Virgin in the Garden*], *Encounter* (May 1979): 72–7.

Rifkind, Donna, 'Victorians' Secrets' [*Possession: A Romance*], *The New Criterion* (February 1991): 77–80.

Rothstein, Mervyn, 'Best Seller Breaks Rules on Crossing the Atlantic' [*Possession: A Romance*], *The New York Times* (31 January 1991): C17; C22.

Schwartz, Lynne Sharon, 'At Home with the Supernatural' [*Sugar And Other Stories*], *The New York Times Book Review* (19 July 1987): 5.

Showalter, Elaine, 'Slick Chick' [*Passions of the Mind: Selected Writings*], *London Review of Books* (11 July 1991): 6.

Smith, Anne, 'Sifting the Ash' [*Possession: A Romance*], *Listener* (1 March 1990): 29.

Spufford, Francis, 'The Mantle of Jehovah' [*Sugar and Other Stories*], *London Review of Books* (25 June 1987): 22–3.

West, Paul, 'Sensations of Being Alive' [*Still Life*], *The New York Times Book Review* (24 November 1985): 15.

## Interviews

'Self-Portrait of a Victorian Polymath', Kate Kellaway, *Observer* (16 September 1990): 45.

## Miscellaneous

*Contemporary Authors* 13–14R; 130.
*Contemporary Authors New Revision Series*, 13; 91–2.
*Contemporary Literary Criticism* 4; 75–8.

I wish to acknowledge the help of Dr Janice A. Rossen, who prepared an earlier draft of these bibliographies; she, in turn, wishes to thank Lisa D. Mossman for her assistance.

## A. S. BYATT

Antonia Susan Drabble Byatt has established a reputation as scholar, fiction writer, and teacher of distinction. Born 24 August 1936 in Sheffield, England, she took a BA (first class honours) from Newnham College, Cambridge (1957) before pursuing graduate work at Bryn Mawr College (1957–8) and at Somerville College, Oxford (1958–9). Byatt then began a teaching career that eventually led to appointment as lecturer in English and American literature at University College, London, from 1972 until 1983. In 1959 she married Ian Charles Rayner Byatt with whom she had two children; the marriage was dissolved ten years later. With her second husband, Peter John Duffy whom she married in 1969, Byatt has two daughters.

Byatt's scholarly reputation rests on two studies of Iris Murdoch, *Degrees of Freedom: The Novels of Iris Murdoch* (1967), the first book-length study of that novelist, and *Iris Murdoch* (1976). She has also published a study of Wordsworth and Coleridge, *Unruly Times: Wordsworth and Coleridge in Their Time* (1970), and pursued an interest in women writers, particularly George Eliot and Willa Cather.

Byatt's fiction – five novels to date – is often compared to that of her younger sister, Margaret Drabble, and to that of Murdoch, for all three women are rigorously intellectual, crafting novels of ideas often set within the Oxbridge academic cloister. In addition to *Shadow of a Sun* (1968), and *The Game* (1968), Byatt has published two volumes of a projected quartet, *The Virgin in the Garden* (1979), and *Still Life* (1985) as well as a number of short stories, some of them gathered in *Sugar and Other Stories* (1987). Nothing, however, has brought her the recognition she has achieved with *Possession: A Romance* (1990), winner of the 1990 Booker McConnell Prize and a bestseller on both sides of the Atlantic.

# 4

# The Real Magic of Angela Carter

## WALTER KENDRICK

The girls stayed at home in their rooms, napping on their beds or repairing ripped hems, or sewing loose buttons more securely, or writing letters, or contemplating acts of charity among the deserving poor, or staring vacantly into space.

I can't imagine what else they might do.

What the girls do when they are on their own is unimaginable to me. (*Saints and Strangers*, 13)

Lizzie and Emma Borden in the long, slow days before slaughter made them famous – unimaginable indeed, even by the narrator of 'The Fall River Axe Murders', the lead story in Angela Carter's *Saints and Strangers* (1986). Not much else escapes, though as the narrator's inquisitive, relentless, unabashedly modern intelligence broods over the legendary house at 92 Second Street, Fall River, and its sleeping inhabitants, two of whom will soon – very soon – die horribly. It is the last instant before 6:00 AM, 4 August, 1892; a hundred factory whistles 'are just about to blast off, just this very second about to blass off . . . ' (*Saints and Strangers*, 12). Carter suspends time, lets murderer and victims sleep, while she ponders, digresses, speculates; long before the end we seem to know exactly why Lizzie will murder her parents, but then, in the last line, magic: 'Outside, above, in the already burning air, see! the angel of death roosts on the rooftree' (*Saints and Strangers*, 31).

Like the seven other pieces in *Saints and Strangers*, 'The Fall River Axe Murders' is billed as a short story, but they're all something much more remarkable: bizarre amalgams of tale and essay, delicacy and grossness, studded with literary allusions and jeweled here and there with poetry. These elements ought not to cohere; they ought to make a mess, not a style. But through sheer braggadocio, the proud refusal to notice incongruities (much less fret about them), Carter triumphs over form, content, structure, tone, every genteel shibboleth. If she had any manners, she'd never manage it. Fortunately, she's ruder than Falstaff; breaking all the rules, she forges new ones.

Born in London in 1940, Carter published her first novel, *Shadow Dance*, in 1965. Since then, she has produced eight more novels, three collections of short stories, a translation of French fairy tales, a study of pornography, and a great number of miscellaneous articles and reviews. She's also written several radio scripts and, with Neil Jordan, the screenplay of her story 'The Company of Wolves' for the 1984 film of the same name. In Britain, recognition came early. Carter's second novel, *The Magic Toyshop*, won the John Llewellyn Rhys Prize in 1967; her third, *Several Perceptions*, picked up the Somerset Maugham Award the following year; and her British reputation remains high, if a bit quirky.

She's been slower to catch on in the United States. Most of her books have been published here, but they came and went quickly, attracting slight critical attention and few readers. Many of those who discovered her, however, became devotees. Until recently, Carter has belonged to the curious American club of 'cult' writers; her admirers valued her chiefly because the sensations she offers, like those of some exotic drug or forbidden sexual practice, appall or confuse the common reader. This is not an inappropriate judgment: Carter's writing is subversive in several senses.

Perhaps her most unsettling quality is that she takes for granted the political nature of sex; she doesn't argue for it, she simply assumes that the body politic is also the individual body and proceeds to play outrageous games with their identity. The generality of American readers, accustomed to fiction that probes the farthest limits of verbal explicitness without denting a single patriarchal cliche, is unlikely to embrace Carter – if only because, in the most fundamental way, it cannot comprehend her.

The widespread critical applause that greeted Carter's eighth novel, *Nights at the Circus* (1985), and the reverence inspired by her third collection of short stories, *Saints and Strangers*, suggest that change is in the wind; her inclusion in this volume is, of course, further evidence. Carter has lately joined the canon, or at least she's well on her way toward doing so; a handful of academic essays has already been written about her, and many more are likely to follow. This, too, is not inappropriate: for all her subversion, for all the Falstaffian rudeness with which she handles the conventions of her craft, she remains a thoroughly conventional writer, in the best sense of that much-abused term. She sees herself, justly, as the heir of literary ages; her rudeness is always a form – perhaps the only valid form – of reverence.

Critical applause, that is, may transform her from a cult writer into a popular one, but it will never make her a rival of Stephen King. Carter can write – which King, despite reams of practice, still can't – and intelligence glares from her books like a spotlight, while his grow steadily duller in their bloated witlessness. Yet there are some intriguing similarities between the two. Both go after the child that inhabits every adult, that sees goblins in the shadows and marvels open-mouthed at fireworks. Both are intensely literary writers, who make no crass assertion that their words mirror real experience, whatever that is. They draw unashamedly on other books for inspiration – King on the mostly twentieth-century genre of horror fiction, Carter on the older tradition of fairy tales. Both writers frequently repeat themselves, but when Carter does so, she seems to be admitting that the world contains about half a dozen stories, which can never be told too often, simply because they're true. Style and wit aside, Carter mines a richer vein. King's originals are polished, processed products, while Carter's embody the nearest any written thing can come to originality.

> There once lived an old widow who had two daughters. The eldest was the living image of her mother to look at, and worse, to listen to; they were both so proud and disagreeable it was impossible to live with them. But the youngest took after her father in gentleness and kindness and she was also very, very beautiful . . .

So begins 'The Fairies' in Carter's version of Charles Perrault's seventeenth-century tale (*Sleeping Beauty and Other Favourite Fairy Tales*, 63). In her fiction, too, Carter has the wisdom to trust that the whole range of human passion is implicit in such a pellucid statement; the storyteller needs only to unpack it, to let the consequences loose. Gentleness will suffer a while, pride will seem to triumph; then comes a test that only the good can pass, and evil will fail. At the end of 'The Fairies', Beauty marries the king's son, while the disagreeable Fanchon 'grew so hateful that even her mother got tired of her, at last, and turned her out of doors. Try as she might, she could find nobody to take pity on her and she crept away and died in a corner of the woods' (*Sleeping Beauty*, 68).

'Marianne had sharp, cold eyes', begins Carter's 1969 novel, *Heroes and Villains*, 'and she was spiteful but her father loved her' (1). This is the same fairy-tale universe, where the same uncompromising values prevail, and again the narrator's task is plain: to tell what tests confronted Marianne and how, after setbacks, she passed them. On the face of it, Marianne's world looks as different as possible from Beauty's – a post-holocaust England divided between Professors in white towers and Barbarians scouring the ruined landscape – but there, as in any enchanted forest, good flourishes under duress while evil falters. On a lark, Marianne escapes from the Professors' antiseptic enclosure; while she frolics outside the walls, news comes that she's lost all reason for returning: 'In a fit of senile frenzy, the old nurse had killed her father with an axe and then poisoned herself with some stuff she used for cleaning brass' (15). So Marianne joins the Barbarians, marries the strange and beautiful Jewel, and at the end seems likely to be named queen of the horde.

Marianne isn't *good* in any namby-pamby sense, but she shares with Carter's other heroines and occasional heroes a tough, even perverse integrity that assures her survival when those about her are getting blown to smithereens. And smithereens abound in Carter's fiction; the violence she portrays would be merely sickening, like Stephen King's or Clive Barker's, if it weren't described in rhapsodic, grand-operatic terms that in their very extravagance promise deliverance from evil:

> A great spurt of blood sprang out as from an unstoppered tap in such a great arc that it drenched us. He must have died instantaneously but some spasm of muscle jerked him to his feet. The juggernaut rose up on his car and stood there, swaying, a fountain of blood, while the crowd moaned and shivered as if at an eclipse. Somehow his uncoordinated shuddering freed the wheels of his trolley and, at first slowly, it began to move. . . . And still the corpse stayed upright, as if rigor mortis had set in straight away. And still it jetted blood, as if his arteries were inexhaustible. So it started on a headlong career, crushing wives and eunuchs and those of his tribe who, maddened at the sight, out of despair or hysteria at the sudden extinction of their autocratic comet, now flung themselves under the wheels of its chariot with maenad shrieks. (*The Infernal Desire Machines of Doctor Hoffman*, 164)

The demise of the cannibal king in *The Infernal Desire Machines of Doctor Hoffman* (1972) – a particularly extravagant scene in Carter's most extravagant novel, but a typical example of her ability to make gorgeous tableaux out of carnage. The worlds into which her protagonists wander or get thrown are wildly violent places; death and dismemberment lurk in every shadow. The special dread that fairy tales invoke, even in adults, is Carter's trademark. Even the shabby South London house in *The Magic Toyshop*, where fifteen-year-old Melanie winds up after her parents are killed, resembles a castle in the Schwarzwald, complete with resident ogre – toymaker Philip Flower who constructs marvellous playthings while plotting the rape of joy. In Carter's recent (and most successful) novel, *Nights at the Circus*, the enchanted forest swells to encompass turn-of-the-century Europe and half of Asia; the errant innocent has grown up into Walser, who has 'survived the plague in Setzuan, the assegai in Africa, a sharp dose of buggery in a bedouin tent beside the Damascus road and much more' (10). Walser thinks he's seen everything, but what he hasn't seen is Fevvers, the Cockney *aérialiste*, toast of London, Paris, and St Petersburg, who really does have wings.

Walser fancies himself jaded, yet 'there remained something a little unfinished about him, still. He . . . had not experienced his experience *as* experience; sandpaper his outsides as experience might, his inwardness had been left untouched' (10). Though he is male – and American – his innocence exactly resembles that of the Marquis de Sade's Justine as Carter broods on it in her only full-length work of non-fiction, *The Sadeian Woman and the Ideology of Pornography* (1978): 'She is always the dupe of an experience that she never experiences *as* experience; her innocence invalidates experience and turns it into events, things that happen to her but do not change her' (51).

The characters who interest Carter most, whose stories she loves to tell and retell, all share this unhatched quality – even Lizzie Borden: 'She traces the outlines of her face with an uncertain hand as if she were thinking of unfastening the bandages on her soul but it isn't time to do that, yet; her new face isn't ready to be seen, yet' (*Saints and Strangers*, 30). In the course of these characters' stories, experiences *as* experience rips them open, spills them out, often with appalling violence and – an unsettling combination – ravishing sexiness.

Carter's sex scenes are just as explicit as her violence and sometimes nearly as violent:

> As soon as they are left alone, no trifling this time; they're at it,
> hammer and tongs, down on the carpet since the bed is occupé.
> Up and down, up and down, his arse; in and out, in and out, her
> legs. Then she heaves him up and throws him on his back, her
> turn at the grind now, and you'd think she'll never stop. (*The
> Bloody Chamber*, 104)

The bed is *occupé*, it should be mentioned, by the still-warm corpse
of the woman's husband, and the floor is littered with dead and
dying rats – the climax of a lighthearted tale called 'Puss in Boots',
narrated by the *soigné* cat who has staged the scene.

Kinky enough, perhaps. But consider the orgy of the clowns in
*Nights at the Circus*:

> A joey thrust the vodka bottle up the arsehole of an august; the
> august, in response, promptly dropped his tramp's trousers to
> reveal a virile member of priapic size, bright purple in colour and
> spotted with yellow stars, dangling two cerise balloons from the
> fly. At that, a second august, with an evil leer, took a great pair of
> shears out of his back pocket and sliced the horrid thing off but as
> soon as he was brandishing it in triumph above his head another
> lurid phallus appeared in the place of the first, this one bright blue
> with scarlet polkadots and cerise testicles, and so on, until the
> clown with the shears was juggling with a dozen of the thing.
> (124)

This is obscenity in the classic, Aristophanean sense: hilarious,
violent, phallic, and treading dangerously on the verge of horror.
Virtually alone among contemporary women writers – one might
say among all women writers since at least Aphra Behn – Carter
appreciates the absurdity of the male sexual apparatus, the ridicu-
ousness of a world-dominating instrument that a simple pair of
shears can slice off.

Carter's women (and men) are resolutely heterosexual, yet their
relationships carry an air of risk that our culture nowadays reserves
mostly for homosexual connections, which are saved from tedium
by their invigorating outrageousness. Carter's men and women

desire each other as if that lust were damned but they'll gladly burn in hell as well as on earth. For such a relentlessly sexy writer, this neglect of the perverted in favour of the merely perverse looks curious. Only in the 1988 'afterword' to her 1971 novel, *Love*, does Carter come close to naming the unnamable variety of that eminently shifty emotion. And then she treats it as a symptom of the 'bleaker' world that has replaced the late 1960s in which the novel is set (113).

The choice is no doubt temperamental, but Carter also doesn't need the sheen of abomination to lend her work an outrageous air. No contemporary writer has a firmer grasp of what's often called the quotidian – the look, the heft, especially the smell of everyday objects and functions – yet Carter never bogs down in the ordinariness of ordinary things. While other writers, especially women, chronicle frustration with reality and excruciating boredom with the phallus and its predictable tyranny, Carter casts glamour over the obvious. Unlike Andrea Dworkin – to choose the most extreme example – she never gratifies the dreams of phallocentrism by hypostasizing the male member into the instrument of irresistible conquest its blindest possessors imagine to be. For Carter, it's a bunch of ballons; her women often love their men, appropriately enough, because they pity them.

Carterian sex isn't always or merely raucous, however; in particular, male sexuality can also be sinister, as in 'The Bloody Chamber', her modernized, eminently adult retelling of the Bluebeard story:

> He made me put on my choker, the family heirloom of one woman who had escaped the blade. With trembling fingers, I fastened the thing about my neck. It was cold as ice and chilled me. He twined my hair into a rope and lifted it off my shoulders so that he could the better kiss the downy furrows below my ears; that made me shudder. And he kissed those blazing rubies, too. He kissed them before he kissed my mouth. (*The Bloody Chamber*, 15)

Comic or ominous, Carterian sex never fails to be robust, high-blooded, and throbbing; when they fuck as when they murder Carter's men and women go about the business with the full vigour of their extremely definite personalities. They take gutsy pleasure in what they do, and even when the scene verges on the nauseating, that pleasure infuses Carter's language and becomes heady delight to read.

Her primary source of inspiration is the Western European fairy tale, the tradition of Perrault, La Fontaine, and the brothers Grimm. But she joins to them an unlikely and much less respectable colleague: Donatien-Alphonse-Francois, Marquis de Sade (1740–1814). The partnership is not so strange as it might at first appear, because Sade's secluded châteaux are, after all, fairy-tale places, where the rules that govern ordinary life lapse utterly. *The Sadeian Woman and the Ideology of Pornography* is an impassioned, muddled defense of the Divine Marquis as, of all things, a liberator of women; it's completely unconvincing on that score, but it reveals clearly enough what Carter *wishes* Sade had been – the fulfillment of her own ambitions:

> The moral pornographer would be an artist who uses pornographic material as part of the acceptance of the logic of a world of absolute sexual license for all the genders, and projects a model of the way such a world might work. A moral pornographer might use pornography as a critique of current relations between the sexes. His business would be the total demystification of the flesh and the subsequent revelation, through the infinite modulations of the sexual act, of the real relations of man and his kind. Such a pornographer would not be the enemy of women, perhaps because he might begin to penetrate to the heart of the contempt for women that distorts our culture even as he entered the realms of true obscenity as he describes it. (*The Sadeian Woman* 19–20)

'True' obscenity, as distinguished from the ersatz variety that gluts our newstands and video stores, represents things that in their extremity – violent, sexy, or both – transgress the borders of propriety and stretch the limits of imagination with a single gesture. The truest obscenity might not even be possible; it might require that an alternative universe be built to house it. Sade tucked his brave new worlds away in fabulous châteaux and monasteries, where covens of inconceivable libertines gathered to perform rites of monstrous cruelty. The real world was too pusillanimous to provide such places, so Sade dreamt them. Similarly, Carter's fiction, however vividly it might invoke realistic details, always combines them with marvels. Amid the teacups and the antimacassars, there's always an angel of death, or a swan-winged *aérialiste*, or an infernal desire machine, to gild reality with wonder.

In this respect, Carter's fiction somewhat resembles 'magical realism', and in interviews she readily admits her affinities to its foremost practitioner, Gabriel Garcia Marquez. She has even done *One Hundred Years of Solitude* the honour of calling it 'the novel that set the tone for the last years of the century' (*The Guardian*, 25 September 1984, 10). She may well be right about the influence and importance of that novel, but Carter's own work – until recently, at least – has been very different. Before *Nights at the Circus*, magic intruded into her fictional world as an uninvited and usually malevolent visitant; there was no sense, as there is in Garcia Marquez and his Latin American colleagues, that reality itself is magical, that to express surprise at the raining of yellow flowers from the sky would be gauche.

Until *Nights at the Circus*, Carter adhered to the North European tradition that inscribed circles to keep the uncanny at bay. Even the most bizarre of her earlier novels, *The Infernal Desire Machines of Doctor Hoffman*, pits dream and reality against each other in clear-cut, if byzantine fashion. At the end, having destroyed the Doctor along with his Machines, Desiderio remarks:

> Nebulous Time was now time past; I crawled like a worm on its belly through the clinging mud of common time and the bare trees showed only the dreary shapes of an eternal November of the heart, for now all changes would henceforth be, as they had been before, absolutely predictable. And so I identified at last the flavour of my daily bread; it was and would be that of regret. Not, you understand, of remorse; only of regret, that insatiable regret with which we acknowledge that the impossible is, *per se*, impossible. (*Doctor Hoffman*, 221)

Doctor Hoffman distinguished himself from the tradition of malevolent sorcerers not because he employed machines rather than magic to advance his ends (the mad scientist of ten thousand B movies is, after all, only the old sorcerer *resartus* in a white lab coat), but because he recognized, like a metaphysician, the temporal structure of desire. Time's arrow, the relentless sequence of past-present-future, is the unacknowledged legislator of the ordinary world; desire, which wills a special future to be present and ignores any past that fails to suit it, subverts 'common time' at every moment; yet it, too, like the flesh it inhabits, remains the slave of time. Doctor Hoffman changed all that and wrought chaos; Desiderio reinstates chronology, and his regret is common, too.

Desiderio's regret at the end of *Doctor Hoffman* is like Coleridge's mixture of disdain and gratitude for the person on business from

Porlock: Carter retains the same English ambivalence about the relative value of intoxicating marvels and secure common sense. The feisty heroines of her fairy tales for adults are distinguished by their refusal to be flummoxed by the most outlandish – and threatening – developments. They carry, even into the ogre's den, a levelheaded air of competence that defeats evil by scaring it half to death. Something similar is true of Melanie in *The Magic Toyshop*, Marianne in *Heroes and Villains*, and even Fevvers in *Night at the Circus* – though Fevvers represents something of a departure, since she herself is a marvel and, for Walser, a bit of an ogre as well.

*Nights at the Circus* is the first of Carter's major works to show any significant affinity with magical realism *à la* Garcia Marquez, because it is her first novel to portray the marvellous not as a frightening incursion into ordinary life but as part and parcel of the ordinary. The fusion is embodied in Fevvers, an unbuttoned woman of the people who nevertheless can fly, and in Fevvers's inseparable companion, Lizzie, who raised her almost literally *ab ovo*. Both characters speak a distinctively Carterian dialect that combines street language with updated Metaphysical poetry, and both treat their own supranormality as if it were the most normal thing in the world.

The double nature of Lizzie and Fevvers is often at odds with itself, but when the fusion is complete, it produces a multiplied wonder that nothing in Garcia Marquez – and, I would venture to say, nothing else in English fiction – can match. The feat is accomplished most fully in a ravishing showpiece, early in *Nights at the Circus*, when the two women take turns recalling Fevvers's maiden flight. After extensive preparation – close monitoring of a pigeon nest, for instance – the moment arrived:

> 'Midsummer,' said Lizzie. 'Either Midsummer's Night, or else very early on Midsummer Morning. Don't you remember, darling?'
> 'Midsummer, yes. The year's green hinge. Yes, Liz, I remember.'
> Pause of a single heartbeat. (33)

Stark naked ('for we feared that any item of clothing might impede the lively movement of the body'), Fevvers let Lizzie lead her across the roof of Ma Nelson's bordello, deep in sleeping London.

At the brink, Fevvers hesitated, gripped by a remarkably philosophical form of fear:

I was not afraid only because the morning light already poking up the skirt of the sky might find me, when its fingers tickled the house, lying only a bag of broken bone in Ma Nelson's garden. Mingled with the simple fear of physical harm, there was a strange terror in my bosom that made me cling, at the last gasp of time, to Lizzie's skirts and beg her to abandon our project – for I suffered the greatest conceivable terror of the irreparable *difference* with which success in the attempt would mark me.

I feared a wound not of the body but the soul . . . an irreconcilable division between myself and the rest of humankind.

I feared the proof of my own singularity. (34)

Finally, however, the feat was 'dared and done' (36), and Fevvers crowned it with a characteristic stroke of brio:

For this first flight of mine, I did no more than circle the house at a level that topped the cherry tree in Nelson's garden, which was some thirty feet high. And, in spite of the great perturbation of my senses and the excess of mental concentration the practice of my new-found skill required, I did not neglect to pick my Lizzie a handful of the fruit that had reached perfect ripeness upon the topmost branches, fruit that customarily we were forced to leave as a little tribute for the thrushes. (36)

An appropriate bit of slapstick followed, as exhausted Fevvers grabbed hold of the guttering and it gave way; but Lizzie pulled her up to safety, as they tell Walser, speaking with what might as well be a single voice. First Fevvers:

And there we huddled on the roof in one another's arms, sobbing together with mingled joy and relief, as dawn rose over London and gilded the great dome of St Paul's until it looked like the divine pap of the city which, for want of any other, I needs must call my natural mother. (36)

Then Lizzie chimes in: 'London, with the one breast, the Amazon queen' (36).

By ordinary standards – or by the standards of ordinary fictional realism – none of this is even remotely possible. It need hardly be said that such things do not and cannot happen, such characters as

Fevvers and Lizzie are said to be could neither have such perceptions nor express them in such highly-wrought, extremely literary
language. They do so, however, convincingly: in *Nights at the Circus*.
Carter finally brings the magical into the real, by means of both her
protrayals and the language that portrays them. She has never mas-
tered dialogue, as Dickens did, or Joyce or D. H. Lawrence; until
*Nights at the Circus*, her characters usually spoke plain English,
leaving the flourishes to the narrator, or else indulged in bursts of
fancy rhetoric that seemed stiff and stilted. In *Nights at the Circus*,
however, the characters' eloquence is fully appropriate to their
magical-realistic nature. Instead of jarring against the narrator's
brilliance or sinking under its weight, the dialogue sings in harmony with it.

In an age of stylistic minimalism, when the goal of many fashionable English and American writers seems to be the whittling down
of language to match the barenness of their vision, Carter stands out
as an anomaly, an intruder from another time or culture. *Nights at
the Circus* is her grandest performance in this regard, too, but the
quality has been with her from the start of her career – a richness
of vocabulary, imagery, and allusion that reflects delight in language itself, and the writer's facility with it, along with unabashed
pleasure in plundering the treasures of the literary past. Despite her
penchant for outrageousness, particularly of a sexy, violent kind,
Carter has been from the start a learned writer who assumes (another unfashionable trait) corresponding learning in her reader. If
her stylistic exuberance sometimes recalls Dickens, her allusiveness
harks back to a yet older phase of the European literary tradition,
the eighteenth-century, the heyday of her favourite Sade and a time
when allusion served to affirm the solidarity of an exclusive,
predominantly male culture.

Carter is emphatically the heir(ess) of that time; her unblushing
claim to its legacy is in fact far more outrageous than the sex and
violence her fiction portrays. It is also the main reason why popularity in the Stephen King sense will probably always elude her. Especially in her earlier work, however, the erudition of the narrative
voice clashes oddly with the elemental story it wishes to tell. The
opening of *The Magic Toyshop* is a case in point:

The summer she was fifteen, Melanie discovered she was made
of flesh and blood. O, my America, my new found land. She

embarked on a tranced voyage, exploring the whole of herself, clambering her own mountain ranges, penetrating the moist richness of her secret valleys, a physiological Cortez, da Gama or Mungo Park. (1)

The Donne paraphrase is exactly appropriate, and of course the reader unfamiliar with 'On Going to Bed' will miss the resonance. That ignoramus may be of no consequence, but it's also far from clear whether this reference is to be understood as mimicking Melanie's thoughts or as a flight of the narrator's imagination. The same is true of the three explorers, and of the other famous names that follow: the Pre-Raphaelites, Toulouse Lautrec, Titian, Renoir, Cranach, D. H. Lawrence, all in the novel's first two pages. *Lady Chatterley's Lover* is definitely part of Melanie's experience; after reading it, 'she secretly picked forget-me-nots and stuck them in her pubic hair' (2). But the ironic tone is the narrator's, and it and Melanie's don't jibe.

The gap heals over in *Nights at the Circus*, which also resolves most of the other contradictions I have described in Carter's earlier work. And, for once, Carter's characters work as both magical and real – especially Fevvers, who leaves the reader feeling that, if no such person ever existed, reality is the poorer. Fevvers is also the fullest embodiment so far of the ideal Carterian heroine, a goal she has been striving toward, in one way or another, from her earliest fiction. According to *The Sadeian Woman*, the moral pornographer aims to 'penetrate to the heart' of Western culture's contempt for women (20). Carter has consistently attempted to fulfill that mission by portraying women for whom contempt is impossible, who'd slap a man senseless if he so much as sneered. Girls, too: whatever their age or station, Carter's females possess a self-sufficient power, an absolutely inviolable integrity, that renders male arrogance futile.

And they're fiercely sexual beings, even her questing virgins; they might be ignorant, yet they're never naive. Carter may think that she's imitating Sade in this, but she's entirely her own woman. For *Sade* in the following passage, read *Carter*:

Women do not normally fuck in the active sense. They are fucked in the passive sense and hence automatically fucked-up, done over, undone. Whatever else he says or does not say, Sade declares himself unequivocally for the right of women to fuck – as if the period in which women fuck aggressively, tyrannously and cruelly wil be a necessary stage in the development of a general human consciousness of the nature of fucking: that if it is not egalitarian, it is unjust. Sade . . . urgest women to fuck as actively as they are able, so that powered by their enormous and hitherto untapped sexual energy they will then be able to fuck their way into history and, in doing so, change it. (*The Sadeian Woman*, 27)

Carter's boldest female fucker so far is Fevvers in *Nights at the Circus*; literally and figuratively, she fucks her way across two continents until at last, in the wilds of Siberia, she wins the man she loves, pins him to the bed, and crouches over him, laughing deliriously for sheer joy:

> The spiralling tornado of Fevvers' laughter began to twist and shudder across the entire globe, as if a spontaneous response to the giant comedy that endlessly unfolded beneath it, until everything that lived and breathed, everywhere, was laughing. Or so it seemed to the deceived husband, who found himself laughing too, even if he was not quite sure whether or not he might be the butt of the joke. Fevvers, sputtering to a stop at last, crouched above him, covering his face with kisses. Oh, how pleased with him she was! (*Nights at the Circus*, 295)

The world-encompassing joke is simply that Walser believed her when she said she was a virgin – a shocking fraud if any ordinary turn-of-the-century woman had played that trick, high hilarity for Fevvers. Carter might intend Fevvers as a model of irrepressible femininity, but she never goes so far as to pretend that such a creature could really walk the earth, then or now. Fevvers has feathers, after all, and she wasn't even born – she hatched.

On all counts, *Night at the Circus* is Carter's most ambitious novel yet; it's also her greatest success and a powerful promise of future achievements. Yet it illustrates on a grand scale her worst failing. After so much praise, I suppose I have to mention it: she can't write a plot, not to save her life. *Nights at the Circus* displays one breathtaking set piece after another, strung on a picaresque string, and girl gets boy at the end, but nothing really accumulates or develops. It's less a novel than a carnival of brilliant tableaux. The same is true, in lesser degree, of Carter's earlier novels: they don't cohere, and on the last page they just stop. When she borrows a fairy-tale backbone as in *The Bloody Chamber*, or writes story-essays like those in *Saints and*

*Strangers,* her fictions turn out as shapely as even Henry James could wish; short forms seem to suit her talent best. Yet she provides such intense and various pleasures in all her books that mere formal inefficiency seems a minor fault indeed.

## A BIBLIOGRAPHY OF WRITINGS BY ANGELA CARTER

*Robert E. Hosmer Jr. and Walter Kendrick*

### Novels

*Shadow Dance* (London: Heinemann, 1966. American edition: *Honeybuzzard.* New York: Simon and Schuster, 1967).

*The Magic Toyshop* (London: Heinemann, 1967. New York: Simon and Schuster, 1968).

*Several Perceptions* (London: Heinemann, 1968. New York: Simon and Schuster, 1968).

*Heroes and Villains* (London: Heinemann, 1969. New York: Simon and Schuster, 1970.

*Love* (London: Hart Davis, 1971; with a new 'Afterword,' 1987. New York: Viking Penguin, 1988).

*The Infernal Desire Machines of Dr Hoffman* (London: Hart Davis, 1972. American edition: *The War of Dreams.* New York: Harcourt Brace, 1974).

*The Passion of New Eve* (London: Gollancz, 1977. New York: Harcourt Brace, 1977).

*Nights at the Circus* (London: Chatto and Windus, 1984. New York: Viking, 1985).

*Wise Children* (London: Chatto and Windus, 1991. New York: Farrar, Straus and Giroux, 1992).

### Stories

*Fireworks: Nine Profane Pieces* (London: Quartet, 1974. New York: Harper, 1981).

*The Bloody Chamber and Other Stories* (London: Gollancz, 1979. New York: Harper, 1980).

*Black Venus* (London: Chatto and Windus, 1985. American edition: *Saints and Strangers*, containing a 'different' [i.e., substantially revised] version of 'The Fall River Axe Murders,' New York: Viking, 1986).

*Wayward Girls and Wicked Women: An Anthology of Stories*, ed. by Carter (London: Virago, 1986; contains her 'The Loves of Lady Purple'.)

'Tis Pity She's a Whore', *Granta* 25 (Autumn 1988): 179–97. Reprinted in *Best English Short Stories 1989*, ed. Giles Gordon and David Hughes (London: Heinemann, 1989. New York: W. W. Norton, 1989): 33–53.

'Ashputtle: or, the Mother's Ghost', *The Village Voice Literary Supplement* (March 1990): 22–3.

## Children's Stories

*Miss Z., The Dark Young Lady* (London: Heinemann, 1970. New York: Simon and Schuster, 1970).
*The Donkey Prince* (New York: Simon and Schuster).
*The Fairy Tales of Charles Perrault*, trans. by Carter (London: Gollancz, 1977. New York: Avon, 1978).
*Martin Leman's Comic and Curious Cats* (London: Gollancz, 1979).
*Moonshadow* (London: Gollancz, 1982).
*Sleeping Beauty and Other Favourite Fairy Tales*, trans. by Carter (London: Gollancz, 1982. New York: Schocken, 1984).

## Poetry

*Unicorn* (Leeds: Location Press, 1966).

## Plays

*The Company of Wolves* (screenplay), with Neil Jordan, 1984.

## Nonfiction

*The Sadeian Woman: An Exercise in Cultural History* (London: Virago, 1979. American edition: *The Sadeian Woman and the Ideology of Pornography*, New York: Pantheon, 1979).
*Nothing Sacred: Selected Writings* (London: Virago, 1982).
'Sugar Daddy'. *Granta* 8 (1983): 179–90.
*Images of Frida Kahlo*, introduction by Carter (London: The Redstone Press, 1989).
*The Virago Book of Fairy Tales*, edited by Carter (London: Virago, 1990. American edition: *The Old Wives' Book of Fairy Tales*. New York: Random House, 1990).
Charlotte Bronte: *Jane Eyre*, introduction by Angela Carter (London: Virago, 1991).
Charlotte Bronte: *Villette*, introduction by Angela Carter (London: Virago, 1991).

## Essays and Reviews

'Bob Dylan on Tour; or, Huck Finn reaches Puberty', *London Magazine* (August 1966): 100–1.
'A Happy Bloomsday', *New Society* (8 July 1982): 65–6.

'Tea and Sympathy' [*A Very Private Eye: An Autobiography in Letters and Diaries by Barbara Pym*], Washington Post Book World (1 July 1984): 1; 5.
'Ludic Cube' [*Dictionary of the Khazars: A Lexicon Novel in 100,000 Words* by Milorad Pavic, trans. by Christina Pribicevic-Zoric], London Review of Books (1 June 1989): 8, 10.
'40 Means You Cry Over Spilt Milk' [*Forty-Seventeen* by Frank Moorhouse], The New York Times Book Review (13 August 1989): 3.
'Brooksie and Faust' [*Louise Brooks* by Barry Paris], The London Review of Books (8 March 1990): 12–13.
'White Nights and Golden Days' [*The Last Voyage of Somebody the Sailor* by John Barth]. The Washington Post Book World (3 February 1991): 1; 10.

# A BIBLIOGRAPHY OF WRITINGS ABOUT ANGELA CARTER

*Robert E. Hosmer Jr. and Walter Kendrick*

## Articles and Reviews

Alexander, Fiona, 'Myths, Dreams and Nightmares', *Contemporary Women Novelists* (London: Edward Arnold, 1990): 61–75.
Bradfield, Scott, 'Angela Carter on the Bawdy Bits', Elle (January 1992): 70.
Bryant, Sylvia, 'Re-constructing Oedipus Through "*Beauty and the Beast*"', Criticism 31, 4 (Fall 1989): 439–53.
Clark, Robert, 'Angela Carter's Desire Machine', Women's Studies 14 (1987): 147–61.
Duncker, Patricia, 'Re-imagining the Fairy Tales: Angela Carter's *Bloody Chambers*', Literature and History: A Journal for the Humanities, 10, 1 (Spring, 1984): 3–14.
Goldsworthy, Kerryn, 'Angela Carter', Meanjin 44, 1 (March 1985): 4–13.
Gorra, Michael, 'Angela Carter's Backstage Magic' [*Wise Children*], The Boston Globe (5 January 1992): B39; B42.
Hamilton, Alex, 'Sade and Prejudice', Guardian (30 March 1979): 15.
Harron, Mary, '"I'm a Socialist, damn it! How Can you Expect me to Be Interested in Fairies"', Guardian (25 September 1984): 10.
Kendrick, Walter, 'Rough Magic: The Many Splendours of Angela Carter', Village Voice Literary Supplement (October 1986): 17–19.
Landon, Brooks, 'Eve at the End of the World: Sexuality and the Reversal of Expectations in Novels by Joanna Russ, Angela Carter, and Thomas Berger'; in *Erotic Universe: Sexuality and Fantastic Literature* (ed. Donald Palumbo) (New York, 1986): 61–74.
Mars-Jones, Adam, 'From Wonders to Prodigies', Times Literary Supplement (TLS) (28 September 1984): 1083.
McEwan, Ian, 'Sweet Smell of Excess', Sunday Times Magazine (9 September 1984): 42–4.
Mortimer, John and Angela Carter, 'The Stylish Prime of Miss Carter', Sunday Times (London) (24 January 1982): 36.

Parrinder Patrick, 'It's Only a Paper Moon' [*Wise Children*], *London Review of Books* (13 June 1991): 3.

Paterson, Moira, 'Flights of Fancy in Balham', *Observer Magazine* (9 November 1986): 42–43; 45.

Punter, David, 'Angela Carter: Supersessions of the Masculine', *Critique: Studies in Modern Fiction* 25, 4 (Summer 1984): 209–22.

Rose, Ellen Cronan, 'Through the Looking Glass: When Women Tell Fairy Tales', in *The Voyage In: Fictions of Female Development*, ed. Elizabeth Abel, Marianne Hirsch, and Elizabeth Langland (Hanover, NH, 1983): 209–27.

Sage, Lorna, 'Angela Carter', *Dictionary of Literary Biography* 14: 205–12.

Sage, Lorna, 'The Savage Sideshow', *New Review* 4 (June/July 1977): 51–7.

Schmidt, Ricarda, 'The Journey of the Subject in Angela Carter's Fiction', *Textual Practice* 3, 1 (Spring 1989):L 56–75.

Stott, Catherine, 'Runaway to the Land of Promise', *Guardian* (10 August 1972): 9.

Warner, Marina, 'That Which Is Spoken' [*The Virago Book of Fairy Tales*]. *London Review of Books* (8 November 1990): 21–2.

Watts, Janet, 'Sade and the Sexual Struggle', *Observer Magazine* (25 March 1979): 54–5.

Wilson, Robert Rawdon, 'SLIP PAGE: Angela Carter, in/out/in the Post-modern Nexus', *Ariel: A Review of International English Literature*, 20, 4 (October 1989): 96–114.

## Interviews

Ann Sintow, 'Conversations with a Necromancer', *Village Voice Literary Supplement* (June 1989): 14–16.

## Miscellaneous

*Contemporary Authors, New Revision Series* 12: 103–5.
*Contemporary Literary Criticism* 1: 75–80.
*Contemporary Literary Criticism* 5: 101–3.
*Contemporary Literary Criticism* 41: 109–22.

## ANGELA CARTER

Born in London in 1940, the daughter of Hugh Alexander (a journalist) and Olive (Farthing) Stalker, she married Paul Carter in 1960, while working as a newspaper journalist. Carter read medieval literature at Bristol University, where she took a BA in 1965, before publishing her first novel, *Shadow Dance*, in the same year. Seven more novels followed, each one further developing her reputation as an iconoclastic mythmaker of daring innovation and bravado. Her translations of fairy stories by Charles Perrault and her own re-writing of classic tales like 'Red Riding Hood' enhanced that reputation. She has also enjoyed considerable success as a writer of short fiction and children's books. Angela Carter achieved widespread popular and critical attention as an original, if occasionally eccentric, artist noted for her independent feminism, Socialist politics, and profuse creativity. She won three of England's most prestigious literary awards: the John Llewellyn Rhys Prize (1967); the Somerset Maugham Award (1968); and the James Tait Black Memorial Black Memorial Prize (1984).

Carter's work in non-fiction included poetry, journalism, and cultural critique as well as radio and television scripts. Angela Carter lived in London, but spent a good deal of time in the United States where she taught at the University of Texas, the Iowa Writer's Workshop, and Brown University. She died in London on 16 February 1992.

# 5

# The Strange Clarity of Distance: History, Myth, and Imagination in the Novels of Isabel Colegate

BRETT T. AVERITT

Perhaps it is because we know nothing first-hand of our own beginning or ending that myths of origin and creation, those of the after-life and resurrection, both delight and comfort us. Other myths, such as romantic and social ones, we often see working in our lives, or if we don't and are oblivious to them, we may suffer their blind-siding. To make things more difficult, social myths which justify the uses of power – imperialism, patriotism, nationalism, social Darwinism, racism, sexism, classism – sometimes compete with romantic myths, such as the myth of the hero and the quest for perfection and the ideal, but they may also be reinforced by them. Sometimes they're substitutes, sometimes complements.

The novels of Isabel Colegate take as their subject the interplay of myth and history, the way in which various kinds of myth (social and romantic ones) are played off against historical reality, especially in the generations just fading from view. It is those past generations of parents and grandparents, English, as is Colegate, members of the British establishment, as is Colegate, who people her fiction. Of her interest in the near past, the period from 1905 through the twenties, she said in a 1985 *Publishers Weekly* interview:

> I think that the period that is just going out of living memory is always rather fascinating. And for Europeans, the first World War was such an enormous cataclysm. From the point of view of social history, nearly *all* the problems which are still besetting us, and which we go on worrying away at, were coming then. It [the Edwardian Age] wasn't a peaceful golden age. Everything was

85

there, beginning to agitate, and then the war accelerated the processes of change (56).

The interplay of social myths and historical reality in the generations preceding our own, in our parents' generation, accounts, in
part, for our own myths of origin, the expectations and assigned
roles we inherit at birth.

In the novel *Statues in a Garden*, published in 1964, Colegate presents
her themes of politics and passion, power and class interest, money
and competition, in a fable of fated obsessions. For Philip Weston,
the nephew and adopted son of Sir Aylmer Weston, a prominent
Liberal politician and member of Asquith's cabinet in the summer of
1914, his assigned role becomes an obsessive one: the role of the
outsider. Philip will never be a true son and heir, and no other
identity seems to matter. Sir Aylmer kills himself after he discovers
that his beautiful, forty-two year old wife Cynthia and their adopted
son Philip are having an affair. It is a story of incest and tragic
suicide. Just as Philip's role of outsider drives his passion for revenge, so Cynthia's assigned role of insider allows it. They are,
indeed, like statues in a garden, frozen in their castings. Cynthia,
who is depicted as one who never dreams, seems to sleepwalk
through their week of passion. She rationalizes that she had always
loved Philip and 'by a sort of ruthless simplicity she would not allow
the shock of discovering that love involved also physical desire to
change its nature. . . . What was impelling her was her love for
Philip, a love she never concealed and which had never been incom-
patible with her love and respect for Aylmer' (127). Never having
questioned the Victorian version of female sexuality, Cynthia knows
nothing of her own desire. She accepts the precept of the veneration
of the female sex as sublime (at least in those who would be wives
and mothers): 'Was it Lord Curzon who was supposed to have said,
"Ladies don't move?"' (127)

She and Aylmer don't talk about their feelings. With Philip, she
discovers deeper delights than she has ever known. Their affair
'made her feel extremely well and happy. Her happiness was of an
immediate nature, and even the fact, of which she must have been
aware, that it could not last, did not mar it. Her sense of physical
well-being made her feel morally in the right' (127–8). A very simple
criterion, indeed. The underside of a social message telling women
that they are not full human beings with sexual desires is that it
allows them to escape the moral responsibility of their sexual ac-

tions. Since she cannot imagine the consequences of her actions, Cynthia moves in a fugue state, unable to tell waking from sleeping.

It is also in this early novel that Colegate identifies the image of love as the shaping spirit of the imagination, what she calls 'our one hope'. Typically, it is the grandmothers in her fiction who speak wisely about love, who have outrun stultifying roles. Lady Weston, Aylmer's eighty-year-old mother, speaks her knowledge down a tube 'across the abyss' to her driver Moberly: '"We have to cling to love," she said. "Our one talent, the shaping spirit of our imagination, our one hope. And we have hardly even tried to find out what it is."' (127). She also wonders if it can be heard if spoken, or whether

> like most messages, incomprehensible except to those who know it already? Well, you see, it is only in old age that the search for sanctions becomes all-absorbing. In youth, there are so many distractions. But your eyes change, you have to hold your book at arm's length in order to be able to read it, and substances change, colours are sometimes brighter and sometimes darker, and you get this strange clarity of distance, men walking down a road along way off, in the sun, between the trees, not knowing why they are going; they are as clear to me as the printed word held at arm's length. (127–8)

The old woman's words echo an irony consistent with Colegate's stance in the novel. That irony stems from the too little-too late nature of wisdom, and the often incomprehensible message that it is love that powers the imagination and provides us with a distancing ego.

In a recent essay in *The Threepenny Review*, Colegate discusses the creative process and dreams, noting that most writers of fiction are aware of the intimate connection between dream and the literary imagination. That stunning separation of ego from affect that occurs during dreaming when the dreamer is removed from judgment by a language that is fresh, original, yet recognizably one's own serves as her analogy. Colegate tells how she came to identify the parallel between her own mind at work on fiction and the process at work in the mind of anyone asleep. Although she says that she is not herself a confessional writer, her own dreams kept turning her deepest preoccupation into stories in much the same way her conscious writing of fiction was doing. It is as if the brain in ceaselessly scanning its environment registers the results of the scan on translation machines, 'one machine using the language of conscious thought and one machine using the language of dream, both dedicated to the search for significance' (10). What she finds fascinating is not that the dream works in a language of symbolism and displacement, but that both literary art and dream seem to be using the same language. In both, she says 'factual description and verbal argument, even where achievable, were inadequate; something else was needed to convey the fullness, the multifariousness, the ambiguity, and at the same time the intensity of the original apprehension and the remembered impression' (10). Both literary art and dream possess an economy which Walter Benjamin called 'chaste compactness', that quality which precludes psychological analysis (*Illuminations*, 91).

Colegate tells of writing down two dreams of a friend which showed her the similarities between the language of art and the language of the dream: both provide distance and through distance, catharsis. In one dream Colegate noticed that rather than her friend's avoiding or defending against something she could not face, she went to sleep facing her problem. 'The dream played her dilemma back to her, using its own language, a language parallel to the conscious language she had been using to herself before she fell asleep. In her dream, she had separated herself from her jealousy . . . .' (10). Colegate asserts that the parallel between dream and a work of art holds if we understand that the mental processes involved in producing the two are the same with the exception that one is willed and the other is not. She calls the work of fiction a conscious, organized dream, moving us to consider 'the proposition that the making of a work of art requires the ability to use images and transpositions in the same way as the language of dream uses them' (10), admitting the need for the other more obvious requirements, technical, intellectual, emotional abilities, as well. Colegate's view of the creative process on the analogy of dream serves to explain the seminal importance she gives these processes in her fiction.

In a telling passage from Isabel Colegate's best-known novel, *The Shooting Party*, Sir Randolph is in his study standing with his hand on a classical bust thinking that the best embodiment of Renaissance man is the eighteenth-century English gentleman. He is looking back to Greece and Athens in a straight line, seeing the British upper class

as the guardians of civilization, placed at the top in the social contract, doing their duty as the stout yeomen do theirs. It was, of
course, the central myth of British society in the golden age of
Edwardian influence when the upper classes filled the role of servants to royalty. In contrast to Sir Randolph's vision, Colegate
shows us a depressing picture of a society trapped in its own myth-
ology, and perhaps most depressing of all, the way servants and
keepers are caught in the web by infatuation with their masters,
especially Cornelius Cardew, who is in some way more trapped in
the system than anyone. Cardew is a stereotype of the nineteenth-
century schoolmaster, the perfect example of an English socialist and
free-thinker, thinking of himself as highly independent yet thrilled
when Sir Randolph pays some attention to him. He envisions their
future meetings as helpful colleagues, equals as men of ideas, pam-
phleteers. Servants love serving. We see John, the hero Lionel
Stephen's valet, copying his master's discarded love letters, and
Tom Harker, the shooting party's accidental victim, sitting up at his
death scene, blessing the British Empire.

*The Shooting Party* was published in 1980 and received the W. H.
Smith Literary Award in England, and when the novel became a
movie starring James Mason and John Gielgud, Colegate's fiction
reached a wider audience. Of the film, which was Mason's last
before his death in 1985, Colegate has said that even though its
director and scriptwriter stuck closely to the pace and themes of
the novel, 'the film and the book are so different. . . . Some of the
irony is lost – inevitably – and the pre-shadowing of the First World
War is made much more of' (Craig, 11).

Colegate published her first novel in 1958 when she was twenty-
seven, and in thirty years since, she has produced eleven novels and
a collection of three long stories, *A Glimpse of Sion's Glory*, in 1985. As
she told Amanda Craig, her output is slow: 'I have to be relaxed
when I write. I get tremendously involved with all the characters,
and this can't be done if I feel at all nervy, or if I'm somehow being
pushed towards pretension' (11).

She married in the middle of her writing career and has three
children. An early trilogy composed of *The Blackmailer* (1958), *A Man
of Power* (1960), and *The Great Occasion* (1962) is published by Penguin in one volume. In 1964 she published *Statues in a Garden*, her
most artistically successful novel to date. A precursor of *The Shooting
Party*, it shares the same period and rich background detail. While
writing *The Orlando Trilogy*, which she finished in 1973, Colegate

suffered what she calls 'a crisis in confidence' (11). The trilogy traces
the rise and fall of a young entrepreneur and member of Parliament
in the 1930s and 1940s. The plots of the novels – *Orlando King* (1968),
*Orlando at the Brazen Threshold* (1971), and *Agatha* (1973) – depend on
seeing Orlando as a hero in search of his origins. With a gloss of
Sophoclean tragedy over three stories, Colegate experiments with
ways to use myth to explore a determined past. Finally, however,
the experiment seems to strangle the life from the characters. In *News
from the City of the Sun* (1979) and in her recent novel *Deceits of Time*
(1988), she explores the very British myths of utopia fomenting
during the thirties as Hitler moved the world toward war. Female
narrators serve Colegate well in these two novels as they create rich
dramatic tension between the unfolding of character and the historical moment.

Three things the new reader of Isabel Colegate should keep in
mind are (1) her special use of the historical setting, (2) her economical use of a cinematic point of view, and (3) most importantly, her
unique use of the theme of creative imagination to examine the
myths governing the lives of her characters and the society in which
they live. Each is developed by the technique of 'interplay' which is
responsible for her subtle handling of themes of power, competition,
and class characterized by an evocative and flinty style. By 'interplay' I mean several things: (1) the way in which various kinds of
myth (romantic, social) are played off against historical reality; (2)
the way in which different kinds of plot are developed simultaneously or side-by-side; and (3) the way in which various parts of the
novel relate to each other or to the whole or to history either metaphorically or metonymically.

Colegate returns again and again to the cusp of history just before
the outbreak of the world wars in England. The First World War
looms as the greater shooting party, but war is not her focus in *The
Shooting Party*. Rather, her focus is on the seeming perfection of a
society just before its demise. The First War brought cataclysmic
changes to all levels of British society; its economic costs were grave,
much graver still the inestimable loss of young men in war. It marked
the end of many things, marking as well the beginning of urban
power, new money, the New Woman, and equalitarian rhetoric.

The traditional shooting party speaks worlds as a typical
Edwardian idea – of elegance, privilege, skill, snobbery, banality,
smugness and fatuity. In the opening scene, Colegate evokes, in deft
description, the drift of days in the autumn, in October 1913, at the

Oxfordshire estate of Sir Randolph Nettleby, Baronet. It is the last weekend in October 'before the outbreak of what used to be known as the Great War'. The story enters the near past, the generation of our parents and grandparents, as the party arrives for the weekend shoot. As readers we feel invited, but if we never feel quite at home, that's because no one should, certainly not from our present-day perspective. With a seductive use of proximity and distance, Colegate interrogates the legacy of a social fabric which must have appeared seamless if one were born to rank, a member of the hereditary landed aristocracy. She opens the novel playing with the contrast of then and now imaged in two kinds of light:

It caused a mild scandal at the time, but in most people's memories it was quite outshone by what succeeded it. You could see it as a drama played out in a room lit by gas lamps; perhaps with flickering sidelights thrown by a log fire burning brightly at one side of the room, a big Edwardian drawing room, full of furniture, tables crowded with knick-knacks and framed photographs, people sitting or standing in groups, conversing; and then a fierce electric light thrown back from a room beyond, the next room, into which no one has yet ventured, and this fierce retrospective light through the doorway makes the lamp-lit room seem shadowy, the flickering flames in the grate pallid, the circles of yellow light round the lamps opaque (a kind of tarnished gold) and the people well, discernibly people, but people from a long time ago, our parents and grandparents made to seem like beings from a much remote past, Charlemagne and his knights or the seven sleepers half roused from their thousand year sleep. (1)

The setting of the novel furnishes the great country estate and our minds with the cast of characters, members of the upper classes, the minor gentry and peers at the pinnacle of their power. Sir Randolph's shooting party is one of the best in the country (Edward, the late King, often shot there), and it brings together, for a test of skill, the nation's sharpshooters, their wives and servants. It is a tribal gathering. The developing rivalry between the men (the two best shots, Stephens and Lord Hartlip, shoot their best records while their loaders overcount to win) is juxtaposed with social competition and sexual intrigues. Relations between masters and servants define the tribal community. Relations between parents and children, between men and women, husbands and wives and lovers, between the cultures of the rural economy and the new urban politics also define the elaborate social rituals embodied in 'good form'.

Colegate's narrative moves from this opening still, a snapshot of the soft glowing scene, the past caught as in old sepia photographs, to a cinematic frame of objective narration. Slowly she brings the faded photograph to life, focusing first on one guest's arrival, and then another's, before panning out across the park from its gardens to the wild, encompassing the grounds, the head gamekeeper's cottage, and the hovel of the poacher Tom Harker, who is destined to be the accidental victim of the shoot. We become privy to the thought processes of Sir Randolph through his notations in the game book and to those of many characters through Colegate's use of soliloquies or interior musings to deal with one person and his or her thoughts. Omniscient narration is limited after the opening panoramic sweep to this 'voice under' technique.

Sir Randolph's quirky, whimsical, often melancholic musings reveal a decent man who rationalizes class interests as necessary for tribal order. Good manners, decency, civility, order and beauty depend as well on hierarchy. But change is encroaching on his image of England in an idyllic past, for 'beyond the boundaries of his own estate, there was a whole clamorous violent process going on which was to bring about the end of an idea, an idea started by people whose combination of poetry and political acumen, curiosity and love of pastoral life, made them seem . . . English' (110).

Urban politics, industrialization, and new money are eroding the values of conservative power vested in the landlord classes; Randolph fears that the succession of values from his generation to the next is at an end. Lionel's rejection of Sir Randolph's way of life signals the impending end of an era; the role he assigns Lionel is that of putative son, but

> instead he [Lionel] saw what was happening, saw that that sort of life isn't the life for a man any more – the sort of life I lead. Everything's against us now. The politicians are determined to turn this country into an urban society instead of a rural one and in the course of the change they think they've got to take away the power of the landed proprietor. . . . 'An age,' he wrote, 'even perhaps a civilization, is coming to an end. . . . In the meantime it is bad for the young men. If you take away the proper functions of an aristocracy, what can it do but play games too seriously?' (28–9).

It is in this context that Sir Randolph reads the escalating shooting competition as a violation of good form.

Sir Randolph sees the passing of the rural gentry and the social values they sustain as a serious loss. The ascendancy of urban life-styles spells an end to an elaborate system of rules crafted through the generations to foster the tribal values of England and of Englishmen. The shooting party is a male ceremony designed to foster the values of gentlemenly competition. The intense competitive spirit and the easy recourse to violence that characterize social life among men is transformed into an emphasis on personal skill in shooting and the slaughter of birds. Cornelius Cardew's comic position in the story is a foil to Randolph's serious role in Colegate's 'plot of argument'. His argument about the rights of animals matches Sir Randolph's word for word, pamphlet for pamphlet.

Olivia, the heroine of Colegate's 'plot of courtship', wonders why men must embrace the letting of blood to confirm their competitive urges and seal their social bonds. Sir Randolph, of course, accepts the necessity of such a blood ritual. He insists that rural England has converted the possibility of divisive competition *between* men to a socially useful competition *among* men with its hunts and shooting parties. For Sir Randolph a fox hunt is not a case of the unspeakable pursuing the inedible, and a shooting party is not simply the bored butchering the defenceless. An organized shooting party engages rural men of all stations in a common endeavour combining a variety of skills (beating the birds, loading the guns, and shooting). Every man has his task that must be pursued with cunning and skill. At a shoot, class station dictates the assignment of tasks, but all of the participants are fully engaged in a dramatic and unifying event.

Of course, the gentlemen who do the shooting carry a special responsibility. They are the stars of the event, so they set the tone. The working-class loader may keep score of the birds killed by his shooter, but the shots themselves must pretend not to keep count. For them it must be an exercise in pure skill and style. And the rules of the game must be strictly observed else the formal shooting party degenerates into a simple bird-kill. When Tom Harker is accidentally killed, Randolph points out that the man who fired the fatal shot did so because he violated a time-honoured rule of the shooting game. He says to Gilbert, 'You were not shooting like a gentleman' (174). The rules of aristocratic rural life may seem arbitrary and childish and possibly even cruel to an outsider, but for Sir Randolph they are a set of directives that convert male violence into a series of ceremonial occasions that transform a potentially fatal male flaw into a force for social cohesion. The ritual of sport sublimates male aggression. Olivia speaks as a woman when she wonders why male relationships must revolve around blood sacrifice. But Sir Randolph accepts violence as part of the male imagination. He fears that the ascendancy of urban politics with its lack of circumscribed male and class ritual will unleash male violence through war, its ultimate form.

When Lionel unwittingly begins to rival Lord Hartlip's shooting record, he does so as he moves into his function of romantic hero in Colegate's 'plot of courtship'. His natural athletic grace becomes quickened by his conquest in love. He and Olivia are in love and she has just realized it and announced her love for him. Olivia, the heroine of the story, is married and has a young son; she is married to the awful snob Bob Lilburn who shoots for social prestige. After Olivia responds in kind to his declaration of love, Lionel, 'his sense of glory endowing him with extraordinary alertness', begins to shoot with complete carelessness and complete accuracy, breaking record after record, stirring up Hartlip's hatred to a frenzy that is equally careless and suddenly deadly.

The courtship in the story represents an escape from the myths of history embodied in the plot of argument (expressed by men and viewed as obsessive and prejudiced). Colegate makes it clear that she intends to treat the myths about the past with irony. She has called herself a historian *manqué* and has said that if she had stayed in school, she might have become a historian; but she does not write 'historical novels'. In her 1985 *PW* interview, Colegate draws a fine line which separates her fiction from novels which are more persuasive as historical documents than as fiction. 'I've written much more about the immediate past and I certainly don't think of myself as a historical novelist. I mean, I'm not pretending that I'm not writing from *now* about it' (56). Certainly compared to a historical novelist such as Olivia Manning, whose three novels published as *The Balkan Trilogy* used real-life events of the early Second World War as a background to her message that never again would Europe, or the world, be able to experience the previous world of stability and order, Colegate challenges the nature of previous myths of order. Even true love does not escape her irony as we have seen. How ironical that Lionel becomes an expert killer because he is in love. Romantic love is a myth which can misfire. Only those characters who have the power to understand how myths are made and with their creative imagination come to see themselves as conditioned by those myths reach something like freedom from the myths of history.

Turning to the structure of the novel, we notice how the ascending romantic plot suppresses the other plots, and how irony is used to interrogate the past as the relationship between history and myth. Olivia is married to a snob. When she asked her husband the 'what if' question – what if there were charming, intelligent people somewhere that we don't know – her probing democratic curiosity is contrasted with his close-minded Tory response: '[Bob had thought for a moment and then he had said,] "It's impossible. But if it were not impossible, then I don't think I should want to know such people. I don't think I should find anything in common with them" (123). And he is the boob who says that 'Art and life are two very different things' (40).

Because art is one of life's richest experiences for Lionel Stephens as it is for Olivia, they become friends who share books and ideas. Lionel is her best friend, so that the discovery that she is in love with him is fraught with ambiguity and unconscious desire. The romantic heroine of the novel puzzles about the way myths work with the man she will soon discover she is in love with:

'I should have thought that every English person's deepest idea of England was of the country. Doesn't England mean a village green, and smoke rising from cottage chimneys, and the rooks cawing in the elms, and the squire and the vicar and the school-master and the jolly villagers and their rosy-cheeked children?'

'It has not existed for many years now.'

'It must exist. How could we all believe in it so if it didn't exist?'

'Exactly. We believe in it. That is why the idea is such a powerful one. It is a myth.'

'If it is a myth, you are part of it.'

Olivia was pleased with the idea. 'You are part of the myth, you see. That's why you say you don't believe in it, because you are inside it.' (108)

Olivia, of course, is caught in myths of her own making. Treated personally, as the romantic plot does treat them, the myths surrounding her marriage and her role as a woman serve as a metonym for these larger themes. How she understands her feelings for Lionel dramatizes the way conventional categories can blind: he is her friend, indeed her best friend. They have so many things in common – a love of reading and literature and more. He gives her the Ruskin essays to which she responds with true aesthetic delight. '"I love Ruskin,' she had said. 'Even when I think he's talking nonsense, I love the sound of it'" (38). Then later, she says again that it is the rhythm of the sentences more than what they say that makes her feel its worth, like music. It is friendship she feels for Lionel, friendship based on shared interests. Later, she calls him her 'long-lost brother'. Surely this may explain her feelings. Beyond that, he is the kind of man she would want her son to become. Olivia analyzes their friendship, sorting the pieces. But the parts must finally be exposed to the whole truth of the heart's affection. As she faces that truth, we see the theme of creative imagination emerging as the moral psychology in the novel.

'Art makes us better, of course. . . . It's the sort of flat truth one's supposed to be too sophisticated to acknowledge (45).' It is Lionel who says this to Olivia before he writes the love letter about truth and beauty, which identifies him, by means of the Keats' gloss, with an awareness of the need for exercising the imagination. It is the authority of the imagination which Colegate uses to control what we come to look at in the novel and how we look at it. The role of the imagination (or what might be called the psychology of the creative process) determines the appraisal of experience that all of Colegate's major novels figure. Colegate manipulates the themes of power and class consciousness, history and myth as well as plotting by the test of 'negative capability', Keats's term for the poet who is 'capable of being in uncertainties, Mysteries, doubts, without any irritable reaching after fact and reason' (*The Letters of John Keats*, Vol. II, ed. E. H. Rollins, 193).

Negative capability is the poet's ability to feel disinterestedly in the creative act, the ability to separate himself from his own powerfully cathected interests and ideas and allow himself to be confronted by new real objects. It is the psychology Keats saw in the great poets and which he knew in himself: an organization of ego fluid enough for new experience to awaken a wide spectrum of unconsciously withheld memories and perceptions and to refocus them into new patterns. The imagination set free by negative capability, what he saw evidenced in Shakespeare's language, reaches existential truth through fusing with the things of experience and the creatures of his imagination in a life of 'allegory'. Imagination makes possible empathetic participation in the existence of other persons and other objects. This is why he wrote of the great poets that they have no determined character, no individuality, because their character is everything and nothing.

Keats's appreciation of identity as a barrier to creative work helps to show the powerful role he assigns to the imagination and negative capability. Colegate's fiction, too, dramatizes how the imagination works to destroy the fixed 'self'. Olivia speaks of how when reading fiction, for example, she identifies with and becomes other 'selves'. True identity is not the innate or early fixed character, but that forged in creative openness. To be personally oneself, to know one's own soul, was for Keats the most important knowledge for the poet, and as Colegate constructs her plots, so should it be for the rest of us. For Keats the imagination takes one on the right journey, the journey where 'the world of Pains and troubles' can school the intelligence and one's true identity can be formed. The poet certainly has negative capability, and creative persons have something akin in their openness to new formative experiences through the working of the imagination.

Not that Colegate centers her fiction on poets or creative artists; Lionel is not a poet, although he writes love poems to Olivia. What we see in the romantic plot are two characters who want to understand their feelings, who are open to experience, and who seek growth in understanding through a wedding of the life of sensations and thought. Both read for this purpose. Olivia is a disciplined, serious reader. She is strict with herself. We know she is struggling to produce an English translation of Lamartine's *Le Lac*. She adores Turgenev for his creation of a true image of women and his true perception about feelings:

> She wished her husband did not despise such reading; it seemed to her very important that people should understand about feelings and recognize them in themselves. By studying feeling, she thought, you would get better at it. It seemed to her as important to feel truthfully as to think truthfully. (74)

Colegate guides the appraisal of character in accordance with Keats's code: the injunction that the role of the imagination is to unite feeling and thought and that truth can dwell in language which speaks directly to our senses. Art makes us better because it instructs us to observe imaginatively, to reach something like neg-

ative capability in an openness to new experiences. This quality is
what Olivia admires in Lionel:

> Lionel Stephens was clever – he could talk about anything. He
> had another quality she liked very much, which was that he could
> think about anything, that was to say there was nothing he was
> not prepared to consider, either seriously or not so seriously, and
> this open-mindedness, or openness to the possibilities of things,
> seemed to Olivia a very attractive quality. (38)

The role of imagery and especially visualization in the novel, the role
of the Keats' s gloss with its allusions to Truth and Beauty, and the
role of memory as the source of art bespeak the themes of negative
capability as a psychology of imagination.

Colegate largely selects her characters from political rather than
poetical realms; they are the chosen members of the British Establishment – the gentry in *The Shooting Party*, political leaders from
the Liberal Party before the First World War in *Statues in a Garden*,
and Conservative MPs before and during the Second War in her
novel, *Deceits of Time*. Catherine Hillery, the central narrating voice
of *Deceits of Time*, is an upstanding widow and grandmother, and
biographer of modest attainments; she is asked to write the author-
ized life of Neil Campion, a World War I flying ace and influential
British politician of the 1930s and 1940s. Was his death an accident?
Is he to be remembered as a traitor to his country, linked as he was
to anti-Hitler Germans and pro-Hitler Englishmen in a politics of
betrayal? Working as a detective sorting facts from rumours,
Catherine comes closest to literary art in her work as biographer
when Campion's story leads her to reexamine her own life story.

> Lives were stories; there was no way out of that. Time and the
> innate human need to give shape to things, to select so as to find
> order, meant that any life was just a story, one's own or anyone's
> else's. Like all stories, the story of a life could only be an approx-
> imation to the truth, or perhaps a parallel. (209)

Hers was a myth of a long and happy marriage turned sour at its end
by her husband Bernard's illness. Worse for Catherine, she reads her
marriage coloured by the shame she feels in their – in her – failure at
parenting.

As Catherine faces her past, she accepts uncertainty; she becomes a distancing ego observing her own myth-making. She realizes that life stories are approximations to the stories of the past and there is no end in testing them

> against such discoverable truths as one could lay one's hands on. For if everyone was to be thought of as more or less an artist by virtue of the construction of their long and sometimes touching tales, redemption for the transient seemed to Catherine, if there were such a thing, to be not so much in the art as in the continuity of the effort to understand. (210)

It is Catherine's life story which produces the needed distance to admit subtle changes and the subtle impact of history on the destinies of individuals.

If a character surely possesses the poetic gift, it is in the future since Colegate spotlights signs of creativity in children; in *The Shooting Party* it is Sir Randolph's young grandson Osbert's passion, *esprit d'jeu*, and his dream which show him to belong to another story, hinted at in the closing words of the novel:

> Sometimes in his [Randolph's] study, looking at the picture over the fireplace of the mysterious rider on the impatient horse and the infinite blue distance, he thought of all the young men who had died and all the endeavours which had failed, and of the cruel wastefulness of a spendthrift nature. More than once at such moments it was Osbert, arrived unexpectedly from goodness knew where, who dispelled such thoughts with his own extraordinary gaiety; but the story of Osbert (who took to Art) belongs to the story of the Twenties, a period which Sir Randolph, despite his deep affection for his grandson, entirely disapproved. (195)

Osbert's dream of the swirling vortexes ('Sometimes I dream of great huge turning circles, thick and blankety and slowly turning, and so, so big, and some have spikes on them and some are smooth and they go on and on forever' (47)) is a nightmare so frightening that the child faces punishment day after day at school for his 'escape' each night. He hides under his bed, in strict violation of school rules, and is found there each morning having to face his headmaster. But at home, at the Park with his grandparents, his dreams are given their worth. He feels safe. Grandmothers in Colegate's three novels under consideration serve their creative grandsons well by abiding, by not overreacting. Minnie in *The Shooting Party* instructs everyone to let him alone, and although she hopes he won't be 'affected', she stands by Osbert by accepting him as he is. Effie does the same for Sam in *Deceits of Time*. He has the same whirling nightmare.

> He avoided all conscious thought of his night dreams, with which had he wanted to he could have frightened himself as much as he like, for he had long been subject to nightmares. These nightmares, which often involved nothing more than vast swirling movements of some kind of circular matter through interminable space but which were always unspeakably terrifying, were never allowed to intrude into his daytime life. (140)

These older women in their roles as grandmothers stand and wait. They do not rush to find labels to affix them on their grandchildren. They tolerate doubts and ambiguities, indeed seem at times the only adults admitting their reality. They have achieved the strange clarity of distance.

## A BIBLIOGRAPHY OF WRITINGS BY ISABEL COLEGATE

### Novels

*The Blackmailer* (London: Anthony Blond, 1958).
*A Man of Power* (London: Anthony Blond, 1960).
*The Great Occasion* (London: Anthony Blond, 1962).
*Statues in a Garden* (London: Bodley Head, 1964. New York: Knopf, 1966).
*Orlando King* (London: Bodley Head, 1968. New York: Knopf, 1969).
*Orlando at the Brazen Threshold* (London: Bodley Head, 1971).
*Agatha* (London: Bodley Head, 1973).
*News from the City of the Sun* (London: Hamish Hamilton, 1979).
*The Shooting Party* (London: Hamish Hamilton, 1980. New York: Knopf, 1980).
*Three Novels: The Blackmailer, A Man of Power, The Great Occasion* (New York and London: Viking Penguin, 1984).
*The Orlando Trilogy: Orlando, Orlando at the Brazen Threshold,* and *Agatha* (New York and London: Viking Penguin, 1984).
*A Glimpse of Sion's Glory* (London: Hamish Hamilton, 1985. New York: Viking Penguin,1985).

*Deceits of Time* (London: Hamish Hamilton, 1988. New York: Viking Penguin, 1988).
*The Summer of the Royal Visit* (London: Hamish Hamilton, 1991. New York: Viking, 1992).

## Articles and Reviews

'The Youngest of the Young', *New Review* (Spring 1978): 19–23.

'Servant to Royals' [*End of An Era: Letters and Journals of Sir Alan Lascelles from 1887 to 1920*], *Times Literary Supplement* (*TLS*) (19 September 1986): 1124.

'How Nice to See Her Again' [*The Life of a Provincial Lady: A Study of E. M. Delafield and Her Works* by Violet Powell]. *The Spectator* (8 October 1988): 34–5.

'Untitled' [*Vanishing Country Houses of Ireland* by the Knight of the Glin, David J. Griffin and Nicholas K. Robinson]. *The Spectator* (18 March 1989): 28.

'Devilish Brown Dog', *The Threepenny Review* (Spring 1989): 10–11.

'One Groom, Two Horses, No Money' [*Walled Gardens: Scenes from an Anglo–Irish Childhood* by Annabel Davis-Goff]. *The Washington Post Book World* (3 September 1989): 1–2.

'The Agonies and the Ex's' [*Ford Madox Ford* by Alan Judd]. *The Spectator* (16 June 1990): 31–2.

'Exaggerations Rather Than Fantasies' [*The Stories of Eva Luna* by Isabel Allende]. *The Spectator* (16 February 1991): 31–2.

'Exceptionally Sane Most of the Time' [*A Passionate Apprentice: The Early Journals, 1897–1909* [Virginia Woolf, ed. Mitchell A. Leaska]. *The New York Times Book Review* (17 February 1991): 5.

'After So Many Deaths, I Live and Write' [*Margery Allingham: A Biography* by Julia Thorogood], *The Spectator* (26 October 1991): 40.

'Writer in Residence: House of Character', *House and Garden* (December 1991): 67–8.

## A BIBLIOGRAPHY OF WRITINGS ABOUT ISABEL COLEGATE

### Articles and Reviews

Beatty, Jack, 'Brief Reviews' [*The Shooting Party*], *The New Republic* (18 April 1981): 38–9.

Bernays, Anne, 'Nancy's Dark and Violent Love' [*A Glimpse of Sion's Glory*]. *The New York Times Book Review* (17 November 1985): 33.

Brookner, Anita, 'The Perils of Biography' [*Deceits of Time*]. *The Spectator* (10 September 1988): 34–5.

Coleman, John, 'Tea in Rumania' [*A Man of Power*], *The Spectator* (29 January 1960): 44.

Craig, Amanda, 'How Isabel Became the Cinema's Shooting Star', *The Times* (6 February 1985): 11.

Crosland, Margaret, 'Some Women Writers' [*The Orlando Trilogy*]. *British Book News* (May 1982): 273–8.

Duguid, Lindsay, 'Barking Outsiders' [*Deceits of Time*], *TLS* (2 September 1988): 953.

Hosmer, Robert E. Jr., 'Isabel Colegate', *British Women Writers: A Critical Reference Guide*, ed. Janet Todd (New York: Continuum, 1989): 151–2.

Hosmer, Robert E. Jr., 'Isabel Colegate', *An Encyclopedia of British Women Writers*, ed. Paul and June Schlueter (New York: Garland, 1988): 115–17.

Jackson, Katherine Gauss, 'Statues in a Garden' [*Statues in a Garden*], *Harper's Magazine* (April 1966): 122–3.

King, Francis, 'Big Shots' [*The Shooting Party*], *The Spectator* (13 September 1980): 25–6.

King, Francis, 'Communal' [*News from the City of the Sun*], *The Spectator* (21 July 1979): 24.

Lesser, Wendy, 'The Character as Victim' [*Three Novels: The Blackmailer, A Man of Power, The Great Occasion*], *Hudson Review* (Autumn 1984): 471–2.

Littler, Frank, 'Sir Aylmer Sees It Through' [*Statues in a Garden*], *The New York Times Book Review* (20 March 1966): 37.

Mallon, Thomas, 'Over Her Head in Nazis' [*Deceits of Time*], *The New York Times Book Review* (11 December 1988): 7.

Mellors, John, 'Living in Love' [*A Glimpse of Sion's Glory*], *The Listener* (30 May 1985): 32.

Motion, Andrew, 'Beaters Turned Game' [*The Shooting Party*], *TLS* (12 September 1980): 983.

Naughton, John, 'Good Shot' [*The Shooting Party*], *The Listener* (4 September 1980): 313.

Parson, Ann, 'Brief Reviews' [*A Glimpse of Sion's Glory*], *Boston Review* (February 1986): 27–8.

Pippet, Aileen, 'The Hero Had Hammer Toes' [*Orlando King*], *The New York Times Book Review* (25 May 1969): 46.

Raven, Simon, 'Outriders of the Apocalypse' [*The Great Occasion*], *The Spectator* (4 May 1962): 597.

Richardson, Maurice, 'Damned Up North' [*The Great Occasion*], *The New Statesman* (4 May 1962): 649–50.

Sage, Lorna, 'Havoc on the Campus' [*The Shooting Party*], *The Observer* (7 September 1980): 29.

Swartley, Ariel, 'Class Acts' [*A Glimpse of Sion's Glory*], *The Village Voice Literary Supplement* (December 1985): 14.

Taliaferro, Frances, 'Colegate's Stories In a Minor Key' [*A Glimpse of Sion's Glory*], *The Washington Post Book World* (12 January 1986): 9; 13.

Turvey, Sarah, 'Isabel Colegate,' *Dictionary of Literary Biography*, Volume 14: 235–43.

Wade, Rosalind, 'Agatha' [*Agatha*], *Contemporary Review* (January 1974): 46–7.

Wall, Stephen, 'New Novels' [*Statues in a Garden*], *The Listener* (27 August 1964): 317.

Webb, W. L. 'Upstairs, Downstairs Before the Fall' [*The Shooting Party*], *TLS* (13 February 1989): 10.

Wickenden, Dorothy, 'Social Climbers, Family Blunders' [*The Shooting Party*], *The New Republic* (28 May 1984): 38–41.

Wilce, Gillian, 'No Abiding City' [*News from the City of the Sun*], *The New Statesman* (13 July 1979): 63.

## Interviews

Hebert, Rosemary, '*PW* Interviews Isabel Colegate', *Publishers Weekly* (13 December 1985): 55–6.

Ross, Jean W., '*CA* Interviews: Isabel Colegate', *Contemporary Authors, New Revision Series*, Volume 22: 84–7.

## Miscellaneous

*Contemporary Authors, New Revision Series*, Volume 8: 108; Volume 22: 81–7.

*Contemporary Literary Criticism*, Volume 36, 108–15.

Thornton, Lesley, 'A Shot in the Park', *Observer Magazine* (20 January 1985): 12–13; 15.

Webb, W. L., 'Upstairs, Downstairs before the Fall', *Guardian* (13 February 1981): 10.

## ISABEL COLEGATE

A novelist of powerful historical imagination, Isabel Colegate uses atmosphere and period detail to dissolve stereotypes about English class and privilege. In her fiction she explores the relationship among those in power, whether titled or untitled, and the politics determining their actions; in the gentry, for example, the ruling class before the First World War, as well as their offspring, their legacy, in the decade leading to the Second World War. Born on 10 September 1931, the youngest of four daughters of Lady Colegate Worsley and Sir Arthur Colegate, MP, Isabel Colegate left school at the age of sixteen and went to London to become a writer. She became a working partner of the London literary agent Anthony Blond and at nineteen wrote her first novel, which has not been published. Blond introduced Colegate to her future husband and published her second novel, *The Blackmailer*, in 1958, after he had set up his own publishing firm. *A Man of Power* (1960) and *The Great Occasion* (1962) complete the trilogy issued together by Penguin in 1984. Likewise, Colegate's fourth, fifth, and sixth novels – *Orlando King* (1968), *Orlando at the Brazen Threshold* (1971), and *Agatha* (1973)– though published separately later appeared as a trilogy (Penguin, 1984).

In 1964 Colegate published the first of three novels that chronicle the impact of the First World War on the lives of the English gentry: *Statues in a Garden*. *News from the City of the Sun* (1979) and *The Shooting Party* (1980) followed; the first and the last have a technical assurance and narrative fluency that particularly distinguish them. *The Shooting Party* was made into a film of the same title in 1985; it starred James Mason and Sir John Gielgud and brought Colegate considerable attention. More recently, Colegate has published a collection of three short stories, *A Glimpse of Sion's Glory* (1985), and another novel, *Deceits of Time* (1988) concerned with war and the myths surrounding war and patriotism, this time in the years before and during the Second World War. Her newest novel, *The Summer of the Royal Visit* (1991), creates an historical moment with intersecting personal fantasies and public myths.

Colegate's themes of money, class, power and mythmaking reveal ironic tension in social as well as individual change. With its patiently accumulated detail, acute psychological perception, ironic acerbity and rich textual strategies, her fiction invites comparison with the work of Elizabeth Bowen and Molly Keane.

Married to Michael Briggs, a successful businessman, and the mother of three children, Colegate makes her home in a 200-year old castle in Midford, near Bath.

# 6

# 'Magic or Miracles': The Fallen World of Penelope Fitzgerald's Novels
## JEAN SUDRANN

Penelope Fitzgerald does not fit easily into the rubric of contemporary British women writers under which these essays are gathered. Born in 1916, she reached adulthood in the decades between the Great War to end all wars and World War Two and published no fiction until 1977 when she was 60. Her closest approach to experiment in the form of her fiction is her frequent use of ironic closures with their attendant ambiguities and a habit of building in very short chapters or simply numbered, seemingly discrete, brief episodes whose sequence creates a significance not apparent in the episode itself. She does not write to explore (or exploit) the wrongs peculiar to female lives, nor is she particularly fond of domestic spaces for her settings. Of the two novels that pay most attention to domestic problems, one, *Offshore*, has for its home-setting a derelict barge named *Grace* moored in the Thames Reach near London's Battersea Bridge, while the other, *Innocence*, set in Florence, keeps up a rapid movement between a decaying family farm, an abandoned villa, and an ancient Palazzo, now divided into flats. The other five novels are primarily set in work-places: a museum, a bookshop, the central London studios of the BBC, a London school for child-actors, and a Moscow printing shop owned in 1915 by a youngish Englishman.

Although there are at least nine runaway wives among the seven novels, only for one of them does Fitzgerald deal in any detail with the domestic difficulty. And while recognition of patriarchal organization is implicit in the work-place settings, it is no part of the function of these settings to provide an arena for a woman's struggle for a room at the top in a male world. Nor do either the work-places or the domestic settings become metaphors of twentieth-century national or global disarray or impending doom. Fitzgerald's novels do not expand in that direction.

How then do they expand, if they grow neither from formal experimentation nor from female interest in female lives? Does she create a world that belongs to the 'contemporary'? Of contemporary women? Of the English? Is there a figure in the carpet of these novels that makes Fitzgerald a novelist of this time, of that place? The answer is an unequivocal 'yes'. These are novels that create through the novelist's meticulously chosen details a variety of instantly recognizable twentieth-century worlds peopled by more or less ordinary twentieth-century characters. I say more or less because many of the characters seem eccentric, sometimes grotesque, while the seemingly motiveless spontaneity of some actions suggests the absurd or, as one of the older characters comments at a gathering of modern novelists, 'they're without the normal safeguards of social life' (*Innocence*, 107). Over these worlds, the voice of the narrator presides – simultaneously compassionate and ironic, above all, witty, and in language so pointed that a whole character unfolds in a phrase, hypocrisy is revealed in a single word, and the immanence of the absurd can be felt in the most matter-of-fact sentence.

That voice, those actions, and the landscapes into which they are set open up for the reader a panorama of fallible human beings whose very lives are at risk in a long-since fallen world. How and to what end they are to manage themselves in the midst of such often unrecognized danger provides a central action for the novels. Recognizing the hazards of so schematic a reading, I propose, nevertheless, to look at the novels from this point of view, first by a close look at *Innocence* to determine the extent to which Fitzgerald really does have in mind a world whose innocence is forever fallen and then by reference to crucial actions, episodes, and characters in the other novels to reaffirm that the simple fact of the fallen world sets the parameters of these fictions. Never once debating the question of 'The Fortunate Fall', Fitzgerald's authorial voice embraces its own post-Edenic role in self-conscious recognition of the challenge the fallen world offers to the maker of truth-telling fictions: how does the writer 'know' the post-Edenic world well enough to be its chronicler, and then how can those earned truths be best communicated in a post-lapsarian world? These epistemological concerns create a subject matter for the novels which relies not only on the tensions between ignorant Innocence and the world of Experience, but also on the internal tensions bred by Ignorance itself guiding the necessarily unexamined life of Innocence adrift in the world of Experience.

In *Innocence*, one of Fitzgerald's most recent novels, certainly her richest and most complex, we find the tightest interweaving of all these themes of her fiction. Set in present-day Florence, reaching back into war-time Florence, beyond that to the calm of the pre-war city and then the legendary past, the novel suggests (rather than traces) the fortunes of the Ridolfi family with its farm of Valsassina in the Florentine countryside; its villa, the Ricordanza, just outside Florence; and its family palazzo on the Via Limbo where the current Count Ridolfi lives in one of the apartments, renting out the rest. Here the elderly Count Giancarlo is bringing up his beautiful young daughter, Chiara, the fruit of a failed experiment in restoring the Ridolfi fortunes by 'following the strongest tradition of the nobility he could think of' (13) – marrying a rich American who then left him as World War Two began. The last of the Ridolfi, the only inheritance of the Contessina Chiara is the 'compassionate heart' of the legendary sixteenth-century Contessina, a midget, born to midget parents 'of the Ridolfi family, certainly' (7), whose whole world, from governess to notary, has been accommodated to her size by her loving parents. When her chosen companion, Gemma, unfortunately grows to full size, the innocence of the Contessina's compassionate heart prompts her to command the amputation of Gemma's legs at the knee and the blinding of her eyes so that she might not have to suffer the lifelong knowledge of her difference from the rest of the world.

With the telling of that family legend as the novel opens, Fitzgerald casts the shadow of our world over the novel's single word title. The central story of Chiara's marriage to Dr Salvatore Rossi leaves the title further shadowed by the accumulation of ironies and ambiguities evoked by the novel's this-worldly setting. Perhaps only Milton has ever succeeded in recreating the human dream of ideal innocence: lovely Eve in her perfect garden. In the light of that legend, the response of Fitzgerald's Professor Pulci to Giancarlo's query about the legitimacy of the Ridolfi myth and the advisability of letting the Florentine Tourist Bureau tinker with it, takes on new dimensions:

The Ricordanza material, including the statuary ['"The Dwarfs' on the highest part of the surrounding wall"(7)], shows that at some unspecified time one branch of your family was considered kindhearted but incompetent, and ill-judged in carrying out their good intentions to a grotesque degree. . . . However, if you are asking me whether the character of a family and perhaps their general prosperity could improve or deteriorate because someone has been allowed to fiddle about with their definition through myth, then I think my answer may surprise you. It is yes. Thirty years ago we none of us believed in either magic or miracles, but I notice that both of them have managed to survive very well without our belief. I should be inclined to leave the story alone. (162)

And that, of course, is precisely what Fitzgerald does. She accepts our fallen world, acknowledging also the survival of the magic and the miracles effected by love.

The Scriptural image of innocence forever lost to man is crucial both structurally and thematically throughout this novel which opens with the Ridolfi legend of the sixteenth-century midget Contessina whose 'good intentions' were implemented to such a grotesque degree. Almost immediately, the novel goes on to describe 'the matter of the missing third and fourth fingers of [Giancarlo's sister's] right hand.' They 'have been taken off with a pair of sharp poultry-nippers by a thief sitting behind her on the 33 bus coming back from Bagno a Ripoli'. The diamond ring given her by her English husband in their happier days was of course the object. 'The incident was not at all an unusual one' (14), the narrator dryly tells us as she embarks on her tale of Chiara's love for her doctor.

Nearly midway through the novel, Chiara, in pursuit of Salvatore with whom she has quarrelled, pauses at Valsassina where her cousin Cesare struggles to maintain the family farm in face of the hostilities of nature and the slyness of local authorities who some two decades ago have gerrymandered the farm's vineyards outside the boundary of the Chianti region. Greeting his visitor, Cesare offers her a walk 'to see the rabbits and doves'. Impatient in her desire to catch up with Salvatore, Chiara rejects the offer. Nevertheless, Fitzgerald gives us a full-scale description of the building.

You could see the tiled roof and the columbarian from the house. It was closed by a solid wooden door which opened in two separate halves. Inside there was a semi-darkness, peacefully reeking

of birds and animals. The squabs muttered from their loft over-
head, feathers strayed down through patches of light and back
into the dark, the broadly palpitating rabbits drowsed in their
pens below. Both the doves and the rabbits were white. There was
no feeling whatever of their fate in store, only a companionable
peace, as though the whole crowded enclosure was breathing in
unison, every creature deeply satisfied with its frowsty living-
space. To children the place was instantly attractive. (95)

I have quoted this passage at length because its rhythms and diction
create a vivid image of livestock being bred for the butchers' stalls of
the Central Market in Florence at the same time that both rhythm
and diction create the perfection of a Peaceable Kingdom, an Eden of
innocence 'instantly attractive' to children who, like the doves and
the rabbits, 'have no feeling whatever of their fate'.

Almost immediately after this description, we find a blissful Chiara
telling her English school friend, Barney – or at least trying to tell her
– how she and Salvatore made love in the Ricordanza. To Chiara's
attempt to describe the ambiguous light of the deserted villa, Barney
responds impatiently:

'Well, then I suppose you thought, what can I do to make him
really happy?'
'No, I didn't think of anything at all.'
Chiara looked composed and peaceful. 'It was very good of you
to come,' she said.
'Cha, just tell me. Just look me in the eyes and tell me this. Were
the beds made up? I mean were there proper sheets . . . After all,
we've both of us got standards.' (109–110)

On the next page, we learn, through a bit of news Cesare leaves
out of a letter he never sends Chiara, that thieves have broken into
dovecote and rabbit hutch – only torn fur and feathers remain. As a
reflection on Chiara's lost innocence the ravaged animals seem as
banal as Barney's insistence on proper sheets is comic; this is, I
think, precisely what Fitzgerald intends. Indeed, she repeats the
episode later when an intransigent young boy wanders away from
Chiara's wedding feast at Valsassina to the re-stocked dove house
and, forcing open one of the louvers, lets the doves escape:

They had only one wing clipped and after soaring boldly out, one after another against the blue winter sky, they reeled sideways like broken toys and lurched towards the ground. Luca was imitating them as they fluttered grotesquely towards the open fields, stretching out his arms like an idiot and stamping his feet. (154)

His two younger sisters report: '"He was driving the birds mad. . . . He told us that he could drive them mad in this way"' (154). This grotesque flight of the doves, parodied by Luca with such wicked intent, is certainly not meant to allegorize the wedding festivities but is deliberately introduced to make us uneasy, to balance the opening paragraph of the wedding party section describing the sunshine of that unexpectedly fine day in February with 'the almond trees in full bloom'. 'Sometimes,' concludes the narrator, carefully restraining the reader from seeing omens where none are intended, 'sometimes you do get weather like that in February' (145). Scattered fur and feathers, birds stolen for market place slaughter or simply let loose to be driven mad by their incapacity for flight, are not, as the narrator has earlier told us, 'unusual' incidents. Only 'sometimes' does the almond tree blossom in February.

The final recall of the love-making in the villa comes just before Giancarlo asks Professor Pulci's advice about the legitimacy of the Ridolfi legend. He phones Chiara to ask her advice about the Tourist Bureau's revisionary history. The query floods Chiara with memories of the villa: the pre-war day-long visit with her father and his guards (Giancarlo was under house arrest in the via Limbo for anti-Fascist protest) and the post-war evening party. During the pre-war visit she walked with Giancarlo around the gardens all day long, Chiara in great discomfort because of the immense difficulty of keeping up with her father's long strides. The image here is of yet another midget Contessina. The celebratory evening party, however, turns the now twelve-year-old Ridolfi into an excited Miranda full of wonder at the brave new world of wine and light and roses where 'human beings . . . speak and behave differently from their everyday or earthly selves' (160). But 'as she listened, anxious to learn, almost all of them turned out to be speaking unkindly about someone else who was present, but out of earshot' (161). Although Chiara had hoped otherwise, the joy of her love-making in the villa does not erase for her the earlier images of distress; even love's radiance cannot illuminate the villa. 'Nothing seemed to have changed . . .

and she only had to shut her eyes to see the unlucky Gemma, the cripple, floundering up the grass stairs' (161).

This simultaneous acceptance of both the fallen world and the magic and miracles of love is the view Fitzgerald offers us from her window in the house of fiction. The world is her stage; the compassionate heart, her protagonist. The tensions between the two – sometimes relaxed into accommodation, sometimes clashing into disaster, often viewed as comic – create the various actions of her novels, each with its different setting and each re-defining and newly elaborating the struggle.

The settings, from the Bloomsbury of her first novel, *The Golden Child*, to the Moscow of the most recent, *The Beginning of Spring* and including the East Anglian Hardborough of *The Bookshop*, the Thames barge world of *Offshore*, the BBC's Broadcasting House of *Human Voices*, and the Covent Garden neighbourhood of *At Freddie's*, all suggest a variousness not unlike the panorama Milton's archangel spread out before Adam to instruct him in the ways of the post-Edenic world. And post-Edenic it certainly is: the cut-throat politics of the Museum world of Bloomsbury, death-dealing storms on the Thames, illicit student printing-presses in pre-Revolutionary Moscow, illegitimate babies born in Broadcasting House, and predatory child actors stealing scenes in the theatre near Covent Garden. Through each of these dangerous worlds an innocent with a kind heart threads his way creating the novel's action.

The range of comic treatment Fitzgerald employs to move her characters on their way is almost as various as the settings she creates for them. Barbs of wit, scenes of slapstick action, images of the absurd, the unexpected action or word which, deflating the cliche, destroys the sentimental, and, perhaps most telling, the complex ironies of her endings – each of these comic modes sharpens the intensity of the action as well as the reader's understanding of that action's intent. The narrator's voice continuously creates ironic commentary, often through its contrast to the characters' actions, thoughts, or appearance as it intervenes throughout the novels to remind the reader that the world of those novels is the world of all of us.

In the opening pages of *The Bookshop* Fitzgerald introduces her protagonist as 'small, wispy and wiry, somewhat insignificant from the front view, and totally so from the back. . . . Everybody [in Hardborough] knew her winter overcoat, which was the kind that just might be made to last another year' (5–6). In *The Golden Child*, she describes the Museum Director whose acknowledgement of the faked artefacts that comprise his great exhibition and his politic regret of his inability to consult the noted and knighted archeologist who first discovered the Golden Treasure because he is not, after all, a 'museum man'. 'The Director's voice,' the narrator tells us, 'trembled with the pride and bitter jealousy which is the poetry of museum keeping' (53). In *Human Voices*, a kindly London lady 'who was generous enough to learn nothing from experience, welcomed a new lodger' (86); in that novel also, a BBC specialist in sound effects, causes 'in spite of his good will . . . as much distress as any perfectionist' (101). In *At Freddie's*, the photographs of the theatrical great are seen by the narrator as 'fixed by an indulgent camera in their best profile. . . . Their faces waiting for the betrayal of the flesh' (45). But Freddie is confident of the immortality of her theatrical school for child actors and its Director: 'Like Buckingham Palace, Lyons teashops, the British Museum Reading Room, or the Market at Covent Garden, she could never be allowed to disappear. While England rested true to itself, she need never compromise' (46). In 1989 as in 1982, the date of the novel's publication, while Buckingham Palace still stands, the Lyons teashops and the market at Covent Garden are only nostalgic memories and the British Museum Reading Room has long since been marked down for removal from its Bloomsbury site, its title already changed to the British Library.

Even as the sheer wit of each of these comments delights us, the narrator's generalizing voice invites us to recognize the world of these novels as our own: the flawed, untrustworthy, mutable world of worn-out winter coats where worn-out good intentions and lofty aims wither into the deadly sins of pride, jealousy, and vanity while the generous who refuse to learn from experience are in for some nasty shocks. The whole method is reminiscent of the Showman of Thackeray's *Vanity Fair*, whose geniality in exposing the Fair serves to distance the reader from the events and whose repeated reminders that he is simply the jester who has taken the puppets out of the box and will return them when the story is told, mitigates any tragic possibilities. Like Thackeray's Showman, Fitzgerald is both of the Fair and stands outside it; unlike her Victorian predecessor, she offers no judgment on its vanities. Instead, the wonderful play of language through which the narrator's this-worldly wisdom is expressed pushes the reader out to a non-judgmental perspective. Because Florence Green is simultaneously an impoverished nonentity and an elderly woman wearing a tatty coat we all recognize as our own, we can neither dismiss her nor sentimentally and condescendingly pity her. But we do want to know more about her. Freddie's high-handed rejection of the signs of vanity and mutability on her office wall, as she declares her own triumph over the fading photographs and faded friends with a grandiose self-defense that equates her school with the eternity of such other institutional manifestations of the English spirit as Covent Garden Market and Lyons teashops, invites the reader to vigorous applause for her zestful vitality, along with mockery of her hyperbole.

The ironic wit which enables us thus to suspend judgment, simultaneously to applaud and to censure, is nowhere more crucial than in the endings of the novels where a complex pattern of cumulative ironies illuminates both the shape and the thematic intent of each novel. Consider the Director's dilemma in *The Golden Child*: either to maintain the integrity of the Museum by concealing the 'great swindle' of the modern replicas which comprise the Museum's exhibition of the ancient Garamantian Treasury, or to maintain that integrity by telling the truth and closing down the Exhibition. In the cold winter rain outside the Museum the public queues up for entrance. Hordes of children, clutching their prepared essays of ill-digested information from Museum educational pamphlets distributed to the schools, are joined by repeat viewers, who, knowing much about the rigors of their pilgrimage, have come protected in their RAF anoraks and Air Warden overcoats, but remember only enough about the exhibit itself to murmur vaguely of 'real gold' to the equally vague newcomers who are 'even perhaps not very interested [in] what they had actually come to see' (110). Should this enduring public, still patiently queued up despite the wet and the cold, be told the truth? Should a Museum official shout out: '"All is not gold that glitters! Please form an orderly queue in the reverse direction! . . . the Director of the Museum will be found kneeling on the steps to apologize!"' (111)

Fitzgerald solves the mystery of the swindle with an exuberant wealth of comic incident which climaxes in a melodramatic porcelain-smashing shoot-out through the corridors and display rooms leading to the Garamantian Exhibit. There, the Director, shooting himself, shatters the central tomb, revealing 'in place of the Royal Child a withered and starved little African who had died not long ago, but was no more than skin and bones, for it had certainly died of hunger' (153). Museum officials work feverishly to re-gild (with genuine gold-leaf) the smashed tomb and image of the Golden Child and the doors are now open to admit the public:

> A patient-looking middle-aged family man, who must have been queuing now for more than half a working-day, was the first, with his two exhausted little girls, to enter the Chamber. They hastened their steps as they turned the corner. . . . In spite of the directing notices, which in any case were practically invisible in the dim light, they went straight to the central case to see the long-awaited Child.
>
> 'Look, real gold!' said the man, turning to the open-mouthed girls.
>
> 'It looks almost new,' he added. 'It might have been done yesterday.' (159)

Beyond the obvious irony of the Public appreciation of the 'real gold' – which is, of course, real though not Garamantian gold, and which does of course look new because it is new – lies the whole irony of the Director's dilemma in seeking to maintain the integrity of the Museum. The replicas are gone, smashed up essentially because of the Director's already noted jealous pride and personal envy. What the Public now views in such a dim light is the result of the devoted work of Museum artists promoted by their love of the artefact and their compassionate knowledge of the public. And if the newly gilded tomb does not hold the body of the Garamantian Child, it does hold a child whose death yesterday equally deserves a Golden Toy as company on the journey to the underworld.

There is nothing ambiguous about this ending. All the loose ends of the plot have been skilfully knit without disturbing in any way the comic texture of the story. The effective leader in the denouement, Waring Smith, the novel's protagonist, 'young, normal, sincere . . . and worried' about his job, his mortgage, and his inability to get home from the Museum early enough to please his wife (19–20), is one of Fitzgerald's Innocents who triumph (for this is a comedy) in the fallen world. His aid in the successful effort of regilding the golden image that graces the tomb of the starved African infant surely has to be included among the yet surviving 'magic or miracles' Professor Pulci describes in advising Giancarlo not to tamper with the Ridolfi legend. And the reader rests easy knowing that the spirit of comedy permits both the truth and the public to be served.

Nowhere else in her work, however, does Fitzgerald permit quite such a triumph. The 'insignificant' Florence Green in her 'worn-out' winter coat leaves the harsh and decaying East Anglian village of Hardborough in the final sentence of *The Bookshop*. Her bookshop has failed. This comes as no surprise to the reader who has been introduced to Florence through her memory of 'a heron flying across the estuary and trying, while it was on the wing, to swallow an eel which it had caught. The eel, in turn, was struggling to escape from the gullet of the heron and appeared a quarter, or half, or occasionally three-quarters of the way out' (5). Florence interprets this recollection to be an image of her own indecision; the reader is more apt to let the image figure as a dismal foreboding of a 'no-win' situation.

That situation reaches its climax when a Parliamentary Bill is passed making Ancient Buildings 'subject to compulsory purchase even if . . . occupied at the moment' (103). Mrs Green's shop premises and home, the Old House, fall directly under the provisions of the Bill. Further Borough regulations make it clear that she will receive no compensation for either house or land. And so, in the final sentence of the novel, Florence leaves Hardborough on the 10.46 to Liverpool Street: 'As the train drew out of the station she sat with her head bowed in shame, because the town in which she had lived for nearly ten years had not wanted a bookshop' (118).

But the truth of Florence's defeat is not so simple. Florence, who 'valued kindness above everything' (113), has an enemy in Hardborough, Violet Gamart, the local *grande dame*, who fancies herself a cultural arbiter, dreams of presiding over a Hardborough Centre for the Arts, and has hoped for some time to raise the money to purchase the Old House for that venture – or at least thinks of it every time near-by Aldeburgh enjoys its summer glory. Mrs Gamart's nephew, 'a brilliant, successful, and stupid young man', and a Member of Parliament, spares her the financial effort when he drafts the Bill on Ancient Houses that dooms Florence to expulsion and raises Mrs Gamart to heights of self-congratulation for her own energy which is so certain to issue into 'a widening circle of after-effects':

> Whenever she realized this she was pleased, both for herself and for the sake of others, because she always acted in the way she felt to be right. She did not know that morality is seldom a safe guide for human conduct. (95)

The irony of the final phrase embraces the whole irony of the conclusion of the novel. Not only did the Parliamentary nephew find in Mrs Gamart's expressed concern a proper vehicle for the advancement of his brilliant career, so too her neighbour, Lord Gosfield, becomes a part of Mrs Gamart's 'widening circle of after-effects' when he decides to take advantage of the new main road through the adjoining village of Saxford-Tye to develop property of his own there. Remembering 'Violet Gamart saying something about a bookshop', he suggests this to his agent as an appropriate development plan. As if that is not enough, we then learn of another significant change, this time in Hardborough itself. Before her final defeat, Florence has had to close the lending library of her shop when Hardborough's first public library is opened. Hard to say who forced the measure through the County Council after so many years of requests. The new library's location had formerly been Deben's wet fish shop, up for sale long before Florence invested in the Old House, suggested to Florence by Mrs Gamart as an alternative and more suitable site for a shop, and later pressed upon Florence by Deben himself at Mrs Gamart's suggestion.

Mrs Gamart's self-styled 'energy' has, then, brought to moribund Hardborough both a public library and a bookshop and has rescued the fishmonger from his failed business. Florence Green has been defeated in part through the promptings toward kindness of her own heart, in part through chance and governmental blundering, and certainly also by the egoism and greed of Mrs Gamart and her Hardborough circle. The reader's foreboding of the 'no-win' situation evoked by the image of the heron and the eel at the opening of the novel is matched, as the novel ends, by the cheerily vulgar advice of Florence's departing accountant: 'my father used to say – if you're down in the mouth, think of Jonah – he came out all right' (102). Thus wryly, with great compassion and exquisite irony, the author forces her reader to a sufficient distance from the bent and shamed figure of Florence Green on her way to London to accept the defeat of Florence Green as both true and not true. There is, after all, a bookshop for Hardborough – but what a bookshop! Fitzgerald has made the 'fallen' truth acceptable.

Penelope Fitzgerald's awareness of the difficulty of knowing the truth, distinguishing the truth from the lie, is manifest in her biography, *The Knox Brothers*. There she tells the story of her grandfather, the Evangelical Bishop of Manchester; her father, Edmund, editor of *Punch*; her uncle Dilwyn, a brilliant classical scholar, war-time cryptographer, and atheist whose attitude was 'always to re-prove [God] for not existing' (72); her uncle Wilfrid, Anglo–Catholic priest and member of the Community of the Good Shepherd among whose members he was known for demonstrating 'how to combine a deep attachment to devotions and liturgical traditions with a totally liberated and fearless search for truth' (163); and her uncle Ronald, received into the Roman Catholic Church and ordained a priest of that church. The family itself, then, both offers an encapsul-ated view of the late Victorian religious scene, and becomes an emblem of searchers along different paths for the different faces of truth. The brilliance with which Fitzgerald organizes the biography to dramatize the collisions of the brothers' careers reaches its climax with her description of the funeral of Edmund's wife:

> Even on such a wretched occasion as Christina's funeral, it was a memorable thing to see all the four brothers together. Wilfrid took the service, Dilly, who rarely entered a church, stood in silent misery at the back, Ronnie, who had not been to an Anglican service for nearly twenty years, knelt in the aisle. Those who saw him, not cut off from the human grief around him, but totally absorbed in communion with God, felt that they had seen prayer manifest. (216)

The Anglo–Catholic priest at the altar, the atheist at the back of the church, the Roman Catholic priest kneeling in the aisle, each ex-pressing his truth in his own way, while the whole picture is held together by the love which for all the rents in its fabric still binds the family; it makes a splendid tableau. Fitzgerald has anticipated its meaning earlier in a comment on the family's reaction to Ronnie's conversion: 'Surely one would think that it must have been as clear then as it is now that if human love could rise above the doctrines that divide the Church, then these doctrines must have singularly little to do with the love of God' (142). In her own voice again, early in the biography, she concludes a chapter on the religious uncertain-ties tormenting all four young men by articulating the fundamental question each of them is asking: 'God speaks to us through the intellect, and through the intellect we should direct our lives. But if we are creatures of reason, what are we to do with our hearts?' (89)

What indeed? Certainly the impulses of the compassionate heart can be, as we have seen, a guide as faulty as any prompted by the reasoning mind. In Fitzgerald's fourth novel, *Human Voices*, the vice of the protagonist, Jeff Haggard, Director of Planned Programming at the BBC, is precisely his uncontrollable propensity to come to the aid of those who need his aid even while he is working, with full loyalty, for a BBC 'dedicated to the strangest project of the war, that is, telling the truth' (20). Jeff himself personifies the same tensions of mind and heart evoked by the tableau of the Knox brothers bearing witness to a death in the family. Successful as he certainly is in furthering the BBC's attempts to broadcast the truth, the movements of his heart are constantly getting him into trouble. Consistent with the tone of the novel, those troubles are embedded in the comic absurdity of day-to-day life inside the BBC London headquarters while outside the bombs fall and human voices fill the air of England with BBC truth-telling: trouble over Jeff's place in the BBC chain of command when he cuts off the air a speech by a French General, escaped from Vichy France, whose advice to the millions of listening English is 'Surrender'; trouble, when he helps the young woman giving birth to her illegitimate child in a concert-room-turned-dormitory of Broadcasting House; trouble, ultimately fatal trouble, as he attempts to aid Sam Brooks, the Director of Recorded Programmes with whom his relationship 'looked like an addiction – a weakness for the weak on Jeff's part – or a response to the appeal for protection made by the defenseless and single-minded' (28). As Jeff's American friend has warned him: 'Helping other people is a drug so dangerous that there is no cure short of total abstention' (134). And Jeff's heart will not let him abstain. Called to the Demos Cafe to come once again to the aid of Sam Brooks, Jeff is blown to bits when, in the black-out darkness, he mistakes an unexploded bomb for the door of his taxi. So much for the power of the human heart.

The ironic final paragraph of the novel presents the reader with the official obituary of Jeff Haggard, written by the Assistant Deputy Director General, who decides that, despite Jeff's long years of service, he does not qualify as an Old Servant. He writes instead: 'His voice, in particular, will be much missed'. This is a simpler and, perhaps, less successfully ironic ending than that of *The Golden Child*. Nevertheless, Jeff's absurd death, coupled with the 'poetry' of the BBC's Assistant Deputy Director General's 'pride and bitter jealousy' (53) work most effectively to sharpen our sense of the hazards and limits of the post-Edenic world, especially for those innocents who are 'generous enough to learn nothing from experience' (86).

Just before Jeff's death, he stands on the curb outside Broadcasting House to look up at its carvings of characters from *The Tempest*, thinking:

> Caliban, who wished Prospero might be stricken with the red plague for teaching him to speak correct English, never told anything but the truth, presumably not knowing how to. Ariel, on the other hand, was a liar, pretending that someone's father was drowned full fathom five, when in point of fact, he was safe and well. All this was so that virtue should prevail. The old excuse. (173)

Jeff may scornfully dismiss Ariel's lying attempt to initiate Prospero's magic as simply 'the old excuse'. For Fitzgerald, however, who knows and expects her reader to know how *that* story comes out, it is simply further evidence of the complex relationship of naked truth to humane lie.

An important aspect of that complexity surfaces in a brief comic episode (almost all of Fitzgerald's truth comes to us in comic guise) in *Offshore*, when Nenna James sharply questions her twelve-year-old daughter, Martha, about whether she and her six-year-old sister, Tilda, are going to end their prolonged school truancy. With some prodding, Martha, characterized as one who sees no need for fictions, replies: 'I shall go, and take Tilda with me, when the situation warrants it'. Further prodded, Martha turns to advise her mother: 'You should tell the truth' (40). Here the narrator intervenes to wonder 'in what way could the truth be made acceptable?' In this case the truth would have to be accommodated to the nuns of the Catholic school the two girls are so assiduously avoiding because of a tempest over a teapot holder Tilda should have been cross-stitching as a present for her father but had, in fact, lost. Tilda, not lying, simply tells a different truth: she 'had never seen her father holding a kettle and . . . Daddy had gone away' (40). She adds that she and her sister pray nightly for her Daddy's return.

The nuns' compassionate response to this substantially true, but hitherto unacknowledged, tale of domestic distress is immediate: every morning 'the whole Junior School pray together that Martha and Tilda's Daddy should come back to them' (41). With the next detail, the 'grotesque degree' to which the nuns carry out their 'good intentions' is clear (162). For after the prayer session, in fine weather, the Junior School proceeds to 'the life-size model of the grotto of

Lourdes which has been built in the recreation ground' for a special prayer that the 'non-Catholic eyes of the absent parent be opened' and 'his tepid soul . . . become fervent'. Martha's unrancorous comment and explanation of the sisters' actions – 'they are good women . . . but I'm not going to set foot in the place while that's going on' (41) has the ring of truth and justice, while through her comedy, Fitzgerald has exposed a profound risk of truth-telling. What 'truth' about the girls' hookey-playing could be told the nuns without the terrible cruelty of mocking the compassion of the 'good women', cutting them, like Gemma, down at the knees. Moreover, Tilda, telling one truth to evade another, has brought down on herself the punishment of their terrible compassion.

At first glance, *The Beginning of Spring*, Fitzgerald's most recent (1988) novel, with its richly detailed Moscow setting, seems remote from all the themes I have identified as central and abiding in her fiction. Indeed, Anita Brookner and Margaret Walters, two of the critics who reviewed the book on its publication, say simply that the novel is about Moscow. Certainly Fitzgerald's picture of pre-revolutionary Russia, ominous with stirrings of political revolt, invested with epic grandeur in its changing seasons and varied landscapes, and populated with exotic images of a dancing bear cub, a pistol-carrying student revolutionary, and a decrepit dacha in whose damp storeroom pickled lemons, cabbages, and mushrooms became infected with moulds and mildew during the family's winter absence create a vivid sensuous frame. It not only invites the reader to put Moscow in the foreground of the novel but also delights him with its evocation of the nineteenth-century landscapes of Tolstoy, Chekov, Dostoyevsky: a literary Moscow. Here the dominant note struck is that of change and renewal within the stable instabilities of 'a country whose nature represented not freedom but law, where the harbours freed themselves from ice one after another, in majestic sequence, and the earth's harvest failed unfailingly once in every three years' (77).

The story of the disruption and renewal of the marriage of Frank and Nellie Reid becomes a part of this earthly rhythm as, in the first paragraph of the novel, Nellie inexplicably walks out of their Lipka Street house, out of the lives of her family, out of Moscow itself at a time when all Moscow's house windows are sealed against the winter's cold, not to be reopened until the beginning of spring. As in the denouement of *The Golden Child*, the comic spirit takes charge of the finale, securing Nellie's equally inexplicable return just as the servants have unsealed the house windows and opened the hen house to let the poultry out for the beginning of spring which, in 1913, begins to stir during Holy Week. Careful to keep this resurrected marriage in the confines of this world, Fitzgerald lets Frank Reid describe Tolstoy's *Resurrection* as '"a new explanation of the gospels. The resurrection, for those who understand how to change their lives, takes place on this earth"' (177). Never blinking her ironic eye, the author lets us know that both partners have been seduced by Holy Russia herself. Nellie's intended flight has been to '"some more free and natural place. Perhaps under the sky in forests of pine and birch"' (181). In the event, her intended companion, Selwyn Crane, Frank Reid's wholly absurd English accountant, 'Russianized', in the Tolstoy fashion, who weaves his own birch-bark shoes and lives on the edge of the Khitrovo market where he can walk about at night '"when the souls of men and women open naturally, as is the case with certain plants"', fails to keep the tryst. But the determined Nellie goes on to 'Bright Meadows', a Tolstoyan community for which he had once given her the address. Left with the three children, Frank makes love – in Chekovian fashion – to the new governess with her 'pale broad, patient, dreaming Russian face' and her hair which 'was parted in the middle and fell in two flaxen pigtails like a peasant's or rather like a peasant in a ballet' (82), who may or may not be a young revolutionary. Selwyn, described in a characteristic Fitzgerald phrase, as having 'the terrible aimlessness of the benevolent' (83) and whom many Russians often think of as 'touched with the finger of God' (84), offers Frank an analysis of Nellie's flight, suggesting that she could not' "as yet, distinguish [the spiritual] from the romantic which casts a false glow over everything it touches"' (180).

The 'false glow' of the romantic is surely one of the snares to entrap the innocents of a fallen world. Once again, then, Fitzgerald has grounded her fiction in the fact of the fallen world, while suggesting a triumph for human love and simultaneously reminding her reader of his own vulnerability in the post-Edenic world by seducing him, as she has seduced her characters, with the romance of

dear, slovenly, mother Moscow, bemused with the bells of its four times forty churches, indifferently sheltering factories, whorehouses and golden domes . . . centred on its holy citadel, but reaching outwards across the boulevards to the circle of workers' dormitories and railheads, where the monasteries still prayed, and at last to a circle of pig-sties, cabbage-patches, earth roads, earth closets, where Moscow sank back, seemingly with relief, into a village. (35–6)

The image of Moscow's 'indifferently sheltering factories, whore-houses and golden domes' belongs with that of the doves and rabbits of the Ridolfi columbarian, and the behaviour of Wilfred, Dilly, and Ronnie Knox at their sister-in-law's funeral, to demonstrate Fitzgerald's continuing epistemological concerns: how do we know the truth, how do we tell the truth, how do we accomodate ourselves to the truth? These linked concerns, each addressing our human heritage of the knowledge of good and evil, underlie all of Fitzgerald's work. From Florence Green in Hardborough to Nellie Reid in Moscow, Fitzgerald's Innocents are self-blinded, moving in their worlds 'without the normal safeguards of social life' (*Innocence*, 107). With no full knowledge of good *and* evil, Florence Green puts *Lolita* on sale in her provincial bookshop without ever reading it; Nellie Reid follows her romantic dream of a 'freer life' into the Russian 'forests of pine and birch' (*The Beginning of Spring*, 181) with no sense that she, like the midget Contessa Ridolfi, is cutting off her family at the knees.

Records of the Ridolfi family history from the surviving sixteenth-century letters in the Biblioteca Nazionale to the twentieth-century Department of Tourism's pamphlet description of the Villa Ricordanza speak as directly to Fitzgerald's concern with the nature of the truth, her own commitment to truth-telling, and her knowledge of the Babylonian confusion of tongues that defines the post-lapsarian corruption of the Word. So too does her use of Ariel's song from *The Tempest* in *Human Voices*. Professor Pulci's reluctant advice in *Innocence* against any tampering with that family's 'definition through myth' even though he has rejected his own earlier study of 'the myth as a justification' (162) points once again to that doubled vision through which Fitzgerald's readers see the Ridolfi columbarian, the Knox brothers, and Moscow. Moreover, it suggests the fundamental integrity of Fitzgerald's pervasive irony. The doubleness inherent in all irony not only mirrors the corruption of the Word after the Fall but also permits the author to withhold judgment, to stress the tensions between Innocence and Experience and to open up panoramas of choice, thus effectively communicating her vision of the fallen world to her fellow-citizens. The choices, both those offered to the reader and those enacted in the fictions, always suggest the simultaniety of knowledge and compassion, of worldly experience coupled with the loving heart, the co-existence of the fact with the 'magic and miracles' which illuminate the post-lapsarian world: the starved African child entombed in real gold; Chiara's recognition that love quiets all warring claims for sympathy, bringing an indescribable sense of tranquillity; Nellie Reid's blithe return home as all of Moscow's windows are being unsealed to let in the spring. In the light of her full knowledge of this world's dangers, Penelope Fitzgerald expresses her love of this world's glories; her novels are the exemplary work of 'a creature of reason' who knows 'what to do' with her heart (*Knox Brothers*, 89).

**Note**

1.  *The Gate of Angels*, Fitzgerald's eighth novel (published after the completion of this essay), tests further the limits both of human rationality and the loving heart in our fallen world. Set in the early years of this century, the novel's action works through beautifully modulated clashes of contingency and grace in a world that encompasses Cambridge dons, nuclear physicists, London working girls, and unscrupulous journalists presented by an author whose ironies once again anchor farce and whose compassion illuminates comedy.

A BIBLIOGRAPHY OF WRITINGS BY
PENELOPE FITZGERALD

**Novels**

*The Golden Child* (London: Duckworth, 1977; New York: Scribner, 1977).
*The Bookshop* (London: Duckworth, 1978).
*Offshore* (London: Collins, 1979; New York: Henry Holt, 1979).
*Human Voices* (London: Collins, 1980).
*At Freddie's* (London: Collins, 1982; Boston: Godine, 1985).
*Innocence* (London: Collins, 1986; New York: Henry Holt, 1986).
*The Beginning of Spring* (London: Collins, 1988; New York: Henry Holt, 1988).
*The Gate of Angels* (London: Collins, 1990; New York: Nan A. Talese/ Doubleday, 1992).

## Books

*Edward Burne-Jones: A Biography* (London: Joseph, 1975).
*The Knox Brothers* (London: Macmillan, 1977; New York: Coward, McMann & Geoghegan, 1977).
William Morris, 'The Novel on Blue Paper', introduction by Fitzgerald (*Dickens Studies Annual: Essays in Victorian Fiction* 10 (1982): 143–51).
William Morris, *The Novel on Blue Paper*, introduced and edited by Fitzgerald (West Nyack, New York: The Journeyman Press, 1982).
L. H. Myers, *The Root and the Flower*, introduced by Fitzgerald (Oxford: Oxford University Press, 1984).
*Charlotte Mew and Her Friends* (London: Collins, 1984; American edition: *Charlotte Mew and Her Friends: with a Selection of Her Poems*. Foreword by Brad Leithauser. Radcliffe Biography Series. Reading, Mass.: Addison-Wesley, 1988).
Mrs [Margaret] Oliphant, *Chronicles of Carlingsford: The Rector and The Doctor's Family*, introduction by Fitzgerald (London: Virago, 1986; New York: Penguin, 1986).
Mrs Oliphant, *Chronicles of Carlingford: Salem Chapel*, introduction by Fitzgerald (London: Virago, 1986; New York: Penguin, 1986).
Mrs Oliphant, *Chronicles of Carlingford: The Perpetual Curate*, introduction by Fitzgerald (London: Virago, 1987; New York: Penguin, 1987).
Mrs Oliphant, *Chronicles of Carlingford: Miss Marjoribanks*, introduced by Fitzgerald (London: Virago, 1988; New York: Penguin, 1989).
Mrs Oliphant, *Chronicles of Carlingford: Phoebe Junior*, introduced by Fitzgerald (London: Virago, 1988; New York: Penguin, 1989).

## Articles and Reviews

'Following the Plot', *London Review of Books* 2 (21 February 1980): 12–13.
'Gringo' [*The Colonist* by Michael Schmidt], *London Review of Books* 2 (21 August–3 September 1980): 21–2.
'A Secret Richness' [*A Few Green Leaves* by Barbara Pym], *London Review of Books* 2 (20 November–4 December 1980): 22.
'Dear Lad' [*The Simple Life: C. R. Ashbee in the Cotswolds* by Fiona MacCarthy: *Philip Mairet: Autobiographical and Other Papers*, edited by C. H. Sisson], *London Review of Books* 3 (19 March–1 April 1981): 16.
'Jerusalem' [*Me Again: Uncollected Writings of Stevie Smith*, edited by Jack Barbera and William McBrien], *London Review of Books* 3 (3–16 December 1981): 13.
'Christina and the Sid' [*Christina Rossetti: A Divided Life* by Georgina Battiscombe; *The Golden Veil* by Paddy Kitchen; *The Little Holland House Album* by Edward Burne-Jones, introduced by John Christian], *London Review of Books* 4 (18–31 March 1982): 21–2.
'Lotti's Leap' [*Collected Poems and Prose* by Charlotte Mew, edited by Val Warner], *London Review of Books* 4 (1–14 July 1982): 15–16.
'Sonata for Second Fiddle' [*A Half of Two Lives: A Personal Memoir* by Alison Waley], *London Review of Books* 4 (7–20 October 1982): 12.

'Keeping Warm' [*Letters of Sylvia Townsend Warner* by William Maxwell; *The Portrait of a Tortoise* by Gilbert White, with Introduction and Notes by Sylvia Townsend Warner; *Sylvia Townsend Warner: Collected Poems*, edited by Claire Harman; *Scenes of Childhood and Other Stories* by Sylvia Townsend Warner], *London Review of Books* 4 (30 December 1982–19 January 1983): 22–3.

'Dear Sphinx' [*The Little Ottleys* by Ada Leverson, introduced by Sally Beauman; *The Constant Nymph* by Margaret Kennedy, introduced by Anita Brookner; *The Constant Nymph: A Study of Margaret Kennedy 1896–1967* by Violet Powell], *London Review of Books* 5 (1–21 December 1983): 19.

'The Real Johnny Hall' [*Our Three Selves: A Life of Radclyffe Hall* by Michael Baker]. *London Review of Books* 7 (30 October 1985): 19.

'Holy Terrors' [*'Elizabeth': The Author of 'Elizabeth and her German Garden'* by Karen Usborne; *Alison Uttley: The Life of a Country Child* by Denis Judd; *Richmal Crompton: The Woman behind William* by Mary Cadogan], *London Review of Books* 8 (4 December 1986): 18.

'Vous etes belle' [*The Lost Domain* by Henri Alain-Fournier, translated by H. Davidson; *Henri Alain-Fournier: Towards the Lost Domain: Letters from London 1905*, edited and translated by W. J. Strachan; *Alain-Fournier: A Brief Life 1886–1914* by David Arkell], *London Review of Books* 9 (8 January 1987) 12.

'Various Women' [*A Voyager Out: The Life of Mary Kingsley* by Katherine Frank; *Marilyn* by Gloria Steinem, with photographs by George Barris; *Joe and Marilyn: A Memory of Love* by Roger Kahn; *I leap over the wall* by Monica Baldwin, introduced by Karen Karmstrong; *Diary of a Zen Nun: A Moving Chronicle of Living Zen* by Nan Shin (Nancy Amphoux)], *London Review of Books* 9 (2 April 1987): 15–16.

'Kay Demarest's War' [*The Other Garden* by Francis Wyndham; *The Engine of Owl-light* by Sebastian Barry; *A Singular Attraction* by Ita Daly; *Cold Spring Harbor* by Richard Yates; *The Changeling* by Catharine Arnold], *London Review of Books* 9 (17 September 1987): 22.

'Dame Cissie' [*Family Memories* by Rebecca West, edited by F. Evans; *Rebecca West: A Life* by Victoria Glendenning], *London Review of Books* 9 (26 December 1987): 17.

'Big Books' [*William Morris: An Approach to the Poetry* by J. M. S. Tompkins], *London Review of Books* 10 (15 September 1988): 23.

'Megawoman' [*Olive Schreiner: Letters, Vol. 1: 1871–1899* edited by Richard Rive], *London Review of Books* 10 (13 October 1988): 11.

'Do You Have the Courage to Cry?' [*The Pilgrim's Rules of Etiquette* by Toghi Modarressi], *New York Times Book Review*, 13 August 1989, 7.

'White Nights' [*In the Beginning* by Irina Ratushinskaya; *Goodnight* by Abram Tertz; *Comrade Princess: Memoirs of an Aristocrat in Modern Russia* by Ekaterina Meshcherskaya], *London Review of Books*, 18 (11 October 1990).

'The Great Encourager' [*Ford Madox Ford* by Alan Judd], *New York Times Book Review* (10 March 1991): 7.

Book Review [*A Very Close Conspiracy: Vanessa Bell and Virginia Woolf* by Jane Dunn], *The Charleston Magazine* 3 (Summer/Autumn 1991): 42–4.

'Luck Dispensers' [*The Kitchen God's Wife* by Amy Tan], *London Review of Books* (11 July 1991): 19.

'Good as Boys' [*The Type of Girl: A History of Girls' Independent Schools* by Gillian Avery; *There's Something About A Convent Girl* by Jackie Bennett and Rosemary Forgan], *London Review of Books* (15 August 1991): 23.

'Fried Nappy' [*The Van* by Roddy Doyle, *London Review of Books* (12 September 1991): 16.

'Children's Children' [*Grandmothers Talking* by Nell Dunn], *London Review of Books* (7 November 1991): 7.

'Lasting Impressions' [*The Kelmscott Press: A History of William Morris's Typographical Adventure* by William S. Peterson], *The New York Times Book Review* (15 December 1991): 19.

## A BIBLIOGRAPHY OF WRITINGS ABOUT PENELOPE FITZGERALD

Brookner, Anita, 'Moscow Before the Revolution' [*The Beginning of Spring*], *The Spectator* (1 October 1988): 29–30.

Brookner, Anita, 'Daisy Pulls It Off' [*The Gate Of Angels*], *The Spectator* (1 September 1990): 31–2.

Byatt, Antonia, 'The Isle Full of Noises' [*Human Voices*], *Times Literary Supplement* (26 September 1980): 1057.

Callendar, Newgate, *The Golden Child*, *New York Times Book Review* (1 April 1979): 21.

Cole, Catherine Wells, 'Penelope Fitzgerald', in *Dictionary of Literary Biography* 14, ed. Jay L. Halio, *British Novelists since 1960*, Part I: A-G (Michigan: Gale, 1983): 302–8.

Glendinning, Victoria, 'Between Land and Water' [*Offshore*], *The Times Literary Supplement* (23 November 1979): 10.

Heller, Zoe, 'Affairs of the Heart in Defiance of Reason' [*The Gate of Angels*], *Independent* (25 August 1990): 29.

Hosmer, Robert E. Jr., 'Penelope Fitzgerald', *An Encyclopaedia of British Women Writers*, ed. Paul Schlueter and Jane Schlueter: 176–178 (New York and London: Garland, 1988).

Hosmer, Robert E. Jr., 'Penelope Fitzgerald', *Dictionary of British Women Writers*, ed. Janet Todd: 252–4 (London: Routledge, 1989).

Kellaway, Kate, 'A Bicycle Made for Two' [*The Gate of Angels*], *The Listener* (23 August 1990): 24.

Kermode, Frank, 'The Duckworth School of Writers' [*Human Voices*] *London Review of Books* (20 November–4 December 1980): 18.

Lee, Hermione, 'Down by the Thames' [*Offshore*], *The Observer* (2 September 1979): 37.

Lively, Penelope, 'Five of the Best' [*Human Voices*], *Encounter* (January 1981): 53–9.

Lively, Penelope, 'Backwards and Forwards: Recent Fiction' [*At Freddie's*], *Encounter* (June–July 1982): 86–91.

Longford, Frank, 'A Unique Quartet of Brothers' [*The Knox Brothers*], *Contemporary Review* (April 1978): 216–18.

'The Old Firm' [*Edward Burne-Jones: A Biography*], *The Economist* (27 September 1975): 119.
'Penelope Fitzgerald', *Contemporary Literary Criticism* 51: 123–27 (Michigan: Gale, 1989).
Plunket, Robert, 'Dear, Slovenly Mother Russia' [*The Beginning of Spring*], *New York Times Book Review* (7 June 1989): 15.
Rumens, Carol, 'Assaults on the Rational' [*The Gate of Angels*], *New Statesman* (1 September 1990): 31–2.
Stead, C. K., 'Chiara Ridolfi' [*Innocence*], *London Review of Books* (9 October 1986): 21–2.
Walters, Margaret, 'Women's Fiction' [*The Beginning of Spring*], *London Review of Books* (13 October 1988): 20.
Ward, Elizabeth, 'Love in Florence' [*Innocence*], *Washington Post Book World* 12 July 1987: 4.

## PENELOPE FITZGERALD

Born in Lincoln, England in 1916, Penelope Fitzgerald, daughter of Edmund Valpy and Christina Hicks Knox, received First Class Honors in English literature from Somerville College (Oxford) in 1939 and married Desmond Fitzgerald in 1941. The mother of three, she did not publish her first novel until 1977, a mystery originally begun as entertainment for her ailing husband who died in 1976. Almost simultaneously with the publication of that novel (*The Golden Child*), she published a Knox family biography, *The Knox Brothers*: the lives of her father, journalist, wit, and Editor of *Punch*, and his three brothers. The turn-of-the-century Knox household – the four boys, together with their father, Edmund Knox, Evangelical Bishop of Manchester, their mother, Ellen (French) Knox, daughter of Thomas French, Bishop of Lahore, and their two sisters – exemplified the mingling of disparate Christian doctrines inherited in part from Victorian religious upheavals in the Anglican Church.

Eleven years after the Knox biography, in 1988, Fitzgerald published her seventh novel and her third biography. Of the novels, two (*The Bookshop* and *The Beginning of Spring*) were short-listed for Britain's Booker prize, while a third (*Offshore*) received that prize. *Charlotte Mew and Her Friends* was awarded the Rose Mary Crawshay Prize.

The settings for the novels, almost all of them workplaces, reflect Fitzgerald's own experience. During World War Two, she worked first for the Ministry of Food, then for the BBC. While she was bringing up her children, the family lived on a Thames houseboat. She has also worked in a bookshop and taught in a London tutorial college. Her novels spring from those experiences as well as her academic training, deep love of literature, and her family heritage of wit and loving accommodation to disparate rational and emotional conclusions.

# 7

# Enclosed Structures, Disclosed Lives: The Fictions of Susan Hill

ERNEST H. HOFER

Susan Hill, now concentrating on writing plays and fiction for children, as well as idylls of country life, is chiefly known for a series of intensely realized narratives composed over a brief six-year period:

> Quite suddenly, a door opened, something fell into place – it's hard to know exactly how to put it – and I began to write as I had known somehow that I could. Between 1968 and 1974 – when I look back, I am astonished at how short a time it actually was – I wrote six novels, two collections of short stories, and half a dozen full-length radio plays. (Family, 31)

During this extraordinary creative period she gained sympathetic critical attention and indeed three major literary awards before passing her thirtieth year. Good reviews, a willing publisher – such encouragement would project the average writer into permanent composition, the next novel always assumed to be on the drawing boards. Unlike her friend Iris Murdoch, however, who manages to publish a new novel as regularly as Christmas, Hill decided to alter course. The so-admired narrative structure of her novels, the distance, 'the simple intensity', disappeared. 'How could a woman so brilliantly imagine a soldier in the trenches of the Great War?' Such questions, asked by astonished critics, became obsolete.

> This is where we get to this question that fascinates me, what was I compensating for, writing fiction that somehow when I was married and had children, didn't need to be compensated for any more and therefore the ability to write fiction, or need to write fiction, whichever, went from me and was replaced by the ability

to go on writing in an off-the-top-need to express myself in this serious fictional form had gone. Why, how, I don't know. (interview, Dr Anthony Clare.)

One wonders about that term, 'serious fictional form'. By comparison one can sense what she means. Her kind of imagination, her discipline, which turned out structures of cool, often somberly understated portraits – as a clinical psychologist might – simply faded as a light fades. From revealing so little, except by controlled indirection and understatement to the perceptive reader, she began to reveal so much in her non-fiction. From the chaste style of her novels, powerful in their suggestiveness, Hill turned into a writer intent on self-revelation: a psychologist this time of self, willing to talk about life in the country and bringing up baby. The contrast – and this is the unique part – could not be more dramatic. For unlike any other current British novelist, this writer deliberately withdrew from the stage where she had been applauded. Withdrew without apology, determined to open a new chapter in her emotional life. Where before that energy went into an intense creative process; now it went into the creation of a family and a pastoral life.

Our task therefore is a peculiar one: to show Susan Hill growing in strength and confidence, producing a prose accepted as individual and unique, and to trace her reasons for abdication as well as, possibly, contradiction.

Susan Hill is at pains to remind us that she was an only child, and that her relatively unhappy youth reflected her solitary predicament as well as a crucial move from her beloved Scarborough to 'a Midland City'. Her days were not spent with playmates, in short. Instead she devoured Hardy, Dickens, the Brontës. These three, particularly Dickens, provided her with early inspiration. Her reclusive youth, especially latterly in Coventry, found her writing vignettes, indeed peopling her world with the playmates she lacked in daily life. In consequence, writing became an outlet for an enclosed, though preternaturally active imagination. No wonder, then, that she wrote and published a novel while still in the sixth form of her grammar school, another before graduating from London University.

*The Enclosure*, she called that first 'novel of apprenticeship', and the term may be applied to the whole panorama of her work.

Though unobtainable today and repudiated by Hill herself, it concerns Virginia (a young writer), so devoted to her craft that she disappoints a young husband. He eventually leaves her to her writing and her pregnancy: 'She seemed to be living in an enclosure which she hated with an agonizing intensity, but out of which she would not let herself escape' (147). Her wish to be a writer, obsessive to a degree, prevented her fulfillment as a person. She became enclosed in a dilemma of her own making. Rosemary Jackson remarked, 'Female freedom or independence is made synonymous with selfishness' (84). True perhaps in a political sense, but the emphasis here seems to be the lure of two modes of behaviour, each in conflict with the other, forming a psychological impasse: to write or to love, both in high gear. To be enclosed in such a dilemma, of course, became the personal problem of Susan Hill herself. Indeed the novel, such as it is, previews the future concerns of its author.

*Do Me a Favour* (1963) is the second novel of apprenticeship, following two years after *The Enclosure*. A similar expression of frustration encloses the protagonist, another woman writer, who this time buckles under the admonition proclaimed by an 'experienced' lady of ideas, Mrs Christoff: 'Your career is important. You write well. But marriage and children is a greater career in the end – for a woman . . . children are a greater gift than knowledge' (39). If Susan Hill could create such a fictional scene at nineteen, it becomes easier for us to understand why it became an *idée fixe* later on.

But the 'serious fictional form' began in earnest in 1968 with *Gentleman and Ladies* and *A Change for the Better*, a year later, both designed to focus on a highly emotionally enclosed – relationship of a mother and son, in *Gentleman*, and a mother and daughter, in *A Change*.

But Gaily, the middle-aged son in *Gentleman*, bonded, actually *enslaved* to his mother since boyhood (we never hear of daddy) manages by a superhuman act of will to break out of the enclosure. He meets Florence Ames in the launderette. She is equally mummified, but equally receptive, her middle-aged loneliness under control, of course. In the second meeting, again doing their laundry, we catch these two forlorn beings trying to emerge from their programmed enclosure into recognition of one another. Hill's method of detached, incisive observation takes the form of dialogue and unemphatic action:

'Oh, I didn't think you would come,' she said, and laughed, not
at all a confused laugh, but quiet, and at herself rather than at him,
looking down at her cupped hands as she did so.
'I'd have to keep a promise.' He stood awkwardly by her table.
'A man of your word,' she said.
'That's it. I hope so.'
'Aren't you going to sit down?' She said that as though she
wondered whether it was the correct thing to say.
'I'll get myself a coffee. Will you have another? You'd no need
to have bought your own.'
'Oh, I had to, in case you didn't come. You can't just sit here.'
'No,' he said. 'No.' (48)

In the cool world of Susan Hill, in the world of enclosure, this is
in a sense a breaking-out of the womb, a first signal that these two
are to be in love, dependent. Florence Ames will be the instrument
of rescue from the mother/son enclosure.

In *Change* Mrs Deidre Fount is an embittered daughter of Mrs
Winifred Oddicott. (We remember the full names: Hill distances
herself from the characters by the constant, formal use of the first
and last names, even 'Mrs'.) James is the son of Mrs Fount. The three
live uneasily together by necessity: Mrs Fount is divorced and needs
to work at the notions' shop run by her mother. The scene is the
seaside resort, reminiscent of Scarborough, so familiar to Hill and
used so often to give accurately her remarkable sense of place.

Further, in *Change*, Hill is concerned to show the effect of the
yoking of three generations, and the voice in the middle, Mrs Fount,
tied to her mother, tied to her son, is a logical choice to carry the
burden of the enclosure. In her consciousness, writ large, we as
readers can observe the building tension, the crisis caused when the
son tries to break out of the enclosure. Poignant perhaps best describes the mounting confrontations which beset Mrs Fount because
she watches with terrible inevitability the very process of her failure
to communicate with James. It duplicates inexorably the sad relationship she suffers with her mother. The enclosure that has en-
circled her is as tight as a boa constrictor.

Hill uses this time the device of a limited stream of consciousness
to advance our understanding of the deteriorating circumstances:

I have done wrong, thought Deidre Fount, when she woke in the
middle of the night, I have done wrong and it is a judgment

upon me. I have quarrelled with my mother and spoken harsh words to her, I have wished her dead, I have made her unhappy and cannot help it. But now my own son will not look me in the eyes, and he will think about me in the same way, and talk about me with his friends. As soon as he is able he will go away. (139)

Finally, in the climax, the enclosure she was born into alienates Mrs Fount completely from the very son she hopes to keep close, within the enclosure. She makes reservations to take him away from his school chum, on holiday alone with herself. But friend Schwartz has already issued a counter invitation. The scene is in the shop; Mrs Fount has reached the point of no return:

> 'Oh go on, go on, do what you like, I do not care for you. You have more feeling for your friend Schwartz than you have for me.'
> James Fount left the shop.
> I am saying all the things to him that I vowed I would never say, thought Mrs Deidre Fount. I am becoming more and more like my own mother was with me and I cannot help myself, for now I understand. I see it all and I am miserable and I am afraid. (183)

As readers we watch her during this view of her consciousness: at last she understands the full consequences of an inherited enclosure.

The question of when the factual experience, the visual record, becomes transmuted into fiction gets explored by Susan Hill in the Introduction to the Longman's edition of her next novel *I'm the King of the Castle* (1970), republished ten years after the Hamish Hamilton first edition.

The setting for *King* is the West Country, near the borders of Dorset and Wiltshire, an area new to Susan Hill. Setting, 'place', always figures importantly in all her works. But after writing four novels and still being in her mid-twenties, she felt need of a change of scene and took a cottage in this 'new' area:

> I had never been to the West Country, and at once loved that very typical, rural corner of it, explored the fields and woods around the cottage, sat and watched deer feed in the evenings, stayed up all night watching for badgers, had a terrifying experience with a crow, one hot afternoon, read and fretted, and wandered about in

that restless way a writer does when things are just starting to simmer deep inside him but aren't yet ready to boil over onto the page. (*Lighting*, 59)

'Hang Wood' bordered the cottage in actuality and turns up later in the novel, as do two boys she casually met: they became prototypes for Kingshaw and Hooper, though metamorphosed into boys totally different from the simple lads who walked down her path. Hardy might have been an influence here (she edited him later), for like his Wessex, the country setting and its inhabitants (Fielding, in King especially) can be identified, though re-focused.

In the Hill novel the two young boys become yoked, enclosed in an enforced relationship that leads finally to the suicide of Kingshaw. The intensity of the incidents leading to the tragedy are dispassionately related, factually noted, and seem to take on a logic all of their own. The public questioned the credibility of a schoolboy suicide, however. Hill defended the conclusion as recently as 1988 in a televised explanation of her narrative strategy. Released by the BBC with Bruce Jamson as producer, this curious televised documentary allows Susan Hill opportunity to recreate the highlights of her story. She talks about the sadistic evil she built up in the words and deeds of Hooper, Kingshaw's ever-present persecutor. She goes on to discuss the claustrophobia of the enclosure:

'It's a book about being trapped,' Hill says on screen. 'No one believed Kingshaw. Probably they *did* believe him, but there was too much at stake.'

What was at stake: the uninspired union, marriage finally, of the Hooper father to the Kingshaw mother. In consequence they fail to listen to Kingshaw's pleas, giving Hooper top billing by virtue of territorial rights, all the privileges of his longevity. 'Go out and play together,' says Mummy in a flash of exasperated unawareness. Conventional, unimaginative, middle-class: all these words spring to mind. Hill never condescends to pen such generalizations. Her narrative subtly loads our consciousness with these terms, however, by highlighting the relationship between the boys, placing the elders in an unfocused authoritarian role.

Kingshaw therefore has no recourse except to try to escape. He runs straight for the dreaded woods. As he starts through the cornfield, the symbolic malevolence of nature then becomes manifest:

He could only hear the soft thudding of his own footsteps, and the silky sound of the corn, brushing against him, then there was a rush of air, as the great crow came beating down and wheeled about his head . . . The beak opened and the hoarse caaw came out again and again from inside the scarlet mouth . . . (30) Then there was a single screech, and the terrible beating of wings, and the crow swooped down and landed in the middle of his back. (32)

The bird recalls the incident Hill experienced the first day she had walked in Hang Wood herself. She transmutes it here into a symbolic incarnation of evil. Indeed the black bird turns up in every subsequent book, even the non-fiction, perhaps most dramatically in *The Bird of Night*.

Later that night, back at Warings, the forbidding house where the boys are 'enclosed', Hooper, who had watched the black bird attack Kingshaw, sneaks into Kingshaw's room with a stuffed crow from the collection displayed downstairs in the 'museum' of his father. He drops it on Kingshaw's bed, its black coat glistening. By such methodical, tension-laden incidents, Hill prepares the reader for the tragic finale. Structure thus supplies data, suggests meaning.

Actually Susan Hill goes a step further in this grisly tale by allowing the reader insight into Kingshaw's mind. We watch the boy's gradual acceptance of the inevitability of his predicament, its no-way-out enclosure. This is perhaps the most poignant aspect of this method of slow revelation, incident piled upon incident. For Kingshaw knows and we know he knows, when he is at last shut out of any parental protection, that he is doomed to the Hooper terror-enclosure. There is no escape now. And so the rush into the woods, to the stream where the boys had been swimming and Kingshaw had previously saved Hooper's life, ends with two sentences which reveal the terrible agony of Kingshaw, and his relief at escape. We understand that the act is deliberate; his dignity remains intact as he seeks peace:

He began to splash and stumble forwards, into the middle of the stream, where the water was deepest. When it had reached up to his thighs, he lay down slowly and put his face into it and breathed a long, careful breath. (222)

The year 1971 saw the publication of *Strange Meeting*, perhaps the most adventuresome imaginative excursion Susan Hill has attempted, both in subject matter and in time warp. To understand what she accomplished, it is imperative to examine the conditioning which prepared a woman of twenty-nine to write a novel primarily about men, set in the trenches of the Great War.[1] The donnee goes back a decade, when the younger Susan visited her eight maternal aunts who could never recover from the loss of their one idealized brother, killed in the 1914–18 conflict. Uncle Sidney Owen became a person eminently worthy of study for Susan. Indeed, she decided to read about everything that happened, politically and personally, to ordinary human victims of that conflagration. A year after her research began – in 1962 – she attended a performance of Benjamin Britten's War Requiem.

It was Britten, the man whose work has had more influence upon mine than anyone else's (including other writers), who first brought me back to my memories of Great Uncle Sidney Owen. In 1962 I went to a performance of Britten's *War Requiem*. I didn't know in advance much about what it was going to be like, or about, I only knew that what music of his I had already heard I had responded to at once, and that it had remained with me, in my mind and my heart, had fired my imagination. But I was not at all prepared for the effect that performance of the *War Requiem* was to have on me. I came out of it feeling dazed, as though something very important had happened – to me, I mean, as well as in musical terms –I can't easily explain it or even describe it. But one result was that I became filled with the desire to write something myself about the First World War. (*Lighting*, 63)

This time Susan Hill rented a cottage in Aldeburgh, home of Benjamin Britten and the Aldeburgh Festivals – a seacoast town again reminiscent of her own coastal childhood and indeed of the setting for *Peter Grimes*. 'I know Aldeburgh through my own emotions and my creative imagination and each book that I [later] wrote there and which has left its mark upon me . . . it is a landscape of the spirit' (*Lighting* 12–14).

After her research in London and elsewhere, the actual writing of the novel took only three months. Sensitive to place, Susan Hill found the Aldeburgh setting ideal for this particular composition. The terrain had echoes of the same war terrain she was trying to re-create:

When it was gray and cold, those marshes took on something of the aspect of the fields of Flanders. Here and there, people had dumped old bicycle wheels and tin oil drums, and they had half sunk in the mud, and rusty metal loomed up out of the pools of water, like the debris of a battlefield. When I took a break from writing, I walked on those marshes, early and late. In the end, I began to hear the boom of guns in the boom of the sea, and the cries of wounded men in the cries of the seagulls, to see blood, not the red of the early sunset, staining the water of the pools and ditches. (*Lighting*, 65)

So the narrative strategy Hill employs in *Strange Meeting* is complex, unlike most modern novels: scholarship, Britten's music, the coastal furniture, plus the 'workings and productions of my subconscious and of my imagination'. It met with a mixed response. One critic found the tour-de-force unrewarding, the structural devices we have noted as disclosing so much about character, less than adequate in *Strange Meeting*. Claire Tomalin felt the 'very restraint and precision of the detail manage to undermine the reality of the central relationship, which fades into a fantasy woven round a discoloured sepia photo of two handsome young Englishmen' (33).

Perhaps we can argue that this same matter-of-fact style manages to keep what might turn into mawkish sentimentality, credible and moving. Without the restraint so typical of Hill, the story (as Kenneth Muir points out) in other hands might turn gruesome or become burdened with sexual innuendoes.

There is considerable space devoted to a realistic depiction of trench warfare in *Strange Meeting*, but that is backdrop for a more intimate drama, stage front, of two young men forced into one another's company by virtue of their army assignment. Hilliard could not be a more cramped, stereotypical English upper middle-class product: he is the senior lieutenant, son of non-communicating parents. He cannot meet people, or indeed even talk to his parents, except in the most level, conventional way. Then Barton arrives in his billet, a newly assigned junior lieutenant, a doctor's son, with none of the built-in hang–ups of class that strangle Hilliard.

But we must build up these impressions from artfully placed details. Back in England these two would never have met, but if they had, would not have been be able to talk, as Hilliard would have been consumed by shyness and inbred prejudice. Here in the novel, at a French farmhouse before going up to the front, the two confront one another. Barton, still idealistic, new to the war, transparently nice, unaffected, has brought a volume each of Henry James and Sir Thomas Browne with him. So opposite in temperament is Barton to Hilliard, that rather in spite of himself, Hilliard opens up to Barton: Hilliard who cannot talk to his own mother (who persists in sending packages from Fortnum's 'to the boys').

Suddenly, in this classless limbo, Hilliard makes a human contact which his family and home (at the top of the village where control was of the highest priority) has never provided. For instance, a day or two into their friendship, Hilliard asks Barton if he always tells people 'everything you're feeling'.

Barton looked around at him in surprise.

'Generally. If I want to. If they want to hear.' He paused and then laughed. 'Good Lord, we're not at school now, are we?'

Hilliard did not reply.

'Besides, it's the way we were brought up. To say things, tell people what you feel. I don't mean to force it on anyone. But not to bottle things up.'

'I see.' (55)

Barton's family, equally 'open', become introduced to Hilliard through correspondence. 'It was as though he had been standing in a dark street looking into a lighted room and been invited in.' Hilliard's life, in fact, is being altered for the better by the war. But Susan Hill's plan is far more complex; she creates a Barton almost prelapsarian in his goodness (but credible nevertheless) in order to make more dramatic the later impact of the stench of death, the discomfort of the trenches, the meaninglessness of individual lives pitched into battle. Then – at the front – the disclosure emerges for us: the roles of the two men become reversed. The more pragmatic, hardened Hilliard must now help the more naive Barton. This spiritual interdependency becomes vivid and indeed possible only because of the sordid conditions.

The first confrontation Barton has with death is so horrifying that it alters his personality overnight. His withdrawal and his silence disturb Hilliard, who has learned to depend on Barton's ebullience and affection. Finally, one wet night before Barton's fatal run into no-man's land on a ridiculous mission to identify dead bodies as German or English, Hilliard manages – with difficulty – to break through to Barton, to talk about death . . .

But the worst of it [Barton says] has been that I haven't known how to face myself. That Private who was snipered . . . looking at him I could have wept and wept, he seemed to be all the men who had ever been killed, John. I remember everything about him, his face, his hair, his hands, I can remember how pale his eyelashes were and I thought of how alive he's been, how much there had been going on inside him – blood pumping round, muscle working, brain saying do this, do that, his eyes looking at me. I thought of it all, how he's been born and had a family, I thought of everything that had gone into making him – and it wasn't that I was afraid and putting myself in his place down there on the ground. I just wanted him alive again. (126)

It is at this point, the personal drama played out against the boom of cannon and the unexpressed recognition that one or both friends may not survive the next twenty-four hours, that Hilliard and Barton communicate best. Must we wait for an emergency to be our best, Susan Hill seems to suggest . . .

The roles of the two men are reversed again: Hilliard now quotes Sir Thomas Brown to Barton, his former teacher, and eventually gets Barton to smile as he looks at the tattered binding of the beloved book which he had hurled into the mud. Hilliard starts to speak –

'Are you afraid of what else is to come?'
'I'm afraid of myself. Of what I am becoming, of what it will do to me.'
'Are you afraid of your own dying?'
Barton's face lighted up at once. 'Oh, no. I've thought about that too. No. I have never really been afraid of that.'
'It is a brave act of valour to condemn death, but when life is more terrible, it is the truest valour to live.'
Barton smiled. 'I've just torn all that up.'
'But I have just learned it by heart.'
'And is it true?' (129)

Susan Hill's use of dialogue here subtly places Hilliard into the role of leader. It is his point of view, now; he controls the action. We as readers must interpret, to assess this passage as crucial in the relationship between the two men. Further, the passage is selective, extremely economical, for the implications are up to us to make: Hill has given us the data, though removed herself. (As Kenneth Muir says, 'Susan Hill gains considerably from her reticence about sex and from her avoidance of psychological analysis' (*Uses of Fiction*, 275).) Then, at the end, when Barton dies and Hilliard, wounded, returns to England, it's first to the home of the Barton family, not to his own. He is met at the station by a friend of the family, and as they drive away, Hilliard names the streets and lanes, much to the surprise of the driver. No, he had not been here before, he answered. 'But then he thought that that was not true, he had been here, he had spent hours here with Barton, as they had talked in the apple loft and the tents and dugouts and billets . . .' (179). Susan Hill, by these quiet structural devices – getting into a car at the station, looking out at the town – conveys to us the depth of feeling, unexpressed, which Hilliard learned about person and place from his friendship with Barton.

The novel, finally, can be dismissed by some for going over material familiar from *All Quiet on the Western Front* onwards; the battle scenes are extremely realistic; the letters home possibly excessive. But *Strange Meeting* covers a far wider canvas. The two main characters, but also the Commanding Officer, and the Adjutant, are drawn with feeling and perspicacity. Factual though the novel essentially is, precise in its details, it likewise possesses an emotional quality not found before in Susan Hill. If it sounds 'like a true story', as the *Observer* critic complained, these 'facts' at the same time disclose latent political and psychological problems, even deep-felt emotion. By talking about the lanes and streets of Barton's Warwickshire, Hilliard discloses his affection and admiration for Barton and all he represents. The enclosure of Barton/Hilliard, indeed, discloses a microcosm of England and war.

Between 1971 and 1975 Susan Hill also wrote a number of memorable short stories, varying in length, and finally collected in two volumes: *The Albatross and Other Stories* (1971), and *A Bit of Dancing and Singing* (1975). Ruth Fainwright declared in the *Times Literary Supplement* that shorter length gave admirable 'restraint' to Hill's talent, particularly in the long story, or novella, *The Albatross*, which she found 'dark and simple as Tolstoy, yet avoiding both the suggestion of brutality and the sentimental moral pleading often found in such tales of elemental relationships' (261).

As in *King*, Hill concentrates on the enclosure of an intensely felt mother-son relationship in *The Albatross*, perhaps the most concentrated and effective of all the tales in these two volumes. She traces, inexorably, the day-to-day deterioration of the enclosed relationship, thus disclosing the real nature of Hilda Pike and son Dafty

Duncan, whose proper name is Duncan Pike. Hill implements her strategy shrewdly, this time encouraging us to make a very difficult judgment. 'Dafty' of course refers to the boy's mental problem: he is 'slow' rather than schizoid, for example, but vulnerable and shy nevertheless. Susan Hill follows the young boy's grotesquely difficult youth in a series of telling incidents which enlist our support for him even to the point of justifiable homicide. We give him a verdict of 'innocent', rather to our surprise.

Again we are on the coast, this time in a sea-swept fishing village. The sea and the often inclement weather combine to become as important as any character in the piece. For weather penetrates the lives of all the inhabitants: boats become endangered by gales; awful winter freezes reduce the townspeople to a sullen acceptance of their lot. The sea pounds the shore, pounds too at them individually, especially if one of the fishing boats has failed to return.

Just so Hilda Pike's words pound at the consciousness of her son Duncan, whom she obviously cannot forgive for being 'slow', but whom she can the more easily dominate. Like the storm, her barrage sets up a rhythm, a bitter obbligato spoken from a wheelchair: she is handicapped. Both as servant and son, Duncan's enclosure with his mother has become suffocating, airtight, constant. That is until Ted Flint, a swashbuckling, easy-going fisherman, offers him a job and unwittingly threatens Hilda's position.

Using the logic of 'what he is', Hilda proceeds to pour scorn on the offer Flint has made to Duncan. What she really fears is long separations, their tight enclosure in the stuffy cottage blasted apart. Her words to Duncan, gathering new storm as the weather also rages, construct a modulated, terrifying coherence. Every word she now utters discloses her true nature. We recall that Hooper gradually beat Kingshaw into submission in *King*. Here too Hilda will accept nothing but total compliance from Duncan.

So this enforced isolation, this unnatural enclosure, becomes intolerable, as it did for Kingshaw. In *King* the result was suicide to escape from enclosure. Here the burden of the albatross (his mother), which he must carry around with him, becomes unendurable. Calmly, deliberately, he overdoses his mother during 'pill time' and then pushes her, 'asleep', off the end of the breakwater wall. A message again seems to rise from these awful incidents – lack of freedom, enforced enclosure, leads eventually to a breaking-point, to death – that final enclosure.

The same formula works for the other stories in *The Albatross*. 'The Friends of Miss Reece', for example, concerns the story of an old woman, Miss Reece, who has one good friend in her nursing home, one fellow conspirator, a small boy. This 'odd couple' became attached through their fear and opposition to a sadistic head nurse, Wetherby. They learn quietly to circumvent her orders, slyly to defy her, but also to reduce her tyranny by being kind to each other. The enclosure this time also results in death, but Miss Reece wants to die. As part of their pact, Miss Reece asks the young boy to open her window against Wetherby's strict orders, and catches a fatal pneumonia. The agent, this small boy, has the same function in the structure of the narrative as did Ted Flint in *The Albatross* or Schwartz, the young friend in *Change*.

Less tragic, more poignant, perhaps, are the stories in *A Bit of Singing and Dancing*, a collection first published in 1973. The title story is particularly affecting, and seems a more benign version of *A Change for the Better*. The enclosure again involves a dominating mother and a subservient daughter bound for economic reasons to live together longer than they should.

Finally in *A Bit*, Esme's mother dies, though her spirit lives on like a ghostly albatross. Nevertheless, Esme decides to break the spell and take in a lodger, a male one at that. Mother's ghost rattles almost audibly for even considering such a step. Esme, however, persists, as Mr Curry appears very correct in dress and manner, an acceptable gent for her part of town, a solidly middle-class area. They set up the arrangement; the rent comes in promptly. One day weeks later Esme stumbles on Mr Curry re-living his earlier music hall professional days at a busy intersection at the seafront. There he is, tap dancing and singing, a cap for coins at his feet. Coins that eventually pay for the rent.

At first she is shocked, realizing that mother was right after all. Why had she strayed outside the enclosure in the first place? As she is about to ask Mr Curry to pack his bags, she reviews her options, her life options, and mother does not prevail.

> She went down into the kitchen and made coffee and set it, with a plate of sandwiches and a plate of biscuits, on a tray, and presently Mr Curry comes in, and she called out to him, she said, 'Do come and have a little snack with me, I am quite sure you can do with it, I'm sure you are tired.' And she saw from his face that he knew that she knew. (119–20)

And so Esme breaks out of the confinement of her enclosure by realizing that the structure of her life – rigid, uncompromising – had little to offer a lonely spinster. She experiences an epiphany in the last scene: her life, its parameters, its shortcomings, are disclosed in a flash of recognition. Just in time she changes course.

But the most extended treatment of breaking down inherited or acquired enclosure occurs in what Susan Hill calls her one frankly autobiographic novel, *In the Springtime of the Year*, a novel which bridges her 'serious' work prior to her marriage in 1975 and her subsequent non-fiction.

It is dedicated to 'the happy memory of David', a man she had loved deeply, and who had died very suddenly. 'Everything I felt and experienced about David's dying went into the novel,' she told Dr Anthony Clare in a radio interview in 1989. 'And I still dream about him once a month, sixteen years after he died,' she continued.

First published in 1974, *Springtime* tells the story of a young forester-husband – Ben – who is fatally felled by a tree, and his young wife Ruth, who is emotionally felled by the incident. This is the final exorcism, Susan Hill tells us further, of the pain David's death had caused, transmuted to the stage of *Springtime*. If, as she has stated in her essays, Susan Hill wrote fiction to make sense of experience, then here, certainly, she is doing so in relation to herself. The voice of her sorrow is Ben's sympathetic, sensitive younger brother; Christianity provides spiritual solace. Slowly, like water heating imperceptibly slowly, Ruth warms to the reality of her loss and gains strength from it.

Spring parallels Ruth's awakening: days are longer; flowers, berries, jams, herbs, windfalls, even cooking in her kitchen again, become objective correlatives symbolic of her groping toward recovery. The awakening from her sad torpor takes specific spiritual form in an epiphany she experiences when she comes upon children in the forest, dressed in white, acting out in nursery rhyme, the ritual of burial. They dig a grave near the fallen elm which crushed Ben and killed him. The leader of the children is Jenny Colt, sister of the young forester David Colt, who first brought the news of Ben's tragic death to Ruth, indeed, had witnessed the death. So the youngsters manage in this symbolic tableaux (in Chapter 6) to direct Ruth's path to spiritual illumination on Easter Sunday, when love overcomes death in the Christian sense and also in her personal return to physical and spiritual fitness.

What triggered this major step in Ruth's return to equilibrium was 'the play within the play' (so to speak) of the children in white at Helm Bottom.[2] Now at long last Ruth can return and look at the tree which had felled Ben, and also talk to David Colt. By extension, by starting to bury the past in this objectification of her grief, Ruth can consider helping others, like the curate and his wife. The beautiful enclosure represented by the marriage of Ben and Ruth had been destroyed by death. By methodically measuring the extent of the enclosure, the extent of the grief, Susan Hill at the same time discloses the secret of a life in process of recovery. The special marital enclosure, at first destroyed by Ben's death, is at the end of the novel rediscovered on a spiritual, Christian level.

*Springtime*, therefore, acts as a transition between the Susan Hill of serious fiction and *The Magic Apple Tree*, a review of country life, with many references to those same windfalls, recipes, and jams that Ruth used as therapy in *Springtime*. Seven years went by, and in 1981, in her regular column called *World of Books* in the *Daily Telegraph*, the following statement appeared in a piece called 'Writing a Book':

I have done with novels, I gave them up seven years ago and have absolutely no intention of returning to them, and no more desire to do so than I have of smoking a cigarette again. Prose fiction of any kind is a chapter of my life closed, as it were, for all manner of reasons I won't go into here. (Lighting, 202)

Two years later in 1983 *The Woman in Black* appeared in the bookstores. Was it a return to 'serious writing', or an experiment in a new genre? A ghost story, a gothic tale, a story within a story, a Jamesian revival: all these critical terms may be applied to this new work. But a word about the circumstances of its composition seems to be in order.

Susan Hill had married in 1975 and soon had one daughter, though like her own mother, she was getting to a period in life, the late thirties, when child-bearing could be risky. But she wanted another child, soon. She tells us frankly in *Family* that a miserable miscarriage then left her bereft, desperate to 'try again'. As she put it, she fretted, examined herself minutely for early signs of pregnancy, eager to conceive so as to eliminate the memory of the miscarriage, and indeed not get beyond the safe age of easy delivery.

It is during this period of heightened stress that she wrote *The Woman in Black*. 'Month after month, I burst into tears of anguish, frustration, misery. I counted ahead – nine months from July – August – September – October, and saw my baby recede into the far future.' (*Family*, 39).

Susan Hill wrote *The Woman* in seven weeks, enclosed, in a manner of speaking, by a burning psycho-physical need. She had to have an outlet. Writing this uncharacteristic piece was the answer. It is (with its archaic language of about 1910) mannered, suggestive, chilling, similar in setting to *The Turn of the Screw*, even to the story within a story and the scene round the fire at Christmas, at the start. Like James again, there is a first-person narrator telling the story within a story, married now a second time and reflecting on horrors which occurred during a previous marriage.

*Woman* received notices calling attention to its atmosphere and that Susan Hill wrote 'like one possessed' (*Punch*). A more extensive review by Stephen Bann appeared in the *London Review of Books*, mentioning its characteristics as a gothic novel, and differentiating it from the contemporary 'horror tale'. But one feels critics simply did not know what to do with this surprising novel which does not in any way resemble the more serious and important achievements of previous novels.

But if *Springtime* by vote of author and critics exorcised the memory of David, then perhaps *Woman* reverberates with a similar personal echo. Critics have avoided the implications of the story itself as related to its author directly. Could it be another exorcism?

The woman in the novel, the lady in black, who hovers frequently around the narrator, appears in the haunted house on the end of the causeway and is obviously overwhelmed with the death of a child, her child. The ghosts of mother and child return regularly to the house, indeed they possess the nursery where the crib is being rocked – empty of child. The lawyer closing 'the estate', sleeping at Eel Marsh House, actually hears the shrieks and yells and strained gratings of the mother, child, horse and trap as they all disappear into quicksand, the driver having lost his way along the causeway, owing to the sudden blanketing of mist. The enclosure of mother-child-house will haunt the area forever, as we are told by all the local inhabitants.

The drama intensifies in London when the lawyer is confronted by the carry-over of the ghostly events into his own personal life: he watches as his own wife and child in pony and trap pass before him, and die as the horse becomes maddened and gallops away, dragging wife and child to their deaths. Fantasy thus turns into reality; the phantoms of the misty causeway turn tragically into the confrontation of death in reality. This re-enactment of the same haunting enclosure first displayed to the lawyer in Crythin, the tiny village on the north coast, provides the chief chill of the novel. The narrator can never be free of this two-tiered memory. He is enclosed permanently in its prison. And perhaps the enclosed structure, the ghostly and the actual represented here, discloses the sub-conscious torment of Hill herself: 'writing like one possessed', or as she says, with 'a need to go on at all costs'. Is the book therefore a reprieve from anxiety for Susan Hill herself?

Finally, to summarize. What must a reader deduce from the strange paradox of Susan Hill's two distinct writing objectives? The one structurally so clinical and objective, the other so intimate and open, both so deliberate and confident?[3]

Simply, at first, in her novels and short stories, Susan Hill kept the reader remarkably distanced. She devised a credible enclosure for her characters, from First World War lieutenants to seaside landladies, where by virtue of the almost relentless objectification of characteristics, the plight of the Important Person was gradually revealed. By so structuring that tight enclosure, its paramaters coolly and effectively measured and planned, Susan Hill's persona come to life. Faithfully adherence to structure, it can thus be said, becomes a dynamic of exposure. We *SEE*.[4]

What has happened after *Springtime* and the maverick *Woman in Black* might be dubbed psychological turnabout. A change in personal goals demolished the writing of 'the serious novel' only to replace it with an entirely different ambition, just as prolific: the antinovel. She no longer needed to project feeling and opinion from the medium of the imagination. When she married Stanley Wells on Shakespeare's birthday, 1975, this author of revealed structures and disclosed lives had undergone a personal revolution:

[She is speaking of her marriage ceremony] The headline read: 'Novelist weds in Stratford.'

Novelist? For a moment, I wondered who they meant. I knew I had told my publisher I would be starting a new book soon, but in truth I wasn't feeling like a writer, a novelist, at all. I wasn't sure I ever wanted to write another word, my mind was on quite other things. (*Family*, 40)

So far only two novels have appeared since the 'ban'. One asks: Is it possible to let an imagination so fertile and inventive as Susan Hill's lie passive, yea dormant, indefinitely? Only the future will tell.

## Notes

1.  Hill herself addresses the question of a writer dealing with the other sex in his/her writing:

    > I am certain now that this gift or talent is absolutely sexless. A great creative writer is, for the purposes of his art, neither male nor female. The woman novelist may write about women, their sens- ibilities and situations, or she may not, but one of the essential marks of the true novelist is the uncanny ability to take the imagin- ative leap, to get under the skin and into the shoes of any other person at all, as different from the writer as may be in sex as in anything else.

    This passage appears in 'Women Writing', an essay in one of the *Daily Telegraph* monthly columns *The World of Books*, 1977–1985, and re- printed by Hill in *The Lighting of the Lamps* (London: Hamish Hamil- ton, 1987): 188.

2.  I am indebted to K. R. Ireland's 'Rite at the Center: Narrative Duplica- tion in Susan Hill's *In the Springtime of the Year*', *The Journal of Narrative Technique*, Eastern Michigan University (Fall 1983): 172–8. Particularly helpful is his analysis of the history and use of the concept of 'play within the play', as applied to Springtime.

3.  Some reviewers have not been happy with Hill's so-called country books. Eric Christiansen, for instance, writing in *The Spectator*, 15 May 1982, calls Hill to task for what she does in *The Magic Apple Tree*: 'The trouble is that depiction of happiness is difficult and apt to be weari- some . . . There is too much wool in her *pensees*. There is also too liberal a dressing of detail . . . Tragedy must be waiting for the lady who uses the words I or me fifteen times in one paragraph (on page 111) in order to explain why she likes but does not grow sweet peas.'

4.  Indeed Hill puts it very well herself in that same essay afore- mentioned, 'Women Writing':

    > There is something magical about this ability both to become other people, to enter fully into them and convince the reader of the imaginative truth of the resulting observations and insights and, at the very same time, to be totally detached, from outside of, above and beyond, all those characters. For detachment, the slightly odd sense of being a participant, but also a witness and recorder, is another of those distinctive marks of the true novelist (188).

# A BIBLIOGRAPHY OF WRITINGS BY SUSAN HILL

## Novels

*The Enclosure* (London: Hutchinson, 1961).
*Do Me a Favour* (London: Hutchinson, 1963).
*Gentleman and Ladies* (London: Hamish Hamilton, 1968; New York: Walker, 1969).
*A Change for the Better* (London: Hamish Hamilton, 1969).
*I'm the King of the Castle* (London: Hamish Hamilton; New York: Viking Press, 1970).
*Strange Meeting* (London: Hamish Hamilton, 1971; New York: Saturday Review Press, 1972).
*The Bird of Night* (London: Hamish Hamilton, 1972; New York: Saturday Review Press, 1973).
*In the Springtime of the Year* (London: Hamish Hamilton, 1974; New York: Saturday Review Press, 1974).
*The Woman in Black: A Ghost Story* (London: Hamish Hamilton, 1983; Boston: David R. Godine) with illustrations by John Lawrence, 1986.
*Air and Angels* (London: Sinclair-Stevenson, 1991).

## Short Stories

*The Albatross and Other Stories* (London: Hamish Hamilton, 1971; New York: Saturday Review Press, 1975).
*The Custodian* (London: Covent Garden Press, 1972).
*A Bit of Singing and Dancing* (London: Hamish Hamilton, 1973).
'Kielty's', in *Winter's Tales 20*, edited by A. D. MacLean (London: Macmillan; New York: St. Martin's Press, 1975).

## Plays

*The Cold Country and Other plays for Radio* (includes *The End of Summer, Lizard in the Grass, Consider the Lilies, Strip Jack Naked*) (London: BBC, 1975).
*On the Face of It* (broadcast, 1975). Published in *Act I*, edited by David Self and Ray Speakman (London: Hutchinson, 1981).
*The Ramshackle Company*, for children; produced London, 1981.
*Chances*, broadcast, 1981; produced London, 1983.

## Radio Plays

*Miss Lavender is Dead* (1970); *Taking Leave* (1971); *A Change for the Better* (1971); *The End of Summer* (1971); *Lizard in the Grass* (1971); *The Cold Country* (1972); *White Elegy* (1973); *Consider the Lilies* (1973); *A Window on the World* (1974); *Strip Jack Naked* (1974); *Mr Proudham and Mr Sleight* (1974); *On the Face of It* (1975); *The Summer of the Giant Sunflower* (1977); *The*

*Sound that Time Makes* (1980); *Here Comes the Bride* (1980); *Out in the Cold* (1982); *Autumn* (1985); *Winter* (1985).

## Television Play

*The Badness Within Him* (1980).

## Other

*The Magic Apple Tree: A Country Year* (London: Hamish Hamilton, 1982; American edition: New York: Holt Rinehart, 1983).
*Through the Kitchen Window* (London: Hamish Hamilton, 1984).
*One Night at a Time* (for children) (London: Hamish Hamilton, 1984).
Bell, Adrian, *Corduroy*, introduction by Susan Hill (London and New York: Oxford University Press, 1986).
*The Lighting of the Lamps* (a collection of essays, introductions, reviews, and plays) (London: Hamish Hamilton, 1987).
*Shakespeare Country*, with photographs by Robert Talbot in association with Robin Whiteman (London: Michael Joseph, 1987).
*Spirit of the Cotswolds* (London: Michael Joseph, 1988; New York: Viking, 1988).
*Family* (London: Michael Joseph, 1989).
*Autobiographic Statement*. Programme notes to the Fortune Theatre production of *The Woman in Black* (London: A Proscenium Production, 1989).
'Reliving a Glorious Past' [*The Shining Company* by Rosemary Sutcliff; *Shadown Under the Sea* by Geoffrey Trease; *Jo in the Middle* by Jean Ure; *The Haunted Sand* by Hugh Scott; *The Conjuror's Game* by Catherine Fisher; *Double Vision* by Diana Hendry], *The Sunday Times* (15 July 1990): 8; 14. (A composite review by Susan Hill.)

## Edited Collections

Hardy, Thomas, *The Distracted Preacher and Other Tales*, edited by Susan Hill (London: Penguin, 1979).
*New Stories 5*, edited by Susan Hill and Isabel Quigly (London: Hutchinson, 1980).
*People: Essays and Poems*, edited by Susan Hill (London: Chatto and Windus, 1983).
*Ghost Stories*, edited by Susan Hill (London: Hamish Hamilton, 1983).
*The Walker Book of Ghost Stories*, ed. by Susan Hill (London: Walker, 1990). Published in the United States as *The Random House Book of Ghost Stories*, ed. by Susan Hill (New York: Random House, 1991).

## A BIBLIOGRAPHY OF WRITINGS ABOUT SUSAN HILL

Atwood, Margaret, 'In the Springtime of the Year', *New York Times Book Review* (5 May 1974): 7.

Bann, Stephen, 'Mystery and Imagination: *The Woman in Black* by Susan Hill and illustrated by John Lawrence', *London Review of Books* (17–30 November 1983): 12.

Brett, Guy, 'Home Truths: New Works by Susan Hill', *Studio International*, 1012,(1986): 60–1.

Christiansen, Eric, 'The Magic Apple Tree', *The Spectator* (15 May 1982): 20.

Clare, Dr Anthony, 'Raw Material', from the interview with Susan Hill 'In the Psychiatrist's Chair', *Listener* (1 September 1988): 14–15.

De 'Ath, Wilfred, 'The Springtime of Susan Hill', *Illustrated London News* 262 (May 1974): 51–2.

Fainwright, Ruth, 'The Albatross and Other Stories', *Times Literary Supplement* (5 March 1971): 261.

Hunter, Jim, 'A Bit of Dancing and Singing', *Listener* (29 March 1973): 423–4.

Ireland, K. P., 'Rite at the Center: Narrative Duplication in Susan Hill's *In the Springtime of the Year*', *Journal of Narrative Technique*, Eastern Michigan University, (Fall, 1983): 172–80.

Jackson, Rosemary, 'Cold Enclosures: the Fiction of Susan Hill', *Twentieth-Century Women Novelists*, ed. Thomas F. Staley (New Jersey: Barnes and Noble, 1982): 81–103.

Muir, Kenneth, 'Susan Hill's Fiction', *The Uses of Fiction: Essays on the Modern Novel in Honour of Arnold Kettle*, ed. Douglas Jefferson and Graham Martin (Milton Keynes: Open University Press, 1982): 274–85.

Nightingale, Benedict, 'A Change for the Better', *Observer* (21 September 1969): 23.

Theroux, Paul, 'The Bird of Night', *The New York Times Book Review* (27 May 1973): 26.

*Times Literary Supplement* (anonymous), 'Gentleman and Ladies', (9 September 1962): 129.

*Times Literary Supplement* (anonymous), 'Strange Meeting', 29 October 1971): 1355.

*Times Literary Supplement* (anonymous), 'Weathering the Calm', (25 January 1974): 69.

Tomalin, Claire, 'Strange Meeting, a Gallery of Types', *Observer* (17 October 1971): 33.

Tomalin, Claire, 'The Albatross and Other Stories', *Observer* (14 February 1971): 24.

Thwaite, Anthony, 'The Bird of Night', *Observer* (20 January 1974): 26.

Trotter, Stewart, 'The Albatross and Other Stories', *Listener* (11 February 1971): 185.

Van Greenway, Peter, 'Gentlemen [sic] and Ladies', *New York Times Book Review* (30 March 1969).

Waugh, Auberon, 'The Bird of Night', *Spectator* (16 September 1972): 434.

## Interviews

BBC Radio 4, Dr Anthony Clare talked to Susan Hill 'In the Psychiatrist's Chair' (31 August 1988).

## Miscellaneous

*Contemporary Literary Criticism*, Volume 4, 226–8.
*Contemporary Novelists* 4th Edition, 417–18.
*Dictionary of Literary Biography*, Volume 14. Catherine Wells Cole, 'Susan Hill' (Detroit, 1983): 394–400.


## SUSAN HILL

Born in 1942 in Scarborough, the resort on the east coast of Yorkshire, Susan Hill attended school there and later grammar school in Coventry. King's College, University of London, then accepted her to read English, though here as in her final year of school, she surprised her teachers by writing her apprentice work, as she calls them: two novels *The Enclosure* and *Do Me A Favour*, both out of print. In 1963 she took her BA with Honours.

After university, Susan Hill continued her apprenticeship in various part-time posts: literary critic for five years to the *Coventry Evening Telegraph* and reviewer for numerous periodicals. From early days in her career she also wrote plays for radio, appeared on talk panels on both radio and television, and composed a monthly column for *The Daily Telegraph* called 'The World of Books'. From 1968 to 1974 she created what she calls her 'best work' or her 'serious books': two collections of short stories, six novels, numerous radio plays.

In 1975, after marrying Stanley Wells, General Editor of the Oxford Shakespeare, now Professor at the Shakespeare Institute, Stratford-on Avon, she tells us, 'I stopped writing serious fiction and turned instead to writing about places and books, country life and kitchens. Lately, I have been concentrating on turning myself into a writer for children.'

In 1983, contrary to her own prediction, Susan Hill composed a ghost story, *The Woman in Black*, which, adapted by Stephen Mallatratt, in 1987, has been seen on stage in Scarborough, the Lyric Hammersmith, and the Fortune Theatre, London. *I'm The King of The Castle* has been made into a play in France.

She has been the recipient of the following honors: The Maugham Award, 1971; Whitbread Award, 1972; Rhys Memorial Prize, 1972. She was made a Fellow of the Royal Society of Literature in 1972, and of King's College, University of London, in 1978.

# 8

# Sex, Snobbery and the Strategies of Molly Keane

## CLARE BOYLAN

The century was four years old when Molly Keane was born in County Kildare in Ireland in a Georgian manor on 300 acres to a father who was a gentleman farmer – which meant he passed his days in energetic sporting recreations – and a mother who was celebrated as the Poet of the Seven Glens, and wrote unswervingly sentimental verse about a loyal and humble Irish peasantry with whom her contact was purely inspirational. Her own children she ignored completely. Like Mummie in *Good Behaviour*, 'she had us and she longed to forget the horror of it for once and for all' (13). Molly was born into a vanishing world of nannies and maids and gardeners and dressing for dinner every day. Now she lives in a seaside cottage with a half door and a daily help. She has enormous wisdom and the ironic wit of having both seen through and seen out an era. Her life and her literature both have been pared down to essentials. 'I have come to believe that the two strongest motivations in life are sex and snobbery,' Molly Keane says; 'and I do *most awfully* believe in love' (Boylan, *Good Housekeeping*, 15).

The Anglo–Irish novelist's eighty-six years span two careers – first as 'M. J. Farrell', author of successful London West End stage comedies as well as nine novels, and more recently under her own name of Molly Keane, author of *Good Behaviour, Time After Time*, and *Loving and Giving*.

A comic writer, she is also a vital recorder of a vanished era but these are just the starting points for an energetic dissection of human nature. From the narrow canvas of an elegant, faded fragment of society (a microcosm of a miniature as the Anglo–Irish were merely a small echo of the privileged English minority of landed gentry), Keane gives us characters that spring memorably to life on the force of their consuming passions.

151

Richly written, from a glowing canvas that is vivid in detail of houses, hunting and the habits of society and fashion, sex and snobbery are what the books of M. J. Farrell and Molly Keane are really all about. Arising out of her personal vision of life, snobbery is their staple diet, sex their midnight feast – and the guileless quest of unlovely people for true love is the thread of humanity that makes her characters as well as her razor-sharp characterisation compelling.

The stamp of most Irish writers is a puritanical approach to sexual matters. Sex is seen as a turbulent youthful force that perverts the course of common sense and results in grief and retribution. Edna O'Brien and James Joyce have a more celebratory approach but their characters still have to bear a Catholic burden of guilt. Molly Keane is quite the opposite. Her characters get away with murder. So, it might almost be said, does she. From the earliest works of M. J. Farrell her heroines have displayed a zest for sexual adventure.

Sex used for power, lust, spite or amusement is deployed for the literary generation of energy, comedy and expose. Adultery (termed as 'light behaviour') and attempted abortion both feature in her 1929 novel *Taking Chances*. 'In those days', she says, 'it wasn't done – but of course it was done' (Virago ed., xii). It wasn't until she returned to fiction after an absence of almost thirty years with *Good Behaviour* – her first novel published under her own name – that eyebrows were raised, when Collins, her old publisher in England, turned down the book as 'too saucy'. An odd judgment in a way, since although the book was all about the pursuit, the defeat and the deceptions of sexual love, there wasn't actualy a steamy sentence in it.

Keane feels it would be untrue to omit from fiction so strong a motivational force about relationships, but she has a golden rule. 'Never write about sex. Describing what people do in bed makes it functional. It kills the magic. I have never seen it work on the page', she says.

She gets around this by snooping around the bed chamber rather than plunging right in, surrounding her lovers with anticipation, recollection, ignorance, malice – sometimes dread – exploring the anxieties that are satellites to the planet bliss. As some of these are common to all of us as readers (whereas all sexual experience is individual and exclusive), she draws in our own imaginations and memories to supply what is unsaid. The reader is left to read between the spare lines and visualize a scenario which Keane astutely maintains would be fogged by descriptive narrative.

A single brief query (unanswered) is the only direct reference to the long-past marriage of elderly, widowed April in *Time After Tine* when the grotesque and spiteful old Leda diverts her friend from her boring health routines. Leda tells us everything of April's numb innocence and leaves us to transport an old lady back to youth and surprising bed, when she says: 'Tell us about your Going Away Dress. How was it after that? Did he pounce? Or was he sweet about it?' (131)

Normally, there is a hard-bitten heroine, who knows and wants everything (like Mary Fuller in *Taking Chances* who decides that 'all men want the same one thing' (37), but concludes: 'Perhaps it's just was well . . . when the world's so hard on sweet young things who can't pay their poker debts' (37)); and one who knows nothing – and finds out the hard way – like Maeve Sorrier in the same novel, who longs for her marriage when: 'each day would be a day to love each other more. And the nights? But Maeve's nice thoughts stopped short there in a mysterious glow' (122–3). Enid in *The Rising Tide* is another doomed innocent. Passionate, willful and pure, she succumbs to her lover, Arthur, to defy her mother. Wreathed in a heat of Edwardian decorum, this sequence manages perfectly to convey, without any description of actual lovemaking, the collision of clumsiness with innocence, in which sex is a fatality:

> She was much too ignorant (innocent was the word perferred by Lady Charlotte) to imagine that such experiences would ever show improvement on the brief horror of this afternoon . . . The only moment she could remember clearly was an hysterical sense of the ridiculous when Arthur, looking woefully ashamed of himself, had mounted his bicycle and ridden away. (50)

Always funny, she is never flippant and does not shirk from the bitter consequences of sexual indulgence among the powerful classes, as in this extract from *Two Days in Aragon*:

> There were noddings and whisperings and tales of childbed in dark corners of the big house, and pale heavy-breasted girls dragging themselves again about their work. Ah, Ann Daly, was a whack-hand at any business like that, and the river is handy for any little things that you wouldn't want to be keeping. 'Dead, dear,' she'd say, and aren't you lucky? Another cat for the river, she'd say, and she'd laugh, she'd glory in it, 'twas like a medicine to her . . . (108).

Perhaps most devastatingly, she writes about the politics of sex – power claimed in alliances and face lost in disadvantageous discovery. 'And, oh my dear, how you do smell', says aristocratic Sylvia Fox in *Two Days in Aragon* (18), greeting her sister Grania who is fresh from an uninhibited romp with an unsuitable rural lover. Grania's disapproval stems not just from the younger girl's moral laxity, but from the unforgivable sin of being attracted to a man not of their class:

> She nipped her thin nose between finger and thumb. . . . 'You smell of musk and, oh, every conceivable awfulness. Put a drop of something in your bath, but not my Rose Geranium'. . . . Grania . . . rushed to the bathroom determined to pour the rest of the Rose Geranium down the sink only to find that Sylvia had removed the bottle and left a small tin of Jeyes Fluid in its place. (19)

In this instance Keane demonstrates that sex and snobbery are by no means inseparable, and social status, which is really her primary theme, is woven into the very air her characters breathe so that it ranges all the way from monstrous prejudice, usually handled as robust comedy with an aftertaste of painful embarrassment, down to minute and barely discernible manoeuvres of displacement.

The writer and critic Polly Devlin, who has written extensively on Keane's early, pseudonymous work, says:

> She writes of narrow horizons, elitist occupations, the preoccupations of a moneyed, hunting, curiously dislocated class of people, floating as it were over the political, angry, geographical reality that was Ireland. In *The Rising Tide* there is no mention of political turmoil although at the time in which it is set the issue of Home Rule was tearing the country apart. In this disregard for the outside world she is akin to Jane Austen: in concentrating on the two inches of ivory of one Edwardian family, in her feeling for the minutiae of human behaviour, she gives an unforgettable picture of a vanished world, the world Home Rule was threatening. (Introduction to Virago edition of *The Rising Tide*, vi–vii.)

But as with Jane Austen, Molly Keane's novels of nasty people with gorgeous manners are more than a shimmering portrait of a vanishing world, and a feast of elegant dialogue and wit. They are also concerned with those spites and yearnings that she has divined as the vital stuff of life. In substance Molly Keane's novels are similar to those of M. J. Farrell. Her characters are the landed gentry, enjoying their privileged lives and taking it all for granted. Into their divinely insensitive world comes an outsider – it might be an innocent who becomes their victim, or more usually, a sophisticate who finds in them an area of naivety. Whereas M. J. Farrell cast a wry but indulgent eye on the naughty doings of the wealthy, Molly Keane's gaze is merciless. The stage curtain was ripped away to reveal some of the cruellest, most selfish, most riveting characters ever contributed to fiction.

Arising out of Molly's personal vision, snobbery is their staple diet, sex their midnight feast. Her readers, blundering through their mysterious code of manners, are drawn, trembling, into a terrifying world where one could fall from grace upon the utterance of a noun deemed improper ('po' is all right, but never, ever 'toilet'); where to weep is bad behaviour, to ride beautifully as vital as life itself.

Keane set herself a difficult task, to establish a vanishing way of life and at the same time to expose it. As Anita Brookner was so devastatingly to do in a number of her novels, and especially in *Look At Me*, she has elected a silent witness, one caught up in, but not involved in, a glittering world. Given the unsympathetic nature of her principal cast Keane could easily win our sympathy for their victims, but she never chooses the easy way out, taking pains to point out that they were victims of their times, just like their victims, so that her most pitiful characters also come equipped with unappealing flaws. The turn of her silver dagger comes with her endowment of the less fortunate with little snobberies and prejudices to echo the enormous ones of the thoughtless privileged. Somehow these petty flaws become greater than the huge incomprehensions of the rich, for they are a mere mime, based on ill-defined envies and fears.

Our pity might have been easily summoned for poor Miss Parker, the little bearded governess, in *Full House*, despised and overworked, compelled to worm the dogs and weed the garden, and pitifully grateful for this abuse for it absolves the loneliness of being excluded. There isn't even a nearby cinema, in which she might have 'spent her emotions on the Stars, their satin underclothes, their astonishing Sex Appeals and Body Urges' (27). There is, of course, a whole bustling downstairs full of amiable servants who would offer her friendship, 'but Miss Parker was terrified of any real intimacy with servants. She clung to her void with pathetic obstinacy' (27).

Even poor Miss Pidgie, the simple-minded aunt living on the family's charity and at the mercy of the despotic housekeeper, Nan, in *Two Days in Aragon*, challenges our compassion, when Nan, asked to deter her from coming to a tennis party, declares with confidence: 'I'll tell her there's a black man coming' (31).

It is almost easier to feel genuine sympathy for the rich and stupid heroine of her most recent novel, *Loving and Giving*, Nicandra, who cries out in grief and pity for the reduced circumstances of the family: 'You don't know, you can't imagine, it was *Indian* tea today' (123). Nicandra is by no means the dimmest of Molly Keane's heroines. Aroon in *Good Behaviour*, Maeve in *Taking Chances*, April in *Time After Time*, are all monumentally stupid women. With her own extraordinary and linguistic fluency, which illuminates narrative, and splits the atom of dialogue so as to demonstrate its true intention as well as its stated one, it is her particular glee to reveal the ruling classes being in command of all before them – except the English language.

'Rawther lovely' (26) is the all-purpose praise from the beautiful Lady Bird of *Full House*, while Jane, the American heiress of *Devoted Ladies*, never gets much beyond proclaiming: 'I feel *horrible*' (43). The snobbish Lady Grizel Massingham of *Good Behaviour* has never quite bothered to master the skill of speech: 'She looked downwards and spoke rather like a child. Quite simple grown-up words, such as "gardening" got lost. Lady Grizel . . . would say instead, "She's diggin' up the garden"' (20).

Molly Keane, never at a loss for words, has revived for us a lost world, in which power is claimed through influence rather than intellect, in which love is the universal yearning and the perpetual sacrifice to pride and prejudice. In reviving the world of the big house she has also magically revealed to us our own, and never-changing world.

## A BIBLIOGRAPHY OF WRITINGS BY MOLLY KEANE

*Robert E. Hosmer Jr.*

**Novels**

*Young Entry* (London: W. Collins and Sons, Ltd., 1928; Virago, 1979. New York: Holt, 1929).

*Taking Chances* (London: Elkin Mathews and Marrot, Ltd., 1929; Virago, 1987. Philadelphia: J. B. Lippincott Co., 1930; New York: Viking Penguin, 1987).

*Mad Puppetstown* (London: Collins, 1931; Virago, 1985. New York: Farrar and Rinehart, 1932; Viking Penguin, 1985).

*Conversation Piece* (London: Collins, 1932; Virago, 1991. American edition: *Point-to-Point*, New York: Farrar and Rinehart, 1933).

*Devoted Ladies* (London: Collins, 1934; Virago, 1984. New York: Viking Penguin, 1984).

*Full House* (London: Collins, 1935; Virago, 1986; Virago, 1986. New York: Little, Brown and Co., 1935; New York: Viking Penguin, 1987).

*The Rising Tide* (London: Collins, 1937; Virago, 1984. New York: Macmillan, 1938; Viking Penguin, 1985).

*Two Days in Aragon* (London: Collins, 1941; Virago, 1985. New York: Viking Penguin, 1985).

*Loving Without Tears* (London: Collins, 1951; Virago, 1988. American edition: *The Enchanting Witch*, New York: Crowell, 1951).

*Treasure Hunt* (London: Collins, 1952; Virago, 1990).

*Good Behaviour* (London: Andre Deutsch, 1981. New York: Alfred A. Knopf, 1981).

*Time After Time* (London: Andre Deutsch, 1983. New York: Alfred A. Knopf, 1984).

*Loving and Giving* (London: Andre Deutsch, 1988; American edition: *Queen Lear*, New York: Obelisk/E. P. Dutton, 1989).

## Books

*Red Letter Days* (with Snaffles, a pseudonym) (London: Collins, 1933; Andre Deutsch, 1987).

*Molly Keane's Nursery Cooking* (London: Macdonald, 1985).

Sybil Connolly, *In An Irish House*, foreword by Keane (New York: Harmony Books, 1988).

Edith Oenone Somerville and Violet Martin Ross, *The Real Charlotte*, introduction by Keane (London: Hogarth Press, 1988).

*The Selected Letters of Somerville and Ross*, edited by Gifford Lewis, foreword by Molly Keane (London and Boston: Faber, 1989).

*The Selected Letters of Somerville and Ross, Through Connemara in a Governess Cart*, introduction by Keane (London: Virago Press, 1990).

## Plays

*Spring Meeting: A Play in Three Acts*, with John Perry (London: Collins, 1938).

*Ducks and Drakes* (1941).

*Guardian Angel* (1941).

*Treasure Hunt: A Comedy in Three Acts*, with John Perry (London: W. Collins and Sons, 1950).

*Dazzling Prospect: A Farcical Comedy in Two Acts* (with John Perry; 1961).

## Articles and Reviews

'Molly Keane's Irish Cottage', *Architectural Digest* 43 (January 1986): 136–9; 173.

[untitled memoir] in *Portrait of the Artist As A Young Girl*, ed. by John Quinn (London: Methuen, 1987).

'The Slow Death of a House' [*Walled Gardens: Scenes From An Anglo–Irish Childhood*]. *The Spectator* (5 May 1990): 35.

# A BIBLIOGRAPHY OF WRITINGS ABOUT MOLLY KEANE

*Robert E. Hosmer Jr.*

## Articles and Reviews

Angier, Carole, 'Kind of Loving' [*Loving and Giving*], *New Statesman* (7 October 1988): 34.

Billington, Rachel, 'Fictions of Class' [*Good Behaviour*], *The New York Times Book Review* (9 August 1981): 13, 34.

Blackwood, Caroline, 'Afterword', *Full House* by M. J. Farrell [Molly Keane] (London: Virago Press, Ltd., 1986; New York: Penguin Books, 1987).

Boyd, William, 'Revenge of the Innocent' [*Good Behaviour*], *Times Literary Supplement* (*TLS*) (9 October 1981): 1154.

Boylan, Clare, 'Introduction', *Taking Chances* by M. J. Farrell [Molly Keane] (London: Virago Press, Ltd., 1987. New York: Penguin Books, 1987).

Brookner, Anita, 'New Interests in an Old Setting' [*Loving and Giving*], *The Spectator* (24 September 1988): 37.

Craig, Patricia, 'Sportive and Sporty' [*Loving and Giving*], *TLS* (9–15 September 1988): 983.

Crisp, Quentin, 'Castle Rackrent' [*Time After Time*], *New York Magazine* (16 January 1984): 60.

Devlin, Polly, 'Introduction', *Devoted Ladies* by M. J. Farrell [Molly Keane] (London: Virago Press, Ltd., 1984. New York: Penguin Books, 1984).

Devlin, Polly, 'Introduction', *Mad Puppetstown* by M. J. Farrell [Molly Keane] (London: Virago Press, Ltd., 1985. New York: Penguin Books, 1985).

Devlin, Polly, 'Introduction', *The Rising Tide* by M. J. Farrell [Molly Keane] (London: Virago Press Ltd., 1984; New York: Penguin Books, 1985).

Devlin, Polly, 'Introduction', *Two Days in Aragon* by M. J. Farrell [Molly Keane] (London: Virago Press, Ltd., 1985; New York: Penguin Books, 1985).

Emerson, Sally, '*Review: Good Behaviour*', *The Illustrated London News* (September 1981): 70.

Glastonbury, Marion, 'Last Judgments' [*Time After Time*]. *New Statesman* (7 October 1983): 27.

Gordon, Mary, 'Vanities of the Hunting Class' [*Devoted Ladies* and *The Rising Tide*], *The New York Times Book Review* (29 September 1985): 43.

Holland, Mary, 'Codes' [*Good Behaviour*], *New Statesman* (13 November 1981): 26.

Hosmer, Robert E. Jr. (with Marjorie Podolsky), 'Molly Keane', in *An Encyclopedia of British Women Writers*, ed. by Paul Schlueter and June Schlueter (New York: Garland Publishing, Inc., 1988): 269–70.

Jefferson, Margot, 'Every Other Inch a Lady' [*Good Behaviour* and *Time After Time*], *The Village Voice* (17 April 1984): 42.

Kierstead, Mary D., 'Profiles: A Great Old Breakerawayer', *The New Yorker* (13 October 1986): 97–107; 111–12.

Kreilkamp, Vera, 'The Persistent Pattern: Molly Keane's Recent Big House Fiction', *The Massachusetts Review*, xxvii (3) (Autumn, 1987): 453–60.

Latimer, Margery, 'Young Folks' [*Young Entry*], *New York Herald Tribune Books* (10 March 1929): 18.

O'Toole, Bridget, 'Three Writers of the Big House: Elizabeth Bowen, Molly Keane, and Jennifer Johnston', in *Across A Roaring Hill: The Protestant Imagination in Modern Ireland: Essays in Honour of John Hewitt*, ed. by Gerald Dawe and Edna Longley (Belfast and Dover, New Hampshire: The Blackstaff Press, 1985): 124–38.

Pritchett, V. S., 'The Solace of Intrigue' [*Good Behaviour* and *Time After Time*], *The New York Review of Books* (12 April 1984): 7–8.

Southron, Jane Spence, '*Valiant is the Word for Carrie* and other Recent Works of Fiction: Shadow of Madness' [*Full House*], *The New York Times Book Review* (27 October 1935): 7.

Tyler, Anne, 'The War between the Swifts' [*Time After Time*], *The New York Times Book Review* (22 January 1984): 6.

Wallace, Margaret, '*Devoted Ladies* and Other Recent Works of Fiction', *The New York Times Book Review* (10 June 1934): 7.

## Interviews

Blackwood, Caroline, 'The Unspeakable and the Eatable', *Harper's and Queen* (November 1985): 200–1; 248; 250.

Boylan, Clare, 'That Certain Style of Molly Keane', *Good Housekeeping* (October 1983): 15; 17; 19–20.

Boylan, Clare, 'A Testament to the Spirit and Endurance of a Remarkable Woman', *The Sunday Times* (11 September 1988): G9.

Devlin, Polly, 'Molly Keane Talking with Polly Devlin', in *Writing Lives: Conversations Between Women Writers*, ed. by Mary Chamberlain (London: Virago Press, 1988): 119–35.

Guppy, Shusha, 'Writers at Work: Molly Keane', *The Paris Review* (forthcoming).

Ross, Jean W., 'CA Interview: Molly Keane', *Contemporary Authors* 114: 264–6.

## Miscellaneous

*Contemporary Authors*, Volume 114, 263–6.
*Contemporary Literary Criticism*, Volume 31, 230–6.

## MOLLY KEANE

Molly Keane, born Mary Nesta Skrine (4 July 1904) to Anglo–Irish gentry in County Kildare, has had an astonishing, if unusual literary career as novelist and playwright. Between 1928 and 1961 she wrote ten novels and four plays. Her novels, all written under the name of 'M. J. Farrell', a pseudonym she concocted from a pub sign ('to hide my literary side from my sporting friends', she has said), brought her more than the dress money she sought to earn: Keane enjoyed a major literary reputation as chronicler of the horse and hunt set of Ireland's Edwardian and Georgian twilight. Her first three plays, all West End smashes directed by her friend John Gielgud, drew favourable comparison with the work of Noel Coward.

The tragic death of her young husband and the failure of her fourth play, *Dazzling Prospect* (1961), described by one its performers, Sarah Miles as 'one of the last times that people actually threw spoiled fruit at actors in a West End production', led to Keane's prolonged withdrawal from the world of letters. Two decades after the publication of her tenth novel, however, Keane reappeared with a stunning bestseller, *Good Behaviour* (1981), shortlisted for the Booker Prize. With that novel and two others, *Time After Time* (1983) and *Loving and Giving* (1988), Molly Keane has resuscitated her literary reputation. BBC dramatizations of *Good Behaviour* and *Time After Time* and considerable media attention, particularly in the United States and France, have given this eighty-five-year old writer a new life.

# 9

# Muriel Spark and the Oxymoronic Vision
JOSEPH HYNES

I

In 1988 Muriel Spark celebrated her seventieth birthday. Interestingly, her writing achievement to that point may be divided into fairly if imperfectly even halves: poetry years and prose years. More accurately and specifically, by 1953 Spark had presumably completed her career as a poet, editor, and general woman of letters. In 1954 she contracted to write her first novel, *The Comforters*, which appeared in 1957. This division of labour is too tidy, admittedly, because in fact her edition of Emily Bronte's letters appeared in 1954 and also because her short stories bridge the two periods and continue to the present time. The years 1953 and 1954 are nonetheless additionally significant as the occasions of Spark's receptions into the Anglican and Roman Catholic Churches, respectively.

Why she shifted pronouncedly from her course as a poet, in which capacity she was honoured,[1] I cannot say. But that she did effect this transition, and that it coincided with her conversion to Catholicism, is noteworthy, and in fact she has made the point that conversion freed her to find her voice and do her proper work.[2] That proper work is her own particular brand of novel. For this reason, and without at all diminishing the interest and value of her *Collected Poems I* (1967), her biography of Mary Shelley (1951; revised in 1987) her drama, *Doctors of Philosophy* (1962), or her excellent short fiction (collected most recently as *The Stories of Muriel Spark* (1985)), I wish to focus in these pages on those stylistic and thematic qualities that characterize Muriel Spark's novels and that signal a moral imagination both delightful and serious. Although I have attempted this task in a full-length study,[3] I wish on the present occasion to use her eighteenth novel, *A Far Cry from Kensington* (1988), as an initial means of demonstrating the persistence of some definite Sparkian preoccupations since 1957. The effect of my investigative cross-referencing will be, I hope, to suggest the uniqueness of Spark's fictional achievement and why this uniqueness matters.

Most of Muriel Spark's novels are written in the third person and many of these focus on the point of view of one or two principal characters. *A Far Cry from Kensington*, however, like *Robinson* (1958) and *Loitering with Intent* (1981), is a first-person narrative. All three feature women narrators. *Robinson*'s January Marlow lives in the 1950s, whereas *Loitering*'s Fleur Talbot and *Far Cry*'s Nancy Todd (Mrs Hawkins) remember the 1950s thirty years later. For all three women London is or was a much-loved home. Moreover, all three are Catholics who either write or work otherwise in the publishing business.

The first-person point of view inevitably gives the reader and each of the three narrators cause to wonder, quite properly, whether the narrator in each book has it right, especially because Spark's books are so filled with mystery even as these protagonists proceed to sort things out capably. In fact, the kind of mystery on display in these three books is, in the main, the kind that can be and is solved. Specifically, Robinson is not dead at all and eventually returns from hiding to teach January a lesson in sticking to provable facts when behaving like a detective. Fleur's theory that the pompously sinister Sir Quentin Oliver is a thieving blackmailer proves to be accurate. Nancy's conviction that Hector Bartlett is a moral thug and a psychological bully is also borne out.

Plot in these three books consists of the presentation of occurrences and surmises leading to the solution of mystery; and the consequent instilling of appropriate lessons concerning the treatment of evidence and regard for fellow human beings. January Marlow learns compassion and comes to respect the kind of mystery that cannot be solved. Fleur and Nancy are proven right and remember with some satisfaction, decades later, both the cost of skullduggery and the pleasure of withstanding and showing up truly evil persons.

Commonly, though not invariably, Spark focuses on a small group of characters with some shared interests, in order to place and limit the temporal plot and activities in her novels. This pattern is certainly true for the three first-person narratives. January, a writer, is one of a handful of survivors literally islanded. Fleur is recalling the autobiographical and fictional events of her early days as a writer among the literarily inclined in the exact middle of this century.

Nancy's recollections similarly concern the publishing business in the 1950s. This small-group pattern obviously extends to the third-person books. *Memento Mori* (1959) gives us a group of persons seventy or older. *The Bachelors* (1960) is in some ways concentrated on its title, just as a delimited group is coloured in *The Ballad of Peckham Rye* (1960). *The Prime of Miss Jean Brodie* (1961) gives us a group of young girls. *The Girls of Slender Means* (1963) raises the age of its group of 'girls'. *The Mandelbaum Gate* (1965) might be said to offer us a number of pilgrims. *The Public Image* (1968) gives us the film industry, from moguls to actors to PR teams to *paparazzi*. *Not to Disturb* (1971) is rooted in the behaviour of a group of domestic servants. *The Hothouse by the East River* (1973) features a handful of the dead – earthbound dwellers in purgatory. *The Abbess of Crewe* (1974) presents nuns politically embattled in their convent. *The Takeover* (1976), like *Public Image*, satirizes *la dolce vita* in its crassness and wastefulness. *Territorial Rights* (1979) offers a similar view, and again within a small international set. *The Only Problem* (1984) involves its microcosm of characters in the terrorist ramifications of that materialism sharply and effectively bashed in so many Spark novels.

The point of laying out this roster of small-group participation is not necessarily to belabour the obvious, but to stress one quite evident characteristic of Muriel Spark's creative procedure in establishing a framework for her plots and characters. More importantly, she declines to attempt the role of 'Mrs Tolstoy' and the writing of thick realistic novels with complicated plots and subplots as well as dozens of carefully delineated characters, even as she aspires to the presentation of 'absolute truth' by means of her spare narratives.[4]

One trait of her spareness is the mileage she gets out of her titles in some instances. *A Far Cry from Kensington*, for example, refers not only to the difference between the life Nancy lived thirty years ago in Kensington and the material and emotional comfort she knows in time present, but also, more poignantly, to Wanda Podolak's cry of the heart to which Nancy thinks she did not adequately respond in 1955. In this way the title neatly intimates both the delights of remembering a happy time, and the importance of remembering Wanda's suffering and suicide and thereby of avoiding the lie that is sentimentality. Similarly, it is both fun to call the fraudulent Hector Bartlett a *'pisseur de copie'* to his face, and a doing of penance or a paying-off of debt to Wanda, driven to suicide by Hector's malice.

In the same way, Spark's *The Comforters* (1957) suggests both the Holy Spirit as 'the Comforter' and Job's comforters, who of course, were no such things for him. In other words, this title refers to the various voices and other sounds, earthly or not, heard by the novelist Caroline Rose. Job figures likewise in *The Only Problem*, the title of which touches on the difficulty experienced by Harvey Gotham in trying to finish his study of the Book of Job when terrorists, moochers, police, and the press keep invading his privacy. The larger value of the title, however, attaches to reflections on the problem of evil, which for Job and Christian metaphysicians alike is indeed often regarded as the only problem. In much the same way, the title of *The Driver's Seat* (1970) looks two ways. On the one hand it evokes the cliché about who's in charge, generally and specificially, of a particular event or set of events. On the other hand, however, it raises the level and increases the scope of that cliché by reviving the tragic conflict between free will and determinism; that is, the title finally asks (as in *The Only Problem*) who or what is *finally* the cause of events. The question prompts reflection, as it did for Job, Sophocles, Aristotle, Aquinas, Calvin, and Kant. The literary-theological imagination is again at work in the title *Not to Disturb*, which, a year after *Driver's Seat*, probes again into the difference between what we may write or otherwise create and what is in fact superimposed despite our sense of authorship. In this vein, the title echoes the 'Be not disturbed' of the Psalms, wherein assurance is provided, not that evil is unreal but that a larger will shapes events, whatever choices we make. Finally, in this titular regard, *Loitering with Intent* is double-edged. It is grounds for arrest (loitering with intent to cause mischief, for instance); but it also intimates Fleur's stage of development as a novelist in the 1950s: she was loitering, or seemingly going nowhere professionally, while all the while she was gathering material for a life's work and in fact writing her first novel.

Spark's liking for multivalent titles is one measure of her economical procedure and of her roots as a lyric poet. Another measure is her remarkable ear, which no doubt accounts to some extent for her popularity. Her novels regularly manifest the conviction that the style is the person, and style is frequently verbal. For example, in *Far Cry*, Nancy states that Hector Bartlett's 'writings writhed and ached with twists and turns and tergiversations, inept words, fanciful repetitions, far-fetched verbosity and long, Latin-based words' (46). To demonstrate, she cites Bartlett's attempt to persuade her to introduce him to Martin York, her employer, so that Martin will introduce Bartlett to S. T. York, the movie producer and Martin's uncle, whom Bartlett hopes to induce to film one of his mistress's novels.

'It would be preferable to procure an introduction from Martin York,' he said. 'It would be let us say a decided feather in Martin's cap. You yourself should have a word in Martin's ear with regard to the possibility of transmuting this fine work of fiction to a saga of the silver screen. Nepotism is still I believe the order of the day.' (49)

Nancy then asks herself, 'How could Emma Loy [his mistress] stand him?' This cliché-riddled 'verbosity' and insincere Jamesian imitation is nicely in accord with Bartlett's downright cruelty and viciousness, on display later in the book. In short, Nancy is a good judge of language and character. She is proven accurate on both counts.

Again, in *The Prime of Miss Jean Brodie*, two of Jean Brodie's little girls create a narrative love-life for Miss Brodie out of their reading of Scott and Stevenson, and from Miss Brodie's account of her romance with Hugh Carruthers, killed in the First World War. The result conveys admirably the girls' age, their curiosity about and virtual ignorance of sex, and the effect of romantic fiction on them. Sandy and Jenny have a fine ear for the grandiosely melodramatic and they indulge themselves in its use hilariously, and innocently, unlike Hector Bartlett.

By their recitations one knows them, we may say of Joanna and Selina, in *The Girls of Slender Means*. Joanna recites bits of *Ode to the West Wind*, *The Wreck of the Deutschland*, and the *Book of Common Prayer*, whereas Selina intones a reminder from her charm school about true poise. Each young woman's behaviour eventually matches her incantations vividly and tellingly. The same device is used in *The Abbess of Crewe* to characterize Alexandra, the title-figure, whose taste in English poetry clashes with her calling to join with her charges in reciting the Latin canonical hours. Credibly enough, Alexandra is presented, in part by this means, as torn between the sacred and the secular; however eloquent and elegant her taste, her vocation is very much in doubt.

Sir Quentin Oliver, in *Loitering with Intent*, likewise tips his character by virtue of his style. He is something of a forerunner of Hector Bartlett. Fleur is on to him as soon as she hears him repeatedly urging his followers to write their autobiographies for him with 'complete frankness'. She senses, correctly, that Oliver will eventually try to use their narratives against them.

Spark's ear and the ears of her narrators are of course not restricted in their use to the detection of frauds and humbugs. Sometimes the narrators simply delight in exotic use of language. Jimmie Waterford, in *Robinson*, for instance, speaks an English influenced by his Dutch origins, his Swiss upbringing, his reading of Renaissance English poetry and Fowler's *Modern English Usage*, and his friendship with American soldiers in the Second World War. Jimmie's marvellous speech includes these examples: 'I did see this chappie . . . and in the moment I behold him I perceive he is not a superior type of bugger. I say to myself, Lo! this one is not a gentleman' (24). Speaking to the sinister Tom Wells in January's presence, Jimmie says, 'Is not to call Miss January honey . . . as if she was a trumpet' (63). January corrects him: 'You mean strumpet.' He continues: 'Strumpet . . . and any indignities vented upon this lady, I black your eye full sore' (65). In one final example of Jimmie's style, we find him telling January of his bad luck with English women:

> In the time of the end of the hostilities I have fallen in love with an English lady . . . of noble blood, and she had declared to me, 'I am not yet old enough to marry without the permission of my pa, but I go on leave to my home and I tell of you to pa. Mayhaps he should desire to meet you, and lo! he shall permit the marriage.' Now I say to this lady,'What is about the ma?' and she has replied, 'Ma has married to another; is necessary only to fix pa.' Alas, then this lady departs to England, and she is writing to me most woeful because the faulty old pa has the plan for his daughter to marry a great lord or mayhaps an American. Then lo! I have a visitor. Is the brother of my lady love, a captain of the English Army. He had declared to me, 'Behold, is five hundred pounds, and you bloody well lay off the girl.' (181–2)

This same delight in broken, archaic, or non-idiomatic English shows up in *Far Cry*'s Cathy and Wanda. It is also on display in the Watergate-like euphemisms and verbal emptiness of *The Abbess of Crewe*, in Rudi Bittesch's Jimmie-like tilted idiom in *Girls of Slender Means*, and in Lina Pancev's charming Bulgarian assault on the English language in *Territorial Rights*. When asked what Robert Leaver does, Lina replies: 'Only loves me. He's a student but not very much

. . . I'm not in rivalry never with no one' (101). In short, Spark has a lot of fun with language, as, finally, in *Not to Disturb*, where she allows a group of 'hip' young men and women to wallow in the mindlessly inexact idiom of discothèque and advertising firm. These speakers, all trying for appropriate verbs to suggest something like Forster's 'connect', offer a series of neologisms: 'correspond', 'coordinate', 'coalesce', 'disparates', 'symmetrises', 'got equibalance', 'pertains', 'cognate', and 'energises'. Like Fleur Talbot, Muriel Spark has a good ear.

Other relatively minor preoccupations recur from *Far Cry* back through Spark's string of novels. I refer specifically, for example, to her interest in blackmail as a manifestation of evil – not merely a sign of bad form, poor taste, or criminal behaviour, but a manipulation or violation of the person, of the right to privacy. This concern is intimately tied to Spark's interest in honesty, again spelled out by Nancy Todd, January Marlow, and numerous other characters. Blackmail, or anti-honesty, steers the plot or subplot in *Far Cry*, *Bachelors*, *Public Image*, *Not to Disturb*, *Territorial Rights*, *Loitering with Intent*, and crops up in other books as well.

Lesser recurrences are similarly characteristic of Spark. I think particularly of her pronounced fondness – through her narrators – for fairy tales, as in *Far Cry*, where Nancy Todd thinks fairy tales an essential part of one's cultural wealth. Again, in *Girls of Slender Means*, the fairy tale frames Spark's book, even as the ballad colours events in Peckham Rye. By extension, predictably, the books are sometimes profoundly immersed in literary echo and allusion as well as in the process of creating books. *The Comforters*, *Robinson*, *Jean Brodie*, *Girls of Slender Means*, *Public Image*, *Driver's Seat*, *Not to Disturb*, *Abbess of Crewe*, *Loitering with Intent*, and *The Only Problem*, all study and lure readers into the intricacies of creating art, especially literature. As I shall suggest, the miracle of creating, of exercising imagination by making plots and characters while also assigning one's creatures the dignity of free will that enables them to make or break themselves and one another – this miracle consistently entices Spark and prompts her fictions.

Before developing this moral-aesthetic point, however, I think it worthwhile to note in passing a few additional recurrent motifs – not really themes, but nonetheless familar to her readers. One of these is the tolerance, charity in fact, shown to homosexuals. Indeed, without at all patronizing them or denying the sadness or sordidness that can typify homosexuals or anyone, the books show a sympathy for them just as they are, for Spark always values seeing the truth, whether good or ill, and showing that truth without sentimentality. Homosexuals she treats as who they are, and what she sees as one's nature she does not vilify or denounce. Indeed, lying, hypocrisy, and other forms of falsehood are usual targets of denunciation for Spark. In *Comforters* the narrative attitude is one of sympathy. In *Takeover*, Hubert Mallindaine is presented as a charming crook. Mark Curran in *Territorial Rights* is an ominous exotic who makes the plot tick. In *Far Cry* the two American fugitives from McCarthyism, Fred Tucher and Howard Send, fight violently but are otherwise as generous and liberal as one would desire of periodical publishers.

Looking back from *Far Cry*, wherein the aging landlady, Milly, plays a humorous part, we recall that Spark is fond of old people, and in particular, of women. Louisa Jepp in *Comforters* is a great pleasure, combining as she does the machinations of an international jewel thief and the tea-drinking gentleness of one's grandmother. Similarly endearing are Auntie Pet, of *The Only Problem*, and Lady Edwina Oliver, of *Loitering with Intent*. Lady Edwina is especially good at feigning senility, outwitting her dreadful son, Sir Quentin, and wetting her pants quite publicly if anyone presumes to cross her. The real feast in this aged regard is of course *Memento Mori*, considered by many to be Spark's best novel. Here virtually the whole cast is over seventy. Spark's accomplishment in this book, written when she was forty, is to have exemplified convincingly a great number of elderly habits even as she wondrously made these old persons representative of *any* human age in any century. Her characters reveal not only who they are in their venerable present circumstances, but who they must have been all of their lives in order to turn out this way. We see who *we* are as we mark Lettie Colston's pitiable worrying, Godfrey Colston's peevish and bullying guilt, Alec Warner's meticulous if eventually empty detachment, and Jean Taylor's Christian calm in the throes of acute suffering.

## II

Reference to *Memento Mori* provides a convenient occasion to develop to some extent the importance of religious belief to the moral and psychological structure and spirit of Spark's work. In *Far Cry*, Nancy Todd attends only glancingly to matters specifically spiritual, but she does have occasion to tell us that she believes in something like destiny. Then in an exchange with her husband William, who says he doesn't believe anything, Nancy says that she cannot disbelieve. These two people are long and happily married, but their psychologies and thus their moral foundations differ dramatically. In this way they typify Spark's consistent tolerance for leaving people's minds and characters alone, so long as these people are honest with themselves and do not violate others. Where she does not find honesty, she can of course become wonderfully satirical.

The old people of *Memento Mori* flesh out this proposition nicely. All of them, given their age, confront the fact of impending death, and each of them reacts uniquely. Nearly all suffer physically or emotionally, most of them respond secularly only, and two respond both secularly and religiously. The books lays out each character sympathetically and amusingly in all its foibles. While the structure gives the believers a fuller view of reality, I suspect that few readers are offended in their own worldliness, so balanced is the perspective, so delighted with individual differences is the narrator. Guy Leet is a lifelong sensualist, Percy Mannering a cantankerous bore, Godfrey Colston something of a lecherous sadist, Jean Taylor an arthritic and somewhat impatient Catholic convert. Spark's tone toward each of them is warm and enjoyable. She distinguishes good from bad not on the basis of a character's membership in the Catholic Church – indeed, Catholic characters overall range typically from minor nuisances to fullblown ogres – but on the basis of integrity in living truthfully according to one's lights, without trampling others. In fact, the book enjoys old Guy Leet and Percy Mannering, who believe in their way of life, and the book understands and sympathizes with Godfrey, whose guilt makes him what he is. Jean Taylor's belief roots her in what the novel offers as a fuller life, one that combines flesh and spirit, but in a sense she is just one of the 'right' characters.

In *Memento Mori*, as elsewhere, actions have consequences, and the characters inevitably die according to how they have lived. The narrative attitude, however, is one of tenderness and sympathy for the most part, whereas in a book like *The Girls of Slender Means*, for all its playfulness and wit, emphasis is much more on the reality of evil in human affairs.

*Girls* is snugly framed by the fairy tale's 'once upon a time', a device that eventually reminds us of how unchildlike and sobering fairy tales can be. This tightly controlled narrative is generated by bits of telephone conversation in time present, which prompt retrospective narrative slices recounting life among the 'girls' in Kensington between VE Day and VJ Day. Telephonic voices alternate with pieces of Joanna's romantic and religious recitations and Selina's charm-school recipe for poise, to set up the good-evil contrast that succinctly alters the life and thinking of Nicholas Farringdon, Selina's lover and the book's protagonist.

In this very impressionistic manner, and without any preachiness – Spark is perhaps the least preachy fiction-writing believer in one's experience (compared, for instance, to Greene or Waugh) – without overt explanation, then, but entirely by virtue of sharply registered experience, Spark makes credible Nicholas's conversion from a typically youthful pagan *joie de vivre* to a conviction of good and evil as spiritual realities dominating his familiar humanistic good spirits. In the fifteen-year gap between Nicholas's conversion and the present-day telephone conversations on the occasion of his death, we know only that he became a Catholic Brother and was martyred for his faith.

Spark's considerable achievement in this extraordinary book is in part to recreate the excitement and idealism and animal high-spiritedness of young people persuaded that despite the Blitz they were on the side of right and would win through. The other part of Spark's genius in this instance is to convince Nicholas and the reader that good and evil are larger spiritual realities that persist, not instead of, but together with the secular ebullience. Nicholas's shocked glimpses of what he regards as evil alert him irrevocably to the reality of original sin. He is not a prude and he does not denounce his friends or regret anyone's happiness. On the contrary, he packs all of his questioning and confusion and joy together with his discovery of the larger spiritual reality, and takes the lot into his new vocation. Typically in Spark's books emphasis is laid not on what is wrong with the secular realm, the here and now, but on the implicitly infinite magnitude of the sacred realm. The trick is to reconcile the lesser with the greater, rather than to repudiate this world. Like Sandy Stranger, in *The Prime of Miss Jean Brodie*, Muriel Spark rejects the world-bashing determinism of Calvin and Knox in favour of a vaster inclusiveness that she finds in orthodox Catholicism.

Indeed it is this insistence on seeing the other side, this adherence to what she calls the 'nevertheless' principle,[5] that marks Muriel Spark's imagination. When, after a period of reading Cardinal Newman and being baptized as an Anglican, she eventually turned to Rome, her reason, like Nicholas's, was not a nay-saying to the secular, so much as an embracing of a view that formalized what she had long accepted as an awareness of the real, but which she had never before been able to draw together coherently on her own. Her psychology directed her to Rome.[6]

Without casting aspersions on other Christian denominations, I think we may liken Spark's religious psychology to that of the Catholic Ronald Bridges, in *The Bachelors*, who states that the 'spiritualist' and the 'Catholic' are the only two kinds of religion. Doubtless it would be excessive to identify Spark with Ronald, and admittedly no course in the history of religion or in the psychology of religion would sit still for such a statement as Ronald's. Nevertheless, as we may say, the statement makes sense in its context.

For Ronald, 'spiritualist' religion is magic and is rooted in the material, the sensibly detectable and knowable. Thus, Ronald's foil, Patrick Seton, who is a thief, a fraud, a liar, and a seducer, is also a medium who holds séances. The characteristic of a séance is its use of a medium as a go-between to connect the bodily conjoined to the realm of the spirit. That is, the medium operates on the assumption that body and spirit occupy separate realms and that his own unique function is to bring these realms together through himself. We know he's been successful when we, holding hands, hear voices or table-rappings, or feel the furniture moving. Ronald considers this sort of thing magic, or false religion, not so much because Patrick happens to be a fraud as because this practice implicitly acknowledges the reality only of what can be known, that is, picked up by the senses. 'Spiritualist' religion is tied to the body in this way and necessarily separates body from spirit. Only the known is true for the 'spiritualist'.

In Ronald's view, the radical flaw in 'spiritualism' is that it denies the inevitable co-existence of matter and spirit. Ronald's 'Catholic' experience is that each of us is body *and* soul, that furthermore each of us co-exists with all other human beings similarly composed, and that all beings live in and with the Being who created us. A corollary of this position is that we cannot possibly know all that is; we cannot be God. Some mystery can be rationally cleared up, as the police know, but some cannot be thus cleared up. This latter variety we simply must believe, since we cannot deny or understand it. Ronald's experience is 'Catholic', therefore, in that it posits the unity of matter and spirit and the rightness of distinguishing between that which we can come to know through the senses and intellect and that which we experience as necessary to account for certain effects but which we cannot detect sensibly or comprehend. The 'spiritualist' operates in the dark and through the body in order to reach a spirit dwelling beyond the body. The 'Catholic', on the other hand, experiences both realms as interwoven, without coming to know the spiritual realm directly. In fact, belief is of that which cannot be seen but the real force of which cannot be denied. 'Spiritualists' accept only what they know; 'Catholics' know some things and also believe what they find real but unknowable.

This distinction is at least implicit in *Far Cry*, where superstitious reliance on and fear of the Black Box leads to Wanda Podolak's surrender of will to the blackmailing *'pisseur de copie'*, Hector Bartlett. Nancy Todd feels guilt because she did not take the trouble to send Wanda's parish priest to her assistance in time to prevent Wanda's suicide. Hector Bartlett is a latter-day Patrick Seton in his promoting of what Ronald would consider 'spiritualist' or magical religion. The occult and what is wrong with it also figure in *Comforters*, *Robinson*, and *Takeover*, and invariably the occult is shown to be evil in that it induces its victims to yield themselves to the 'spiritualism' espoused by this or that blackmailing magician. Commonly, for this reason, evil is shown to be the attempt to take over human beings, to manipulate the personhood which is not the 'spiritualist's' to tamper with. Ronald and, I think, Spark would include among 'spiritualists' all who in one way or another presume to play God, to act as Creator among uniquely individual creatures, and to do so by paralyzing, distorting, or bending those creatures' wills. To take away freedom of choice, however one might come to use that freedom, runs obviously counter to what Ronald or anyone else means by 'Catholic' religion.

To sustain and convey this religious position in her fiction Muriel Spark not surprisingly uses paradox, which is assuredly an important characteristic of her sensibility. Thus, for example, in *Memento Mori*, Inspector Mortimer, who has spent his professional career tracing telephone calls and apprehending criminal callers, advises those whose callers' message is, 'Remember you must die', to attend to the message and forget about the caller. This is clearly the theme of the book. Once again, in *The Prime of Miss Jean Brodie*, after Sandy Stranger does the 'right' thing by stopping Miss Brodie from interfering in the lives of her pupils, Sandy nonetheless appears to feel guilt, very likely because she herself has interfered rather self-righteously in the life of another. Spark is not the kind of author who rounds things out and resolves complexity, although she is a writer of comedy in large part. Rather, she delights and instructs precisely by laying things out in their diversity, however unknowable they may be in their causes, and then letting it be understood that her imagination is attached by whatever she discerns – by what is real, whether or not it can be tidied up or fitted into a pattern. She writes about what she knows and about what she believes.

Paradox abounds for the most part because Spark insists on Ronald's religious view and thus on what she regards as the realistic oneness of the mundane and the spiritually absolute. Nancy Todd believes in destiny and chooses her own way vigorously. Caroline Rose, in *Comforters*, listens to her voices and/but creates her own novel. The characters in *Hothouse by the East River* cling avidly to their temporal life until they recognize the rightness of acceding to demands of the spirit and moving on to the purgatorial existence proper to the dead. In *The Abbess of Crewe* Alexandra is situated ambivalently between her religious vocation and her passion for creature comforts of a refined nature. To make this paradoxical point finally, however, we might look at *The Mandelbaum Gate*.

The protagonist of *The Mandelbaum Gate*, Spark's longest novel, is Barbara Vaughan, an oxymoronic wonder. Like Muriel Spark, Barbara Vaughan is the daughter of one Gentile and one Jewish parent. She is in Jerusalem, itself split, by the gate of the title, into Jordanian and Israeli sections. Barbara is a recent Catholic convert torn between her Catholic faith on one hand and her wish to marry Harry Clegg, whose marriage may or may not be annulled by Rome, on the other hand. With this novel, in its lavish detail, Spark comes as close as she has ever chosen to come to being 'Mrs Tolstoy', yet even here she typically insists that Mrs Spark needs to fit all the realistic detail together with Ronald Bridges' vision of the larger reality. In the course of the book Barbara comes to experience oxymoronic reality acutely:

For the first time since her arrival in the Middle East she felt all of a piece; Gentile and Jewess, Vaughan and Aaronson; she had caught some of [her friend and English escort] Freddy's madness, having recognized . . . that he had regained some lost or forgotten element in his nature and was now, at last, for some reason, flowering in the full irrational norm of the stock she also derived from: unself-questioning hierarchists, anarchistic imperialists, blood-sporting zoophiles, sceptical believers – the whole para-

doxical lark that had secured, among their bones, the sane life for
the dead generations of British Islanders.

She . . . felt all of a piece, a Gentile Jewess, a private-judging
Catholic, a shy adventuress. (144)

This passage admirably suggests, in typically compact fashion,
the essence of Spark's 'nevertheless' idea. Characteristically her books
manifest and applaud efforts to live on two planes simultaneously,
or, more accurately, to combine the values of both planes in one's
life. Before his conversion-making vision of evil, Nicholas Farringdon
flirted with Communism and Catholicism, with homosexuality and
heterosexuality, with militarism and pacifism, and with monarchy,
fascism, and anarchy. In short, he was split up and torn in several
directions; he had no ground for a consistent life. Barbara Vaughan
is the same sort of person. Her particular euphoria in this passage
arises from the exhilarating realization that however difficult it may
be to live the oxymoronic life, one will certainly never succeed by
playing it safe and seeking the blandly theoretical median. She experiences the moral thrill of the passage cited when she realizes,
happily, the need to live actively, venture forward, take real risks.
She needs to give to each claim its due, to enhance every variety of
truth, to walk both sides of the street and never ineffectually stroll
down the middle. Indeed, she converts Freddy, who then re-
converts her, to the force of God's statement in the Apocalypse:
'Being what thou art, lukewarm, neither hot nor cold, thou wilt
make me vomit thee out of my mouth.' Barbara's psychology and
religious belief, like those of her creator, are one.

### III

Creating, or making, is perhaps Muriel Spark's profoundest concern.
In a number of works it is tangentially or secondarily important,
while in a few it occupies her centrally. As we have noted, *Far Cry*'s
protagonist works in the publishing business and plays detective to
discover how voices and words expose their creator's character and
wreak havoc. Hector Bartlett's style is himself: intrusive, lying, seductive, self-centered, evil. The charlatan Hubert Mallindaine's
pagan fundamentalist revival session creates a riotous fervour akin
to that induced by current televangelists. The blackmail fictions,

various other letters, novelistic excerpts, and ballad bits in *Territorial Rights* demonstrate not exclusively the fraudulence that occupies Spark's attention, but the contrast between fiction as genuine attempt at truth and fiction as deliberate falsehood. This is the same creative contrast that concerns January Marlow in *Robinson*. In *Bachelors* Patrick Seton actually sells himself on the right-mindedness of his convincing and homicidal behaviour. The Abbess Alexandra in a very real sense consciously creates herself for public and even personal consumption. Harvey Gotham, in *The Only Problem*, is aware of everyone's ability to rationalize personal behaviour or even to proceed without any need to create good reasons. He is himself an example of such rationalizing, for good or ill. In *The Driver's Seat* Lise creates a scenario for her own death and its aftermath. The characters in *Hothouse by the East River* have willed a temporary earthly existence decades after their own demise. Dougal Douglas's presence, if not his efforts, induces those he encounters to behave in some grisly and several more amusing ways that bring about a comic ending for *The Ballad of Peckham Rye*. The ultimate point of the phone calls in *Memento Mori* is that those receiving the 'same' message create or re-create for the reader the history of their different lives, which are not the same at all. *Memento Mori* is the assemblage of these various reactions: by the characters' behaviour Spark builds her book and her thesis, and indirectly gives a boost to supporters of reader criticism.

The foregoing instances are relatively peripheral or minor in comparison to other concerns in the books cited. On the other hand, in a few additional novels creating or making is more nearly central. As its title implies, *The Public Image* is about almost nothing but the relationship between 'seem' and 'be'. This is Annabel Christopher's book, a *Bildingsroman* tracing in a depth both detailed and economical her gradual understanding of how reputations and even persons can be created by studio publicity departments as well as by individual imaginations (the *Memento Mori* theme again). Annabel must then decide, alone, who she is apart from who the studio and movie magazines say she is, and must confront the cost of abandoning her public image in favour of recapturing and reviving the private person who is always revered in Spark's novels.

Something like the same entanglement confronts Fleur Talbot in *Loitering with Intent*. Here the spirit is lighter and more farcical than in *Public Image*, which is decidedly darker, grimmer, even suicidal. Fleur, like Annabel, must cope with blackmailing, but the real connection between the two books lies in the complexities of discerning truth from falsehood, or honest writing – whether novel or autobiography – from dishonest writing. Because it is obvious that the public hardly cares about such a distinction or indeed comprehends it, Fleur is left to her own devices to fight Sir Quentin Oliver, who regards creativity as valuable only to the extent that it leads to financial profit, and who eagerly distorts the innocently constructed autobiographies of his duped literary society, intending to blackmail these poor souls. Fleur, on the other hand, is shown to be an honest editor in improving the primitive style of the club members' writings, and in writing an entirely fictitious book of her own, a novel. The borderline between fact and fiction, between lie and novel, becomes humorously and interestingly blurred when Oliver and Fleur steal and re-steal each other's manuscripts and when Fleur thereby has occasion to consider how or whether her editing of Oliver's devotees' work has influenced the making of her own book. As in *Robinson*, fiction, or the thing made, may have either falsehood or truth as its goal. Spark always strives for the latter.

With her very first novel, *The Comforters*, Spark tackled the double mystery of how fictions get made and of how, once made, they inevitably go on being re-made according to who reads them at any given time. Caroline Rose, a recent Catholic convert interested, like Spark, in absolute truth, is both a novelist and a student of fiction. *The Comforters* is the novel that Spark's narrator creates from the embattled tussles between Caroline's extra-authorial doings and her typewriting and speaking muse. Caroline is both driven by her voices to write what she writes, and insistently free to shape her own novel. The book we read is simultaneously the record of that ever-blurred contest and an invitation to contemplate what happens when we ingest this artifact. Caroline is fascinated by her committed belief in absolute truth, but the novel appears to prove her not so much defeated in her effort to convey absolutes as necessarily stuck with the fact that any conceivable absolutes will have to be carried by the chemistry that resulted in her novel when that chemistry encounters the mystery that is a reader's own aesthetic and moral chemistry. Any absolute will have to emerge from the interworkings of such a number of relatives. We're on our own as readers, but not for lack of Caroline's and Spark's efforts to guide us.

To conclude this essay I want to look at *Not to Disturb*, surely one of Spark's most ingenious and delightful works, and one that sums up for me the characteristics of her art. *Not to Disturb* is typical of Spark in being hyper-economical. It occurs overnight in one place, features a small cast of characters, impresses us as both ominous and hilarious, and leaves us pondering precisely what about these comparatively few gracefully styled pages has held out attention.

The plot is triggered, so to speak, by a crime of passion. Three people who are sexually involved with one another meet in a locked room and at some time during the night of their encounter die violently. The book, however, is the novel created by Spark's narrator from and about the various narratives and the film that the group of servants creates about the trio's relationship and demise and about their own involvement as servants. *Not to Disturb* manifests the creative process at work and the vivid-murky ties between this process and getting at the truth. Because Spark's is an absolute view, bolstered by Catholic belief, this novel shows us much of the flash-forward technique regularly found in these books. It is typical of Spark's narrators to give us certain outcomes casually, to remove suspense early on. In *Not to Disturb* this practice is one that the servant-creators of their own fictions indulge in happily. The servants treat as a *fait accompli* the slaughter to be revealed to the police the next morning. Consequently, the servants use tenses and moods interchangeably, as if they were divine, living an eternal now. This is puzzling or exasperating unless the reader is paying attention, but if the reader is alert this practice makes Spark's kind of sense and is very funny besides. For example, one servant says, 'There might be an unexpected turn of events' (68). To this, Lister, the butler, responds, 'There was sure to be something unexpected. . . . But what's done is about to be done and the future has come to pass' (68). In one sense, of course, this means merely that they've all finished their versions, and these are what will eventually be published or shown as definitive. In another sense, however, Spark is working with the familiar theological debate between God's knowing, forever now, what creatures have done and will do, and those creatures' treating their choices as free and necessarily past, present, or future in time. Time is not eternity, despite another servant's wonderful remark that 'To put it squarely . . . the eternal triangle has come full circle' (29).

*Not to Disturb* is clearly an exploration into the delights and mystery of making, of fictioning. The servants make fictions of the trio's demise and its accompanying flurry. The narrator gives us the servants' careers as artists and creators. Spark invents that narrator. The whole onion-skinned composite becomes a different whole fiction for each of us who discovers and re-creates it. Finally, given Spark's psychology and theology, over or within all these planes or spheres is the first and last Creator, the Maker of all. For this reason it is appropriate, rather than flippant or presumptuous, to speak of Spark's 'divine comedy'. The meaning here is of course not that Spark's work is indistinguishable from Dante's, but that her aesthetic-theistic vision is one that posits, indeed necessitates, the Being whose existence accounts for all other beings, and whose eternal purpose overlies all our temporal purposes. Thus the 'divine' element. The 'comedy', as for Dante, fits because of the implicit belief that, for all the evil that we are free to choose, God's master plan is good. We are not to be complacent or stupid, of course, but neither are we to be 'disturbed' if we have faith and do right.

Muriel Spark would almost certainly never write anything as doctrinaire-sounding as the preceding paragraph, and in fact a book like *The Driver's Seat* shows her awareness of the tragic sense untouched by Christian belief. Nevertheless, underlying her books is a consistent Dantean comic view of all that is. She has faith that there's a reason for what happens, whether we know the reason or not. It is not her philosophy that makes her a splendid writer, obviously; yet without that view she would perhaps not be a writer at all. I hope I have given some reasonable indication of why we should all be grateful for her writing.

### Notes

1.  In 1947 Muriel Spark became a member of the Royal Society of Literature. In 1949 she became an honorary member of PEN and was named a Fellow of the Royal Society of Literature.
2.  See 'My Conversion', *Twentieth Century* 170 (Autumn 1961): 58–63; and 'Keeping It Short – Muriel Spark Talks about Her Books to Ian Gillham', *The Listener*, (24 September 1970): 412.
3.  *The Art of the Real: Muriel Spark's Novels* (London and Toronto: Associated University Presses, 1988; Rutherford, New Jersey: Fairleigh Dickinson University Press).
4.  See Frank Kermode's interview with Spark in 'The House of Fiction:

Interviews with Seven English Novelists', *Partisan Review* 30 (Spring 1963): 79–82.
5. 'Edinburgh-born', *New Statesman* (10 August 1962): 180.
6. 'My Conversion' 60.

## A BIBLIOGRAPHY OF WRITINGS BY MURIEL SPARK

### (Hardback editions)

### Novels

*The Comforters* (London: Macmillan, 1957; Philadelphia: Lippincott, 1957).
*Robinson* (London: Macmillan, 1958; Philadelphia: Lippincott, 1958).
*Memento Mori* (London: Macmillan, 1959; Philadelphia: Lippincott, 1959).
*The Ballad of Peckham Rye* (London: Macmillan, 1960; Philadelphia: Lippincott, 1960).
*The Bachelors* (London: Macmillan, 1960; Philadelphia: Lippincott, 1961).
*The Prime of Miss Jean Brodie* (London: Macmillan, 1961; Philadelphia: Lippincott, 1962).
*The Girls of Slender Means* (London: Macmillan, 1963; New York: Knopf, 1963).
*The Mandelbaum Gate* (London: Macmillan, 1965; New York: Knopf, 1965).
*The Public Image* (London: Macmillan, 1968; New York: Knopf, 1968).
*The Driver's Seat* (London: Macmillan, 1970; New York: Knopf, 1970).
*Not to Disturb* (London: Macmillan, 1971; New York: Viking, 1972).
*The Hothouse by the East River* (London: Macmillan, 1973; New York: Viking, 1973).
*The Abbess of Crewe* (London: Macmillan, 1974; New York: Viking, 1974).
*The Takeover* (London: Macmillan, 1976; New York: Viking, 1976).
*Territorial Rights* (London: Macmillan, 1979; New York: Coward, McCann & Geoghegan, 1979).
*Loitering with Intent* (London: The Bodley Head, 1981; New York: Coward, McCann & Geoghegan, 1981).
*The Only Problem* (London: The Bodley Head, 1984; New York: Putnam, 1984).
*A Far Cry from Kensington* (London: Constable, 1988; New York: Houghton Mifflin, 1988).
*Symposium* (London: Constable, 1990; New York: Houghton Mufflin, 1990).

### Stories

*The Go-Away Bird and Other Stories* (London: Macmillan, 1958; Philadelphia: Lippincott, 1960).
*Collected Stories I* (London: Macmillan, 1967; New York: Knopf, 1968).
*The Stories of Muriel Spark* (New York: Dutton, 1985).

## Poetry

*The Fanfarlo and Other Verses* (Aldington (UK): Hand & Flower Press, 1952).
*Collected Poems I* (London: Macmillan, 1967; New York: Knopf, 1968).

## Play

*Doctors of Philosophy* (London: Macmillan, 1963; New York: Knopf, 1966).

## Biography

*Child of Light: A Reassessment of Mary Wollstonecraft Shelley* (Hadleigh (UK):
    Tower Bridge Publications, 1951; Revised as *Mary Shelley*, New York:
    Dutton, 1987).
*John Masefield* (London: Peter Nevill, 1953; New York: Coward & McCann,
    1966).

## Essays and Articles

'The Religion of an Agnostic: A Sacramental View of the World in the
    Writings of Proust', *Church of England Newspaper* (27 November 1953): 1.
'The Mystery of Job's Suffering', *Church of England Newspaper* (15 April
    1955): 7.
'How I Became a Novelist', *John O'London's Weekly*, 3 (61) (1 December 1960):
    683.
'My Conversion', *Twentieth Century*, 170 (Autumn 1961): 58–63.
'Edinburgh-born', *New Statesman*, 64 (10 August 1962): 180.
'The Brontës as Teachers', *New Yorker* (22 January 1966): 30–3.
'What Images Return', in *Memoirs of a Modern Scotland*, ed. Karl Miller
    (London: Faber and Faber, 1970), pp. 151–3.
'The Desegregation of Art', The Blashfield Foundation Address, *Proceedings
    of the American Academy of Arts and Letters 1971*, pp. 21–7.

## Miscellaneous

*Tribute to Wordsworth: A Miscellany of Opinion for the Centenary of the Poet's
    Death*, ed. with Derek Stanford (London: Wingate, 1950).
*A Selection of Poems by Emily Brontë*, edited with an introduction (London:
    Grey Walls Press, 1952).
*The Brontë Letters*, edited with an introduction (London: Peter Nevill, 1953;
    Norman, Okla.: University of Oklahoma Press, 1954).
*Emily Brontë: Her Life and Work*, ed. with Derek Stanford (London: Peter
    Owen, 1953; New York: Coward, McCann, 1966).
*My Best Mary: Selected Letters of Mary Shelley*, ed. with Derek Stanford
    (London: Wingate, 1953).
*Letters of John Henry Newman*, ed. with Derek Stanford (London: Peter Owen,
    1957).

*Voices at Play* [Stories and radio plays for the BBC] (London: Macmillan, 1961; Philadelphia: Lippincott, 1961).
*The Very Fine Clock* [children's book] (London: Macmillan, 1969; New York: Knopf, 1968).

## BIBLIOGRAPHY OF WRITINGS ABOUT MURIEL SPARK

### Bibliographies

Magill, Frank N., ed., *Magill's Bibliography of Literary Criticism*, Vol. 4 (Englewood Cliffs, New Jersey: Salem Press, 1979).
Pownall, David E., *Articles on Twentieth Century Literature; An Annotated Bibliography 1954–1970* (New York: Kraus-Thomson Organization, 1978).
Schwartz, Narda Lacey, ed., *Articles on Women Writers: A Bibliography* (Santa Barbara and Oxford: Clio Press, 1977).
Tominaga, Thomas T., and Wilma Schneidermeyer, *Iris Murdoch and Muriel Spark: A Bibliography*, Scarecrow Author Bibliographies, no. 27 (Metuchen, New Jersey: Scarecrow Press, 1976).

### Books and Monographs

Auerbach, Nina, *Communities of Women: An Idea in Fiction* (Cambridge: Harvard University Press, 1978).
Bold, Alan, *Muriel Spark*, Contemporary Writers Series (London and New York: Methuen, 1986).
Bold, Alan, ed., *Muriel Spark: An Odd Capacity for Vision* (London: Vision Press, 1984. Totowa, New Jersey: Barnes & Noble, 1984). This volume contains: Hart, Francis Russell, 'Ridiculous Demons', pp. 23–43; Hubbard, Tom, 'The Liberated Instant: Muriel Spark and the Short Story', pp. 167–82; Massie, Allan, 'Calvinism and Catholicism in Muriel Spark', pp. 94–107; Menzies, Janet, 'Muriel Spark: Critic into Novelist', pp. 111–31; Perrie, Walter, 'Mrs Spark's Verse', pp. 183–204; Pullin, Faith, 'Autonomy and Fabulation in the Fiction of Muriel Spark', pp. 71–93; Randisi, Jennifer L., 'Muriel Spark and Satire', pp. 132–46; Royle, Trevor, 'Spark and Scotland', pp. 147–66; and Shaw, Valerie, 'Fun and Games with Life-stories', pp. 44–70.
Edgecombe, Rodney Stennings, *Vocation and Identity in the Fiction of Muriel Spark* (Columbia and London: University of Missouri Press, 1990).
Hynes, Joseph, *The Art of the Real: Muriel Spark's Novels* (Rutherford, New Jersey: Fairleigh Dickinson University Press; London and Toronto: Associated University Presses, 1988).
Kemp, Peter, *Muriel Spark*, Novelists and Their World Series (London: Paul Elek, 1974).
Little, Judy, *Comedy and the Women Writer: Woolf, Spark, and Feminism* (Lincoln and London: University of Nebraska Press, 1983).
Malkoff, Karl, *Muriel Spark*, Columbia Essays on Modern Writers Series (New York and London: Columbia University Press, 1968).

Massie, Allan, *Muriel Spark* (Edinburgh: Ramsay Head Press, 1979).
Page, Norman, *Muriel Spark*, Macmillan Modern Novelists Series (London: Macmillan, 1990).
Perelman, Mickey, *Reinventing Reality: Patterns and Characters in the Novels of Muriel Spark* (New York: Peter Lang, 1989).
Richmond, Velma Bourgeois, *Muriel Spark* (New York: Frederick Ungar, 1984).
Stanford, Derek, *Muriel Spark: A Biographical and Critical Study* (includes a bibliography by Bernard Stone) (Fontwell: Centaur Press, 1963).
Stubbs, Patricia, *Muriel Spark*, Writers and Their Work Series (Harlow: Longman, for the British Council, 1973).
Walker, Dorothea, *Muriel Spark* (Boston: Twayne Publishers, 1988).
Whittaker, Ruth, *The Faith and Fiction of Muriel Spark* (New York: St. Martin's Press, 1982).

## Articles and Book-Segments

Adler, Renata, 'Muriel Spark', *On Contemporary Literature*, expanded edition, ed. Richard Kostelanetz (New York: Avon Books, 1969).
Baldanza, Frank, 'Muriel Spark and the Occult', *Wisconsin Studies in Contemporary Literature* 6 (1965): 190–203.
Berthoff, Warner, 'Fortunes of the Novel: Muriel Spark and Iris Murdoch', *Massachusetts Review* 8 (1967): 301–32.
Blodgett, Harriet, 'Desegregated Art by Muriel Spark', *International Fiction Review* 3 (January 1976): 25–9.
Bradbury, Malcolm, 'Muriel Spark's Fingernails', *Critical Quarterly* 14 (1972): 241–50. Reprinted in Bradbury's *Possibilities: Essays on the State of the Novel*, pp. 247–55 (London, Oxford, New York: Oxford University Press, 1973).
Byatt, A. S., 'Empty Shell', *New Statesman* (14 June 1968): 807–8.
Byatt, A. S., 'A Murder in Hell', *The Times* (24 September 1970): 14.
Byatt, A. S., 'Whittled and Spiky Art', *New Statesman* (15 December 1967): 848.
Casson, Allan, 'Muriel Spark's *The Girls of Slender Means*', *Critique* 7 (Spring-Summer 1965): 94–6.
Cruttwell, Patrick, 'Fiction Chronicle', *Hudson Review* 5 (24) (Spring 1971): 177–84.
Dobie, Ann B., 'Muriel Spark's Definition of Reality', *Critique* 12 (1970): 20–7.
Dobie, Ann B., '*The Prime of Miss Jean Brodie*: Muriel Spark Bridges the Credibility Gap', *Arizona Quarterly* 25 (Autumn 1969): 217–28.
Dobie, Ann B., and Carl Wooton, 'Spark and Waugh: Similarities by Coincidence', *Midwest Quarterly* 13 (July 1972): 423–34.
Duffy, Martha, Review of *The Driver's Seat*, *Time* (26 October 1970): 119.
Enright, D. J., 'Public Doctrine and Private Judging', *New Statesman* (15 October 1965): 563, 566.
Feinstein, Elaine, 'Loneliness Is Cold', *London Magazine*. n. s. 11 (February–March 1972): 177–80.
Gifford, Douglas, 'Modern Scottish Fiction', *Studies in Scottish Literature* 13 (1978): 250–73.
Greene, George, 'A Reading of Muriel Spark', *Thought* 43 (1968): 393–407.

Gross, John, 'Passionate Pilgrimage', *New York Review of Books* (28 October 1965): 12–15.

Grosskurth, Phyllis, 'The World of Muriel Spark: Spirits or Spooks?', *Tamarack Review* 39 (Spring 1966): 62–7.

Grumbach, Doris, Review of *The Mandelbaum Gate*, *America* 113 (23 October 1965): 474–8.

Harrison, Barbara Grizzuti, review of *Loitering with Intent*, *New York Times Book Review* (31 May 1981): 11.

Harrison, Bernard, 'Muriel Spark and Jane Austen', *The Modern English Novel: The Reader, the Writer, and the Work*, ed. Gabriel Josipovici (London: Open Books; New York: Barnes & Noble, 1976): 225–51.

Hart, Francis Russell, 'Region, Character, and Identity in Recent Scottish Fiction', *Virginia Quarterly Review* 43 (1967): 597–613.

Hart, Francis Russell, *The Scottish Novel: From Smollett to Spark* (Cambridge: Harvard University Press, 1978).

Holloway, John, 'Narrative Structure and Text Structure: Isherwood's *A Meeting by the River* and Muriel Spark's *The Prime of Miss Jean Brodie*', *Critical Inquiry* 1 (March 1975): 581–604.

Hosmer, Robert E. Jr. 'Writing with Intent: The Artistry of Muriel Spark' *Commonweal* 116 (21 April 1989): 223–41.

Hoyt, Charles Alva, 'Muriel Spark: The Surrealist Jane Austen', *Contemporary British Novelists*, ed. Charles Shapiro (Carbondale and Edwardsville: Southern Illinois University Press, 1965): 125–43.

Hynes, Joseph, 'After Marabar: Reading Forster, Robbe-Grillet, Spark', *Iowa Review* 5 (Winter 1974): 120–6.

Hynes, Samuel, 'The Prime of Muriel Spark', *Commonweal* 75 (23 February 1962): 567–8.

Jacobsen, Josephine, 'A Catholic Quartet', *Christian Scholar* 47 (1964): 139–54.

Karl, Frederick R., 'Muriel Spark', *A Reader's Guide to the Contemporary English Novel*, revised edition (New York: Farrar, Straus and Giroux, 1972).

Kelleher, V. M. K., 'The Religious Artistry of Muriel Spark', *Critical Review* (Melbourne) 18 (1976): 79–82.

Kennedy, Alan, 'Cannibals, Okapis, and Self-Slaughter in the Fiction of Muriel Spark', *The Protean Self: Dramatic Action in Contemporary Fiction* (New York: Columbia University Press, 1974): 151–211.

Kermode, Frank, 'The British Novel Lives', *Atlantic Monthly* 230 (July 1972): 85–8.

Kermode, Frank, *Continuities* (London: Routledge and Kegan Paul, 1968). Reprints two reviews under the titles of 'To *The Girls of Slender Means*' and 'Muriel Spark's *Mandelbaum Gate*', pp. 202–16.

Kermode, Frank, 'Diana of the Crossroads', *New Statesman* 91 (4 June 1976): 746–7.

Kermode, Frank, 'Foreseeing the Unforeseen', *The Listener* 86 (11 November 1971): 657–8.

Kermode, Frank, 'God's Plots', *The Listener* 78 (7 December 1967): 759–60.

Kermode, Frank, 'Judgement in Venice', *The Listener* 101 (26 April 1979): 584–5.

Kermode, Frank, *Modern Essays* (London: Collins Fontana Books, 1971). Reprints of the two reviews in *Continuities* (above) and a review of *The Public Image*, pp. 267–83.

Kermode, Frank, 'Sheerer Spark', *The Listener* 84 (24 September 1970): 425, 427.

Keyser, Barbara Y., 'Muriel Spark, Watergate, and the Mass Media', *Arizona Quarterly* 32 (1976): 146–53.

Laffin, Garry S., 'Muriel Spark's Portrait of the Artist as a Young Girl', *Renascence* 24 (Summer 1972): 213–23.

Leonard, Joan, 'Muriel Spark's Parables: The Religious Limits of Her Art', *Foundations of Religious Literacy*, ed. John V. Apczynski (Chico, California: Scholars' Press, 1982): 153–64.

Little, Judy, *Comedy and the Woman Writer: Woolf, Spark and Feminism* (Lincoln and London: University of Nebraska Press, 1983).

Lodge, David, 'Change from the Best', *Tablet* (12 May 1973): 442–3.

Lodge, David, 'Passing the Test', *Tablet* (10 October 1970): 978.

Lodge, David, 'Prime Cut', *New Statesman* (27 April 1979): 597.

Lodge, David, 'Prime Spark', *Tablet* (7 December 1974): 1185.

Lodge, David, 'The Uses and Abuses of Omniscience: Method and Meaning in Muriel Spark's *The Prime of Miss Jean Brodie*', *Critical Quarterly* 12 (1970): 235–57. Reprinted in Lodge's *The Novelist at the Crossroads and Other Essays on Fiction and Criticism* (London: Routledge and Kegan Paul, 1971): 119–44.

Malin, Irving, 'The Deceptions of Muriel Spark', *The Vision Obscured: Perceptions of Some Twentieth-Century Catholic Novelists*, ed. Melvin J. Friedman (New York: Fordham University Press, 1970): 95–107.

Malkoff, Karl, 'Demonology and Dualism: The Supernatural in Isaac Singer and Muriel Spark', *Critical Views of Isaac Bashevis Singer* (New York: New York University Press, 1969): 149–69.

May, Derment, 'Holy Outrage', *The Listener* 89 (1 March 1973): 283–4.

Mayne, Richard, 'Fiery Particle: On Muriel Spark', *Encounter* 25 (December 1965): 61–8.

McBrien, William, 'Muriel Spark: The Novelist as Dandy', *Twentieth-Century Women Novelists*, ed. Thomas F. Staley (Totowa, New Jersey: Barnes and Noble, 1982): 153–78.

Metzger, Linda, 'Muriel Spark', *Contemporary Authors*, new revised series, vol. 12 (Detroit: Gale Research Co., 1984): 450–7.

Miller, Karl, 'Hard Falls', *New Statesman* (3 November 1961): 662–3.

Murphy, Carol, 'A Spark of the Supernatural', *Approach* 60 (Summer 1966): 26–30.

Naipaul, V. S., 'Death on the Telephone', *New Statesman* (28 March 1959): 452.

Ohmann, Carol B., 'Muriel Spark's *Robinson*', *Critique* 8 (1965): 70–84.

Petersen, Virgilia, 'Few Were More Delightful, Lovely or Savage', *New York Times Book Review* (15 September 1963): 4, 5, 44.

Potter, Nancy A. J., 'Muriel Spark: Transformer of the Commonplace', *Renascence* 17 (1965): 115–20.

Quinton, Anthony, Review of *The Ballad of Peckham Rye*, *London Magazine* 7 (May 1960): 78–81.

Quinton, Anthony, Review of *Memento Mori*, *London Magazine* 6 (September 1959): 84–8.

Raban, Jonathan. 'On Losing the Rabbit', *Encounter* 40 (May 1973): 80–5.

Raban, Jonathan, 'Vague Scriptures', *New Statesman* 82 (12 November 1971): 657–8.

Ratcliffe, Michael, 'Hell and Chaos as Farce', *The Times* (1 March 1973): 14.

Raven, Simon, 'Heavens Below', *Spectator* (20 September 1963): 354.

Ray, Philip E., 'Jean Brodie and Edinburgh: Personality and Place in Muriel [*sic*] Spark's *The Prime of Miss Jean Brodie*', *Studies in Scottish Literature* 13 (1978): 24–31.

Reed, Douglas, 'Taking Cocktails with Life', *Books and Bookmen*, 17 (11 August 1971): 10–14.

Richmond, Velma Bourgeois, 'The Darkening Vision of Muriel Spark', *Critique* 15 (1973): 71–85.

Ricks, Christopher, 'Extreme Instances', *New York Review of Books* (19 December 1968): 31–2.

Rowe, Margaret Moan, 'Muriel Spark', *Dictionary of Literary Biography*, vol. 15, Part 2: *British Novelists, 1930–1959*, ed. Bernard Oldsey (Detroit: Gale Research Co., 1983): 490–507.

Sage, Lorna, 'Bugging the Nunnery', *Observer* (10 November 1974): 33.

Sage, Lorna, 'Roman Scandals', *Observer* (6 June 1976): 29.

Schneider, Harold W., 'A Writer in Her Prime: the Fiction of Muriel Spark', *Critique* 5 (1962): 28–45.

Sears, Sallie, 'Too Many Voices', *Partisan Review* 31 (Summer 1964): 471, 473–5.

Soule, George, 'Must a Novelist Be an Artist?', *Carleton Miscellany* 5 (Spring 1964): 92–8.

Stanford, Derek, *Inside the Forties: Literary Memoirs 1937–1957* (London: Sidgwick and Jackson, 1977).

Stanford, Derek, 'The Work of Muriel Spark: An Essay on Her Fictional Method', *Month* 28 (1962): 92–9. Reprinted in slightly altered form in Stanford's *Muriel Spark* (op. cit., above).

Stubbs, Patricia, 'Two Contemporary Views on Fiction: Iris Murdoch and Muriel Spark', *English* 23 (1974): 102–10.

Swinden, Patrick, *Unofficial Selves: Character in the Novel from Dickens to the Present Day* (London: Macmillan, 1973).

Thomas, Edward, Review of *The Driver's Seat*, *London Magazine*, n. s. 10 (October 1970): 95–8.

*Times Literary Supplement* (*TLS*), 'Crabbed Age and Youth' (17 April 1959): 221.

(*TLS*), 'Faith and Fancy' (4 March 1960): 141.

(*TLS*), 'Grub Street Gothic' (12 November 1971): 1409.

(*TLS*), 'Hell in the Royal Borough' (20 September 1963): 701.

(*TLS*), 'Meal for a Masochist' (25 September 1970): 1074.

(*TLS*), 'Mistress of Style' (3 November 1961): 785.

(*TLS*), 'Questing Characters' (22 February 1957): 109.

(*TLS*), 'Questions and Answers' (27 June 1958): 357.

(*TLS*), 'Sense and Sensitivity' (19 December 1958): 733.

(*TLS*), 'Shadow Boxing' (2 March 1973): 229.

(*TLS*), 'Shallowness Everywhere' (13 June 1968): 612.

(*TLS*), 'Stag Party' (14 October 1960): 657.

(*TLS*), 'Talking about Jerusalem' (14 October 1965): 913.

Updike, John, 'Between a Wedding and a Funeral', *The New Yorker* 39 (14 September 1963): 192–4.
Updike, John, 'Creatures of the Air', *The New Yorker* 37 (30 September 1961): 161–7.
Updike, John, 'Fresh from the Forties', *The New Yorker* 57 (8 June 1981): 148–56.
Updike, John, 'A Romp with Job', *The New Yorker* 60 (23 July 1984): 104–7.
Updike, John, 'Seeresses' *The New Yorker* 52 (29 November 1976): 164–74.
Updike, John, 'Topnotch Witcheries', *The New Yorker* 50 (6 January 1975): 76–8.
Waugh, Evelyn. 'Something Fresh', *Spectator* (22 February 1957): 256.
Waugh, Evelyn. 'Threatened Genius: Difficult Saint', *Spectator* (7 July 1961): 28.
Whittaker, Ruth, '"Angels Dining at the Ritz": The Faith and Fiction of Muriel Spark', *The Contemporary English Novel*, eds. Malcolm Bradbury and David Palmer, Stratford-upon-Avon Studies 18 (New York: Holmes and Meier, 1980): 157–79.
Wildman, John Hazard, 'Translated by Muriel Spark', *Nine Essays in Modern Literature*, ed. Donald E. Stanford (Baton Rouge: Louisiana State University Press, 1965): 129–44.
Wilson, A. N., review of *Loitering with Intent*, *Spectator* (23 May 1981): 20–1.
Wilson, Angus, 'Journey to Jerusalem'. *Observer* (17 October 1965): 28.
Wood, Michael, review of *The Takeover*, *New York Review of Books* (11 November 1976): 30.

### Interviews

Armstrong, George, *Guardian* (30 September 1970): 8.
Barber, Lynn, 'The Elusive Magician', *Independent on Sunday* (23 September 1990): 8–10.
'Bugs and Mybug', *Listener* (28 November 1974): 706.
Daspin, Eileen, 'Good Old Girls', *W* (21–8 January 1991): 14.
Emerson, Joyce, 'The Mental Squint of Muriel Spark', *The Sunday Times* (30 September 1962): 14.
Gillham, Ian, 'Keeping It Short – Muriel Spark Talks about Her Books to Ian Gillham', *Listener* 84 (24 September 1970): 411–13.
Glendinning, Victoria, 'Talk with Muriel Spark', *New York Times Book Review* (20 May 1979): 47–8.
Hamilton, Alex, *Guardian* (8 November 1974): 10.
Holland, Mary, 'The Prime of Muriel Spark', *Observer* (Colour Supplement) (17 October 1965): 8–10.
Howard, Elizabeth Jane, 'Writers in the Present Tense', *Queen*, Centenary Issue (August 1961): 136–46.
Kermode, Frank, 'The House of Fiction: Interviews with Seven English Novelists', *Partisan Review* 30 (Spring 1963): 61–82. The Spark interview covers pp. 79–82.
Koenig, Rhoda, 'Bella Donna Muriel Spark', *Vogue* (UK edition) (September 1990): 368–9; 420.

Lord, Graham, 'The Love Letters That Muriel Spark Refused to Buy', *Sunday Express* (4 March 1973): 6.

Muggeridge, Malcolm, 'Appointment with . . .', Granada Television (2 June 1961) Unpublished.

Sage, Lorna, 'The Prime of Muriel Spark', *Observer* (30 May 1976): 11.

Toynbee, Philip, *Observer* (Colour Supplement) (7 November 1971): 73–4.

## MURIEL SPARK

Muriel Sarah Spark was born on 1 February 1918, in Edinburgh, to a Jewish father, Bernard Camberg, and a Gentile mother, Sarah Elizabeth Uezzell Camberg. From 1924 to 1936 she attended James Gillespie's School in Edinburgh. In 1937, in Rhodesia, she married S. O. Spark and bore a son, Robin. In 1938 she was divorced.

In 1944 Spark returned to England from Africa and worked in political intelligence for the government. In 1945 she worked as a press agent and founded a literary magazine, *Forum*. This was her poetry period. In 1947 she was an editor of *Poetry Review* and became a member of the Royal Society of Literature. In 1949 she was named a Fellow of the Royal Society of Literature, General Secretary of the Poetry Society, and an honorary member of PEN. In 1950 she became Review Editor of *European Affairs*, and co-edited *Tribute to Wordsworth*. In 1951 she won the *Observer* prize for 'The Seraph and the Zambesi', a short story, and published her biography of Mary Shelley. In 1952 she published *The Fanfarlo and Other Verses* and a selection of Emily Brontë's poetry. In 1953 she wrote a biography, *John Masefield*, co-authored an appreciation of Emily Brontë, co-edited a collection of Mary Shelley's letters, was received into the Anglican Church, and began reading Newman's works.

In 1954 Spark became a Roman Catholic, edited selected letters of the Brontës, and received an advance from Macmillan for a first novel. In 1957 *The Comforters*, her first novel, appeared, and she co-edited Newman's letters.

From 1958 to 1988 she published eighteen additional novels. *The Stories of Muriel Spark* (1985) is the latest compilation of her short fiction. She has lived in Israel briefly (1961), in New York City (1962–6 and since 1988, intermittently), occasionally in England, but mainly in Tuscany (since 1966). Her play, *Doctors of Philosophy*, was produced in 1962 and published in 1963. She received awards for *The Mandelbaum Gate*, and several of her novels have been filmed. In 1967 she was named Commander, Order of the British Empire.

# 10

# 'See Me As Sisyphus, But Having A Good Time': the Fiction of Fay Weldon

JENNY NEWMAN

Fay Weldon writes survival manuals for women. Her fiction demonstrates the value of female independence, not only financial, but emotional. Even her luckiest characters live precariously. Sooner or later a heroine's husband will run away with a younger woman, or a damaging secret come to light from the past, or her boss give her the sack in a fit of sexual pique, or her landlord will evict her for the same reason. Then she will find out about life 'down among the women', a phrase made famous by the publication of Weldon's second novel. Here circumstances are reduced and the wages exploitative; friends gossip and old lovers find good reasons for not helping. But Weldon's overall message is optimistic, and escape routes are provided for any woman who realizes that she is in part responsible for her own destiny.

Weldon writes mainly about women, without ever idealizing them. Her characters fall in love with clumsy, callous or expedient men, their pregnancies are unplanned, their children sometimes neglected or, worse, lost altogether. In every novel women let each other down, begrudging the looks and despising the talent of their friends, stealing their husbands – and even their children – if they can get away with it. In other words, they often behave just as badly as any of Weldon's male characters.

Usually, as with the eponymous heroine of *Praxis*, feminism sneaks up on them unawares. Without ever becoming ideologues, Weldon's characters are willing to change once they have seen the point of sisterhood. 'When women can survive by themselves,' she claims, 'and have a man as a matter of choice, an optional extra, women are far less ready to see men as possessions or other women as competitors or rivals' (Interview with John Haffenden in *Novelists in Interview* (London and New York; Methuen, 1985) (hereafter Haffenden): 315). Her men never develop, and we are seldom told why they act as they do. If male readers find these characters exceptionally weak, says Weldon, it is because men are accustomed to seeing themselves represented as 'noble heroes, carrying the action along': 313. She aims to redress the balance.

Fay Weldon began her working life answering problem letters for the *Daily Mirror*, then writing what she now describes as propaganda for the Foreign Office, and then, most importantly, as an advertising copywriter (hers was the famous Sixties' slogan, 'Go To Work On An Egg'). Writing television advertisements led, by her own account, to writing plays: 'Television commericals are tiny little plays selling a product, and I worked up to longer plays selling ideas, which was much more gratifying' (*Boston Globe*, 3 April 1988: 73).

The plot of Weldon's first novel, *The Fat Woman's Joke* (1967), looks lightweight compared with her later fiction, perhaps because it began life as a radio play. Esther partly resembles C, an aspect of the author's own temperament she once personified in an interview, who spends a lot of time staring into space and eating too much bread and butter (Wandor, 162). The voice of Esther herself dominates one of the novel's two strands, as she is cajoled by her *soi-disant* friend, Phyllis, into divulging the reasons for her flight to Earl's Court.

As a device this is clumsy, because Esther is astute enough to see that her confidante is both devious and 'invincibly stupid' (8). But intimate conversations are to remain part of Weldon's technique for some time, her dislike of interior monologue making them an indispensable means of describing her characters' inner lives. Not until the surrealistic heroines of her later fiction does Weldon attempt to create a psyche through revealing its thought processes. In *The Fat Woman's Joke*, the cosy talk enjoyed by this improbable pair is not to be jeopardized – even when Esther divines Phyllis's adultery with Alan, Esther's husband.

The second narrative voice is wittier and brusquer, a chronicle of the past in the Sussman household, and at Alan's office, from day one to the final day eight of the fateful diet which led to the breakdown of the Sussman marriage. Here we watch the interplay of social forces, including the Esther of a few weeks earlier, as the basement present is contextualized by the domestic past – until the two strands coincide with Alan's arrival at the basement where Esther and Phyllis sit talking.

Esther's addiction to food began as a housewife's route to creativity through cooking, and ended in the emblematically female space of her damp, dark basement as an atavistic urge to engross everything in sight, 'frozen chips and peas and hamburgers, and sliced bread with bought jam and fish paste, and baked beans and instant puddings, and cakes and biscuits from packets' (7). It is in part a regression to nursery fare; in part a strictly adult pleasure, registered as both sensuous and forbidden, a secret love affair undermining all the ideals of the homemaker: 'There is nothing, she would think, more delicious than the icing of bought chocolate cake, eaten in the silence and privacy of the night'; and finally, such eating suggests what a later character calls 'blowing up' (*The Heart of the Country*, 27) – a female rage which Weldon highlights by isolating her heroine and then adding to her psychological weight by contrasting her with the meretricious Phyllis.

By becoming unacceptably large, Esther flouts society and re-asserts her own integrity, while adulterous Phyllis and adulterous Susan, both of whom attempt to undermine her position as wife, remain thin. It is monumental Esther, purged of the desire to overeat by telling her story, who is validated at the end of the novel when her husband renounces extra-marital sex and asks her to come home.

Esther arrogates to herself the role of narrator in the opening pages:

> Then I will tell you about it . . . It is a story of patterns but not endings, meanings but no answers, and jokes where it would be nice if no jokes were. You have never heard a tale quite like this before and that in itself you will find quite hard to endure. Are you sitting comfortably? (13)

In the conversations which dominate the narrative present, the wry note in Esther's voice often resembles Weldon's own. But there is too much of a jump between this sturdy, judgmental recluse and Esther of the little-girl lisp in the second narrative skein, where she figures as Mrs Sussman.

Weldon believes that readers like writers to be cleverer than they are (*Letters to Alice*, 139); yet she seldom adopts the role of the omniscient narrator. For her the challenge lies in inventing a character bright enough to dazzle the reader while remaining flawed enough to be interesting.

By the time she reaches *Praxis* (1978), Weldon has resolved two problems apparent in *Down Among the Women* (1971) and *Female Friends* (1975): for the first time, the unfolding tale has helped to shape the 'I' who reflects on it, and vice-versa; and she has dropped her experiment of interspersing the narrative with short extracts written in play format in favour of spare, polished, plot-propelling dialogue. Light years away from the stultified talk of *The Fat Woman's Joke*, it is evidence of the writer's continuing involvement in the theatre despite the difference in layout, and marks the beginning of her great middle period.

Weldon's early years in advertising are still apparent in her staccato prose, and the technique she began using to good effect in *Remember Me*: isolating carefully honed phrases from the rest of the page to maximize their effect. It may be a little fanciful to claim, as Olga Kenyon does, that this use of double spacing is 'postmodernist' (126). Weldon herself, often the best commentator on her own work, gives a lucid description of the advantages of her early training:

> Designers and topographers actually teach you the look upon the page. Words are given resonance by their positions, they must be displayed properly. If you wish to give something emphasis, you surround it by space (Haffenden, 320).

In order to make a success of her own career in advertising, Praxis too acquires the skill of honing and fining sentences down 'to fill the brief and fit the space available' (218). Yet Weldon's own attitudes to this world remain sceptical, despite – or perhaps because of – her own early experience. In *The Fat Woman's Joke* she poked fun at Alan, so suggestible he thinks he may have been sold a car by his own copy. Often she presents the copywriter – manipulating consumers and purveying received ideas – as the antithesis of creative artists such as David Evans in *Female Friends*; or else the tension exists within a single character, such as Kim in *Down Among the Women*, or Alan himself, who started out in art school, and still fancies himself a painter *manqué*.

Praxis's slogans read like a travesty of the creative impulse of her author, who claims to write books with intent to reform (Haffenden,

308). Women who read Praxis's copy are encouraged to depend on a man to support them – a tendency all women need to struggle against, in Weldon's view (Haffenden, 312). Her success shows that language is as powerful when used for trivial and immoral ends as for good. '"God made her a woman," [Praxis] wrote blissfully, "love made her a mother – with a little help from electricity"' (218).

Praxis herself is by this time juggling a job with a complicated family life. When she tries to target working mothers like herself, the company resists as part of a backlash against women's growing independence. Although Praxis continues to work there, Weldon is not too hard on her heroine's doublethink, because she is by now supporting not just one family but two. The confrontation between Praxis – in high heels, black mesh stockings and an Ossie Clark dress – and a roomful of angry feminists is one of the most ideologically pointed in the book. Between them lie cuttings of her advertisements, 'scored with red markings and indignant exclamation marks' (231). Praxis does, in time, come to think more and more like Irma; but she is by no means routed by her first brush with the sisterhood.

Weldon has counted herself a feminist from the beginning of her career; but not a feminist writer 'because that would imply the novels were written because I was a feminist' (Haffenden, 313). A dislike of fanaticism often surfaces in her work, along with the suggestion that a strong commitment to feminism can de-sex or even dehumanize. In *Down Among the Women*, for instance, Byzantia, now a young adult, despises her mother and her mother's friends for continuing to see success in terms of men. She is like her grandmother, but 'where Wanda struggled against the tide and gave up, exhausted, Byzantia has it behind her, full and strong' (233). This makes for an inspiring end to their saga; and yet the final message, 'We are the last of the women', coming from a member of her mother's generation, implies that Byzantia is not fully female. The same suspicion of confident young women is re-echoed in the ageing Praxis's view of her fellow-passengers on the bus:

> They are satiated by everything, hungry for nothing. They are what I wanted to be; they are what I worked for them to be: and now I see them, I hate them. They have found their own solution to the three-fold pain – one I never thought of. They do not try, as we did, to understand it and get the better of it. They simply wipe out the pain by doing away with its three centres – the heart, the

soul and the mind. Brilliant! Heartless, soulless, mindless – free! (14).

Sometimes Weldon goes so far as to make feminist ideologues seem physically repellent. Praxis's response to the unaccommodated femaleness of Irma and her new friends looks forward to Ruth's responses to the feminist collective in *The Life and Loves of a She-Devil*: Praxis sees

> a great many brownish, sinewy, sweaty arms in the room: too many rather large, shiny noses, strong jaws, wild heads of hair, intense pairs of eyes, pale lips, and rather dirty sets of toes cramped stockingless into sandals (231).

By comparison with Praxis they all seem inhuman, and Irma's expectation that Praxis will go on supporting her and her children with her earnings from the vilified advertising agency typifies a hypocrisy far smugger and more grating than Praxis's own.

Perhaps this suspicion of thorough-going feminists springs from Weldon's belief that art and ideology do not mix. 'Fortunately,' she claims, 'in fiction there are this week's truths and next week's truths' (Haffenden, 314). As Praxis's name suggests, her grasp on life is not theoretical, but practical. Her education has come through experience – of war, illegitimacy, incest, adultery and madness. Her Greek name, her inadvertent sexual encounter with her father, even her big toe, pulped by one of the New Women on the bus, all suggest that she is a contemporary Oedipus. But in this female version of the myth we are more than the sum of our pasts. Knowledge means survival, not death, and women blinker themselves to it at their peril.

Weldon's heroines, like the author herself, believe in passing on their learning to other women. Gemma in *Little Sisters* told young Elsa her life story in fairy-tale form, the better to instruct her. But often Gemma's judgment is as misleading as the advice of Jane Austen's Emma to Harriet Smith. Nor could Phyllis in *The Fat Woman's Joke* be expected to take Esther's advice seriously. But in *Praxis* the instructions are directed at the reader, striking a new note, more urgent and solemn than before: 'Watch Praxis. Watch her carefully. Look, listen, learn' (109). This is the heroine grown old, cutting into the third-person narrative of her young life; a good device, because it is the way the child develops through adulthood into an old woman that makes this strong, sombre story cohere like no earlier Weldon novel.

The organization of her next book, *Puffball*, marks another new departure. Set in the vicinity of Glastonbury Tor, it reflects both the move of the Weldon family to Somerset, and Weldon's own experience, like her heroine Liffey's, of a *placenta praevia*. Pregnant at the time, she wrote *Puffball* believing she was going to die.

Unlike Praxis at twenty-eight, Liffey is immature, and her dearth of experience has left her without much food for thought. The red star, Betelegeuse, has been replaced by the earthier puffballs as the novel's central symbol, to which Liffey's responses are physical rather than intellectual. 'The smooth round swelling of the fungus' (19) makes her think of a belly swollen by pregnancy, whereas her husband, Richard, thinks of a brain in a laboratory jar. When Tucker, a neighbouring farmer, kicks the fungus into smithereens, Liffey feels a pain in her middle which is proleptic of her pregnancy which is to dominate the rest of the novel.

Praxis's lawless side – the woman who notes her hands growing darker, older and more her own, and later uses those same hands to murder a baby – has no counterpart in Liffey. Instead we have Mabs, the local witch, Tucker's wife and Liffey's enemy. Weldon engineers some striking contrasts between these two versions of female power:

> Liffey bent to riddle the fire and her little buttocks were tight and rounded. The backside of a naughty child, not of a grown woman, who knows the power and mirk that lies beneath, and shrouds herself in folds of cloth. So thought Mabs (43).

Liffey is too much the child-bride to gain an easy victory. 'Does infidelity matter?' asks the heroine of a later novel (*The Heart of the Country*, 25). It is a question worth asking, because most of Weldon's plots hinge on adultery, what she describes in *The Shrapnel Academy* as a decade's fidelity flashing into infidelity 'within the drunken silvery hour' (63). What Weldon concludes there holds good for Liffey after Mabs has manoeuvred Tucker into seducing her new neighbour on the kitchen floor, so that Richard will never know for certain who is the father of the baby: 'Yes, is the answer. Yes, yes, yes' (63).

'Novels for me,' Weldon has said, 'usually have a proposition which you examine in literary terms, without being sure of the

answer' (Haffenden, 307). The proposition in *Puffball* is that women
are victims of their own biology, a view already expressed graphic-
ally by Praxis:

> Nature does not know best, or if it does, it is on the man's side.
> Nature gives us painful periods, leucorrhoea, polyps, thrush,
> placenta praevia, headaches, cancer and in the end death (147).

Originally, Weldon has intended to explore this conflict by writing a
gynaecological handbook on one side and a story on the other, just
to keep readers interested, but in the end she had to interweave them
(*Women's Review*, 9: July 1986). The 'Inside Liffey' chapters comprize
the textbook strand, describing the gradual but dramatic development of the foetus. Over its battle for survival Zature reigns supreme
– that is, Nature with its initial N turned on its side by Weldon to
remind us that the 'wide-eyed, clear-eyed, purposeful Nature' that
we prefer to see is an illusion, because there is no purpose. Zature is
a blind mistress. Ostensibly Liffey has ethical decisions to make. At
the same time, her hormones are shown to be propelling her towards
conceiving a child by the nearest man to hand.

*Puffball* was in general well reviewed, with Jim Crace, for instance,
saying he was tempted to call it faultless (*Quarto*, March 1980: 15).
Subsequently Weldon said the novel (her favourite among her own
works) seemed to her 'a very complex book, far more complex than
when I wrote it, a pattern of opposites and contradictions and
polarizations' (Haffenden, 307). But some of these contradictions are
never adequately resolved. We can accept that the foetus, which
figures quite prominently, has no choice but to fight for survival. But
it is harder to understand why the two main adults are likewise
ruled by a biological imperative – reproduction – as Weldon rein-
forces the dangerous assumption that women have a special connection with nature. One woman's dedication to wrecking the life of
another sits uneasily with the novel's social side, cast as a modern
morality tale with all its attendant notions of choice, and the triumph
of Good over Evil after a pitched battle between Liffey's sweet
generosity and Mabs's malevolence.

Weldon is a prolific writer who continues to find satisfaction in
learning new ways of communicating, turning her hand, as she says,
'with what seems to some as indecent haste, from novels to screen-
plays to stage and radio plays' (Wendy Brandmark, *Fay Weldon*
(London: British Council, 1988) (hereafter Brandmark)). Elsewhere

she explains that each new genre demands a different technique, difficult to master at first, but afterwards as easy as throwing a switch (Haffenden, 318).

Of the three separate strands of *The President's Child* (1988), the idea for a thriller came first – the story of a woman, Isabel Acre, who has told no-one that her six-year old son, Jason, is the result of an illicit sexual idyll with Dandy Ivell, who is now being groomed for the United States Presidency. Jason is growing to look dangerously like his father. The attempts of the hit men, Joe and Pete, to solve through violence the problem of Dandy's past, demonstrate the vulnerability of women and children who get in the way of a man's rise to power.

The second strand is domestic, the home life of Isabel in Camden Town with Homer, her husband, met on her return flight for America after that fateful fortnight. The third skein is that of Maia, who comes closest to standing in for Weldon herself. Housebound, it is predictable that she should become Isabel's confidante, so her role as narrator is more convincingly shaped by her present circumstances than even Praxis's was, as she dishes out great slabs of Isabel's past to the neighbours. Maia's own reflections – on Isabel, on the neighbours themselves, on the favourite Weldon topics of men, sex, children and marriage, and on the nature of her own hysteric blindness – punctuate the narrative and strike its most literary note. Emphasizing her resemblance to a choric commentary on the action are exclamations, echoes and repetitions: *'Pit-pat, spitter-spat.* Listen! How the wind blows against the window-pane' (5). She is an author-surrogate, wise in spite of herself owing to the blindness which accords her a special status as the community story-teller.

'Is it true about Isabel?' asks Hilary. 'Or will you be making it up?' (6). As a narrator, Maia has granted herself the license to do either, and so compelling a Scheherazade is she that the glissade from first to third person which jars in *The Fat Woman's Joke* and *Down Among the Women* becomes utterly convincing here, as we forget that neither Maia nor Isabel nor any other character could have known about half the episodes in her story, including the plot of Joe (Potato) Murphy and Pete (Kitten) Sikorski to kill Isabel and Jason. Maia's recovered sight at the end of the novel comes as a striking affirmation of the enforced inwardness of a story-teller's life: time spent interpreting the lives of other women leads to a dramatic renewal of vision.

In *Puffball* Liffey's unborn child is a magical ally. Even in her crisis, when Mabs has slammed the door on her and there is a trail of blood whenever she moves, Liffey feels the touch of his spirit, 'still clear, still light and bright, almost elegant' (251), before he emerges from the womb to smile with uncanny beneficence on his arch-enemy. And as he strongly resembles Richard the happy ending is complete, with Weldon revising her original thesis that the father is the enemy of the unborn child.

In *The President's Child*, Weldon reverts to her first position; and far from making things better, Jason's growing likeness to his father – unbelievably it becomes obvious to the public after photographs of father and child appear on different pages of *Cosmopolitan* – becomes a testament to the lie on which Isabel has based her marriage, and precipitates a near catastrophe. Even so, Jason is Weldon's most engaging child character, and what tension there is in the thriller plot mounts because he may be at risk.

Weldon approves of women with a strong maternal instinct. Yet her fictional mothers often fail to take much interest in their progeny. Conveniently, their children either leapfrog quickly into adulthood, like Byzantia, or else they vanish, like Little Nell in the later *Hearts and Lives of Men* (1987), who does not reappear until she is fully adult and exceptionally talented. Frequently they develop a Dickensian gift from bringing themselves up, like Praxis and Hypatia, miniature adults both; or else, like Praxis's own children, Claire and Robert, they are so boring that their mother, Moll Flanders-like, contrives to forget about them when she moves on to her next marriage. But Jason, roaring, stamping and charming his way through the novel, becomes impossible to forget. Like his mother, the reader is duped into believing he is a delinquent. But here Weldon admits to what she herself describes a 'rather sneaky trick' (Haffenden 307).

By the end of the novel Homer stands revealed for the monster he always was; but that does not mean that it was right, in the beginning, for Isabel to attempt to deceive him. Elsewhere, Weldon proposes that the writers who get the best and most lasting response from readers are those who 'offer a happy ending through some kind of moral development' (*Letters to Alice*, 83). Maia has added to her stock of wisdom, and so have we. But we also need to know what Isabel has learned from her past, and if Jason was harmed by her early ruse, and Weldon's failure to tell us seems like a failure in responsibility.

There is an ethical question at the core of Weldon's ninth novel, likewise, but here her approach to the issue is more direct, even though the heroine's actions are far more controversial than Isabel's. *The Life and Loves of a She-Devil* (1983) succeeded in 'frightening men and amazing feminists' (*Boston Globe*, 3 April 1988). Its mainspring is the classic Weldon rivalry between the ugly, discardable wife and the glamorous mistress, both updated since Weldon first pitted them against each other in *The Fat Woman's Joke*.

Weldon is a partisan, unashamedly on the side of women like Esther, or Madeleine, the divorced wife in *Remember Me*, whom she regards as one of an economic sub-group whose members are doomed to eke out their lives in dreary flats which form the starkest possible contrast to their ex-husbands' opulent homes, their only crime a failure to arrest time and stay forever young. Her first wives usually combine moral authority with a more robust intelligence than the second ones – like Wanda, who has the guts to say to Kim he is becoming a sham of a painter, while Susan cannot tell one canvas from another; or Ruth herself, who can write just as good a romantic novel as Mary Fisher, but disdains to have it published. Ruth is in part responsible for telling her own story, whereas Mary Fisher, like all the other mistresses and second wives, is denied access to the authority of a first-person narrative. Notable exceptions to this rule, like Praxis, and the heroine of the later *Leader of the Band* (1988) are made to learn the error of their ways, and by the time they speak as 'I' they already know better than to steal another woman's husband.

For the first part of *The Life and Loves of a She-Devil*, hulking Ruth with the hairy moles on her chin behaves just as a feminist should, says Weldon, purposefully putting the past behind her as she sets fire to the suburban home that used to absorb so much of her energy, dumping her children (another unlikeable pair) on her husband and his mistress, and setting out to make her fortune.

But Weldon has grown less optimistic about what women want, and how likely they are to get it. Her first heroine, Esther, treated her rival, Phyllis, with undisguised contempt for having had plastic surgery: 'That you, a decent woman . . . should be so seduced by masculine values that you allow your breasts to be split open and stuffed with plastic' (The Fat Woman's Joke 103).

Bobbo, unlike Alan, will never return to his wife while she remains fat and ugly. But Ruth still loves Bobbo and wants him back. Her 'cosmetic' operation means future pain when walking, and a dangerous circulation problem after the necessary looping and folding of the nerves and muscles. This is more than any foolish concession to masculine taste; yet in a later article Weldon defends Ruth's decision:

> I'm glad she did it. I'm on Ruth's side though I get a lot of tut-tutting from right-minded readers. Irresponsible. Dangerous. Ruth should have done what she *ought*, faced up to things, not what she *wanted*, side-stepping God's will. But that's always said of women, isn't it; they're expected to carry the moral burden of the world, allowing men to walk free. And now in novels too.
>
> Nobody tells men writers, I suspect, what their characters *ought* to do ('Suture Shock', *Mirabella* July 1989).

If Praxis was a female Oedipus, and the dead Madeleine a woman Dracula returning to trouble the bourgeois home, then Ruth's story becomes a version of the Frankenstein legend. Which one is the monster? Mrs Black frequently calls her surgeon husband Frankenstein, and expects to see in Ruth a monster 'with the plates of her scalp pinned together by iron bolts' (223). Ruth can also be seen as the maker, paying for her own female flesh to be recreated, not in God's image, or Adam's, but that of another woman. With her capacity for suffering the sign of an unconquerable determination, Ruth makes it clear she is a Prometheus yet more modern than Mary Shelley's, explicitly taking up arms against God himself: 'Lucifer tried and failed, but he was male. She thought she might do better, being female' (82).

Ruth brings a brooding intensity to her she-devil reflections which punctuate the narrative. With her cold blood and slow pulse she succeeds in becoming 'heartless, soulless, mindless – free' in a manner even Praxis could never have envisaged as she watched the young women on the bus. For once, the heroine has no confidante. Ruth briefly befriends Nurse Hopkins, then passes on. A female friend is no more essential to Ruth's grand plan that it was to Medea's or Joan of Arc's. Her energy is focussed on Bobbo, and her determination to win him back turns the narrative into one woman's hymn of hatred for another: 'I hope the tower burns and Mary Fisher with it, sending the smell of burning flesh out over the waves' (14).

Weldon's first heroine triumphed by making herself larger than life. By the time we get to Ruth the comic turn has indeed, to quote the closing words of the novel, turned serious, making the first fat

woman's refusal to diet look naively optimistic. Ruth's plastic surgery is not, as Patricia Waugh suggests, 'the first step towards
deconstructing the sado-masochistic ties which bind men and women
unhappily together' (194), but a final step instead, and a metaphor
for the changes women will inflict upon themselves when they see
no possibility of changing the world. Ruth's is a pyrrhic victory. By
deciding to look like Mary Fisher she reaffirms a stereotype of feminine beauty, keeping Mary Fisher's beauty alive in a very literal way.

Finally Ruth comes to believe that it isn't a question of male and
female after all, just power. First Bobbo had it all, then she took it
away from him. Power-play continues to dominate Weldon's next
novel, *The Shrapnel Academy* (1986). Here the battle between the sexes
is examined in the light of military history – its widest context yet in
Weldon's fiction. Accounts of famous battles punctuate the story of
the Shrapnel Academy guests' interpersonal skirmishes in the same
way that *Puffball* was sliced with gynaecology:

> A quick description of the Battle of Borodino, on the way to
> Moscow? You can bear it? The ins and outs have been fascinating
> the owners of lead soldiers and the players of computer war
> games ever since. Does that tempt you? (177)

In such passages the author is making her presence felt directly for
the first time, with no character-narrator as intermediary. The chirpy
note contrasts oddly with the gravity of the subject matter. But it is
important to be personal about it, claims Weldon, 'because the whole
way people deal with war is to depersonalize it' (*Boston Globe*,
3 April 1988).

Parts of the novel read like a parody of military tactics: dinner
party seating drawn up like a plan of battle; the thirteen timeless
verities of combat exposing the fallacies of this particular sample of
military intelligence; and the events of Saturday morning listed like
a soldier's campaign timetable. Towards most of her characters
Weldon adopts an oppositional stance: 'If we are to get the better of
Joan Lumb,' she remarks in her authorial role, 'we must know more
than she does: that is why we have had these boring lectures on
Tiglath-Pileser, Adolphus, Augustus, and so forth' (70). And indeed,
she identifies Joan's weak spot precisely: besotted with Murray
Fairchild, the famous veteran, Joan fails to note the disappearance of
the servants in time to forestall disaster.

Weldon's use of satire cuts her characters down to the same size as the above-mentioned lead soldiers – although they still manage to inflict considerable damage through their stupidity and xenophobia. Apart from Mew, one of Weldon's few likeable feminists, all the middle-class characters in *The Shrapnel Academy* are refugees from a civilian life where they could only be judged inadequate. These heedless, pugnacious people are contrasted with the Family of the Unknown, the immigrants, mostly illegal, who are crammed into every available cupboard and bed alcove in the cellars, many of them unknown even to Joan Lumb, the resident administrator.

At times *The Shrapnel Academy* reads like a grim parody of a famous British television series for which Weldon wrote the first instalments: *Upstairs Downstairs* dealt with life in a large Edwardian household; but there our attention was almost equally divided between life above and below stairs. In her fiction, however, Weldon seldom writes about the working-class, because, she says,

> if you're dealing with people who are not practised in dealing with abstract thought or see no virtue in it, or who aren't practised in expressing their thoughts with any subtlety, you have to spend your entire time with internal monologue, which I don't particularly enjoy writing. (Haffenden, 311)

In one of her many direct addresses to the reader, the author points out that the hands that serve us are mostly female, and usually brown, and for the most part go unnoticed, thus positioning her reader among the middle-class White academy guests rather than the immigrants in the cellarage; and indeed we, like them, find it difficult to tell the Black characters apart, they are given so rudimentary a psychology.

Weldon is often described as a political writer. But she is less interested in the belief that justice is worth fighting for, than in observing how any struggle for power will corrupt – which is why Acorn, the Black butler from Soweto, soon becomes as bad as the whites, with one or two variants such as rolling eyes which do little but endorse an outworn racial stereotype.

Mew is the one person who wants to do better than this, and her silent address to the Family works coincidentally as a sharp critique of white, middle-class feminism (89). Believing that we look too eagerly to 'isms' in general to explain society's ills, and fail to recognize the hate, spite and anger within ourselves (*Puffball*, 72), Weldon, writing in the liberal humanist tradition, attaches an almost mystical importance to the actions of individuals. At the end of the political fracas of *The President's Child*, for instance, it is all that is left. Says Maia:

> The habits of culture and kindness are catching – it is one of the few hopes we have. New ideas drop like juice into icing sugar, and behold, everything changes, and is better (218).

But it was good luck, not good deeds, that saved Isabel's life; and in *The Shrapnel Academy* 'the habits of culture and kindness' look flimsy when set against what Panza sees as the unchanging nature of man, and man's 'employment of lethal instruments to force his will on other men of opposing points of view' (101); or against the other guests' treatment of Mew, as they strip her naked in a fit of paranoia, and shove her down the laundry shaft, to be followed by a canister of C. S. gas.

Through the story of she-devil Ruth she showed that women will grab at power if they dare. Ruth gets away with it, perhaps because she specifically defines the nature of her strength as female. Joan Lumb, merely a military man *en travestie*, is blown up along with the rest.

In her novels of the early and middle eighties, Weldon's tone grows more astringent, and her optimism is increasingly carefully qualified. *The Heart of the Country* (1987; written first as a television play in 1986), shows women still struggling for the rights that Byzantia and her friends believed to be almost won. This is a Britain of dole queues and social security snoopers, and as women fight for social and economic survival, the men grow more prosperous – and even more ruthless – than ever.

The narrator – anonymous at first – has a tendency to be arch, dotting the text with exclamations such as 'Whew!' or 'Wouldn't she just!' As early as Chapter Two she divulges her identity:

> There, I have blown my cover. The 'I' who speaks to you is Sonia. In my quest for sanity and self-improvement I do my docile best, as instructed by my psychiatrist, to objectivize myself and see myself as others see me – that is to say in the third person – when and as I enter Natalie's story (17).

This strategy allows Weldon a technique she has favoured from the beginning of her career: a free movement from third-person narrative to statements in the first person by a character who turns out to be telling the story. But the glissade from third person to first is just as awkward as ever, with Sonia's tendency to interrupt looking more like authorial self-indulgence than creative writing therapy.

Mad prophetess or moral arbiter, Sonia pops in and out of the novel at will. Conveniently instructed by her psychiatrist to 'establish a moral framework for our existence, to decide exactly who to blame for what' (25), Puritanism runs riot through her description of 'the pleasures of adultery', with her culinary metaphor shedding a hellish glow over our memory of Maia's lemon drops of culture and kindness:

> Pleasure I said, pleasure I meant. Adulterate means to spoil, to pollute. It also contains the sense of dilution by poison. It's dropping a spot of cochineal into the white icing sugar and water mix and watching the colour spread – great streaks of vile red circling out with the first stir from that single central drop, gradually easing and diluting as you work into bland universal pink (17).

Her scepticism about the prevailing order ('Adultery's worth it. That's what I think' 17), her financial insecurity and her conviction that it is necessary but dangerous to make choices link her with the great Puritan heroines of the past, in particular eighteenth-century parvenues such as Moll Flanders and Pamela, as does her careful consideration of the doctor's marriage proposal. But her message is modernized and pushed to its limits, like Betelgeuse's to Praxis when he leant down out of the sky, 'all spears and pale fire' (127) to dispense advice.

'I told them about the wickedness of men and the wretchedness of women . . '. (192). As Angus's effigy blazes in a simulacrum of hellfire, Sonia's rhetoric from the carnival float becomes a latter-day Jeremiad on the cruelty and coruption at the heart of the country – or the pocket of the country, as she sometimes calls it. For Natalie, there will be no more sexual bargaining. But Weldon rewards her determination to survive by granting her fulfilment with Bernard in his latter-day Eden by the rubbish-dump, half empty after the demise of Flora, the pretend-virgin goddess who once presided over the polluted countryside.

Sonia, whose council house is on a ley line, lives before her incarceration between the Mendip Mast and Glastonbury Tor, that same Tor that Madge used to smile at as a friend, thus disturbing Tucker. Sonia proposes the ancient hummock, with its crumbling tower on top like a nipple on a breast, as a female symbol; and the Mast, 'streaming out Dallas and Robin Day' as male, like the tower blocks, or 'rearing phalluses of man's delight' (61) in *Down Among the Women*. Like Mabs's witchcraft, this ancient lore can be seen either as a religion, or as a metaphor for the way those who are marginalized try to change existing belief systems – or at least counter them in their own minds. It is Liffey who is ignorant of witchcraft and who is, like Natalie, secure in her urban brand of sexual appeal. Mentally, she dismisses Mabs as a 'smiling, friendly country-woman with a motherly air and no notion at all of how to make the best of herself' (43). Natalie, too, can afford to disregard natural magic. For her, men will always be the main route to money and luck. Yet when she commits adultery again at the end of the novel – in exchange for free accommodation from the local auctioneer – she appropriately chooses to seal her bargain at the foot of the Mendip Mast as it transmits its 'uneasy mixture of sentiment, world-liness and greed' (170); rather than by the Tor, where, says Sonia, 'she knew well enough she'd be struck dead for unrighteousness, for confusing sex with a business arrangement' (169).

Weldon never allows over-reachers like Sonia to exceed what is politically possible with their primitive magic. Women with awak-ened strengths and energy may wish to change the world, but witch-craft is not a shortcut to ruling it. And it may all be nonsense after all. Sonia is mad, and it could be said that Mabs's chthonic power works in collusion with nothing but Liffey's heightened hormonal activity. And as for Ruth's she-devil grace triumphing over nature: not all the female magic in the world is enough to subvert men's preference for trivial blondes who have learned to look up to them appealingly.

Jan Freeman believes that 'as Weldon's vision has expanded, characters have shrunk, as if to make room for more important guests' (*Boston Globe*, 6 November 1988). In her latest fiction – the novella, *The Rules of Life* (1987), and the novels, *Leader of the Band* (1988) and *The Cloning of Joanna May* (1989) – every paragraph be-comes a distillation of the heroine's own psyche, with the supporting cast dwindling into negligibility. *Leader of the Band* is Weldon's first novel to be told entirely in the first person. Here she gives the narrating 'I' to Starlady Sandra, the sort of woman Weldon dislikes most – rich, successful, pleasure-loving and childless. At the end we are asked to believe that Sandra has changed into the kind of charac-ter preferred by her author – pregnant, and ready to let her lover return to his wife. But the change is difficult to take seriously, because Sandra's hallucinations in the Hotel de Ville are no substitute for the self-recognition, painfully gained, of a Praxis or an Isabel.

Starlady Sandra is the daughter of a half-gypsy upon whom her Nazi father conducted his experiments in genetic engineering, a science which in Weldon's hands becomes yet another means of exploring the construction of the feminine personality in a patriarchal world, and the latest in a series of devices – such as weightgain, witchcraft, madness or cosmetic surgery – to bestow upon her female characters a preternatural size and importance while holding their identity up to question.

Weldon has always been a shrewd exponent of sexual politics. At points during her career (in *The Shrapnel Academy*, for instance, or 'Ind. Aff.' *Vogue*, January 1989) she has successfully located the sex war in a wider political arena. In these later novels her concerns grow still broader, even cosmic in their dimensions. In *The Cloning of Joanna May* the heroine is, like Starlady Sandra and her earlier predecessors in *Down Among the Women* and *Puffball*, aligned not with nature but with science. But the link with genetic engineering looks glibly depoliticized by comparison with her gritty analysis of male and female power ploys; and by comparison with Weldon's earlier heroines Sandra, Gloria, and Joanna look vapid, scarcely more individualized than Joanna's clones.

*The Cloning of Joanna May* takes its place in a long series of novels where Weldon uses her favourite technique: proceeding by shifts between a third- and first- person narrative. Although less successful here than previously, because of the novel's general air of breathless haste, it retains its major advantage as a narrative strategy: generating a tension between the readers' vision of the heroine as the world perceives her, and our sympathy for a woman attempting to explain herself. One of the author's most successful devices, it takes its place alongside her sharply-honed dialogue, her carefully burnished phrases often isolated from the text to heighten their effect, her use of refrains, songs and exclamations, and her densely interwoven time schemes which serve as a constant reminder that the past is a living influence on the present: all add up to a distinctive but flexible style which makes Weldon one of the most innovative and popular writers in Britain today.

In *Letters to Alice* Weldon says, 'Readers need and seek for moral guidance. I mean this in the best and even unconventional sense.

They need an example, in the light of which they can imagine themselves, understand themselves' (83). Using her 'twin prongs' of psychoanalysis and feminism, she provides her readers with just such examples, believing that 'people will put up with a lot if they are entertained' (*Observer*, 30 April 1989: 41). It may be that she believes, along with one of her characters in *The Rules of Life*, that fiction has replaced Christianity without anyone noticing; and that its priests (that is, writers) must conduct themselves with due regard to their responsibilities (56). Elsewhere she remarks, 'See me as Sisyphus, but having a good time' (Brandmark).

From the beginning, Weldon has defined the purpose of reading and writing as self-discovery. Despite her growing tendency to sound brittle, and to preach, and her intolerance of certain kinds of women, she still retains much of her early inventiveness and zest. Her books illustrate well the main tenet of the Great New Fictional Religion in *The Rules of Life* – 'acceptance and self-understanding', and, above all, its credo 'that we must strive to understand the sub-text of our lives while delivering the text with gusto and without doubt' (45).

## A BIBLIOGRAPHY OF WRITINGS BY FAY WELDON

### Novels

*The Fat Woman's Joke* (London: MacGibbon and Kee, 1967; Coronet, 1988. American edition: . . . *And the Wife Ran Away*, New York: McKay, 1968).

*Down Among the Women* (London: Heinemann, 1971; New York: St. Martin's, 1972; Penguin, 1987).

*Female Friends* (London: Heinemann, 1975; Pavanne, 1987. New York: St. Martin's, 1975).

*Remember Me* (London: Hodder and Stoughton, 1976; Coronet, 1988. New York: Random House, 1976).

*Little Sisters* (London: Hodder and Stoughton, 1978; Coronet, 1980. American edition: *Words of Advice*, New York: Random House, 1977).

*Praxis* (London: Hodder and Stoughton, 1978; Coronet, 1980. New York: Summit, 1979).

*Puffball* (London: Hodder and Stoughton, 1980; Coronet, 1981. New York: Summit, 1980).

*The President's Child* (London: Hodder and Stoughton, 1982; Coronet, 1983. New York: Viking, 1983).

*The Life and Loves of a She-Devil* (London: Hodder and Stoughton, 1983; Coronet, 1984. New York: Pantheon, 1984).

*The Shrapnel Academy* (London: Hodder and Stoughton, 1986; Coronet, 1986. New York: Viking, 1987).

*The Rules of Life* (London: Century Hutchinson, 1987; Arena, 1988. New York: Harper and Row, 1987).
*The Heart of the Country* (London: Century Hutchinson, 1987; Arrow, 1988. New York: Viking, 1988).
*The Hearts and Lives of Men* (London: Heinemann, 1987; Fontana, 1988. New York: Viking, 1988).
*Leader of the Band* (London: Hodder and Stoughton, 1988. New York: Viking, 1989).
*The Cloning of Joanna May* (London: William Collins, 1989. New York: Viking, 1990).
*Darcy's Utopia* (London: Collins, 1990. New York: Viking, 1991).
*Life Force* (London: Penguin, 1992. New York: Viking, 1992).

## Stories

*Watching Me, Watching You* (London: Hodder and Stoughton, 1981; Pyramid, 1988. New York: Summit, 1981).
'The Man Who Liked Swimming', *Ms.* (June 1981): 61+.
'Birthday! '*Winter's Tales* 27, ed. Edward Leeson (New York: St. Martin's Press, 1982): 165–78.
'The Gift of Life', *Fiction Magazine*, 2.2. (Autumn 1983): 37.
'The Officer Takes a Wife', *Redbook* (October 1984): 72+.
*Polaris and Other Stories* (London: Hodder and Stoughton, 1985; Coronet, 1988. New York: Penguin, 1989).
'Ind. Aff.', *Vogue* (January 1989): 183+.
'Love Among the Artists', *The Times* (27 December 1991): 78.
*Moon Over Minneapolis: Or Why She Couldn't Stay* (London: Collins, 1991. New York: Viking, 1992).

## Plays

*Permanence* (in *Mixed Doubles: An Entertainment on Marriage*: London: Methuen, 1970), 1969.
*Words of Advice*, 1974.
*Moving House*, 1976.
*Mr Director*, 1978.
*Action Replay*, 1980.
*After the Prize*, 1981.
*I Love My Love*, 1984.

## Miscellaneous

'Me and My Shadows', in *On Gender and Writing*, ed. Michelene Wandor (London: Pandora, 1983) 160–5.
*Letters to Alice, on First Reading Jane Austen* (London: Michael Joseph, 1984; Coronet, 1988. New York: Taplinger, 1985).

*Discipline: by Mary Brunton,* 'Introduction', by Weldon (London: Pandora, 1986).

*A Small Green Space,* libretto, music by Ilona Sekacz. First performed by the English National Opera, London, June 1989.

'Suture Shock', *Mirabella* (July 1989): 52+.

*Sacred Cows: Counterblast No. 4* (London: Chatto and Windus, 1989).

'Saintly Passion', *New Statesman & Society* (15 December 1989): 10–11.

'Talk Before Sex and Talk After Sex' [*Deception* by Philip Roth], *The New York Times Book Review* (11 March 1990): 3.

'A Single Shining Muscle of a Girl' [*Body* by Harry Crews], *The New York Times Book Review* (9 September 1990): 14.

## A BIBLIOGRAPHY OF WRITINGS ABOUT FAY WELDON

**Articles and Reviews**

Alexander, Fiona, 'Fiction and Sexual Politics: Fay Weldon', *Contemporary Women Novelists* (London: Edward Arnold, 1990): 51–60.

Amis, Martin, 'Prose Is the Leading Lady', *The New York Times Book Review* (2 October 1977): 13; 52.

Birch, Helen, 'Wife v. Mistress' [*The Hearts and Lives of Men* and *The Rules of Life*]. New Statesman (11 Septemebr 1987): 28.

Blodgett, Harriet, 'Fay Weldon', *Dictionary of Literary Biography,* Volume 14: 750–9.

Blue, Adrianne, 'The Servant Problem' [*The Shrapnel Academy*], *New Statesman* (11 July 1986): 33–4.

Brandmark, Wendy, *Fay Weldon* (London: British Council Publication, 1988).

Briscoe, Joanna, 'Sweet Anarchy, Poisoned Utopia' [*Darcy's Utopia*], Guardian (19 September 1990): 17.

Brookner, Anita, 'The Primrose Path of Dalliance' [*Leader of the Band*], *The Spectator* (9 July 1988): 62; 65.

Brookner, Anita, 'The Return of the Earth Mother' [*Puffball*], *Times Literary Supplement, (TLS)* (22 February 1980): 202.

Chesnutt, Margaret, 'Feminist Criticism and Feminist Consciousness: A Reading of a Novel by Fay Weldon', *Moderna Sprak* 73 (1979): 3–18.

Crace, Jim, 'Autobiology' [*Puffball*], *Quarto* (March 1980): 15.

Craig, Patricia, 'Hostilities on All Fronts' [*The Shrapnel Academy*], TLS (11 July 1986): 766.

Craig, Patricia, 'Wife into Gorgon' [*The Life and Loves of a She-Devil*], TLS (20 January 1984): 70.

Dinnage, Rosemary, 'The Corruption of Love' [*Praxis*], *The New York Review of Books* (8 February 1979): 20–2.

Drexler, Rosalyn, 'Looking for Love After Marriage' [*The Life and Loves of a She-Devil*], *The New York Times Book Review* (30 September 1984): 1; 47.

Dunford, Judith, 'Losing to Despair' [*The Cloning of Joanna May* and *Leader of the Band*], *The New Republic* (20 and 27 August 1990): 40–2.

Freeman, Jan, 'Laughter in the Dark' [*The Heart of the Country*], *The Boston Globe* (6 November 1988): B18.

Freeman, Jan, 'Most of Them Live in a Mellow Submarine' [*Polaris and Other Stories* and *Leader of the Band*], *The Boston Globe* (11 June 1989): B18.

Glendinning, Victoria, 'The Muswell Hill Mob' [*Remember Me*], *TLS* (24 September 1976): 1199.

Glendinning, Victoria, 'Novel of Scrambled Egos, Women, Ideas, and Oracles' [*Darcy's Utopia*], *The Times* (20 September 1990): 20.

Gerrard, Nicci, 'The Fay Weldon Academy of Laughter', *Women's Review* 9 (July 1986): 10–11.

Gerrard, Nicci, 'Fay Weldon: *The Heart of the Country*', *Women's Review* 17 (March 1987): 36–7.

Guest, Harriet, 'Laundry' [*The Rules of Life* and *The Hearts and Lives of Men*], *London Review of Books* (10 December 1987): 14–16.

Hislop, Ian, 'Writing about Novels' [*Letters to Alice*], *Books and Bookmen* (June 1984): 16–17.

Hollinghurst, Alan, 'Post-War' [*Puffball*], *New Statesman* (15 February 1980): 251–2.

Houston, Robert, 'Her Sisters, Herself' [*The Cloning of Joanna May*], *The New York Times Book Review* (25 March 1990): 7.

Ingoldby, Grace, 'Dear Heart' [*The Heart of the Country*], *New Statesman* (6 February 1987): 27–8.

Jones, D. A. N., 'Warnings for Women' [*Female Friends*], *TLS* (28 February 1975): 213.

Jones, Lewis, 'Airport' [*The President's Child*], *New Statsman* (24 September 1982): 30.

Kakutani, Michiko, 'In Fay Weldon's New Novel, The Devil Is a Man' [*The Cloning of Joanna May*], *The New York Times* (16 March 1990): C34.

Kemp, Peter, 'Go to Work on an Ovum' [*Puffball*], *The Listener* (21 February 1980): 254–5.

Kemp, Peter, 'Packaging from the Pulpit' [*Watching Me, Watching You*], *TLS* (22 May 1981): 562.

Kenyon, Olga, 'Fay Weldon', in *Women Novelists Today*, ed. by Kenyon (Brighton: Harvester, 1988): 104–28.

King, Francis, 'Obstetricks' [*Puffball*], *The Spectator* (1 March 1980): 22.

Kitchen, Paddy, 'Conjuror's Trick' [*Letters to Alice*], *The Times Educational Supplement* (11 May 1984): 27.

Krouse, Agate Nesaule, 'Feminism and Art in Fay Weldon's Novels', *Critique: Studies in Modern Fiction*, 22, no. 2 (1978): 5–20.

Lasdun, James, 'Pig Stys' [*Watching Me, Watching You*], *The Spectator* (11 July 1981): 22.

Lipson, Eden Ross, 'The Life and Loves of Fay Weldon', *Lear's* (January 1990): 112–15.

Maddocks, Melvin, 'Mothers and Masochists' [*Down Among the Women*], *Time* (26 February 1973): 91.

Motion, Joanna, '*Letters to Alice: On First Reading Jane Austen* – Fay Weldon', *TLS* (6 July 1984): 763.

Naughton, John, 'Family Lives' [*Watching Me, Watching You*], *The Listener* (28 May 1981): 717.

Prose, Francine, 'The Future Imperfect' [*Darcy's Utopia*], *The Washington Post Book World* (10 March 1991): 1–2.

Rafferty, Terence, 'Books: She-Devil' [*The Hearts and Lives of Men*] *The New Yorker* (1 August 1988): 66–8.

Rich, Frank, 'Fay Weldon Offers "After the Prize"' ['After the Prize'], *The New York Times* (24 November 1981): 22.

Rinzler, Carol E., 'Hell Hath No Fury' [*The Life and Loves of a She-Devil*], *Washington Post Book World* (30 September 1984): 1–2.

Sage, Lorna, 'Aunt Fay's Sermons' [*Letters to Alice*], *The Observer* (13 May 1984): 23.

Sage, Lorna, 'Soul Sisters' [*The Cloning of Joanna May*], *Observer* (7 May 1989): 32.

Shrimpton, Nicholas, 'Bond at 70' [*Watching Me, Watching You*], *New Statesman* (22 May 1981): 21.

Simon, John, 'Soldiers and Sisters' ['After the Prize'], *The New York Times Magazine* (7 December 1981): 159; 162.

Smith, Joan, 'The Four of Us' [*The Cloning of Joanna May*], *Guardian* (5 May 1989): 29.

Sternhell, Carol, 'Fay Weldon's Dangerous Dreams' [*The President's Child*], *The Village Voice* (19 July 1983): 34.

Walker, J. K. L., 'Sinners against Women, Nation and Nature' [*The Heart of the Country*], *TLS* (13 February 1987): 164.

Ward, Robert, 'Never Ready for Love' [*Polaris and Other Stories*], *The New York Times Book Review* (4 June 1989): 1.

Waugh, Harriet, 'Unbelievable' [*The President's Child*], *The Spectator* (2 October 1982): 24–5.

Waugh, Patricia, 'Fay Weldon: Contemporary Feminist Gothic', in *Feminine Fictions: Revisiting the Postmodern* by Waugh (London: Routledge, 1989): 189–96.

White, Diane, '"I Write the Books I Want to Read": Fay Weldon Speaks from the Heart', *The Boston Globe* (30 March 1988): 67+.

Wilde, Alan, 'Bold, But Not Too Bold: Fay Weldon and the Limits of Poststructuralist Criticism', *Contemporary Literature* 29, 3 (Fall, 1988): 403–19.

Wright, Sarah, 'Nice and Grown-up' [*The Cloning of Joanna May*], *Observer* (30 April 1989): 41.

Zeman, Anthea, 'Fay Weldon', in *Presumptuous Girls: Women and Their World in the Serious Woman's Novel* (London: Weidenfeld and Nicholson, 1977): 64–5.

## Interviews

Brown, Craig, 'Fay Weldon', *Vogue* (January 1989): 182+.

Dunn, Elisabeth, 'Among the Women', *Sunday Telegraph Magazine* (16 December 1979): 55; 58; 61; 64.

Haffenden, John, 'Fay Weldon', in *Novelists in Interview*, ed. John Haffenden (London and New York: Methuen, 1985): 305–20.

Heilpern, John, 'Facts of Female Life', *Observer Magazine* (18 February 1979): 36–7.

Kenyon, Olga, 'Fay Weldon', *Women Writers Talk*, ed. Olga Kenyon (New York: Carroll and Graf, 1990): 189–207.

Neustatter, Angela, 'Earth Mother Truths', *Guardian* (20 February 1979): 24.

Peters, Pauline, 'The Fay Behind the Puffball', *London Sunday Times* (17 February 1980): 36.

Purvis, Libby, 'The Case for Utopia Unlimited', *London Times* (17 September 1990): 18.

Steinberg, S., '*PW* Interviews: Fay Weldon', *Publishers Weekly* (24 August 1984): 83–4.

Turner, Jenny, 'Say What You Mean, Mean What You Say', *The Listener* (20 September 1990): 24.

## Miscellaneous

*Contemporary Authors, New Revision*, Volume 16.
*Contemporary Literary Criticism*, Volumes 6, 9, 11, 19, 36.

## FAY WELDON

Fay Weldon was born in England in 1931, emigrating with her parents to New Zealand in early childhood, and returning to England with her mother at ten, after her parents' divorce. Her graduation from the University of St Andrews was followed by an unsettled decade, with early attempts at novel-writing but no publications, and a young son to support without any clear sense of direction at work. She earned her living successively in market research, on the problem page of the *Daily Mirror*, in the Foreign Office, and finally by the work which was to have most influence on her eventual career as a writer: advertising copywriter.

In 1960 she married Ron Weldon, a jazz musician and antique dealer, with whom she has had three more sons. Now she divides her time between the family home in Somerset, and a terraced house in North London, where she devotes herself to writing. Prolific and above all else professional, she is one of the best- known living British writers. Versatile from the outset of her writing career in 1967, when she adapted her first novel from a radio play, she has written radio, stage and television plays; serials for television and a woman's magazine, television adaptations, an opera libretto, numerous short stories and, with her growing reputation as a polemicist, some controversial articles on a wide range of issues. But Weldon remains best known for her novels – fifteen to date. Her work has been translated into many languages, and *Praxis* (1978) was shortlisted for the Booker Prize.

# Index of Names